Sweetness #9

Sweetness #9

A Novel

STEPHAN EIRIK CLARK

Little, Brown and Company
New York Boston London

Copyright © 2014 by Stephan Eirik Clark

Little, Brown and Company
Hachette Book Group
237 Park Avenue, New York, NY 10017
littlebrown.com

First Edition: August 2014

Little, Brown and Company is a division of Hachette Book Group, Inc. The Little, Brown name and logo are trademarks of Hachette Book Group, Inc.

The publisher is not responsible for websites (or their content) that are not owned by the publisher.

The Hachette Speakers Bureau provides a wide range of authors for speaking events. To find out more, go to hachettespeakersbureau.com or call (866) 376-6591.

Library of Congress Cataloging-in-Publication Data
Clark, Stephan Eirik.
  Sweetness #9 : a novel / Stephan Eirik Clark.
    p. cm
  Sweetness number nine
  ISBN 978-0-316-27875-1
    1. Weight gain — Fiction. 2. Eating disorders — Fiction. 3. Sweeteners — Fiction. 4. Family life — Fiction. I. Title. II. Title: Sweetness number nine.
  PS3603.L36877S94 2014
  813'.6 — dc23   2014018060

10 9 8 7 6 5 4 3 2 1

RRD-C

Printed in the United States of America

For Nastia,
Моя сладкая

All great change in America begins at the dinner table.

— Ronald Reagan

CONTENTS

PART ONE

ANIMAL TESTING

Summer 1973

WHEN I SAY IT ALL began with monkeys, I don't mean to issue another rallying cry in the ongoing Culture Wars. I only mean to say it began in the Animal Testing labs at Goldstein, Olivetti, and Dark, to which I was shown after filing my thesis on the biophysics of brie and being graduated from the food science program at Rutgers University.

Goldstein, Olivetti, and Dark. They were no less an industry giant then than they are now, with five thousand employees worldwide and production facilities on every continent but one. I certainly felt a good thrill in joining their number. As I first pulled up to the gate of their ocean-side complex in Jupiter Park, I believed myself just as important as one of the policy wonks inside the Beltway or an engineer bent over a slide-rule at NASA. It was the summer of 1973 and I too was doing my part to win the Cold War, for if anything other than an ICBM could clear the Berlin Wall, it was the taste of a smuggled Ho Ho or Ding Dong — flavors that suggested a life freer and more limitless than any possible under the grey yoke of Communism.

After parking, I was met in the lobby by one of the men who'd interviewed me, a middle manager with the company's Laboratory for the Development of Substitute Materials. A short, round fellow with a tonsure of dirt-brown hair, he was constantly hoisting his belt or running a finger around inside his tight collar. I'd forgotten his name (it was either John Rogers or Roger Johns; he was one of these blue-blood types), so for fear of making a mistake I called him "sir."

"Just this way now, Leveraux."

"Yes, sir."

"Here we are."

3

He moved across the red carpet into a bay of wood-paneled lockers, found the one he was looking for, then fished a key out of his pants pocket and gave me a wink.

"Well?" he said. "Shall we? Hmm? Hmm?"

At the age of twenty-four, my most natural expression was a kind of smile-in-waiting, the face of someone politely anticipating a punchline to even the most poorly told joke.

"Yes," the middle manager said, as he popped open the locker and reached inside for a white lab coat that was hanging motionless on a pink plastic hanger. "Give 'er a whirl."

I switched out of the blue blazer I'd worn from home, then stepped up to the small panel mirror attached to the inside of the locker door. My name had been stitched in blue thread over the breast pocket: *David Leveraux, Flavorist-in-Training.* I went to trace my finger across it, but before I could, John Rogers slapped me hard on the shoulder, knocking my hand off course.

"A million dollars, Leveraux! A million dollars!"

He led me out of the dressing room and down a long checkerboard hallway to a sign jutting out over a far door: ANIMAL TESTING, it read in red-on-white letters. The middle manager ushered me into the lab with a sweeping gesture of one hand, telling me as I passed before him that I'd be working with rats and monkeys.

I turned beaming to him after I'd stepped inside, my eyes as shiny as the Vitalis I combed through my hair each morning. "Rats and monkeys?" It was my introduction to the American economy. "Splendid," I said. "*Splendid.*"

And how couldn't I be so thrilled? It was a wonderful time to embark upon a career in the flavor sciences — a Golden Age, I can't help but think now. Just consider: in the nineteenth century, the industry existed solely for the benefit of the baker, confectioner, and soda maker, but following the end of the Second World War, the profession experienced a great westward expansion as a result of the TV dinner — a Louisiana Purchase that was drawn in the shape of a four-compartment aluminum tray. This was added to in short time by the launch of the first domestic microwave, a Sputnik-like event that caused young men such as myself to heed the call of the nation's top food science programs. I was now on the other side of my Master of Science degree and being asked to start in Animal Testing, but this was in no way unexpected. Animal Testing at Goldstein, Olivetti, and Dark was like the mail-room at the old William Morris Agency; even those recruited out of the Ivy League started here.

"Well?" With another sweep of his hand, Roger Johns revealed the world my dedicated scholarship had won. "What do you think? Hmm?"

Two island work stations rose from the center of the room, their black counter-tops holding microscopes and Bunsen burners and stainless steel sinks. To our right was a wooden maze on a thigh-high table. To the rear, two doors, one marked PRIMATES, the other RODENTS. The door to the primate room stood ajar, allowing the screeches of a more primal tongue to reach my ears. Hearing this, I pushed at the bridge of my glasses and squinted behind their thick black frames. I could make out only the first of the floor-to-ceiling cages inside, but I saw the beasts so clearly in my mind: rattling their doors, jumping up and down, exposing the pinks of their gums.

"Chimpanzees, are they?"

"Mmm."

"Lovely," I said, though in truth that shrill glottal sound, the screaming of the jungle...Some men dread clowns or midgets, others a ventriloquist and his dummy. For me, it has always been monkeys, monkeys by any name. I feel their presence like a cold finger pressed into the base of the spine, and so for a moment, just an involuntary flash, I wished I had joined a smaller outfit, one that would've dispensed with the cage cleaning and other rites of passage and let me begin as so many other would-be flavorists did, by mixing chemical compounds in a 250 cc beaker.

But then I had prepared myself for this and was ready with all the necessary rejoinders. At the end of six months, certainly no more than a year, I would be transferred into the Flavorings Division on the third floor, where I'd be assigned a mentor in the specialty of my choosing, most likely Breakfast Cereals. And here I would be able to dream bigger, because Goldstein, Olivetti, and Dark not only possessed state-of-the-art laboratories; they offered access to an unrivaled Research and Development Department. Just the previous summer, the company had floated an air balloon across a stretch of dense and virginal jungle in Papua, New Guinea. The team had drifted over the treetops, hovering in place and dropping a long vacuum-driven tube each time it wanted to capture a specimen from beneath the lush green canopy below. More than two hundred fruits, flowers, barks, pods, and mushrooms had been collected, along with at least five new plant specimens and one frog whose skin was reportedly covered by a sweet-tasting mucus.

I challenge you to find the young man schooled on Guenther and Bedoukian who could resist such talk during his interview. After all, though Gas Chromatographs and Mass Spectrometers had become commonplace in the last decade, these instruments were only as valuable as the information you fed into them; and by this stage of our country's culinary development, no one company alone had tagged and quantified more than fifteen hundred volatile flavor chemicals. That meant if you injected a sample into the GCMS—a pot roast, let us say—the computers would only be able to identify the most obvious peaks and valleys of its flavor profile. It was no more helpful than a seismograph that could record an earthquake only if it shook the decorative plates off your shelves, because to produce a truly remarkable flavor, one that left even its creator confused as to its origins, you had to know what a sample's subtlest notes were comprised of, and this in many ways was a godly task. Consider the humble pot roast. It is a sublime creation rising up from more than six hundred different flavor molecules—and that's before it's served alongside a dollop of garlic mashed potatoes and a pile of pork-fat green beans. So, no, I didn't come to Goldstein, Olivetti, and Dark because they had an impressive fleet of technological hardware; I came because they knew what their machines were saying. With such vast resources and so many privately held compounds, Goldstein, Olivetti, and Dark boasted a veritable Book of Life. I wanted to lick their frog. Call it youthful exuberance if you must, but I wanted to taste the sweetness that had been sequestered for so long in nature and now called Jupiter Park home.

A man emerged from the primate room holding a clipboard down at one side. As I'd later learn, he had a Purple Heart from Vietnam, a GED he'd earned while recovering at Walter Reed, and a technician's license from the American Association of Laboratory Animal Sciences.

"You must be our latest victim," he said.

He wasn't much older than me, but already he moved like a fearsome old mariner. His right foot swung out at his side as if to follow the rounded edge of a protractor. There was a little play in his right pant-leg as well. The fabric pushed in against the metal rod that had replaced his flesh and bone from foot to knee. My manners failed me twice: first when I stared at his prosthetic limb, and then again when I looked up from it pretending not to have done just that.

"Charles Hithenbottom," he said, extending his hand.

"David," I answered, smiling with my teeth thrust forward in my mouth like something too hot or too large to swallow, this the sad consequence of an otherwise welcome English birth. "David Leveraux," I said, pumping his hand.

John Rogers threw his arm around me and whispered in my ear, "People call him Hickey." Then he slapped me on the bottom and threw his voice out to my new lab-mate. "Leveraux's the biophysics of brie, Hickey!"

"Oh?" He'd been sweating; here, he began patting his face and neck dry with a handkerchief. "You raised some very interesting questions about surface-enhanced Raman scattering."

"You read my thesis?"

Roger Johns goosed me in the side. "Hope you don't mind if we passed it around."

"No. No, of course not."

They said a few more things then, but I was lost to the thrill of it all, smiling like a blind man at a concert. You must understand: this was the end of a very gratifying period in my life, one that had begun when my thesis adviser met with me to discuss my completed research. "You're going to cause a bidding war," he'd said. "Do you know that?" And he was grinning so widely I thought the corners of his mouth might dislodge his ears. "If only I could be in your shoes, a young man again with the whole world of flavor still in front of him. Oh, Leveraux, I envy you!"

Roger Johns sent a wet fingertip into one of my ears. "Now listen, you ever have a problem" — he hiked up his belt — "come see me."

"Yes, sir."

He ran two fingers around inside his collar, then pointed to the ceiling. "I'm on four."

"You mean five," Hickey said.

"Right." He chuckled and went again for his belt. "Five. Or is that six from the basement?"

"I don't know, sir."

We laughed and nodded some more, and then, after another playful slap on my cheek and a final poke in my ribs, John Rogers was disappearing behind a door that eased shut on a hydraulic hinge.

Hickey crossed to a stool at one of the island table-tops, the oversized shoe of his artificial leg squeaking against the polished epoxy floor. He leaned into the lens of his microscope then and addressed me in a way that was both distracted and firm. "Don't touch the monkeys."

"Pardon?"

He looked up, his expression no less unyielding. "Don't touch my monkeys. You're working with the rats."

"Oh, yes." I looked to the rodent room. "Splendid."

EACH DAY AFTER HANGING UP my lab coat, I rushed off to my beautiful young wife, who like me dreamed of a large family and a home that wasn't graced by that saddest of residential digits, the fraction. Our life at 345¾ West Orange Avenue was very simple: we ate and had sex, and I worked so we could continue to do this again and again. Though it was a routine, it was far from monotonous, because while it was a baby we were after, it was a male fantasy that was taking us there. Betty met me at the door each night wearing heels and a frilly pink baby-doll negligee. "There's my hubby," she'd say, pushing up on her toes to give me a kiss, and then off she'd go, making a quick orbit of the living room—dropping a Mantovani record on the hi-fi, fixing a drink at the bar trolley—before catching up to me at the mouth of the hall, where I'd accept my stinger while pulling at the knot of my tie.

Some evenings, after leading her into the bedroom in back, I'd lie with my arm around her and stare up at the cottage cheese ceiling wondering how it could possibly get any better. A post-coital cigarette? Since college, I had liked to imagine my life as a French film, but I knew I couldn't fill my days with smoke, no matter how romantic the image might be. Cigarettes damage your organoleptic senses, and a flavorist is nothing without his nose.

That I could find such happiness at the cramped Lido Village apartment complex was likely a consequence of my early troubles at the state university, where only two years previously I had feared my loneliness was a terminal condition. Since arriving on campus in 1967, I had walked the streets of Battle Station wanting nothing more than a pretty young girl on my arm, someone I could pass a fork to at ethnic restaurants and practice French with from beneath the tangles of my musty bed-sheets. But despite these longings, or perhaps because of their strength, I remained a virgin on into graduate school. It was so very disheartening. The more I looked at women, the more they reacted to me like a shortstop to a throw from center field; they were all instinct and motion, turning from me as if to gun down a runner racing for home.

But then there she was, Betty Lynne Elliot Webb, standing beside me in the co-op bookstore. It was January of 1972, and she was a freshman reaching across me for a thesaurus, while I was a first-year grad student going the other way for a hardcover dictionary. Our skin touched in the crossover, my elbow to her forearm, and as it did we shared a brief smile. I dropped my eyes to the cover of the dictionary in my hands, as if hoping to find an instructive blurb, but I couldn't focus. Her scent dizzied me. It was a jasmine-imbued fragrance—Chanel No. 5, I knew—that was so thick and heady, so exotic and sultry, it all but roared, "I am woman!" So powerful was the scent that when I turned to the holder of it, I realized she was already gone, moving off toward the far sign that read FAMILY/CONSUMER SCIENCES.

I walked to the front register with halting steps and while in line flipped open my book. One word jumped out at me bolder than all the rest: "**fuck** (fŭk) *Obscene. v.* **fucked, fucking, fucks.**" I widened my eyes to sharpen my focus. "-*tr.* **1.** To have sexual intercourse with." The young woman in front of me glanced back over one shoulder, a black patch obscuring her eye. The words in my dictionary seemed to vibrate and glow. "**2.** Used in the imperative as a signal of angry dismissal." Fuck! What was I doing? I glanced to Family/Consumer Sciences, but I couldn't see her; I might as well have been alone. "-**fuck** *n.* **1.** An act of sexual intercourse. **2.** A partner in sexual intercourse." The man at the register called me forward. "-*phrasal verbs.* **fuck off.**" I had to find her. I had to reach for her elbow and speak to her with hushed, insistent tones, to persuade her to leave with me and conjugate, to conjugate, that most natural of acts. "**3.** To masturbate." I couldn't leave alone. Not again. But the man at the register called out to me insistently, saying did I want anything or not, so I stepped toward him, reading one last entry before handing over the book. "**fuck up. 1.** To bungle. **2.** To act carelessly, foolishly, or incorrectly."

The register dinged. I paid my money. And then I was out beneath the bruised and battered clouds, carrying so many empty and unused words in a bag that banged against my leg.

"Fuck," I said. "Fuck, fucking, fucks."

I couldn't explain it. My toothy smile and the heavy black frames of my glasses spoke of those years I'd spent in my mother's England under its system of National Health, but I wasn't entirely without my charms. In high school, I had been found sturdy enough to serve as a blocking tight end on more than one crucial third down. The very thing that had once made me so self-conscious, my flared feet, had blessed me with an almost preternatural balance on the gridiron. So what was it?

"You're a square," my roommate said the afternoon I returned from the bookstore. "Do you even know it's not 1957 anymore?"

I turned over on the bunk beneath him, regretting that I had confessed my lustful passivity.

"Look at you." He jumped down from the top bunk and sat on the edge of my mattress. "You're a dinosaur." He rubbed at my flat-top, a style I wore in honor of my dead father. "I'm rooming with Johnny Unitas!"

I sat up and swung my legs to the floor. I wore grey woolen slacks, a matching cardigan over a black short-sleeve mock turtle-neck, and a pair of zip-up Chelsea boots that I polished with the dedication of a soldier. I thought I looked good. Certainly decent. But my roommate was bell-bottomed and dimpled, a chemistry major with long hair and dubious educational motives.

"The world's changing, man. Chicks want a cat who's wild, someone who'll talk about the revolution and our brother the Viet Cong. You dig?"

No, I did not dig. But for a few hours that night I did try. I went with him to one of the less reputable houses off-campus, a dingy place off Somerset where all the women walked braless and bouncing from one hushed and earnest conversation to the next. On three occasions I was offered a marijuana cigarette; each time I politely declined and bled into the next room, looking for a bottle of scotch. When I had made a full circle and returned to the front foyer, I saw my roommate at the base of the stairs, talking to a blonde who had a flower in her hair. She led him up the runner of red carpet into a bedroom, leaving me, as the door closed behind them, to move out onto the street coupled only with a feeling of loss.

I wasn't like these people. I couldn't conjure a sexual union with little more than the words "free love" and a harsh rebuke of Nixon. I was a member of the Silent Majority who feared the Domino Effect and supported the war in Vietnam. Perhaps most of all I preferred the breasts of my youth, the missiles of Marilyn Monroe and Jayne Mansfield that stood out in stark contrast to the careless and collapsed styles of my contemporaries.

Back in my room, I lay in bed chewing on buttons of licorice as bitter as death while staring up into the latticework of the empty bunk above mine.* My mind was a wintry soup, thick and bubbling. I questioned everything, even my career path. My ambitions had been set as far back as 1953, when sweet rationing had ended in England and Hitler was finally put to rest. Then a boy of only three or four years, I felt so unprepared for this unprecedented burst of flavor. It is my first memory, one that is so strong that it precedes any other by at least two years. In it, I am sitting on the living room rug in our riverside home in Wargrave, surrounded by the colorful curls of foil I'd torn from the many chocolates and hard candies that my father had brought back for me from London on the train. It is a celebration of scent: my father sits behind me smoking his pipe and reading the paper, as my mother hums along to the radio in the kitchen while doing the dishes, the perfume of our Sunday roast still hanging in the air.

Many years later, after we'd moved to the States and my parents had met their tragic end (a clock tower in Texas, a grad student with a rifle), I realized it wasn't only Jesus who'd been given the power to bring back

---

* Licorice, I've learned, has been linked to lower testosterone levels. I won't say this was the cause of my loneliness in college, but I do think it interesting that I was such an avid fan of the candy at this loveless time in my life.

the dead. My father was the easiest to revive. He had been an import-export man who'd made his name in coconuts after the war; to get him to rise up before me, all I had to do was run a knife down the middle of a bag of coconut shavings and push my nose inside. Mother was more difficult. She was locked away in the smell of all those Christmas dinners and rhubarb crumble pies that no one else had come close to reproducing in the handful of years since her death. I had chased her memory into the lab, thinking I would one day stumble upon that elusive chemical combination that'd bring her back to me again.

But oh how foolish I'd been. As I lay in my dorm room in the dark, sucking on another button of black licorice, I was no closer to success than I had been when I'd signed up for my first chemistry class. I should've chosen a different direction, I realized. Should've tuned out, dropped on, whatever. Gotten laid, that's what I should've done. Not stayed in the lab both night and day, my one eye pinched over the lens of a microscope. Sex. That's what I wanted. To fuck from the front and the rear, the top and the bottom, on Fridays and Saturdays and high holy holidays as well. A fucking fuck — was it so much to ask for on an overpopulated planet? Wasn't there one woman out there for me? Just one?

I turned over in the dark, fearing one's sex-life was like poured concrete: something that once laid would forever be set. A virgin. I closed my eyes at the thought of it — I'll die a virgin! — then wondered if perhaps I could still save myself by leaving this instant on a Greyhound bus. I could join an ashram out west and adopt an Indian name, and maybe find some barefooted girl who'd introduce me to more than just a strict dietary regime. Love. The physical and spiritual wonders of love. It was all out there, just waiting for me, but it was also a fleeting fantasy. I wasn't the type to walk with dirt between his toes, so when I awoke the next morning, still hung-over with disappointment, the inertia of my old life had already recaptured me. Go west? I could barely get out of bed.

For the next month I lived a double life of sorts, working in the college lab mornings and afternoons, and then abandoning my rôle as scientist and going out in the evenings to a local café. I wore an authentic French beret that I'd bought from the back pages of *The New Yorker,* and I said over more than one cappuccino to anyone who'd listen, "It may work fine in practice, but it just doesn't work in theory." I'd always considered myself more of a Brit like my mother, but by leapfrogging my father's New Jersey and playing up to the Gallic ancestry of my last name, I thought I could attract the type of woman who believed a Frenchman so talented in bed.

I looked for love as a statistician might, by exposing myself to more "events." I prowled the library and browsed the stacks, being sure to always comment on the books being read across from me. On the quad, I suffered a flat nearly every day, if only so I could kneel down beside my ten-speed and wait for some pretty young thing to pass me by with a comment of concern or support. Beautiful girls were everywhere, but never with any greater frequency than in the language lab. Through its doors came young women dreaming in Romance languages, girls who wore knee-high socks and Sunday school shoes and sat down before a reel-to-reel to practice rolling their *r*'s. I spent whole weekends in there, turning at the sight of every short skirt or hint of strong perfume. But still, no matter how many times I extended my headphones saying you have to hear this, my act was nothing more than a succès d'estime: not one girl accepted my offer to listen to a song by Edith Piaf.

There was only one logical conclusion to draw from all of this: I was homosexual. Of course I was. Those men who were had simply proven themselves unsuccessful with women. Scientific fact. They got together to form a lonely hearts club, and spent their days playing bridge and drinking too much sherry. The morning I accepted the truth of this— "Scientific Fact!" I said aloud—I threw off my covers, stabbed my legs into my pants, then stood before my roommate's empty bed, slowly buttoning up my shirt while seething with an unexpressed rage. His latest conquest had kept him away through the night. I hated him— hated him so much I thought I should go to Residential Life and request a change of roommates. I wanted someone who used a wheelchair or an iron lung or at least limped noticeably. But it was wishful thinking, I knew. They'd never approve my transfer, so I messed up his sheets, then grabbed my coat and went out across the dewy campus to the dining hall.

It was there, while snatching a tray still moist and warm from the wash, that I saw her again. Betty Lynne Elliot Webb. I had forgotten her face. It had faded from my memory, leaving only a dull, familiar ache in its place. But when I saw her again, sitting there with two friends at a table in the middle of the room, I felt that same sharp carnal impulse that had come over me in the bookstore. I wanted to clear the room and have her on the table right then and there, amidst the clutter of salt and pepper shakers and sticky condiment bottles. So I left my tray behind and walked directly to her, a little too stiffly perhaps, as if carrying a jug of water on top of my head, but with great purpose, too.

"Pardon," I said. "So sorry. Don't mean to interrupt."

Her friends whispered; Betty looked up at me and asked, "Can I help you?" I smiled to keep from showing that I was cursing myself inside. I had lived in Wargrave, on the western outskirts of London, until the age of twelve; only then did my father move us to the other side of the Atlantic, saying I had better learn to be an American before it was too late. It had taken a year in front of the television for me to lose my English accent, but now it was back, like some streaker set loose on the set of *Benny Hill. Pardon. So sorry. Wouldn't happen to have seen my pruning shears around here, would you? Seem to've lost the silly little buggers somehow.* And I couldn't deviate from it now. She'd think I was mad — British one minute, American the next — and she was too beautiful for that, with her sculpted blonde hair curling up over the shoulders of her blue dress in a way that brought to mind a young Jacqueline Onassis, and breasts — breasts as pointed and firm as the fantasies of my youth. I'd fake it. In a moment I knew I'd fake my accent forever if only I could unhook her brassiere and fall asleep with the feel of her warm flesh cupped in my hand. So I let my silence linger until it had turned from an expression of timidity into a bald and pulsing statement of fact. Then I spoke. "I wanted to find you," I said. "That day in the bookstore."

Her friends shared another whisper, but Betty held my attention, looking at me with blushing cheeks and skin so clear and eyes so white.

15

"Whilst standing in line," I said, "I opened my dictionary, and the word that I saw," and here she lifted her chin ever so slightly, her lips parting to release the soft hiss of a warm breath, "that word was 'fate.'"

The moment stretched between us like taffy being pulled apart at the county fair, then she bit into her lower lip and glanced away, restraining the coyest of smiles. It was all the encouragement I needed to sit down beside her — and if she had said nothing more in the next five months that we dated, it would have been all the encouragement I needed to drop down to one knee and say, "Betty, I love you. Will you be mine?"

IF GIVEN THE CHOICE, I would have lived a life of quiet domesticity, benumbed by the banality of my daily routine. I never wanted to go poking at my past as the cook pokes at the cut of grilled meat to see if it's done; I wanted to have kids and a buy a barbecue and follow an American football team with the same passion I'd once given The Tractor Boys of Ipswich Town. And yet here I am banging away at the keys of my old IBM Selectric as if I were a failed ex-president with a deadline for a bloated memoir.

What happened? you say.

One thing: Sweetness #9.

It was my task at Goldstein, Olivetti, and Dark to conduct a chronic toxicity test of this artificial sweetener prior to our submitting it to the FDA for approval. For this, I bred eight pairs of Sprague-Dawley rats, those red-eyed albino creatures that are so commonly used in toxicology studies because of their calm demeanor and excellent reproductive performance. Within days, vaginal swabs in each of the females in estrus showed the presence of sperm, a reliable indicator of conception, and the males were eliminated from the colony. Gestation cycles ran between twenty-one and twenty-three days and resulted in the birth of seventy-four pups across eight litters. When the males were once again eliminated, there remained thirty-nine test subjects, one of which was cannibalized by its stressed mother before it could open its eyes at two weeks.

The rats were housed independently in plastic tubs on one of two wheeled storage shelves that occupied the back wall of the rodent room. Each tub was secured from above by a metal grate and equipped with

17

an overhanging water bottle; the rats were fed standard rodent chow *ad libitum* and given one of four doses of Sweetness #9. The control group was given no amount of The Nine, as we had taken to calling the sweetener. One-third of the remaining population was given the equivalent of 75 mg/kg BW/day (more than fifteen times the estimated daily human intake of the sweetener), while another third received 1,600 mg/kg BW/day, and the final third enjoyed a dose of 8,000 mg/kg BW/day. To offer perspective, if the group receiving the least amount of Sweetness #9 was ingesting the equivalent of a sweetened bullet every twenty-four hours, the middle third could be said to be absorbing one of the conventional bombs dropped on Dresden, while those receiving 8,000 milligrams per kilogram of body weight per day were taking in something approaching the combined power of Fat Man and Little Boy.

For the first four weeks of my planned twelve-month study, I administered the sweetener by feeding tube. After my rats were weaned from their mothers, I added The Nine to their rodent chow and mixed it in with their water, leaving me to calculate the amount of the test substance assimilated each day.

I would be remiss if I did not mention here the existence of one last test group, however unofficial and poorly tracked it was. This group consisted of two people: me and my wife. That this went against protocol goes without saying. I just couldn't help leaving the lab with a little vial of sweetener stashed away inside my coat pocket every third or fourth day. I felt proud to be wearing my lab coat and performing this work, which would help bring about a future in which diabetics and the calorie-conscious could enjoy a sweetened drink or snack without fear or guilt. And besides, this wasn't a drug study whose results were in question from the start. Previous short-term tests had already determined the maximum dosage I was to deliver, beyond which a large mortality rate could be expected. So when I took home that first vial of The Nine and sweetened my wife's coffee one Saturday morning, I didn't think to discuss its dangers. I only lifted my cup to hers and toasted to progress and new ideas.

Betty giggled as if we were teenagers sneaking alcohol. "It certainly is sweet," she said, after taking a wide-eyed sip.

"One hundred and eighty times sweeter than sugar," I told her, "and at a fraction of the cost."

"Progress and new ideas," she echoed, clinking her cup against mine once more.

While I consumed the sweetener twice per day (first with my morning coffee, then in the evening with a cup of Earl Grey), Betty ingested the substance at a somewhat higher rate, as she had inherited a taste for sweet tea from her Virginia-born father and drank no fewer than four or five cups of the stuff each day. So.

If gaining access to Sweetness #9 years before the public would was a perk of my new career, the excitement this afforded me soon wore off. In fact, by the end of my first month, the novelty of my newfound professionalism had disappeared entirely, and I was looking at my job as a factory worker might. It was the same thing day after day. Each morning I'd pull the rats out of their tubs by the base of the tail and check for anomalies in appearance or behavior. Illness can overtake a rodent quickly and without warning; for this reason it is important to know your test subjects intimately, right down to the consistency of their stool samples. I would touch each specimen's nose and stare deep into its red eyes, looking for any sign of nasal or ocular discharge; then, after rubbing its tail between my fingers to determine if it was running a temperature, I'd set the rat down upon the wire roof of its tub and apply a stethoscope to its chest, listening for the tell-tale signs of congestion or wheezing. Once this task was completed, I'd palpate the rat's lumbar spine and pelvic region to assess its Body Condition Score, a five-point scale that runs from "emaciated" to "obese" and helps identify an animal's general health status. Finally, I'd set the test subject down in the communal glass tank with anywhere from one to three other members of its cohort, and observe its sociability and response to external stimuli, being sure to record all of my findings in the marbled notebook that I stored in the top drawer of my desk.

Rats, as Hickey was kind enough to inform me after the fact, are less prone to biting if you handle them in silence; as a consequence, my days became muted by design. Even those few hours I spent at my desk, writing up my daily observation reports or eating the sandwich I'd brought from home, passed without much more noise than the thrumming of the building's HVAC system. Hickey rarely spoke, perhaps owing to my initial reaction to his prosthetic limb. On several occasions I tried to draw him out on the subject of Vietnam, wanting to learn how he'd lost his leg. But it only seemed to push him farther away. Thinking I should meet him halfway, I spoke freely of my undergraduate adventures as a reporter for *The Daily Targum*, when I'd been assigned to what my editor had called "the draft-card-and-bra-burning beat." I was on his side, I wanted him to know, but still he responded to me as if I had challenged him to a breath-holding contest.

It began to affect my judgment. When it was time to run my rats through the wooden maze (a task I'd perform once a week with a stopwatch in hand), I often couldn't help but say a few encouraging words to one of my test subjects as it moved off toward the piece of cheese I'd set down at the finish line. (Coach Dix had done the same for me the summer before my junior year of high school, after I'd defied my mother's wishes and baffled my closest friends by signing up for the football team. I suffered through a few rather unfortunate acts of hazing before emerging out beneath the lights of Friday night, but the ends, as they say, always justify the means.)

I grew so desperate for conversation that I finally brought a transistor radio from home and tuned it in to the Watergate hearings.

"Are you a Nixon man?" I asked Hickey.

"Mmm."

"Horrible, this thing they're dragging him through, don't you think?" It was the day that former White House counsel John Dean testified, implicating Nixon in the cover-up. He'd prepared a 246-page opening statement, in which his powers of memory were so great that some newspaper columnists had taken to calling him The Human Tape Recorder. "Enemies lists and hush money—what nonsense! Do you believe a word this man says?"

Hickey turned round in his seat, running a handkerchief across the back of his neck. At first I'd thought he perspired so profusely because the primate room was kept at a more tropical temperature than the one housing my rats. But after seeing him wipe his face dry after return-ing from the cafeteria or attending to himself in the men's room, I had come to the conclusion that he simply had overactive sweat glands.

"It's one man's word against another's," I said, "and the word of a disgruntled former employee at that. Who but a madman writes a two-hundred-and-forty-six-page opening statement? Can you tell me?"

Hickey turned back to his paperwork, his voice almost lost in the drone of the air conditioner. "Turn the radio down, will you?"

In a way, it was a triumph. Usually he gave me no more than a word or two. "Lunch," he might say at midday, or "Checking out" near five o'clock. But here? Six! A triumph indeed.

Conversations with my wife were barely better anymore. One evening in late June, I came home to find her sitting in the dark in the living room, wearing a pair of my grey sweat pants and an oversize T-shirt. Streaks of mascara ran from her eyes; a field of used Kleenexes, like so much scattered dandelion fluff, lay all about her on the sofa.

"That bastard!" she said, as I moved in from the door. "How could he be such a bastard?"

It was her father. He had left her mother for a younger woman and fled to a pied-à-terre in Philadelphia.

"Can you believe it?" she said. "She's only three years older than me!"

The four of us had planned to celebrate the Fourth of July together with a cruise of New York Harbor; when we'd first spoken of it over glazed ham at Christmas, I'd imagined lifting a glass of champagne to what I'd assumed would be the inevitable news—we're having a baby! But instead, as we rode the *Spirit of New Jersey* on the evening of Inde-pendence Day, it was just three of us, regardless of your views on the beginning of life.[*]

That evening, Betty and I might as well have been sailing away from

---

[*] In this regard I am not quite a fundamentalist. Life, I say, at least any sense of life that rises above the mere biological, begins after conception, most likely during the seventh week of pregnancy, when a fetus develops taste buds and first senses the sweetness of the amni-otic fluid, thereby establishing a flavor preference that will later be reinforced by the equally sweet taste of mother's milk. What is flavor perception if not the first hint of a soul?

our life as newlyweds, because as the fireworks erupted over the Statue of Liberty, her mother stood wilted at the ship's railing, staring down into the flashes of light that spread out in blurry bursts across the water.

"I think I'm going to vomit," she'd say, as Betty rubbed her back. "I think I'm going to vomit."

Had I known that grief and sorrow can be contagious, I would never have allowed my wife to spend so many countless hours that summer in the hot zone of her childhood home. I thought I was being supportive each time I told her yes, of course, go away for a day or two. But then back she'd come to punish me for another man's crimes.

July was as passionless as it was unbearably hot. When Betty was home, long stretches of silence passed between us, interrupted only by the hum of the refrigerator or the whirring of the window A/C unit.

I began to live in my head more than anywhere else. At work, after Alexander Butterfield testified that Nixon had recorded all the conversations in the Oval Office, I even stopped turning on my transistor radio. Maybe if Hickey had been a better conversationalist, I would have been fine. That wasn't the case, though. And so I descended deeper and deeper into my muted world, a place where every sound became all the louder as a consequence of the deafening silence that surrounded it. Most unnerving were those cries I heard coming from the primate room, especially those that sounded after Hickey had slipped away to perform his morning's toilet or grab a bite to eat.

One day, sure the screeching of the chimpanzees had never before reached such heights, I called for Hickey moments after he'd stepped out into the hall.

"But I've got to go!" he said.

"It'll just be a moment."

A great huffing sigh propelled him back into the lab, then he stood at my side, looking at me with restrained violence. I held up one finger to ask for his patience, and stood there with my head cocked toward the door of the primate room. "There!" A screech—not quite as hideous as it had been moments earlier, but plaintive and terrible all the same. "Did you hear that?"

"They're monkeys," Hickey said, wiping the sweat from his brow. "What do you want?"

"But they've been getting worse, haven't they? Louder, I mean."

He just looked at me. Sometimes I thought he had a glass eye, though maybe it's only in retrospect that I've begun to think this.

"You should hear them when you leave the room," I said.

"When I leave the room?"

"As soon as you're gone"—I pointed—"it sounds like someone's protesting ritual slaughter in there."

He exhaled and turned back for the door. "I have to go."

"But don't they sound angry?"

"I'm no expert."

"You work with monkeys!"

He threw a hand up over his shoulder, saying maybe they just needed a snack. This was his answer to everything. If I said they were making a horrible noise, or he emerged from the primate room and conceded they were a little restless, he'd head off to the cafeteria for another box of milk and a crate of bananas. I never dared watch him feed them; they took their milk from a baby's bottle and this seemed somehow grotesque, considering what Betty and I were trying for at home. But one afternoon, after the monkeys had started cackling and Hickey had gone in there to placate them, I did dare step up to the door and peek through its window—right as a monkey's face filled the glass, its eyes wild, its chin doubled, its cheeks as fat as a baby's.

I spun away from there just as Hickey turned in front of the window holding that monkey over one shoulder (was he burping him?), and then I sat down at my desk, too overcome by my primal fear to focus on the notebook open before me.

It was August before Betty and I touched each other again, and then we only did it because we felt we had to: it was our first anniversary. In retrospect, I see we should have gone somewhere after the French restaurant, a Holiday Inn perhaps, because as we lay together in our bedroom, my attention moved to the wall over our headboard, through which could be heard the voices of our neighbors in 345½. Such a jeremiad! He railed against her meatloaf ("Not again!") as she went on about his drinking ("Never stops!"). Listening to this, I rolled away from Betty, unable to finish, and looked up to the ceiling. What did I really know about my wife? Only recently had she started defecating when I was under the same roof as her; on our honeymoon in Hawaii, she'd taken the ice bucket as cover each morning and used the facilities in the hotel lobby. Had we married too soon? I feared asking the question was answer enough.

"I'm sorry," I said.

"No, it's me," she answered, before adding in a smaller voice, "We won't wind up like them, will we?"

I rolled my eyes into the back of my head, looking up at the wall over the headboard. "*Them?* No."

"Or my parents," she said.

We were like all young people, I suppose, certain we wouldn't repeat the mistakes of the past, that our family would be stronger, healthier, more loving. I reached for her hip. "I love you," I said. I kissed her. "Do you hear? We'll be fine. Better than fine."

And then we turned out the lights, and our despair recaptured us in the dark.

Not long after this, I accompanied Betty to a doctor's office and learned that my wife's uterus was heart-shaped and blanketed by an abnormally thick mucus at ovulation. Betty fled into the hallway in tears and convulsed violently in my arms near the elevator while repeating the words the doctor had told her. "'Have you considered adoption?' *Adoption?*" She might as well have been saying "cancer" or "double homicide." And for good reason, too. We wanted children, *our* children, so we went for a second opinion, and this time heard my sperm described as "sluggish" and "listless" — everything but alcoholic and unemployed. "You should consider adoption," the doctor said.

Instead, Betty insisted we redouble our efforts at baby-making, which immediately rendered our sessions in bed more workmanlike and desperate. She stopped wearing those sheer outfits of pink and yellow chiffon that had once made my groin thrum like a struck tuning fork; now the pendulum had swung back in the other direction, so far so that one evening I found my wife in bed in a white bra and her every-day panties, with a bowl of Rocky Road ice cream balanced on her belly. When she saw me in the doorway, she licked her spoon and set the bowl on the bedside table, then lifted herself up at the hips to slide her panties free. "We have to try extra hard tonight," she said, a phrase that troubled me even then as a fit young man. "Extra hard," she said, bringing to mind the piece of graph paper, stashed in her bedside drawer, on which she charted her basal temperature.

At times such as these, when our likelihood for conception was increased, I knew we'd be going at it every thirty-six hours, until we'd passed back through into a period of reproductive doubt. Betty was relentless. Not even sleep would slow her. More than once I awoke in the middle of the night to find her moving atop me like a figure in a dream, here and then gone, my memory of this uncertain by morning, when I'd be yawning over my first cup of coffee at work and being reminded of the excellent reproductive performance of my rats.

One sleepless morning I set E3CL9, a rat I'd taken to calling Louie, into the wooden maze and watched him turn round in a slow circle near the starting line. It was strange behavior, considering he had for several weeks been racing off toward the cheese he knew would be waiting for him at the end.[*]

I drove home slowly that night, stopping for milk at one convenience store and eggs at another. Since the death of my parents, I had become a master of compartmentalization. But no matter how bad things had ever been, I had always had a sanctuary, a place where I could box myself off from worry and doubt. Before I joined Goldstein, Olivetti, and Dark, it had been my studies and dreams of becoming a flavor chemist, and before that — my grandfather's shoe store. It was there that I had settled for a year after graduating from high school. While all my

---

[*] Louie is a strange name for a female rat, I confess, and one that no doubt could cause certain members of our nation's professoriate to parse out the differences between the homosocial and the homosexual. But if I am to make this my first attempt at full disclosure, I suppose I had better not allow myself to edit even those details that I believe are inconsequential or not connected to the story of The Nine.

peers launched off into college life, I stayed at my grandfather's side and learned how to hold a woman's ankle and smile whenever she insisted the shoe I'd slipped on her foot was a half-size too large, never too small. Now, though, where but in my car could I find any peace of mind? At home I had to bunker down in front of the TV or roll over in bed and pray the magical spell of sleep would hold, while at work I needed to avoid looking into the window of the primate room and concentrate on my rats.

That evening, I expected to come home and find my apartment darkened, as it had been so many nights of late. Instead, it was all lit up, no different from my wife's face.

"C'mon," she said, grabbing me by the hand and leading me back out through the door. "We've been down in the dumps long enough. We deserve a night out."

It was only a Wednesday, so I thought the Howard Johnson's out by the interstate would suffice, but Betty had me take note of her makeup and hair and insisted we treat ourselves to something more extravagant than that.

"How about Le Petit Cochon?"

"French?"

"Why not? I'm worth it, aren't I?"

"Yes, but…"

"We're young, David. Let's live."

So on we went, and then we were sliding into a corner booth and sharing a memorable roast duck with a side of buttered turnips. It was delicious, as good as you could get in North Central New Jersey at the time, and then it only got better. When I reached for the decanter in the center of our table and went to pour my wife a second glass of house red, Betty raised the flat of one hand and couldn't help but grin.

"A baby?" I said.

She nodded. "I'm two weeks late. I wanted to wait until Dr. Orrey could say for sure, but he's away at a conference until next week, and I just couldn't keep it to myself any longer. I know it, though," and she smiled as she had on our wedding day. "I've never been late like this before."

"Oh, Betty!" I squeezed her hand, and then, to the great horror of the maître d', ducked down beneath the table-top and buried my face in her lap. "A little Baby Leveraux, at last!"

Believing this was just the start, I fell asleep that night picturing a teeming family reunion in the country. Betty and I sat at a long wooden table decorated with a gingham table-cloth, watching as our many sons and daughters and grandchildren passed fat pies back and forth. We took a walk through the arbor after dinner, the young following the old as birds swooped down over our shoulders, jealous of the fruit that was so ripe it dropped from the trees and rolled to a stop at our feet. Paradise.

The following evening Betty and I went to the supermarket together, though usually she completed this chore alone. How could I want to be apart from the family? That little force of life in her belly was like a magnet pulling me toward her, so as she filled our cart with jars of pickles and a pyramid of canned soups that were unconscionably salty, I smiled and nodded at passing shoppers, rejoicing at my wife's new-found "cravings" no less than she enjoyed describing them to me.[*]

These developments on the domestic front left me feeling so refreshed and renewed that when I next sent Louie through the maze and saw him give up after only a few steps, I dropped my face down over him like some benevolent god descending from the clouds and offered him a few encouraging words: "C'mon, Louie, you know how it's done! Left, right, left, c'mon, now!"

Moments later, Hickey emerged from the primate room, scribbling onto his clipboard.

"He won't run the maze," I said.

My lab-mate looked up from his work, distracted.

"It's taken him longer and longer each week," I said, "and now he won't even give it a go."

Hickey glanced back into the primate room, and only then did I re-

---

[*] The increased blood flow of pregnancy dilutes a woman's normal level of sodium, triggering the craving for salty foods.

alize it myself: they weren't making any noise. Hadn't made any all day, in fact, perhaps all week.

Hickey walked to his desk shaking his head. "They just sit there and stare right through me."

"The monkeys?" I followed him over, so glad to hear the strain in his voice—it wasn't just in my head, then! I thought this might be our breakthrough. Silent monkeys and apathetic rats! We'd be like Crick and Watson, volleying wild conjectures back and forth over pints of warm bitter. But then Hickey draped his lab coat over the back of his chair and continued around me to the door.

"Calling it a day," he said.

Nothing more. Not even an encouraging word about the weekend.

IN MY YOUNGER AND MORE impressionable years, a classmate of mine felt something turning over in his stomach before at last he leaned forward and vomited. This was at an assembly, when I was still just a lad in short pants at infant school. I don't remember exactly where I was sitting in relation to the sick child, but I know it was close enough that I could smell the bitter odor of the slick of vomitus on the hardwood floor. In America, this would have been cause for a riot. But in England, after my fellow students and I had allowed ourselves a quiet collective gasp, the headmaster clapped his hands and called us to attention, saying there was nothing to be alarmed about. Just as quickly, sawdust, kept nearby for just such an occasion, I suppose, was poured over the offending item, and I was pulling the end of my striped tie away from my mouth and nose, the assembly continuing as if nothing had happened.

When I tell people I consider myself more British than American, if only because my most formative years were spent in England, I often think of this scene. It happened long before Lady Di's untimely death sent the country wailing out into the streets, back in that era when memoirs were still written only by explorers and great men of state. All of which is to say that while I may have been developing suspicions in Animal Testing, I felt no need to share them with my wife. A good man didn't bring his work home with him, least of all if it was troubling. He deposited the money in the bank and provided for his family as best he could. We were going to have a baby, remember. So what Betty needed was comfort and shelter, not a steady diet of darkness and doubt.

But, of course, if there is one thing I've learned after all these years, it's that darkness and doubts will visit you no matter what, and that's exactly what happened to us.

The Sunday after we visited Le Petit Cochon, I stood at the stove cooking bacon and eggs for breakfast when I heard a sudden half-muffled yelp over the sound of the popping grease. I shut off the fan, then turned round holding the spatula up in one hand as if it were a torch. There it was again, a little louder this time. I turned the stovetop to low and followed the sound to the door of the bathroom, from behind which running water could be heard.

I knocked with the knuckle of my index finger. "Betty?"

Like a gymnast thrown higher by a trampoline, her yelping soared. I pushed inside and found her crying at the sink, wearing only one of my undershirts. She'd gotten out of bed a minute or two earlier and was standing there with her panties in her hands, washing them beneath the faucet. I didn't have to ask. I could see it well enough myself: a spot of blood.

Foolishly, I thought we should rush to the hospital, but what could they do? Deliver a fetus at six weeks, before it could tell the difference between bitter and sweet?

"Maybe it's just spotting," Betty said. She threw her panties down into the bowl of the sink—a loud, wet smacking sound that told me how little she believed her own words. "You hear about women who accidentally get pregnant," she sobbed, "or teenage girls who…" The thought trailed off; she shook her head and looked at me with her washed-out eyes. "Why is it so hard for us? Why?"

I still had the spatula in one hand, the eggs and bacon crackling in hot grease behind me. I stepped toward her and wrapped her up in one arm, my body there beside her but my mind thrown back to the summer before my senior year of high school, when I'd last felt such grief. "There, there," I said. "There, there."

As a Fighting Quartermaster assigned to the 3032nd Mobile Baking Division, my father led a trailer-mounted dough mixer, divider, and rounder into the horrors of Buchenwald. A nominal Catholic at the time of his enlistment, he turned his back on organized religion after

walking away from the spent loaves of the battlefield, and began to retreat, in either mind or body, to the cathedral that was Yankee Stadium,
a place where he would rise at one with the crowd and feel the thrill of
hope each time a foul ball came arcing up through the air toward him.

I was not very different. Though I had been raised singing alongside
my mother in the Church of England, I too preferred a religion of my
own creation, one that came to me with the same power of revelation
that I suspect Joseph Smith and William Miller must have felt. It happened in a Waffle House on Guadalupe Street, the morning after my
parents had been shot at the University of Texas.

Pimply and seventeen, I sat in a booth by the window, facing an old
army buddy of my father's who had come up from San Antonio to comfort me until my grandfather could fly in from the coast.

From my seat I could see a newspaper vending machine on the sidewalk outside, complete with the day's most obscene headline framed
in its window: Sniper in U.T. Tower 'Fortress' shot after 90
minutes of terror. Student slays wife and mother, Kills 13,
wounds 31 on campus. I had found myself standing before it while
my father's old friend circled round from the driver's seat of his Cadillac, and though I should've known better, I hadn't been able to look
away. The day of death: See pages 17, 18, 19. I could resist the pull
of these words no more than I'd been able to resist watching Chet
Huntley the night before, the opening remarks of his newscast still
looping round in my mind all these hours later: *For an hour and a half
today, the normally placid university and capital city of Austin, Texas,
was held in the grip of a terror that began in killing and ended in killing.
A maddened former marine, a twenty-four-year-old student in the architectural school...*

Inside the restaurant, when I wasn't picking at my pecan waffle and
staring out the window, I was reading those pages of that morning's
Austin American that my father's old army buddy had deemed fit for
my perusal. The sporting news offered a few diversions, but nothing ap-
pealed to me as much as the almost twenty inches of print given over
to a profile of The World's Oldest Man, a Bulgarian by the name of Kiril
who had stood on this spinning planet for more than 113 years.

"I owe it all to yogurt," he said. "Each day, I eat no less than three cups."

The Waffle House, as those of you familiar with the American South no doubt know, does not serve yogurt, or at least it most certainly did not in 1966. When I asked for a cup, our waitress looked at me as if I'd just requested directions to the offices of the local branch of the NAACP. Still, even after being rebuffed, I knew I had found the rock on which I could build a new life. What could possibly matter more? I wondered. That the meek would inherit the earth? That the Yankees would win another World Series? Or that a man as old as the sky and the air swore by the life-giving properties of the *Lactobacillus bulgaricusa* culture?

Later that same day, when I met my grandfather at the airport, I had that newspaper clipping tucked away in my back pocket; it was the first of many such profiles that I stored in an old MJB coffee can that I kept beneath my bed. Especially in those years directly after this crisis, I followed the comings and goings of the world's oldest citizens as my father had once followed the seasons of Mickey Mantle. I wanted to know how they did it, what they thought of dancing and laughter, cigars versus cigarettes, caffeine. If a super-centenarian had something to say about moderation, I'd meditate upon it while brushing my teeth. If another believed life had been better under Benjamin Harrison, I'd check out a biography at the library, or perhaps dash off a letter to a local scholar. More than anything, I coveted their thoughts on food. If The Oldest Man in America attributed his advanced age to eating figs and rainbow trout, I filled my shopping cart accordingly. If The World's Oldest Woman warned about the evils of cheap whiskey and stinky cheese, I recoiled from these items as if from a flame.

When I learned from Betty that our dreams of parenthood were dashed, I dumped the bacon and eggs I had already prepared and fixed us a breakfast consisting of white fish, white potatoes, and white milk.

"Eat," I told my wife. "That's an order."

Since first reading about the dietary habits of the current Oldest Man in America, a stolid Norwegian immigrant from St. Olaf, Minnesota, I had filled our freezer with the work of the Gorton's Fisherman. Betty was in no way a convert to my system of faith, but on this woeful morning she agreed that a few fish fingers and a side of hash browns couldn't possibly hurt.

After she had cleared her plate and downed a second glass of milk, she said, in a small voice that made this sound like a question, "I'd like to spend the day with my mother." I didn't object; I encouraged her. Considering the many mysteries of the female anatomy, I assumed my mother-in-law would be a greater service to my wife than I would be. So I drove Betty inland to Battle Station (the midpoint between Jupiter Park and her mother's home in Montclair) and made the exchange in the parking lot of a Holiday Inn.

By then it was lunchtime, but instead of returning home for a sandwich, I thought of my rats and drove out to calculate their daily intake of Sweetness #9. When I'd finished, I ate a bag of chips and a candy bar from the vending machine, then stayed in the lab another hour or two and observed my test subjects as they moved about the communal glass tank. Such a transformation I saw. They had once been blind, needy pups no heavier than the air in my hands, but now they were growing into adulthood, many of them already nearing the 200 grams of weight that signified maturation.

I found myself ready to cry when I considered how it wasn't just their bodies that were growing. One rat, who was in the group receiving the highest dose of The Nine, had in recent weeks begun to show evidence of rage issues; another from his cohort slept for hours at a time on the exercise wheel, though near the start of the summer she'd spent just as much time with her little legs blurring upon it. No less troubling were two rats who previously had exhibited homosexual tendencies; this afternoon they showed not the slightest inclination to frolic and play. Louie, though—he was somehow the worst. Louie was crying blood. I knew better than to think of it like this. Within the eye's orbit of every Sprague-Dawley rat there exists a Harderian gland which produces a pigmented substance that, once secreted, has the appearance of dried blood; but still I couldn't help it. As I wiped the "tears" from Louie's coat and set him down in the tank, I sucked in a jagged breath of air, then watched as he slunk over to the tank's far corner and rolled onto his back, as if he were some delinquent French philosopher lounging about in the fields.

"Oh, Louie," I said.

He was an easy mark. The rat who'd been experiencing rage issues pounced on him, causing me to pull them apart and get bitten in the thumb in the process. Minutes later I was out in the main room, pinning back the skin of the offending party in a dissecting tray. My autopsy was not an act of retribution; it was part of a continuing and planned process of scientific inquiry that had already reduced my population of test subjects by approximately 20 percent. I don't know what I expected to see magnified on my glass slide that afternoon — tumors and misshapen organs, holes in the brain — but everything checked out fine: the rat's bladder was as smooth as the skin of a chestnut, and its brain as pink and fluffy as grade-A ground round.

I wanted to make sense of all the changes I'd observed, but I couldn't detect any consistency in the symptoms or find a correlation between the dosage and its effect. The rat whose brain was on my slide had been receiving a dose of Sweetness #9 six times as large as Louie's, but I wasn't sure he was any worse off because of it. I could say with no greater certainty that this was all in my head.

Desperate for corroborating evidence, I went to Hickey's desk and looked all over for his notebooks. Only his pencil drawer was unlocked, and it held little of interest: a prescription bottle of Quaaludes, a pornographic postcard, Asian in theme, stuck inside a copy of *Jonathan Livingston Seagull*, and a letter from his mother that described her worries: *You should find a nice girl, it doesn't matter how she looks, someone who cooks.*

I stashed the letter back in its envelope before I could finish reading it, but minutes later, after I'd pulled away from the parking lot and arrived at the first four-way stop down the road, my memory wouldn't let me forget what I'd seen. As I idled there with my left indicator flashing, and by no means eager to spend the day alone with my thoughts, the looping letters of Hickey's mother's handwriting appeared in my mind's eye, and I pulled up on the lever to make my right indicator flash, just before I turned away from my home toward his.

HICKEY'S NEIGHBORHOOD OF SMALL RANCH-STYLE houses was some-how sadder than my own apartment complex, perhaps because of its suggestion of greater permanence. I parked across the street from his neighbor's house, which had a blue tarp fluttering loose at one corner of its roof. No fence ran between this home and Hickey's, at least not in the front yard; the property lines in the subdivision were revealed by lawn-mowers at those points where one homeowner chose to stop cutting his grass, bringing his neighbor's delinquency or diligence into stark relief.

As soon as I got out of my car, I spotted Hickey in his backyard, wearing madras shorts and spraying lighter fluid onto the coals of a black Weber barbecue. I didn't think anything of this until I had stepped up onto the sidewalk and realized he was alone. I'd still be puz-zling over this a few hours later, but already it slowed and then stalled my steps. We owed so much to the discovery of fire. It brought our early human ancestors together, first for the hunt, then the chore of cooking. You had to skin the game and soften its meat by pounding on it with a stone, then you'd pierce its flesh with a stick and set it out over the open flame. Conversation developed as a result of these chores, our very first communities; you couldn't do everything by yourself, af-ter all, and if you worked closely with others, your grunts and groans would naturally develop into a shared tongue. Fire is what made us human. Because smoked meats last longer than those that are raw, fire provided us with our first free time, allowing us to forget about our survival for a minute and dream up the first of those niceties — a wheel! — that have made our civilization so civilized. But Hickey,

35

Hickey—the thought pierced me like a spear to the gut: he was barbecuing alone.

I looked back to my car, but then he spotted me, and I returned his tentative wave and moved forward smiling until we were shaking hands beside the Weber.

"Well." I turned to face his home, as if I were on a tour of architectural marvels. A black flag hung from the window of the door to the kitchen. It showed a crestfallen soldier in silhouette, standing before a watchtower and a couple of strands of barbed wire. POW*MIA, it read. YOU ARE NOT FORGOTTEN. "Hope you don't mind my dropping by."

"No, not at all." He ran a handkerchief across his forehead, mopping up the sweat that had gathered there. "You hungry?"

It was a strange time for a meal, somewhere in that grey zone of hours between noon and five o'clock, when so many bachelors, realizing they've forgotten to have lunch, spoil the prospects of a proper dinner by consuming a large meal.

"Famished," I said.

He didn't have any more ground beef thawed out, but he did have some cold lunch meat and a couple of slices of white bread that were surprisingly fresh, considering he didn't know how long they'd been languishing on his kitchen counter. After I'd slathered on the mustard and mayo, I followed Hickey back out into the yard and sat with him beneath a sun umbrella, drinking cans of Budweiser he fished from an ice chest near his feet.

"I apologize for coming over unannounced like this," I said at last. "Betty and I have been…" I shook my head, then bit into my sandwich. "We're going through a difficult time."

He reached into the cooler—"Incoming!"—and set a can down before me.

"I'm not even done with my first one yet," I said.

"Then you had better catch up."

I don't know if it was the drinking that did it, or if perhaps he was on the pills I'd seen in his desk drawer, but he spoke as he never had before in my presence. It was as if he'd been hiding his words in his backyard all this time, and now that I had come upon his stash, he had no choice but to show them to me. He spoke of an absent father and an overbearing mother, then went on — and on — about his miserable time in high school. (He was the uncoordinated kid whose flop sweat was the subject of universal ridicule.)

"When I signed up for the army," he said, "I thought I'd finally be able to start over." But he was neither brave nor daring, and the fellowship of man was no more automatic in the swamps of Vietnam than it had been in the corridors of his old high school. "My fellow soldiers refused to learn my name because they were certain I'd get sent home in a box or on a gurney before I'd made the effort worth their while. And they were right, too." Hickey rapped his knuckles into the side of his artificial leg. "Happened on Day Four. I walked away from the others to piss, so shy about pulling myself out in front of them that I forgot about the dangers of a land mine." He lifted his beer can to toast. "Live and learn, right?"

I sat there silently, nodding as if I were a priest receiving confession.

"I'm not a happy man," he said. "I don't know that I've ever been happy."

I laughed nervously; then joked that maybe he was just coming down with a bad case of Sweetness #9 poisoning.

He crushed his empty can in one hand, then tossed it over his shoulder into the wilds of his lawn. His pinched expression said it all: What do you mean?

So I shared my suspicions, telling him what I'd observed that afternoon and in the preceding days and weeks, too. "I think it's safe to say they're all affected." I counted the symptoms off on one hand. "I've noticed anxiety, lethargy, unexplained anger, reduced intellectual acuity."

Hickey leaned back in his chair, sighing. "Oh, Leveraux, don't tell me you're one of these goofy types."

"But Louie's the worst."

Hickey crossed to the Weber and closed its lid. "How many times do I have to tell you? Use numbers, not names. Otherwise you'll swing the results."

"You should see him," I said. "It's plain as day. He's come down with what I can only describe as a generalized dissatisfaction with life."

"Then put down that he's suffering from the American Condition and be done with it."

"I mean it, Hickey." I'd had only one beer for every three that he had consumed, but still that was one or two more than I usually had. I took a sip and continued: "I'm worried about him."

"And I'm worried about you. Do you know what you're doing?"

I didn't, but the element of menace in his voice made it perfectly clear: a lot was at stake. Millions had been invested in The Nine, but billions more were forecast on the other end. Just the soda pop and table-top markets alone were expected to generate a fortune greater than that of any remaining European king or queen, and it was all there for the taking, if only cancer didn't halt its advance into America's supermarkets, restaurants, and homes. The disease had already placed the future of saccharin in doubt. In 1960, lab tests had linked the popular product to bladder cancer in rats—a clear violation of the newly enacted Delaney Clause of the Food, Drug, and Cosmetic Act, which prohibited the use of any food additive known to cause cancer in man or animal. The only reason saccharin hadn't immediately been pulled from the shelves was that it couldn't be replaced. It was the only artificial sweetener then on the market, something we at Goldstein, Olivetti, and Dark knew full well and were racing to undo.

Hickey reached for another beer and popped it open. "Have you put any of your rats under the microscope?"

I nodded.

"And what does it say?"

I shrugged.

"Then stop your worrying."

"But Hickey."

"What?"

It would have been blasphemous for me to think this only a few weeks earlier, but now I wanted to speak to him about the dangers of a lifetime of exposure to food additives, a chemical residue that builds up like silt in a stream. I kept thinking back to something I'd learned as a graduate student. At the start of the century, when the unscrupulous were fortifying your flour with sawdust and using embalming fluid as an anti-curdling agent in your milk, Dr. Harvey Wiley, chief of the FDA's forerunner, the U.S. Bureau of Chemistry, tested a variety of potentially harmful substances then in the U.S. diet, including borax, sulfuric acid, and formaldehyde. His methods would be impossible now, for he added these substances to home-cooked meals that he served to young civil servants who had volunteered their time. "Dr. Wiley's Poison Squad," as the press came to call this group, was supposed to have stayed together for five years. But before the experiment could continue as long as that, the volunteers began complaining of nausea and vomiting, of various mental afflictions and a perhaps not too surprising loss of appetite. For some, these problems started only after chronic exposure; for others, one meal was more than enough.

And my rats could be the same. Had they been able to speak, they might have told me there was more to food safety than looking for tumors and cancers and misshapen organs—all the stuff of the Delaney Clause. Perhaps they felt shooting pains in their sides or suffered from numbness in the extremities. They could have unexplained cramping, or feelings of vertigo or tinnitus. There was blurred vision to consider, fuzzy memory, slurred speech; joints that creak while you walk, shortened attention spans, bouts of panic. Perhaps they were seeing an atomic whirl at the periphery of their vision, perhaps only at certain times of day or night. There were so many things we didn't or couldn't test for: mood changes, phobias, difficulty swallowing; too much thirst and hunger, too little. They could be feeling godlike and unreal, confused and lost in a fog, unable to think straight—or worse.

"I think Louie might be suicidal," I said.

"Oh dear god." Hickey stood and turned toward a row of bushes that ran away from his tool-shed. "You're obviously drunk."

"What?" I went to follow him, realizing too late, as he was unzipping his shorts and then dipping his one good knee to pull himself out, that he was urinating. "He sleeps with his face pushed down into the sawdust. He'll suffocate. But what's worse is, I don't think he even cares."

"You're serious?" He shook, then turned round, listing to one side as he zipped himself up. I looked two doors down, where a neighbor lady was collecting her wash from the laundry line. "You've had him on the couch then, have you?"

"Listen, I know we can't give him the Minnesota Multiphasic."

"Because do you really want to go to the fourth floor with this?"

"The fifth."

"'Leveraux's mouse is depressed, fellas.'"

"My rat."

"'Better pull the plug.'"

"I've been working with him for weeks. I know."

"'Forget the millions you've pumped into R&D.'"

"He just lies there!"

"'The rat can't get out of bed!'"

"Some days he doesn't even eat, Hickey!"

"Well, good! It is a no-calorie sugar substitute, remember! Someone's gotta lose weight!"

As he brushed past me back toward the table, I remembered the fat face I'd seen in the window of the door to the primate room, when Hickey had been in there burping one of his monkeys. But he wouldn't say anything more. After finishing the last of his beer, he saluted his POW*MIA flag and started indoors, saying he was calling it a night.

After the screen door had slammed shut behind him, I started toward my car with as much purpose as I had lacked on my walk in from it earlier. Betty was at her mother's; there was no reason to rush home. So I drove back out toward the ocean, parked after waving hello to the night guard at the gate, then walked into the lab and went straight to the door beneath the red-on-white sign marked PRIMATES. Hickey had rolled a TV in there during the week, and as I pulled at the door, I could hear two men speaking in cartoonish German accents.

I found each monkey pushed back into the darkened corner of his cage. They all looked alike. They sat with a bottle of sweetened milk in one hand, surrounded by a scattering of banana peels. Their eyes were fixed on the TV in front of them, and whenever I passed before it or blocked the screen, they leaned to one side or the other, trying to maintain their line of sight.

A narrow gutter cut across the concrete floor in front of the cages, ending at a drain. A gutted cardboard box lay next to it with an empty bladder of milk spilling out from inside. The monkeys had kept Hickey busy. He'd been running back and forth between them and the tap, silencing their cries with another round of sweetened milk and a bunch of bananas, until only their silent appetites remained.

I looked over my shoulder to the television. Jerry Lewis sat in the backseat of an open-roofed Mercedes-Benz, dressed like a Nazi general, as he argued with a soldier at a checkpoint. I recognized the scene from when I'd seen it in the theaters. *Which Way to the Front?* I turned off the television, but the screaming of the monkeys—I can hear it even now—sent me scrambling to flip it back on.

As my breathing returned to normal, I found the courage to look, to really look at the monkey directly in front of me. It was akin to staring at a total lunar eclipse; it filled me with such dread and awe. You see, after almost four months of The Nine and all the bananas he could take, this monkey was pot-bellied and thick-limbed, sitting there with an oddly swollen face. His breathing slowed, became shallow. He looked through me, lost in an unblinking daze.

I fell down out of my crouch and felt the cool of the concrete floor rush up to meet me.

These monkeys; they were no different from four out of every ten Americans today.

They were not simply overweight. They were obese.

HICKEY WAS ALREADY THERE WHEN I came in to work the next morning, but we didn't talk as I gathered my things at my desk and then crossed into the rodent room. Our first words were exchanged near lunchtime, after he had emerged from the primate room holding a diapered monkey and feeding it from a bottle. I wouldn't have been more surprised if he'd reemerged cradling a baby in his arms.

"Where'd you get that one?" I said.

The monkey was thin, disturbingly so—anorexic compared to the ones I'd seen the night before.

Hickey sat at his desk, with his back turned to me.

"Did they expand your test group?" I asked. "Deliver him this morning?"

He spoke over his shoulder. "You stopped in here last night?"

"I left a few things behind. Now, c'mon, tell me. Where'd you get him?"

He didn't answer. Just turned away from me. So I strode out the door, telling him he wasn't the only one I could ask, and took the elevator up to the fifth floor, where I was met by a smiling secretary.

"John Rogers, please," I said. And when she just looked at me blankly, I held my hand out even with my shoulder as if to remind her of his height. "Maybe I mean Roger Johns? It's important," I added.

A man stepped into the doorway of the office behind her and fixed me with an appraising look. "You mean Billy?"

Now it was my turn to look confused. "Billy?"

He chuckled and explained it was an old prep school name. "You won't find him around here anymore, though. He's joined the other side."

42

Thinking this might be a corporate euphemism for death, I affected a look that was suitably mournful and, when invited, followed him into his office at a slow, funereal pace.

"I'm sorry to hear about Billy," I said. "I didn't know him very well, but he seemed like such a good fellow."

He showed me to a chair before his desk, saying I shouldn't feel too sorry for him. "Nothing beats government work, eh? Or is it the other way around? 'It sure beats government work?'" He waved it off, saying that probably explained why he'd agreed to come here. "I didn't know the answer, did I?"

I smiled, but even so he saw the need to elaborate.

"He's joined the FDA," he said. "Which I just left."

"*Billy?*"

"Likes to joke he got traded for a player to be named later and an undisclosed amount of cash. Well" — he turned his palms to the ceiling — "here am I. Just don't go asking about that money."

He laughed loudly. I showed a jagged mouthful of teeth, trying unsuccessfully to do the same.

"Candy?" He sat up from his seat and extended a dish of cut crystal. I reached for a butterscotch. He was chewing his before I could even get mine unwrapped.

"So is this normal?" I said. "His, you know, going there, and your…"

He was already nodding. "Business and government: they need to work together to provide safe, beneficial products that can be delivered to the market at an inexpensive but reasonable price. Don't you agree? A reasonable price."

I had come up here with a feeling of great urgency, but now I felt ready to sink through the bottom of my chair. There was something hypnotic about his voice. Something captivating about his dark, swept-back hair. I had thought him Irish at first, but now, looking into his mesmerizing deep-set eyes, I felt certain he was German.

He spun round in his chair and opened the lowest drawer of a green filing cabinet, then turned back to me and laid a manila folder on his desk. After opening it and reading for a moment, he said without looking up, "You're Leveraux, right? Down in Animal Testing?"

"Yes, a flavorist-in-training," I answered.

"Right, right" — he turned over a piece of paper, his eyes racing down the next page as he skimmed its contents — "don't tell me: you're the aerodynamics of Stilton."

I wrinkled my nose, pushing the frames of my glasses up into my brow.

He looked at me. "Rutgers, right?"

"Oh!" Now I understood. "Yes, but it was the biophysics of brie."

"That's it." He tapped his finger into the document opened before him, then threw it out toward me like the barrel of a gun. "But you lived in England, where they make Stilton."

"That's right, yes." My voice had slowed; I leaned forward in my seat, trying to see what he was reading. I didn't remember saying anything about England on my CV.

The man closed the folder then and threw a thumb back over one shoulder. "Baseball fan?"

In a photo on the wall, he stood alongside Bing Hardwell in foul territory of Philadelphia's Veterans Stadium.

"Yes," I said, "but the Yankees are my team. Passed down with the X chromosome."

"Well, you may have more pennants than us, but one thing you do lack" — and here he turned his smile toward the picture — "is a man who can barbecue like that."

"You don't say?"

"You're not a vegetarian, are you, Leveraux?"

"I'd rather die charging the last cow."

"That's what I like to hear. We'll have to play hooky tomorrow and take in a game. I'll introduce you."

"To Bing?"

"Great guy." He gave the file on his desk another glance. "Now, what brings you up to menswear, David? I thought you lab coats liked to stick to yourselves."

I almost didn't want to say anything anymore. Bing Hardwell! I'd never met a real live baseball player before, let alone a former MVP who was as good with the barbecue tongs as he was with a Louisville

Slugger. I stammered out my response: "It's just a few concerns, is all."

He tapped the file. "You're working on The Nine?"

"That's right."

"Problem?"

"No. No, I don't know if I would call it that. Some concerns, though. A few concerns."

His mouth hung open thoughtfully. I charged into it with a rambling talk about perceived personality changes, lowered test scores, and Louie's difficulties in the maze. "The monkeys are no less disturbing. At first they went all but silent, and now they've grown considerably overweight. You could even say obese."

I expected him to respond in some way, but he didn't blink or move his head; he just looked at me, a faint smile held on his face. I cleared my throat (I am the type of man who clears his throat) and continued. "I thought to discuss this with Hickey—my lab-mate," I said. "He has more experience with these things. But he's not the greatest conversationalist, I'm afraid."

"So you came up here?"

I nodded. "I couldn't sleep last night. I got to thinking maybe The Nine triggers a primitive desire to eat."

He turned in his chair to face the window. "A primitive desire to eat?"

"I checked my rats again this morning, and their BCS scores are in no way promising. At least half the population is leaning closer to obese than emaciated. The problem's not quite as pronounced as it is with the monkeys, but it's there all the same, and as The Nine is a no-calorie sugar substitute, the last thing we'd want is something that promotes weight gain."

He nodded—this man whose name I realized I hadn't been told. I looked in the direction he was looking, out to the surf silently pounding into the shore beneath a line of roiling grey clouds that looked like so many brains set up in a row, each heavy with the mysteries of the weather. We didn't speak for a minute or more, and when at last he did continue, I realized I was holding my breath.

"Well," he said, "I'm sure we could throw some money at it. The primitive desire to eat?" He swiveled his chair in my direction. "But what good would come of it? Who can say where the primitive desire to eat is located, or if we're ever turning it on or off? Can you?"

I looked to the floor. I held my hands in my lap.

"The brain is like the Amazon, Leveraux. Ten steps in and we're lost. Can't see the sun, can't hear the voice of your guide if he's more than a machete whack away. There's no north or south, no right or left — it's all madness in there." Again, he targeted me with a finger gun. "Cancer, though — cancer we can see. Cancer moves like a fire through the hills." He pointed to the ceiling. "'Look, there! Cancer!' It's easy. But everything else" — he shook his head — "it's like a scuttling sound on the jungle floor, something that shakes a bush or runs up a tree just moments before you can identify it. It's a shadow, Leveraux. A blur. And what are we supposed to do about that? 'The primitive desire to eat.'"

He all but spat these last words out. I nodded. Then he rose from his chair and started round toward me. "What do you say we go get some lunch? I hear they have enchiladas today."

I stood, but remained rooted to the floor. "I just can't get past this one last thing. The monkeys were watching television. A Jerry Lewis movie. It seemed to calm them. But when I turned off the TV..." I frowned. "The most awful screams."

He placed his hands on my shoulders and turned me toward him until we were looking at each other eye to eye. "Let's not get ahead of ourselves, okay? Because what do we have here? A few fat monkeys, some apathetic rats? This is fine. Expected even. But you have to remember the scientific process, because until we have repeatable results —"

"Yes, of course."

" — we can't go off screaming into the wind."

"Oh, I do hope I didn't give that impression."

"Because I'll tell you something." He led me out toward the elevators, his voice dropping to a whisper. "There are investors in this world so savvy they can pick up on the faintest psychic tremors emanating out from the centers of industry." The elevator opened with a ding. He sent me in with a slap on the back. "Now, you remember to bring your glove tomorrow." He pointed as the doors closed between us. "And I'll call Bing and have him slow-cook us a brisket!"

BETTY VISITED THE DOCTOR that day with her mother, and was home by the time I arrived in the early evening. I found her on the sofa, lit up by the glow of the TV and wearing one of the baby-doll outfits I hadn't seen since the start of summer. I thought this a positive sign until I sat down beside her and saw she was drinking something clear, on the rocks, with an olive in it.

I reached for her thigh. "How did it go at the doctor?"

She kept her eyes on the evening news and took a sip of her drink, the alcoholic intake telling me all I needed to know: it had been a phantom pickle, no baby all along, or perhaps just not one anymore.

"We can try again," I said.

And that's when she told me. "I need an intellectual life."

Nothing could have confused me more. She'd majored in Family-Consumer Sciences and navigated our brief courtship with all the skill of someone completing the thesis for her MRS degree. But now she was saying she was thinking of going back to school in the fall, this time as a business major. She'd already placed a call, and because she was a former student, it was just a matter of completing some paperwork.

I looked to Dan Rather for consolation. He stood reporting the news from Vietnam, a village burning behind him.

"All I have is silence," she said. "It'd be enough if I could just hear a baby scream." She looked at me. "You have your work. I need something, too, David."

I looked back to the television and the jungle atrocities that would trouble my sleep that night. "An intellectual life," I said.

We watched the village burn.

* * *

The next morning I drove in to work with my Yankees cap on the passenger seat, thinking I'd stop into the lab for only an hour or two before heading up to the fifth floor and offering to drive Billy's replacement to the park. As it so happens, I wasn't there even that long.

When I entered Animal Testing, I heard the sounds of The Carpenters ("We've only just begun") coming from a radio inside the primate room. As the door was ajar, I poked my head inside and found Hickey dancing with one of the monkeys as a grandfather might dance with his granddaughter. The monkey was standing on his shoes and holding his hands, the two of them seemingly having a grand old time. I stepped inside, smiling, and then I noticed the monkey's profile: thin, not fat. What's more, when he turned to face me, I saw he had bright, lively eyes and cheeks that were far from bloated. They were so drawn, in fact, that I could see the outline of the monkey's skull.

"Is he the one from yesterday?"

Hickey's expression hardened into a mask of B-movie sincerity. "What do you mean?"

"Don't play dumb with me." As he returned the thing to its cage, I looked at all the others—and they all had changed. Standing, walking in circles, shaking at their screens—they were lively, loud, and above all else thin.

"Repeatable results." I turned to face him. "If that's what we're after, who are we testing? Hmm? The monkeys or me?"

"I don't know what you're talking about."

"Don't play with me."

"What makes you think I'm playing?"

"That playful remark. What did you do? Make a phone call after I visited you on Sunday? Say I was out of control?"

"I really don't know what you mean."

I turned from him and marched into the other room. The rats were no different. One drank freely from a vertical bottle; another ran on an exercise wheel. And Louie! Oh, Louie! There was a yellow clip attached to the rat's left ear identifying him as E3CL9, but when I had him out and was holding him up before my nose, it was as if I was looking into the eyes of one of those pod people in the movies. "What have you done with Louie?" I said.

Hickey stood at the door, struggling to speak. I set the rat down in the communal tank and bumped out past him.

"Where are you going?" he said. "Let's talk. What are you gonna do?"

"You'd like to know, wouldn't you?"

I stopped at my desk for a framed photo of Betty, then pulled open the pencil drawer and grabbed a roll of quarters I kept there for the vending machine.

"You just need to calm down."

"Calm down?" I turned to face him, but there was nothing to say. I added only one word as I moved around him. "Lunch," I said. And then I was slamming the door behind me — or trying to; I had forgotten about the hydraulic hinge.

I crossed the parking lot as erect as a soldier on parade, knowing full well the part that I was to play — that of the brave whistle-blower, the man who goes without sleep and forgets to shave, sacrificing everything in the name of a grand ideal. *A cover-up! A cancer in the industry! People needed to know the truth!* Then I stopped, remembering the marbled notebook in which I'd entered all of my observations and readings. There was nothing more galling than an anti-climactic flight, but I was sure I'd need it for evidence, so I turned round and went in again to Animal Testing.

As I pushed through the door, Hickey and the man I'd spoken with the day before were talking at Hickey's desk.

"What's your name?" I said.

Billy's replacement gave me a smile I'm sure he thought was pacifying. "I hear you're in quite the state, Leveraux."

"I'm not in a state. I'm reacting as any sane man would." I pointed to the door of the primate room. "Those monkeys are thin, and they were obese only two days ago. It can mean only one thing."

Hickey spoke to the man as if I weren't there. "He showed up at my house on Sunday drunk."

I stepped toward them. "What?"

"Is this true, David?"

"I had one for every three that he had!"

"He's been having family problems," Hickey continued. "He and his wife can't conceive."

"Now wait a second, that doesn't have anything to do with this."

"It's been affecting his work," Hickey said. "He told me so himself."

"Will you stop!" I turned to face the man whose name I didn't know. "I only told him about my wife because he was going on and on about his own sad and pathetic life."

"There's no need for name-calling, David."

Hickey mopped his brow with a handkerchief, while the nameless man held up his hands as if I had approached them with a knife and not the truth. "What do you say you just take a few days off?" he said. "A little vacation."

"I don't need a little vacation."

"Just long enough to get your mind back in order."

"My mind is perfectly ordered. It's Hickey's that's out of whack."

"If you won't let us help you, Leveraux, you can't help us."

I looked at him as if he'd grown a third arm and a second nose. "What on earth does that mean?"

At this moment, a security guard entered the room with an empty banker's box balanced on his belly. He was a young, plodding fellow whose brain seemed to trail him by a good four or five steps. The man whose name I didn't know pointed him to my desk, saying he should collect my things.

I followed him over and reached for my marbled notebook before he could grab it from the desk's drawer.

"That's company property," Billy's replacement told the guard, who snatched it out of my hand and set it down in his box.

"This is absurd," I said.

"You're out of control, Leveraux. You're refusing help. What would you have us do?"

"Are you firing me? Did you just fire me? Because if you fired me, I want it known that I quit. Do you hear?" I sent my hand into the banker's box as the guard reached for the doorknob to leave, but as soon as I grabbed my marbled notebook, the executive whose name I didn't know stepped forward to yank it out of my hands—just a second before Hickey tackled me to the floor.

I landed with a thud, and spoke through a wheeze. "What are you doing?"

The security guard was standing over us, fumbling to unbutton his gun.

"Get off of me!" I said. "This is an outrage! You think you can silence me?"

"Take him to his car," the executive told the guard. "And make sure you watch him drive off the lot."

"I know what happened here!" I said. I spoke back over my shoulder to Hickey, who lay on top of me, struggling to hold my arms behind my back. "Dean may not be a human tape recorder, he may get a few of the details wrong, but if he's anything like me, he remembers the big things. The sky is blue. Water's water. Nixon is or is not a crook." The executive helped Hickey pull me up by the armpits and throw me into the arms of the guard. "Those monkeys were fat," I said. "They were fat, I know it—and now they're thin."

I didn't say another word. While the security guard escorted me out to the parking lot, I tried only to remember everything I'd need to say. *We could throw some money at it?* Such insanity! Because if we understood so little about the human brain that we couldn't even test the effects of Sweetness #9 on it, what were we really doing?

"It's this one," I said, pointing to my station wagon.

The guard stood nearby as I started the car, then watched as I backed out and turned toward the gate. As I approached it, I thought there might as well be a sign arching up over the entrance: INNOVATE AND PROFIT—AND RECALL ONLY IF THEY RAISE A STINK!

I stopped to wait for the guard in the booth to lift the traffic arm. I'd seen him countless times before, but we'd never spoken. "I just quit," I said. "And do you want to know why? You want to know what's going on back there?"

The security guard was a black man with frosted hair and a thick mustache. He looked at me as if he were a marble statue contemplating the risks of coming to life.

"It's not justice," I said, "I can tell you that. They use 'innocent until proven guilty' like some men use the pointy end of a stick."

Finally, he spoke through a crack in his window. "This America, baby. You think anything's fair? Why you think at fifty-three I'm sitting on a hard chair with my face in the wind? I'm a college-educated man. How old are you?"

"Twenty-five."

"You a baby, baby."

He looked off toward the main entrance of the building. I glanced in the rear-view mirror and saw the security guard approaching us slowly on foot.

"Can I give you a word of advice?" he said. "Don't let 'em do it."

"Do what?"

"*It.* Whatever it is that I don't wanna know about. 'Cause they gonna try. They gonna try and make you believe all kinds of things. It'll get to where you don't know top from bottom or left from right."

I was shaking my head. "Won't happen. I saw this with my own eyes."

"Your own *lying* eyes, they'll say." And then, with another look toward the guard—he'd started to jog now—he lifted the traffic arm and told me, "You best git."

And that's just what I did, too: I got.

I DROVE AWAY LIKE STEVE MCQUEEN in a chase scene, thumping the flat of my hand into the steering wheel and shaking my head. The notion of food safety was a complete mirage! As long as a powdered beverage didn't eat away at your flesh, or a candy bar didn't instantaneously inflate your feet to four times their normal size, it was considered safe, perfectly suitable for the marketplace, because if it did anything else — brought on dark thoughts, triggered the primitive desire to eat — the crime would never be known or investigated, or if it was, it'd be many years later, when the crime scene was so cluttered and cold there'd be no telling if the gelatin dessert had done it with the artificial sweetener or if the butler had done it with the candlestick. Cancer, that was all they cared about. Cancer, because it was all they could possibly know.

I imagined walking up the steps of the Capitol and sitting down before a congressional committee. *Fat monkeys and apathetic rats, that's right, Senator. Perhaps it's a Communist conspiracy.* I saw it all so clearly: the microphone and my nameplate, my lawyer leaning over to whisper into my ear, and the senators sitting high above me, including the one from New Jersey who had always parroted the industry line: "Food is a wild mixture of substances designed for non-food purposes, namely its own survival and reproduction. People have always eaten at their own risk, and they always will." I was ready to throw myself into the open maw of all this, but then my vision expanded to include my family in the front row: there was Betty, sitting with a white leather purse piled up in her lap, and our two children, a young boy in his first suit and a beautiful little girl in a crinoline dress and a pink bow in her hair.

I pulled to the shoulder of the road and pushed the button to get my hazards blinking. My throat went dry; my Adam's apple struggled to settle into place. I was no whistle-blower, was I? Because what would happen if I talked? Once people learned I'd met with a congressman's aide—or worse, some bearded journalist drunk on the truth—I'd never find another job in all of New Jersey. All the dreams I'd poured into a test tube—I might as well dump them down the drain and start selling refrigerators at Sears, Roebuck. And where would my family be then?

I punched off my hazards and turned on my blinker, then leaned forward into my side-view mirror, looking for a break in the traffic. When it came, I gunned it, the acceleration throwing me back into my seat.

Minutes later, when I saw the green sign moving in toward me, I let my foot up off the gas, ready to merge over toward my exit. But it wasn't even ten o'clock; Betty wouldn't be expecting me for another seven hours yet. So I pushed down on the accelerator and drove onward, first toward Canada, then Key West. My course only grew more precise as my gas tank neared empty. Then, pulling off the Parkway to fill up at a Texaco station, I spied a bowling alley down the street and thought it would be as good a place as any to have lunch.

Inside, a young man stood at the front counter spraying disinfectant into a long line of tri-colored shoes. He was taller than me by several inches, and had the lean looking-glass appearance of a boy who's just been stretched out by an especially strong growth spurt. After reassuring me that the kitchen was indeed open (the only other person in here was the mechanic waxing the lanes), he took my order for a hamburger, then asked if I planned to bowl.

I realized the extent of my ambitions only then. "Do you offer any kind of discounts?" I said. "For those who bowl a lot, I mean." He communicated almost entirely by relaxing or tightening the muscles in his jaw and around his eyes. "I'd like to stay here all day," I explained. "At least until five."

Saying we could work something out, he gave me a pair of size tens and I went looking for a ball that'd get the pins a-clattering. The charade would be easy enough to pull off, I thought. Each morning I'd simply give Betty a kiss at the door and leave in my suit and tie for a job that no longer existed. "I'll call if I'm going to be late," I thought I'd say, and then off I'd go in the car to rent my pair of shoes and try to master the 7–10 split. It'd be easy. All I'd need to do was keep up the expected small-talk and petty complaints that are the stuff of our workaday lives. "You won't believe what Hickey did now…." Then, once I'd found suitable employment, I could sit her down on the sofa and tell her the truth. "Seeing as how we've been trying for a baby, I didn't want you to worry. But truth of the matter is, these last couple of weeks I haven't been working at Goldstein, Olivetti, and Dark."

Yes, I thought, as I held my hand over the dryer, it'd be a funny story we'd retell through the years, and then I stepped up to the line and rolled a strike.

When I stepped through the door that evening pulling on my tie, Betty stood up from the sofa and spoke to me in a confused tone of voice.

"What's going on?" she said.

"What do you mean?"

"What do you mean what do I mean? Your shoes."

I followed her eyes to the floor: bowling shoes; I was still wearing bowling shoes. I'd prepaid for the day and walked out at five o'clock, so immersed in my thoughts that I'd left my Florsheims behind.

"Oh, Betty." It was as if I'd been deboned. "I've had the worst day."

I staggered past her to the bar trolley, cringing at all of her questions: "What happened?" "But why?" "Are you serious?"

It was then that the lies began. "I'd never be happy there," I said. "I should be mixing flavors, not feeding rats. I'm an artist."

"Yes, but?"

"But what?" We were out of brandy. I poured two fingers of white crème de menthe, then turned to her, wincing at the too-sweet taste. "Would you rather I make the break five years from now, when we've got kids and a mortgage? It was now or never."

"So you just walked out?"

I moved around her toward the hallway. "What did I say?"

"I don't know. You quit?"

"I walked out, yes. Now, don't you want me to be happy?" I stopped at the door to the bedroom. Betty remained at the mouth of the hall-way, staring at me incredulously. "If I make a mistake, one bad decision," I said, "am I supposed to live with it for the rest of my life? It wasn't the place for me. That simple. End of story."

"I just can't believe you'd do this without talking to me first. Should I cancel the check?"

She wore a pair of denim gaucho pants and a tight white T-shirt, neither of which I'd seen before.

"I signed up for a night class," she said.

I groaned. "And this is your back-to-school outfit?"

"I wanted to look nice. Should I return it? I've still got the receipt."

I set my drink down on the dresser inside the bedroom door, then started back toward her and began working at the metallic buttons of her pants. "Keep it," I said. "It's nice."

"But can we afford it?"

I pushed my hand inside her jeans. "Let's make a baby."

"Don't be ridiculous."

"I had more than a dozen interviews this year. We'll be fine."

"Not now!" She hit me, first in the back, then the chest. "Stop it, I said!"

So I let her go, and she stepped away from me shaking her head.

"I can't believe you just quit."

I stood there, slump-shouldered and sexless, full of desire and confusion, a young man who'd had the world of flavor taken away from him on the same day he'd bowled no better than a 125.

"I guess this means no more Sweetness #9 in our coffee?" she said.

I turned back for the bedroom, telling her she wouldn't have to wait too long. "It'll probably be on the market in another year or two."

THERE WAS NO SHORTAGE OF flavor houses in New Jersey. Though the American flavor industry had gotten its start on the edges of New York City's garment district, soaring real estate prices had sent it scrambling into the Garden State shortly after the war. By the time I was hiring a typist to copy out my résumé and a telephone service to field my calls, there were no fewer than fifty flavor companies between the ocean and the Turnpike. In addition to its main research and production facility in Jupiter Park, Goldstein, Olivetti, and Dark had a manufacturing center off Exit 10 of the New Jersey Turnpike in Perth Amboy. The Dutch, meanwhile, the mighty, mighty Dutch, had long staked their claim to Teterboro in the north, just a short drive from which you can still find the pride of Passaic, Tanko-Shinju, the venerable Japanese firm whose name I've heard translated as both "pink pearl" and "two men commit suicide in a coal mine." After that, there was Sensations, Inc., F. F. Schlosser & Company, and National Perfume and Chemical, one right after the other almost in South Plainfield, East Orange, and Jersey City. In all, two-thirds of the flavor additives consumed in this country originated in New Jersey, and yet by the end of September, I was thinking my home state must be more famous for manufacturing rejection.

"You have to understand," Fleming Van Moorsel told me after I'd called the Dutch five or six times and he'd finally agreed to see me. "Times have changed. There's no position for you anymore."

His corner office was small and decorated tastefully with wooden tables and low-slung chairs that dipped and curved to meet the lines of your body. Dutch modern: hardly the thing for a display of rage.

I surged forward in my chair, my knees reaching almost as high as my ears. "Understand? I understand that not even a year ago you were fall-ing over yourself to talk to me about the use of a company car, and now?"

He slumped back in his chair, throwing up his hands helplessly. "You talk as if I were a part of some great conspiracy."

"Interesting to hear you put it that way."

He looked at me for a long moment, testing the limits of a strained smile. "David, I like you, I do, and I wish I could help, but I can't."

I lowered my voice. "They were too rigid over there, Mr. Van Moorsel. I don't know what you've heard, but that's the whole story. They were forcing me to move into Breakfast Cereals, and I've always dreamed of being a generalist. It's that simple."

He nodded.

"I'll conform," I said. "I'm no trouble-maker. I'm a company man, but you have to understand: A company man is nothing without a com-pany."

"*You* have to understand. It's the economy, that simple. The weather's bad, the crops are small, the price of food commodities is going through the roof." His voice became a whisper. "I'm not even sure our side is winning anymore."

"Sir?"

He reached for a magazine on his desk. "In Portland and Chicago there are stores selling horse meat — in the United States of America! Horse meat! Tell me, what can our industry do about that? Ten years from now a Communist might be sitting in this chair, reassigning you and me to a career in a factory. We could be given an axe and told to go fell trees.

"Read about Minneapolis." He rolled the magazine up like a club and smacked it into his open hand. "There's a black market for beef. People are selling ground round out of the boots of their cars. Could it be any worse in Moscow? In Kiev or Minsk?"

He tossed the copy of *U.S. News & World Report* up onto his desk. The cover's headline spun round toward me: WHY A FOOD SCARE IN A LAND OF PLENTY?

"I'd love to hire you," he said. "There's no one I'd like to bring on board more. But if I did, I'd get a call in the middle of the night from my boss in Wageningen, and then we'd both be out of a job. It's the economy, David. That simple."

I left scratching my head and leaving a snowy wake. Dandruff. I'd developed a case so severe that in the coming days I sought the care of a doctor, fearing cancer of the scalp.

"Seborrheic dermatitis," my doctor told me. I repeated his diagnosis ominously, prompting him to add, "A bad case of dandruff, nothing more."

I got it in my eyebrows and mustache (which I'd grown thinking a change would do me good), and then my skin began to deteriorate as well. It was like I was a teenager again; when I wasn't popping a pimple, I was marveling at the first splotches of eczema I'd ever seen. They appeared on and around my nose, and made the sides of my index and third fingers raw and painful. I couldn't hide it. Soon a red scaly spot the size of a quarter had even appeared on the underside of my foot.

"It's just stress," Betty told me. "You'll find work soon enough."

I would have found these words more encouraging if I hadn't felt the need to be no less encouraging to her. She was gaining weight, you see. She'd pulled out a muumuu I'd bought her as a gag gift on our honeymoon, and now she wore it while doing household chores and even running errands. I would have thought she was hiding herself from me if it weren't for the fact that she'd corner me every now and then in the bedroom while we were changing into or out of our clothes. "Look at this," she'd say. "Do you see?" And then she'd reach for those portions of her body that had changed, naming them as if she were a bombed-out Londoner marveling at the extent of Hitler's blitzkrieg. Warsaw, Brussels, Paris. Her hips, her thighs, her ass. "Look at this." But I would do everything I could to avoid just that, because seeing her like this, I couldn't help but think of her as overinflated, the features and form of my beautiful young bride lost in the thickening folds of her flesh. The only thing worse than thinking all of this was realizing that if beauty is in the eye of the beholder, I was someone whose love was apparently skin-deep.

One morning Betty confessed her innermost fears to me in the kitchen as we sat eating our cereal.

"You're going to leave me for another woman," she said.

"Don't be ridiculous. I love you."

"You love the woman I was. *I* love the woman I was. Look at this." She grabbed her side, pinching at a bulge of fat beneath her flower-print muumuu. "I've become the fatter older sister I always wanted. Do you see?"

"Stop. If anything, you're the one who's going to leave me. All those men in your classes, strung out on hormones."

"Please. They see my wedding ring."

"Yes, and it tells them you could teach them a thing or two. That you're a woman of the world."

"You should eat more," she said. "It's only fair. If I'm going to get fat, we both should."

"Betty."

"Have some ice cream."

I was eating a bowl of Cheerios. "It's eight o'clock in the morning."

"Don't you love me?"

"Of course I do."

"We've got Rocky Road."

I pushed my bowl away, then kissed her and left for an interview that didn't exist. It was too difficult to stay at home, and not only because I'd found myself getting hooked on the same soap operas as my wife. Betty's face sometimes unnerved me. Once or twice a day she'd turn from the sink while doing the dishes, or look over to me from the sofa, and for a moment, just a blink of the eye, I'd see a monkey staring back at me.

Had The Nine, or perhaps her withdrawal from it, triggered in her a primitive desire to eat? Or was my own short history of using the sweetener to blame? Had it perhaps made me as anxious and depressed as one of my former test subjects, causing me to see a rat where once I had known only the face of my beloved?

I drove each morning as if to race away from these questions, drove for more than an hour or two some days just to receive an informational interview or learn firsthand about an unpaid internship I wouldn't have considered in the spring. Things got so bad that by late

October I had started driving by the offices of Tanko-Shinju, even though they were notorious xenophobes who ran a closed shop. Today I can see this as evidence of my impending collapse, but back then, as I sat in my parked car each morning watching the Hondas and Datsuns and Toyotas pulling into Tanko-Shinju's gated lot, I actually believed I was exhibiting the persistence and optimism of an achiever.

The last morning I idled there, I laid on my horn like a latter-day Commodore Perry, refusing to be ignored any longer. After maybe five or ten minutes of this, a polite man in a white lab coat walked out smiling and bowed before my opened window, low enough to show me the part in his hair.

"Please leave," he said. "Thank you, good-bye, thank you."

IF BETTY THOUGHT I WAS going to run off with a prettier woman, I was sure she'd leave me for a richer man, because in the end the only work I could find was at a gas station, a Mobil franchise six exits south of Jupiter Park. Taking this position was only slightly less humiliating than staying home to clip coupons and watch daytime TV, or so I thought before coming to appreciate the full impact of the OPEC oil crisis.

Each day, I sat on a stool inside a booth near the pumps, making change or asking the customers if they'd like the carbon with that. Because I had the least seniority, I was also the one who had to drag the sign out of the garage (NO GAS TODAY!) and set it down in front of the long line of waiting cars whenever there was another shortage. For this I received curses that rarely were so sophisticated as to be directed at the oil-producing nations of the world and a variety of obscene gestures informed by America's great ethnic and cultural diversity.

Prices soared. They quadrupled from the same time the previous year, sending gas to a previously unimaginable high of one dollar per gallon. By the time a barrel of oil cost eleven bucks, some angry customers were leaning down to the little silver trough where I left their change and screaming a few choice words at me.

"If it's OPEC's fault, why are gas company profits on the rise? Tell me that, Fucko!"

I wasn't the only one who believed we should be given hazard pay. After learning my master's degree had earned me fifteen cents above the minimum wage, a young black co-worker tore off his grease-stained coverall and walked away, saying *fuck it, fuck this,* and *fuck you* — never had I heard such a torrent of profanity. I'm told he didn't even come back to pick up his last check. They say he caught a bus that same afternoon to the nearest military recruiter, believing he'd be no worse off fighting in the malarial swamps of Vietnam.

It was shortly after he left that I suffered my own breakdown, one brought on by a customer whose accent I couldn't place. "How much are the small ones worth?" he said, while puzzling over the coins in his hand, and the foreignness of his voice caught me so unaware — was he from Switzerland or Germany? — that my mind, as if looking for a connection, fell back to 1966 and the equally far-off land of Texas.

We had traveled there so my father could visit an old army buddy who lived in San Antonio, but it didn't make for much of a family vacation. While he got to stay up late in the breezeway, drinking bourbon and swapping war stories, my mother and I had to settle for a tour of the Alamo and a side trip to the original Dr Pepper bottling plant in Waco. In between, we slapped mosquitoes and marveled at "Uncle Charlie's" ability to live in this heat and humidity with only the benefit of a thundering swamp cooler. My father took pity on us the morning of our fourth day. Though we weren't scheduled to fly out of Houston for another seventy-two hours yet, he rented a car and said we'd spend the time between now and then taking a tour of all the most modern, air-conditioned hotels in Texas's Hill Country.

On the second morning of this ramble, a Waffle House waitress in Austin suggested we take in the view from the university's clock tower. I can only imagine what would have happened to me had I not begged out of this excursion by saying I'd like to inspect the library. I had started sifting through college brochures earlier that summer, you see, and though I had no intention of leaving the Northeast — or even attending a college outside of New Jersey — as we stepped onto the sprawling campus, I struck a pose as a potential applicant to the flagship institution of the University of Texas system.

Near eleven thirty that morning, while I was hidden away in the stacks reading passages from Henry Miller's *Tropic of Cancer*, Charles Whitman pushed his footlocker on a dolly into the lobby of the clock tower building. He wore a flattop and coveralls and gave the appearance of a maintenance man as he rode the elevator some 300 feet to the top.

My parents took the stairs. My father had jogged before it was fashionable. "It'll save your life," he used to say. "Just a mile or more a day. Isn't your life worth that?"

Whitman came prepared. He packed food (two tins of condensed milk, honey, Spam, sweet rolls, Planters Peanuts, sandwiches, and a box of raisins) and gear: binoculars, a plastic compass, two 3.5-gallon jugs (one filled with water, the other gas), several lengths of rope (both cotton and nylon), ear-plugs, an extension cord, kitchen matches, a flashlight, and (for reasons I still dare not dwell on) a deer bag.

After getting off on the twenty-eighth floor, from which you took a short flight of steps up to the viewing deck, Whitman hit a secretary on the back of the head, presumably with the butt of his rifle; then he shoved that woman's desk against the stairwell door—just moments before my father pushed into it with his shoulder.

Whitman was an honor student and an ex-marine. He held the observation deck for ninety-six minutes, wounding thirty-one and killing thirteen, including a pregnant woman and a Peace Corps trainee. It was ninety-eight degrees out, and in his footlocker there were weapons both primitive (a hatchet, a hammer, a hunting knife) and modern: a Magnum .357 Smith & Wesson revolver, a 6mm Remington bolt-action rifle with a four-power Leupold scope, a .30-caliber M1 carbine, and the sawed-off twelve-gauge shotgun, bought at Sears, Roebuck, which he used on my parents while I was furtively masturbating in the library.

"My father took the stairs," I said in my booth at the Mobil station, as the heavily accented tourist, maybe a Frenchman or an Italian, stood puzzling over the dimes he thought were nickels and the nickels he thought were dimes. "Whitman had been complaining of headaches, you know. Left a letter asking that an autopsy be performed. Thought science might be able to learn from him. It's remarkable, isn't it? Off to do what he did, and still thinking of the public good."

The tourist smiled as only a foreigner can, perhaps not understanding more than one out of every three words that I said; then he was gone and another customer had taken his place. I reached for the flexible neck of my microphone and continued as if he'd heard it all.

"And they did find a tumor, you know. About the size of a walnut. Take a guess where." It had started to snow. The world was spinning around me as I sat motionless on that stool. "Right here." I tapped at my skull. "In the part of the brain responsible for emotional associations with memory."

The customer gave me his credit card. I laid it down in the manual imprinter, then placed a carbon over it. "But this is what gets me most," I said. "He wore a white headband. Can you believe it? Up there on the clock tower, a marksman, an ex-marine, wearing a headband. What could be more terrifying?"

I spoke non sequiturs much of that evening, to one driver after another:

"Of course, it's not just the limbic system that's associated with emotion and memory. If you've read your French literature, you know the power of a good biscuit."

"Spam, canned food, deodorant. Who can say what causes these things?"

"Some say it must've been the saccharin in his diet soda. In the letter he left for the police, he said he drank more than six cans of Tab a day. Do you think that's too much?"

I finally lost my balance and fell to the floor, the stool ricocheting against the wall and dropping on top of me like a wrestler going for the pin. My breathing slowed and became more shallow. White flakes of dandruff spiraled down through a slant of light, growing as large in my eyes as the snowflakes falling outside. Then a man rapped his keys against the thick sheet of glass, and a voice came tumbling down over me like an echo in a cave, the accent from Staten Island or Brooklyn.

"You all right down there? We gonna need an ambulance? I need a fuckin' fill-up on three!"

WHEN I CAME TO, a man in a saucer-shaped hat stood over me, crouched down like a referee ready to count a boxer out.

"Can you tell me the name of the president?" he said. "With which country are we at war? What do you think of Soviet Russia?"

A golden triangle floated over the brim of his black hat; he wore a dark tie and a military-style jacket. I lay speechless beneath him, as if I'd been reborn into a fascist mirror world. Then I heard the wail of an approaching ambulance, and I realized he was a state policeman.

"Soviet Russia is a place totally lacking in freedom and liberty." I sat up. "President Nixon's right to be in Vietnam. If we don't stop the Communists there, they'll be knocking at our back door next."

The trooper turned nodding to the man from Brooklyn or Staten Island—"He's fine"—and then he stepped aside to let a paramedic come rushing through. This man said I shouldn't drive and recommended I go with him to the hospital for additional testing, but I refused his advice and the trooper's offer of a ride home, and insisted on calling Betty and having her come for me in a taxi.

Before this, my wife had believed that my parents died in a tragic if otherwise unremarkable auto accident. It was only after she drove us home that evening that I told her the truth.* Betty didn't feel betrayed. On the contrary, she marveled at how I'd kept it to myself. But then I barely gave her a chance to scold me. I cried and howled and made

---

* Minus the masturbation, that is.

noises like a drowning man coming up for air. "Just let it go," she said. "Get it all out. It's your parents; of course it hurts." Then she put me to bed early as if I were the child we still so desperately lacked, and it was only after I had awoken the next morning ("Would you like some tea?" "Maybe a couple of eggs and a short stack of pancakes?" "How's over easy?") that I remembered I still hadn't told her everything. Fat monkeys and apathetic rats. When would I tell her about them?

I wanted to lose myself in my work to avoid these thoughts, but I couldn't. When I reported to the Mobil station that afternoon, I saw an unfamiliar man in the glass booth. I searched for answers in the service bay, and there found only my final paycheck.

At home, I wept freely once again, the sound of my yelping growing louder and more forceful each time I tried to stop myself. "Oh, Betty," I said, but she didn't let me speak. She led me back to the bedroom, and the lovemaking that followed was so charged through with a jolt of electricity that I thought for sure we must have created a baby. "I love you," I said, and these words seemed somehow new. "I love you, too," she answered, and the night would have been perfect if only we'd stopped there, if only we'd turned out the lights and willed ourselves to sleep in the soft and beautiful silence. We didn't, though. My mind wouldn't allow anything as peaceful as that. So as Betty lay with her head on my chest, I spoke of my grandfather, who just that week had sent me a copy of Napoleon Hill's *Think and Grow Rich*. A note had accompanied his package, one that read, in full, "You think I got my three shoe stores by rolling over in bed one morning and farting? I made a plan. The shortest distance between two points is a straight line. Make a plan, David. Love, Grandpa."

"You know I love that man," I told Betty. "He took me in when my parents died, has always treated me like a son. But how am I supposed to make a plan when every time I step away from Point A, Point B disappears? Can you tell me? Even the crow meets the curve of the planet, Betty. There are no straight lines, I'm saying. And how's a man supposed to make the rent in a world like that? How?"

Her voice was quieter than mine, more tentative. "Couldn't you just go back to Goldstein, Olivetti, and Dark?"

I snorted. She pushed up onto her elbow and ran her fingers across my chest.

"Tell them it was a mistake. You weren't thinking. Can't you do that?"

I rolled away from her then, reaching for the light, and though I could have told her everything here, I couldn't get the words out of my mouth. *Betty, you don't understand what I saw. I could never go back.* I was afraid if I told her what I'd been through, she'd consider me weak—or worse, crazy. *You quit the company softball team for that!? Men are dying for their country in Vietnam, and you get scared by a couple of overweight monkeys?*

"I think maybe we should start being more cautious," she said.

I don't know how long we had been lying there silently, but when she spoke, I rolled back onto my other side and looked at her as if she'd receded into the distance.

"We could use condoms if you don't mind, or I could get fitted for a diaphragm," she said.

"A diaphragm? I thought you wanted a baby."

"Yes, but..."

"What?"

"Forget it."

"Forget it? How can I forget it?"

She rolled away from me. "Let's just sleep," she said. "Sleep."

But now it was impossible, not just that night but each successive one. Anxiety builds on anxiety. Each workless day that I carried the secrets of Animal Testing inside me, I felt like a drunk who is compelled to go out and do something horrible, if only to take his mind off the horrible thing he'd done the night before. Betty noticed. Seeing me sulk and finding me quick to anger ("Yes, Betty—fish again!"), she thought I must still be hurting from the memories stirred up by my fall at the gas station.

One Sunday morning she suggested we try church. She'd been raised Episcopalian, and though she was by no means a fervent believer, she was more than happy to return to the fold if it'd get me smiling and small-talking with strangers again. "You haven't left the house in days," she said. This may have been true, but it was also the wrong Sunday to try and convince me of theism. When she made her suggestion, Betty was in the kitchen, brewing a cup of coffee, while I was at the breakfast table, reading the front section of the Sunday paper. My Norwegian had died, my stolid, fish-eating Norwegian had passed in the night three days previous, and now the *Times* was ready to reveal the identity of the nation's newest oldest man (if you'll forgive the apparent oxymoron). He was a gentleman of more rarefied tastes, those he had cultivated as a missionary, first in the Kingdom of Kongo (1889–1893) and then Siam (1896–1904).

I stood, tightening the belt of my bathrobe, and asked Betty if she loved me.

She came over to the table, smiling tentatively as she set down our mugs of steaming coffee. "Of course," she said, and gave me a peck on the cheek.

"Then I need you to do something for me. I need you to find some plantain leaves and as many cassavas as you can carry."

"Cassavas?"

"No less than a dozen. You do know what a cassava is, don't you? Not a sweet potato, not a yam—a cassava. Here, let me draw you a picture. Okay? Yes? Now once you've picked up those—and get two dozen, if you can—find some coconut milk. It's absolutely imperative that you find some coconut milk. Should I write that down?"

Betty looked at the shopping list I handed her as if it began with King Arthur's sword and ended with the Ark of the Covenant.

"But, David, I don't think they carry any of this at the Acme."

This was true. She would have been lucky to find taco shells and a bottle of La Choy sweet and sour sauce. That's why I told her she should take the train into New York City.

"There's sure to be an appropriate ethnic market in Brooklyn or the Bronx."

"You want me to go to the Bronx? Alone?"

"You know I'd go with you, Betty, but that city"—I returned from the kitchen with the scissors and started cutting out the profile of my latest super-centenarian—"and how my nerves are on edge as it is, I just can't do it. You'll be fine, though. It's a perfectly sunny day."

I don't know what happened in the city that day, but when Betty returned home that night after sundown, she set a bulging shopping bag down on the kitchen table, went into the bathroom to shower, and then promptly went to bed. When Christmas arrived later that week, we celebrated alone over a dinner of cassava porridge and a dessert of sweetened rice wrapped in plantain leaves.

New Year's Eve was far less exotic, for Betty had insisted she wouldn't be going into New York City again. That evening, before the ball could drop on 1974, we dined on Hamburger Helper and drank too much champagne, and my wife asked if maybe it wasn't time I got professional help.

I knew where she was going with this—or, rather, where she'd have me go. A couple of weeks back, when we'd gone together to the local Episcopal church's annual Christmas bazaar and rummage sale, I had bought a historical society's monograph on Greystone Park Psychiatric Hospital, or the State Lunatic Asylum at Morristown, as the institution had been known when the book was published. The hospital stood at the end of a long tree-lined street high in the leafy mountains of northern New Jersey, and the many black and white photos in my book made it look more like a resort than anything else. The guests, as they were known, were housed two to a neatly furnished room and given the same privileged treatment regardless of their economic standing in the outside world. Ornate rugs ran down the corridors; stuffed divans, bright curtains, and fresh flowers filled the day rooms; and if the on-site bowling alley didn't interest you, surely one of the regularly tuned pianos would. Everyone looked so content. Men in suits and ties were shown walking the trails through the surrounding woods, while women in ankle-length dresses lay on chaises and read edifying books. Most memorable to me were the shots of the community garden, in which a handful of stout souls worked with their sleeves rolled up and their hands sunk deep down into the earth's warm and regenerative soil.

"It wouldn't be forever," Betty said.

"Of course not."

"Just long enough to get you back on your feet."

I was nodding. "Like a little vacation."

"That's right. A little vacation. And there's no shame in it."

"No, no. Like National Health, isn't it? There to give you a little boost when you need it."

And need it we did: our insurance had been taken away, and the end of our savings account was already in sight.

She finished her champagne, adding almost as an afterthought, "But all the same, it probably would be best if we kept this to ourselves. Do you think we could do that?"

I smiled. It was the easiest question to answer all night. "You can tell your mother I went to a dude ranch out west."

THE DAY BETTY DROPPED ME OFF at the hospital, I was interviewed by a jowly man with salt-and-pepper hair and hound dog eyes. A doctor here for more than thirty years, he loosened his tie and held up the flat of one hand after I'd spoken to him for no more than a few minutes.

"Let me stop you right there," he said. "There's no garden anymore."

"Pardon?"

He dropped his forearms onto his desk. "Ruling came down a couple of years ago. Courts said we must be exploiting our patients. You know, forcing you to grow your own food and not paying you a nickel to do so." He threw his index finger out toward me. "Goldwater would've put a stop to this nonsense. We wouldn't have half the problems we've got today if only we'd put a good man like him in the White House."

Sitting there with my suitcase on my lap, I tried a hopeful chuckle. "Well, at least the lawyers can't take away the libraries."

In fact they could and they had, if not the lawyers, then the accountants, because while the thinking of Moral Treatment had held for a time, allowing the sick to look out the windows and see fountains and rolling green lawns, soon overcrowding had forced the state to consider other demands. By the mid-fifties ("when we even had that Communist Woody Guthrie in here"), some seventy-five hundred men and women were being housed at the asylum—more than ten times the number the facility had been designed for.

"And so you'll excuse us," the doctor said, "if your bed's in a former reading room. But if you'd like, I could ask the nurse to scrounge up a couple of Reader's Digests for you. I'm sure we've got a few copies lying around here somewhere."

72

* * *

My room held three bunk beds and thankfully no more than five men. After being shown to it by an orderly, I took a top bunk and spoke briefly with the patient below me, a graphologist who stood no taller than five foot two and claimed to have killed six Bolsheviks in the Crimea before his twelfth birthday. I told this White Russian I'd come here because the economy was poor and the application deadline for Ph.D. programs had passed. He said the self-admits were crazier than the committeds and that he had a deep distrust of academics.

We quickly hit it off and spent our days playing chess and dismantling Marxist theory. One moonlit evening as we sat playing on his bed, he studied my handwriting between moves and pointed to my routine shifts between cursive and print. "You're an emotionally labile, nervous writer whose irregular baseline suggests a tendency to drift between fact and fantasy."

I moved my rook into position and enraged him by saying he'd once again failed to protect his king.

"As for your willingness to ignore the truth, that can be seen in the large circling loops of your *y*'s and *g*'s. You're probably a closeted homosexual."

I took the medication they provided me, telling myself this would be my counter-culture, my sixties. I'd never smoked a joint, after all, or eaten a tab of lysergic acid. I'd always worked, worked, worked, and where had it gotten me? Nowhere. So down it went twice a day with a little Dixie cup of water: 50 mg of chlorpromazine, which was good enough to get the muscles in the back of my neck to pull away from my spine. There were a few side-effects — sensitivity to light, constipation and urinary retention, an increased appetite and weight gain — but this was a small price to pay for peace of mind. I spent my days like a schoolboy, curled up in a chair and reading Alistair MacLean.

One evening in the dining room, I found myself sitting across from an old man whose intellect or medication kept his face locked in an intimidating, toothless smile. It was from him that I learned of the state's other psychiatric hospital, in Trenton, where earlier in the century the

r. Henry Cotton, believing tooth rot the cause of insanity, ...eved a much-lauded cure rate by leaving his inmates without so much as a molar or canine with which to chew their daily gruel.

Near this time I read in the papers that Sweetness #9 had been submitted to the FDA for approval, and I tried to tell the doctors about the many rats and monkeys I'd known. I used clinical terms only those employed in my field would have had at their command, but whenever I said anything especially meaningful ("They replaced the fat monkeys with thin ones"), my doctor shared a look with his Pakistani internist that made me push my tongue up over my front teeth. I didn't want to be branded a paranoid schizophrenic and kept here forever; I just wanted a nice little rest. So I began to strike a balance between world-weary and deeply troubled, and I left the true talk of my past to my hushed late-night conversations with the White Russian.

He thought it absurd. Because if they'd replaced the fat monkeys with thin ones overnight, that meant they either kept a few spare monkeys in the basement for just such a purpose or had called someone who specialized in the express delivery of primates. And who was this, some cleaner who gets paid handsomely for erasing all evidence of corporate crimes? A man whose name moves with a whisper from the lips of one CEO to the next?

"Are you telling me there's a psychopath out there with ties to both the Fortune 500 and the zoological communities? Tell me," he said. "I need to know." He thought it more likely that my mind had played tricks on me. "You were tired, sleepless, drinking too much caffeine, possibly sterile. Your wife had just lost a baby, you were alone and half-drunk. Am I wrong or am I right?" He led me through my recollections, reminding me that the first time I'd seen those monkeys, they'd been sitting in the shadows of their cages. And the following morning, the monkey I'd thought too thin had been out and dancing on Hickey's shoes, its body stretched to its full height. "Couldn't it be a question of shadow and light, of posture? Or what? Are you telling me there's a handful of fat monkeys lying in a shallow grave somewhere in South Jersey? I'm crazy," he said, tapping at his barrel chest. "I've got the paperwork to prove it. But if sanity's what you'd have me believe, I don't want anything to do with it. I'll ask for another pillow and serve out my time here."

My god, I thought, what have I done? And for the first time it wasn't the memory prompted by this question that troubled me, but the uncertainty of that recollection. What *had* I done?

All through that winter, with the exception of one Saturday when an ice storm made the roads impassable, Betty came on visiting day and sat with me for an hour or two in the day room. Sometimes we simply stared out the window, as silent as a couple married for fifty years; other days she'd do all the talking, telling me about the course in marketing she was thinking about taking or how many miles she'd jogged that week.

When the snow receded and the sun began to rise higher over the hills, my mood improved, and we started to take long, meandering walks through the slow-blooming forest.

Once, in March or April, we even ran off the designated path and up over a dale to a hidden alcove beneath the exposed roots of a toppled tree. It was like we were young lovers again. Betty giggled when she saw me staring at her and realized my intent, and then, with spring's first rush of warm air exciting our bodies, she tore at my clothes as fiercely as I pulled at hers. Crows cawed from the trees; raccoons and rabbits scurried by. I turned Betty round to take her in a way I'd never done before, and then, as a deer froze on the horizon, realizing our presence, we joined in on the natural cacophony and threw our sounds of pleasure into the wind.

It was just that one time, though. When on the following weekend I led her in the same direction, we both knew what was coming and couldn't help but react awkwardly. Betty worried about ticks. I kept hearing footsteps.

By late spring, Betty had had enough. One afternoon in the day room, she moved her wicker chair in front of mine and spoke to me slowly, carefully, as if she imagined me lost behind a haze of pharmaceuticals. "This has to stop, David. You've been here long enough. Now, will you leave with me?"

"How's our savings account look?"

She fell back in her chair. "Grim," she admitted.

"And so is that why you need me to come home? So I can find a job and provide for you?"

"David."

"Until you get your degree, that is, and can provide for yourself."

"What are you saying?"

"I think you know what I'm saying."

Having so much time to myself had allowed me to work on this thought until it was frayed like a piece of rope. Betty was going to leave me as soon as she had her degree. That's why she was jogging and beginning to lose weight. She was preparing for her reentry to society.

"You're being cruel, David. For five months I've stuck by you, and now you're being cruel."

We sat together for another minute or more, silently, and then I watched as she walked the length of the day room floor and pushed through the double doors past the nurses' station. It was for the best, I told myself. When she sent me a letter later that same week, saying she wouldn't be coming to visit me anymore, I told myself what I'd been telling myself since I'd last seen her: it was most certainly for the best. Because where could I go? What could I do? She wanted a family, a proper family, and could I provide for one while working at a gas station? Or feel good about myself if she was bringing home the bacon and frying it up in the pan? Today, stay-at-home fathers who measure out their lives in dirty diapers are looked upon with kindness, not pity. Back then there was only one word for them: bums. So I decided it was better to let her go and find a new life rather than be weighed down by a man like me.

As the dog days of summer arrived, I paced the halls grinning and medicated, spending more than my fair share of hours studying the dust motes twirling down through a slant of light. At one point my doctor told me that Sweetness #9 had been approved for use in dry foods and powdered beverages. He thought hearing this would be therapeutic. "The government says it's safe, now don't you think you can, too?"

If it wasn't that same evening that I went into the day room and heard the conflicted cries and curses of a roomful of idiots, it has become that way in my memory. Nixon was speaking down at us from the television: "I will resign the office of the presidency effective immediately." Amidst all the cackling and throwing of pillows, all the hee-hawing and stomping at the floor, I thought I might as well be in a roomful of monkeys, and I laughed.

It was a strangely freeing moment. Standing there staring up at the TV, I realized the truth doesn't matter, only your relationship to it does. Because even if I wanted to do something about the rats and the monkeys, could I anymore? Who would ever ask me to testify in court? "Now, Mr. Leveraux, before we return to what you *say* you saw in Animal Testing, can you please tell the jury a little bit about your stay at the State Lunatic Asylum? I'm sorry, Your Honor, I stand corrected: at Greystone Park Psychiatric Hospital."

An unreliable witness. This is what I'd become. It was another way of saying it had never happened. And wasn't that what America promised us all anyway? A second chance? A new life? So I had swallowed my whistle on that drive away from Jupiter Park. That didn't mean I couldn't still lead a happy life. I only had to learn to monitor my breathing. To avoid a sudden rushing intake of air that'd agitate that whistle hidden deep down inside me and cause it to release its shrill and treasonous cry. It's not a matter of truth and consequences, I told myself. It's only a matter of control.

They say that when the student is ready, the teacher will appear. The same must be true for the employee and the employer. How else to explain that just a couple of weeks later a nurse was tapping me on the shoulder in the day room and telling me I had a visitor?

I HEARD THE CANE FIRST, a rhythmic *tap-tap-tap* that turned me round from the large picture window overlooking the basketball court. For a moment, my visitor appeared as if through a brilliant sparkly haze. Then my eyes adjusted to the dim interior light and I saw him.

He was a diminutive man of fifty-some years, dressed in green woolen pants and a jacket of Harris tweed, though summer was still in full force. His cane had a gold tip and a gold handle, matching the color of the tie that showed from beneath the green V-neck sweater he wore inside his jacket.

As he stopped before me and appraised me with a warm smile, I became conscious of my own appearance: blue pajamas and a striped terry-cloth bathrobe, my bare feet stuck into a pair of open-heel slippers. He extended his hand as I reached for the top of my head, eager to pat down the stray hairs that I knew must be there.

"Ernst Eberhardt," he said.

We shook. "The FlavAmerica Ernst Eberhardt?"

His smile brightened. "You know of us, then?"

I certainly did. I'd sent him a résumé, twice now, and never received a response.

"I hope you don't mind," he said, "but an old girlfriend now living in Parsippany invited me for coffee. I thought while I was so close I should take the chance to speak with you about a job."

In my seven or eight months at Greystone Park, I had never believed myself worthy of commitment until now. Had I sent him a résumé from here? Complete with a return address?

He smiled as if reading my mind. "I spoke with your wife," he said. "She told me when visiting hours were."

"Wonderful," I said, as I glanced to the nurses' station, wishing I had time to ask for the clothes I'd been wearing when I'd been admitted. "I only wish Betty had thought to tell me."

Quick with a smile and a tap of his cane, he glanced past me to one of the two wicker chairs set out at an angle in front of the window. "Shall we?"

"Of course, of course!" I followed him over, then invited him to sit down.

Before he did, he reached into his coat pocket for a stiff piece of paper with an accordion fold, its text accentuated by several full-color photographs. "As you'll see," he said, as I inspected the brochure, "we're a full-service flavor production house, located just across the river from downtown Battle Station. A bit of a specialty in vanilla, but that doesn't stop us from taking on any flavor between A and Z—or apple to zucchini, as the literature says."

I smiled, glad to see he appeared as eager as I was to imagine we were somewhere else. He glanced out the window then, saying he was "a great admirer of sport."

I stashed the brochure in the breast pocket of my pajamas and looked where he was looking. A game was under way on the basketball court outside—a tense and spasmodic contest of two-on-one that pitted a short, fat black man and a tall schizophrenic against a man in a wheelchair who no one wanted to play with because he was such a terrible ball hog.

"But let me begin," he said, before at last getting down to what he said was his "true reason" for coming here. "My orange is not fit for the American market. The flavor is too harsh, astringent. Americans expect an orange that is sweeter, brighter, somehow more hopeful. This is why I have always needed a Yankee Doodle Dandy at my side to calibrate my senses."

His smile faltered here, and his blue eyes strayed to a point over my shoulder. A rail-thin man stood at the window, turning something invisible round in his hands and nibbling at it as if he were a squirrel with a nut.

I tried a little chuckle. "Fascinating, isn't it? The human mind. Where it can take you. How it can leave you behind."

Ernst nodded, then nodded again, then finally smiled and continued. "Yes, as I was saying, I arrived from Germany after my mouth and nose were already set. You can smile if you wish, but it is true. Your country stays with you like sand after a trip to the beach. Even when you bathe and think you've shaken it free" — and here his jaw hung open in a sort of listless smile — "even then it is there, hidden away from you."

I sat in my chair with my every muscle clenched, fearing sand would come pouring out around my ankles if ever I dared stand up. Such a fraud I was! Since misspeaking in the cafeteria that day I met Betty, my accent had turned back toward my mother's England. It hadn't quite reached the misty land of Albion yet, but it wasn't within sight of America anymore either. It had drifted out between the continents, off in the middle of the blustery Atlantic, near the islands that had once served as a way station for the slave trade. This was my sonic home, a slippery place leagues from the nearest Yankee Doodle Dandy.

"So if you are wondering why I have come for you," Ernst said, "the answer is simple." He poked his finger into the air. "I have friends at Goldstein, Olivetti, and Dark." His voice dropped to a whisper. "We talk. I've learned a few things about you."

I sank down in my chair, fearing now that this was all a cruel joke. In this nose-diving moment, it seemed entirely possible that I might have somehow been selected to serve as the plaything for various Captains of Industry, men who could unwind only by using a fellow human being as a dog might use a chew toy.

Ernst continued in a bolder voice, "Raised in a village west of London, brought to America when you were still in short pants." He tapped the floor with his cane and shook his head, grinning widely. "Any company can go to the University of Iowa and hire a corn-fed American. I need a flavorist who has been a student of the culture since he was a young boy. And that's you."

My mouth opened to reveal a woozy smile, even though I didn't quite understand it all just yet. I *had* been a student of the culture, though. When I'd been transplanted to my father's New Jersey in the middle of the seventh grade, I'd had an accent as thick as the frames of the glasses given to me by National Health. There had been only one way for me to fit in: to sit in front of the TV and take notes. So in the company of boys no one else would befriend at Joyce Kilmer Junior High School, a ragtag crew of asthmatics and ninety-seven-pound weaklings who visited the same uninspired barber and were constantly wiping at their noses, I took in horror movies on Friday nights, baseball games on Saturday afternoons, and westerns any chance I could get. For my friends it was mere entertainment, but for me—a cultural reeducation camp. I learned the difference between Deputy Dawg and Huckleberry Hound, and mimicked the voices of Elvis Presley and John Wayne. Finally, near the start of my sophomore year (when, tragically, I learned an English accent would have helped me fog the back windows of a Chevy Bel Air), I had so thoroughly cleansed myself of my past that you would have known I'd once lived in England only if you'd pumped me full of sodium pentothal and asked me arcane trivia questions about the Queen.

"You're just what we need," Ernst was saying. "When others were watching TV, you had a pencil in hand and a pad of paper at the ready. You've been a scholar longer than any Ph.D."

Later, I'd learn that as a young child in Germany, Ernst Eberhardt had been given the nickname "Sonny Boy" because of his blond hair. People had stopped calling him that in the thirties, when Al Jolson's Jewish heritage had made the pet-name problematic, but on this afternoon it was perfectly suited to him. His hair wasn't a muted grey anymore; it appeared to me as a transcendent burst of light, one I would have gladly thrown myself into.

Ernst pushed himself up with the help of his cane, asking—and he apologized for having to do so—if I was taking any medication. I told him I had stopped a couple of weeks before.

"It's easy to do if you've seen the right movies or TV shows," I said.

My answer seemed to please him. He led me to the double doors, saying he'd like me to do one thing before we met for a final follow-up interview: write a three-thousand-word essay on sugarless bubble gum, the use of cut fruit in molded Jell-O, and the love songs of Gordon Lightfoot.

"You are aware that Mr. Lightfoot is a Canadian?" I said, and hearing this, Ernst pumped my hand more swiftly, smiling as he told me he had a good feeling about this.

Two Sundays on from this he was back and fanning his face with my over-caffeinated prose, telling me I'd need to come in and get fitted for a lab coat. I almost cried as he slapped me on the back and congratulated me. It had been one hell of a year. I just wanted to start over. I certainly didn't want to question my good fortune or his logic in interviewing me at Greystone Park. It's called dumb luck for a reason. If you get too smart, if you think about it too long, it just might disappear. "You won't be sorry for this," I told him, as we moved out past the nurses' station and continued down a hallway lit on one side by a long row of windows. "I'll give you everything I've got."

He nodded, and then we shook hands once more and I watched him walk out through a final set of double doors, beyond which was the hospital's main entrance.

It was then that I heard the voice.

"David," it said.

Betty rose from a hard plastic chair pushed up against the wall, then turned this way and that to show off her new figure. One of my legs buckled; the knee felt like a pancake on a cushion of maple syrup. "Oh, Betty," I said. Because she looked like a young co-ed again. Her hair was done, and she wore heels and a form-fitting navy blue skirt that showed off plenty of leg.

She came over smiling. "How's my man?"

I fell into her as if throwing myself into an abyss.

"I'm so sorry," I said. "I only ever wanted to provide for you."

"Hush," she said. "Don't worry. Just tell me you're ready to come home."

I pushed her back at arm's length, looking her in the eyes.

"I was a self-admit," I reminded her. "I just have to pack a bag."

ERNST EBERHARDT FOUNDED FlavAmerica (the "a" in "Flav" rhymes with "crave") in 1949, the same year he became a naturalized citizen of the United States. He certainly didn't lack the expertise to lead such a company. Before his skills were reappropriated by the war effort, he had been employed as a flavor chemist by Pabst, Pfaff & Pfeiffer in Wiesbaden. Talent, however, only gets you so far, as he learned while struggling through his first year of business in America. He had no connections here, no network of friends and colleagues to call upon as he would have had in Germany had Hitler not reconfigured his future. Sales were so poor he finally called *Food & Flavor* magazine to pull the ad he'd been running at a cost of five dollars per issue. He couldn't afford it anymore. He was going to take down the tri-colored sign hanging over his front door and return to the rubble of his homeland, where at least he'd be able to understand the bus driver and buy a decent schnitzel on the street corner.

The salesman who fielded his call that day would have reacted differently if Ernst had asked to open an account. But because he was ending his relationship with the magazine, he didn't see the harm in saying what he said: "I can't help but notice your accent. You didn't happen to serve in the war, did you?"

It was then that Ernst first used the line that three generations of American flavor chemists would come to know: "Serve? I didn't just serve in the war, I served Hitler his dinner!"

Before this, he hadn't told anyone about his life in Germany, least of all how he'd been assigned to the bunker in the last days of the war to lift Hitler's spirits by delivering more concentrated flavors to his food. But he too saw no reason to hold back at this point, so he entertained the salesman until finally the man interrupted him, saying he'd like to pass this call on to a reporter. It happened so quickly that Ernst barely had the time to realize his good fortune. The reporter came to visit him that same week with a photographer at his side, and by the middle of the next month, the cover story was going out in the mail to more than three thousand institutional subscribers. ERNST EBERHARDT, the headline read. FROM HITLER'S BUNKER TO FLAVAMERICA!

"Ever since," Ernst said on my first day on the job, "the phone hasn't stopped ringing." We stood in his office, beneath the framed cover of *Food & Flavor* magazine which he kept hanging on the wall by the door. "Even now everyone loves to talk about Hitler. 'Did he like cats or dogs?' 'Was he really a vegetarian? I find it strange he didn't eat pork.' What am I supposed to do? I talk. I tell them everything I know, and sometimes"—he smiled—"a thing or two I don't, because at the end of each conversation I can expect an order. Back then, I needed everything I could get. My client list began and ended with an ice cream shop in Queens—barely enough business for a good night of beer, let alone a career. But now look at us."

He led me out through the front foyer and down a blue-carpeted hallway into the flavor development studio, a humble lab that had an E-shaped work station running the length of one wall. One flavorist stood working at the granite counter-top, holding a glass pipette over a test tube. A cluster of small brown bottles stood near his work station; hundreds of others crowded the tiered shelves that lined the walls. "I hope you'll soon feel proud to be working among us," Ernst said, giving a squeeze to my forearm. "We may not land the biggest contracts or hold the fanciest employee retreats." Here the flavorist looked up from his test tube, his eyes widening beneath the pair of protective goggles that he wore. "Hello, Holiday Inn Newark!" he said. "We just put our heads down," Ernst told me, turning us back toward the door, "and do our part to make palatable all the foods and beverages that drive today's fast-paced lives and economies. We make ourselves useful, yes? And there's nothing wrong with that."

We stopped next at the flavor application studio, which would have looked very much like a kitchen in a model home were it not for the scales and bags of white powder crowding its shelves and counter-tops. By the close of the following decade, after the Krafts, Nestlés, and Unilevers of this world had scaled back or eliminated their food product design teams in the name of an improved quarterly report, two more kitchens would be connected to this one, and our team of food scientists would triple in size. At present, only an Australian expat named Anthony spent his days here, making sure the flavorings created across the hall did not break down on their journey from the beaker to the oven, microwave, or Deep-freeze.

After circling away from here, Ernst pushed through the double doors at the end of the hall—"We call this the killing floor," he said—and led me out into a vast open room where a dozen or more employees in gloves, goggles, and blue jumpsuits were performing a variety of tasks. One worker stood at an island counter-top, pouring an off-white powder through an aluminum cone into the mouth of a plastic five-gallon jug below. Two others stood on the far side of the room, tending to a fifty-five-gallon barrel beneath a large silver brewery vat.

Ernst removed a hair-net from a Kleenex-like dispenser on the wall and handed it to me. "To remind us that we are in the kitchen to the world," he said. Once we were both suitably attired, he continued toward a series of metal shelving units where all the many chemical components used in the flavor development studio were stored in bulk.

"You'll see we have everything you could ever need."

There were dry mixes in large plastic jugs and jars (used to flavor soups and baked goods) and clear colorless liquids in glass containers (for ice creams and microwaveable dinners). Each was but a single letter in the flavor alphabet, a thing of infinite combinations, like the colors on a painter's palette.

He grabbed a jar of a dry powder and studied its dot matrix label—calcium 5'-ribonucleotides, perhaps, or wild mushroom extract—then put it back after a moment's contemplation, saying he'd be interested to see what I could do.

"Well, I can only hope to approach some of your achievements," I said.

He smiled shyly and gently touched my back, guiding us toward the double doors. "I'm more an administrator these days than a flavorist," he said.

"I doubt it, and even if that were so, you'd always be remembered for NoNilla®."

We stopped as a beeping forklift passed before us, taking a crate of small blue barrels wrapped in cellophane to the back of a truck waiting at the open loading bay door.

"That was just something I dreamed up in response to the Global Vanilla Crisis of 1963," Ernst said.

"You're too modest."

And he was. NoNilla®, the all-natural, non-characterizing flavor that "apes" the vanilla or vanillin into which it is added, made it possible for flavor perception to remain the same—and at a much better price point—even when a product contained only half its original amount of vanilla flavoring.

"There are only enough vanilla beans grown in this world to satisfy a country the size of Germany," I said, "and here we are in the vanilla-dependent United States, where less than two percent of the world's beans are grown but more than three out of every four are consumed, and still you say you did nothing?"

His smile gained a little confidence. "You've been doing your homework."

"Because of you, we no longer have to fear a cyclone's path across the vanilla fields of Madagascar or worry that drought or revolution will destroy the lesser crops in Mexico, Bali, or Java."

He clapped me on the back and pushed through the double doors, saying now we only had to convince the world's leading food manufacturers to get over their prejudices and reformulate their brands. This was no easy task then, when sales of NoNilla® were limited to companies that made generic cookies and off-brand ice cream, and it's even more difficult now that we have entered into the post–New Coke world. Today, CEOs know to expect a customer uprising in response to every break from tradition, even if that break could only be detected by those in possession of the rarest mouth and nose.

"If NoNilla® doesn't bring in the profits it should," I said, "your peers know what you've done. You're a flavorist's flavorist, Ernst. A flavorist's flavorist."

JUST WEEKS AFTER I HAD BEEN fitted for my lab coat, I was feeling assertive enough to argue that FlavAmerica should redirect its limited research and development dollars toward our industry's holy grail, the buttery artificial that is identical in taste to nature. One of my new colleagues, "Tennessee" Terrence Matthews, to this day the best sweet-brown man I've ever known, was not alone in dismissing me as "just another young flavor chemist tilting at cows." But I'd learned my lesson; I'd no longer withhold my voice. So in one of the company-wide memos it was my job to compose as FlavAmerica's lead cultural commentator and seer, I wrote:

> *Understand. Microwaves will be like public pay phones. In the near future, certainly no later than Orwell's imagined 1984, you will be able to find one on every street corner alongside a vending machine that will offer you a dish you can pull from a box. People will deposit a few quarters and eat dinner while waiting for the train. Goulash, sweet and sour chicken, Dutch apple pie. Sometimes a snack will suffice and consumers will push a button to select their favorite brand of popcorn from a bag. It will take less than five minutes to cook, and corporate allegiances will be formed on the basis of the quality of the buttery taste.*
>
> *There is a revolution coming to the dairy aisle. Let FlavAmerica be the first to rush the ramparts and raise its flag.*

I proved myself no less valuable to the company in the eighties, as Reagan and Thatcher (with the occasional able-bodied assist from the pope) reshaped the world with a wave of merger madness. As Betty continued on at Rutgers for her MBA, I told Ernst Eberhardt that we could overcome the changes coming to our industry if we paid greater attention to those "mom-and-pop" shops that could no longer meet the minimum order standards of the consolidating multi-nationals. Here I am reminded of a Hasidic man from Williamsburg who appeared in my office one humid afternoon to send his thick, callused fingers worrying around the brim of his black hat. He had little more than a dream and an empty ten-ounce bottle in his battered black leather briefcase, but the words he spoke to me were still powerful enough to make my forehead perspire beneath the hum of the air conditioner.

"Flavored seltzer water," he said.

It may sound simple now, but all revolutions are simple in the end. No more kings. Let's divide the money evenly. Black cherry–flavored seltzer water.

No sooner had he left his card than I was pulling off the cover of my IBM Selectric and banging away at the keys.

Look into the future with me. People will tire of colas. Their color is dark, ominous. They bring to mind shadows and doubt, things untrustworthy, the hidden rivers of the mind.* In this more optimistic decade, under the leadership of The Great Communicator, Americans will demand a beverage that is clear, something that steers us away from the turbulent sixties and all the turbid years that followed.

Seltzer water. It is a beacon of purity. Observing its clear, colorless liquid and believing it will work on the soul, consumers will drink three, maybe four units a day. This is no false Cassandra's cry. Raspberry. Root beer. Vanilla. Black Cherry. Shoppers will leave the supermarket with multiple six-packs and go home to tell their friends and families what they have found.

By this point, the FDA had extended its approval of The Nine to carbonated beverages and other liquids, something I couldn't ignore be-

---

* You can always count on a flavorist for a fancy prose style.

cause of my wife. Each night when I returned home from work, Betty would be waiting for me at the door, dressed in leg warmers and a striped leotard and drinking from a can of diet cola. "Now with Sweetness #9," the commercials had started to say.

For a brief period of time before this, it had been possible for me to keep The Nine out of our lives by patrolling the pantry and policing the fridge. When Betty first came back from the store with a powdered pink lemonade and a gelatin dessert, I'd told her not to buy these products again. "I just don't have a taste for them," I'd said. But now that was impossible; now The Nine was everywhere, multiplying as quickly as the Tribbles in *Star Trek*.

I tried to convince her to go back to drinking an endless cup of sweet tea, but I might as well have asked her to quit the aerobics classes that helped her keep her weight down. She was sure the sweet tea had been responsible for her putting on all that extra weight when I was looking for work. The sugar in it had produced cravings for other sweets, she said. And so she left each night for aerobics drinking from her fifth or sixth can of diet cola. Do you think that's too much?

At the same time that Sweetness #9 was approved for use in carbonated beverages, it was also allowed to enter the table-top marketplace, making it so that at every diner, restaurant, or truck stop in the nation you could find a packet of sweetener waiting for you in a little porcelain holder. If you're old enough to remember, you'll know that these packets glowed warmly from within, as their granulated contents were dyed bright pink—a visual testament to what the adverts urged consumers to do: "Pour a little cheer in your life."*

When Betty wasn't drinking from a can of diet cola, she was empty-

---

* Sweetness #9's pink glow faded for good in 1994, at which point The Nine's "natural, dye-free" alternative, first introduced five years earlier, became the only one sold in stores (outside of Mexico). It's been said that sales alone drove this decision, but judging from the nostalgic frenzy you can still observe on eBay, where one hundred–count boxes of "Mexican Nine" go for exorbitant prices, I believe it's more likely that the company's analysts, having observed the rise of Alice Waters out west and seen the musings of agricultural theorists supplant profiles of French restaurants in the pages of *Gourmet* magazine, forecast the coming of the next great awakening in the country's food consciousness and suspected the consumer would soon no longer tolerate an artificial sweetener that was so visibly artificial.

ing a packet of sweetener into her coffee and wondering why I wouldn't do the same. She remembered only the good times, those days when we were young and in love and sneaking the sweetener I'd brought home on the sly from Goldstein, Olivetti, and Dark. "You should turn that frown upside down," she'd say, "and pour a little cheer in your life." I didn't know what to tell her, or at least I didn't know the best way to do it, so I'd simply say I preferred my coffee black. "That way you can taste the flavor of the bean."

I knew this was wrong, and I wanted nothing more than to protect her—you must believe me when I say that. But before I could find the courage to act—and I know this sounds convenient, but it is the truth—Betty came home from what I had believed was a study session at the library (it was the summer of 1981, just before she was scheduled to begin the final year of her MBA program) and told me she'd been to the doctor.

"Are you sick?"

"I'm three months pregnant," she said.

The news lifted me as high as I'd ever been, higher even than the first time I'd learned I was going to be a father, if only because this time it was so unexpected. But then, like Icarus when he felt that first rushing singe of hot wax, I fell from these heights into a depth of anxiety like none I'd ever known. I wished I had told her everything, because she and the baby were already sharing the same blood. But at the same time I feared what would happen if I told her anything at all. You have to remember our history. Carrying a baby to term would be like carrying an egg on a spoon for nine months. I didn't want her to worry—to become uncertain in her steps. So I stood by her silently, convinced I could tell her about my experiences once I knew everything was okay. But then even that proved to be a lie, for once I was holding that pink bundle of joy in my arms and looking down into the eyes of our baby girl, Priscilla Reagan Leveraux—even then new fears came rushing in, one after the other after the other, my worries as relentless as the tide. The first few years of a baby's life are filled with enough questions and doubts. Once you count fingers, thumbs, and toes, you ask one another if the baby's walking and then talking on schedule, and then if she can handle blocks as well as the toddler down the road. I didn't want to add to this list of concerns; and what's more, I wasn't sure I could say anything meaningful if I did. I hadn't studied the prenatal risks of ingesting Sweetness #9; that had been outside the purview of my chronic toxicity test.

So we returned to the little house we'd bought in South Battle Station Township, a family of three now, and Betty felt so unexpectedly blessed that she turned her back on a job she'd been offered with the Chamber of Commerce and devoted herself entirely to the upbringing of our daughter. After that, things just kind of slipped away from me, at least where Sweetness #9 was concerned. You see, just months after Priscilla's birth, the Japanese, those bloody Japanese, reached for the centrifugal separator and announced that Sweetness #9 was as well suited to commercial kitchens as high-fructose corn syrup. Almost as quickly the FDA awarded it a blanket approval for all uses, making the sweetener's expansion into the marketplace complete. By the time we were celebrating Priscilla's first birthday in January 1983, The Nine was so ubiquitous that the town of Cottonville, Alabama, was renaming itself Sugar Hill in a desperate effort to be selected as the site of the product's new North American production facility.*

I suppose that by the time a second miracle was sending us back to the hospital (a boy this time, named in honor of the man who'd resurrected my career: Ernest Everest Leveraux), I could have sat my family down and told them to avoid several hundred food products. But by then too much momentum had built up behind my denials, and telling the truth made as much sense for me as it did for Goldstein, Olivetti, and Dark. It'd be a confession of liability, exposing me to the threat of marital bankruptcy, a dissolution of all the familial bonds we'd been trying for so many years to forge. So again I kept my silence, telling myself that even if I did attempt to admit the truth, I couldn't possibly substantiate my claims.

---

* It was selected, too, though any history of Sweetness #9 would be incomplete without a mention of the Mexican state of Michoacán, to which production was shifted only a decade later, after the governor there had unilaterally renamed Ciudad Hidalgo, a centuries-old city honoring a Mexican revolutionary hero, Montaña del Azucar.

I don't mean to sound like every scandal-plagued politician or athlete who's ever tried to save face in public, but you have to see my point: it was now the mid-eighties, and I was removed from Animal Testing by more than a decade. I felt no more certain of what had happened than I did after waking from an especially troubling dream. There were transitions I could no longer explain, half-remembered details I remembered well enough only to know I didn't remember them well enough at all. What could I possibly say? Especially when so many people were telling me that Sweetness #9 was a modern wonder of the world! A product whose significance lay somewhere between the splitting of the atom and the pest-free peace of DDT! Hadn't you heard? Freezer-burn was a thing of the past because of it, baked goods kept their bronzed, just-from-the-oven appearance months after they'd been put on a shelf or plopped inside a vending machine, and production values—they were so improved that microwave dinners and boxed macaroni and cheeses could be sold in larger and larger portions at ever-decreasing prices. Everyone spoke of its benefits. Marxist scholars convened at a conference in Paris to discuss how the sweetener would help facilitate the transition to global Communism, while survivalists and Mormons eager to stock an underground shelter praised it no less than the nation's dieting housewives. Even *Time* magazine got in on the act, naming Sweetness #9 its Man of the Year in 1985, an honor previously bestowed outside of humanity on only The Personal Computer. So great was the influence of The Nine that when I returned to my alma mater in 1988 to deliver a guest lecture in a graduate seminar on theoretical flavor chemistry, I ended with more than two minutes on "that godsend, Sweetness #9" and could be seen taking questions afterward while chewing on an energy bar and sipping from a can of diet soda.

How is this possible, you say? How could I have so thoroughly erased my past that I no longer had any fears at all about the safety of this food additive? Perhaps memory is like a book written in ink that fades. Perhaps every time I thought back on what I'd observed in Animal Testing, I discovered another alarming passage had been removed, allowing me to pen a more hopeful one in its place. I'm sure the victims of any great trauma would agree it shouldn't be any other way. For if not by forgetting, how else are we to recover and find peace?

Then again, maybe this is all too forgiving, and I was simply being pragmatic. After all, more and more of the flavorings I was creating at work were going into products containing Sweetness #9. It was a matter of utility and survival to think as I did. I had a wife and kids to support. I couldn't regret; I couldn't succumb to anguish and doubt. I had to act like one of the strap-down men responsible for securing the prisoner before he receives the lethal injection. I had to concentrate on the task at hand (just secure the left leg), because to think of the big picture, to see how my work contributed to a larger whole...only madness could be found there.

So I concentrated on my job and didn't let my thinking push out beyond the confines of my test tube. It was easy, and I suppose in this regard I was no different from my mentor. Like him, I wouldn't have worried about what was going on behind the barbed-wire fence on the outside of town; I would have joined the masses in the streets, lured by the spectacle of the parade and all the wild cheering. A good German, content never to speak about the war, or at least those parts best kept to oneself—this is who I had become, and it served me well, too.

My life improved. I bought a set of golf clubs and a new Volvo every three years. I felt better. Where once I had suffered under the weight of anxiety and guilt, now I believed I was rightfully reaping the benefits of a lifetime of dedicated work. Shortly after my son Ernest was born, Betty and I even closed on our dream home, a two-story Colonial Revival on a tony tree-lined street in the best neighborhood of South Battle Station Township. Topped by a side-gabled roof and covered in white wooden siding, this five-bedroom house had dramatic Tuscan columns that framed a wide front door crowned by an elegant swan's-neck pediment.

By the time we were settling into it, Betty had nursed our son through his first three months and landed a job as a tourism development analyst for a company recently relocated to downtown Battle Station, not far from where I worked. To accommodate her new career, we acquired the services of a housekeeper, a plump and affable woman who had escaped persecution in her native Guatemala and been recommended to us by a lady Betty met in aerobics class. Aspirina Barriga Gómez del Campo Martínez moved into the small bedroom in the back of our home, and soon was just another member of the family. She always had a pot simmering on the stove, and if ever she suspected one of us of harboring a dietary deficiency, she was quick to corner the offending party in the kitchen and make herself clear with a few fierce movements of a slotted spoon.

We had the best of both worlds: home-cooked meals and satisfying careers. On the weekends, we'd often celebrate this fact by having friends, family, and co-workers join us for a fancy dinner or a barbecue. Aspirina would be there to clean up and help out, but Betty and I always took the lead, cooking in between glances at a recipe in a glossy magazine. If someone was with us for the first time and impressed by the view (our home overlooked a state park thick with trees), I'd mention that at almost three hundred feet above sea level, we stood higher than all but a few points in Middlesex County. I'd say this as off-handedly as possible, but while lifting a glass to make a toast or cleaning the barbecue grill afterwards, I'd recall these words and feel a warm flush of satisfaction. Higher than all but a few points in Middlesex County...It wasn't just a geographic statement, I thought; it was a metaphoric one.

I recall one such day when I felt so enthused. It was the fall of 1994, not long after the Flav-R-Savr tomato had debuted in our local supermarket, and more than a dozen of us had gathered round the barbecue on the patio in back. Tennessee and his wife, Jean, were there, as were the Ikedas from across the street and the Wilsons from next door. It's the Wilsons I remember most. They brought their daughter that evening, a mopey girl with long, lanky hair who had just returned from some fresh trauma. I don't recall the whispered particulars; nor did I make any mention of them in the diary I had started to keep in the Reagan years.* Despite this, I know her misfortune left me acting overly cheery in her presence, as if to compensate for the abortion or stint in rehab she had suffered.

If eating is still as communal as it was during the fire-driven days of the Stone Age, the Wilson girl did everything she could to show us that she wanted nothing to do with our company. When I announced to the crowd that we were enjoying the bounty of the world's first commercially grown genetically modified crop, she set down the tongs she'd been holding and moved away from the wooden salad bowl with an empty plate. "You've got to eat something," her mother said, but no, while Priscilla crunched through her own bowl of lettuce and chopped tomatoes, and Ernest made quick work of a hot dog that Aspirina had slathered in ketchup for him, the Wilson girl sank into a saggy lawn chair at our periphery and sulked like some grim figure in a Russian novel. "It's Frankenfood," she said.

As her parents apologized by offering me a pained look, I smiled and raised my voice so it'd reach the girl. "You shouldn't be afraid of progress and new ideas, you know. Why, even your regular everyday tomatoes are picked green to prevent bruising and spoilage during shipping. They only get their traditional red color" — and here I smiled round at all my guests — "and that's all it is, you know, *a tradition,* they only get that way after the distributor has gassed them with ethylene."

I had hoped this would reassure her, but instead the girl popped up from her chair and said she was going for a walk, which we all understood to mean a smoke. I must admit, it felt good to have a hushed conversation with her father near the end of that evening, for while telling him he shouldn't worry, that it was just a phase all children had

---

* Like the president who inspired me, I did not take copious notes, and often included the events of several days in one entry. The following, dated 5 July 1989, serves as a representative sample: "Bought a batting tee over the weekend and went out to Mill Pond Park with the family. Ernest refused to use anything other than a cross-handed grip before finally abandoning baseball to chase butterflies. Priscilla asked for a try and twice nearly groined me with a line-drive. Betty says she wants to sign up for Little League next year, but I fear baseball might be a gateway sport, and I'd hate for her to develop the shoulders of a swimmer or terrify the boys in the lowest weight class of her high school wrestling team.

"Lovely parade in Battle Station on the 4th! So nice to see so many friendly folk crowding into downtown again. Redevelopment is looking up. Onward, Battle Station!"

to go through, I imagined myself lucky in comparison. When the Wilsons left (and they didn't even wait for the hand-cranked ice cream that the Ikedas had brought over), young Ernest was popping up from Aspirina's lap and biting into a quartered tomato. "It's alive! It's alive!" he said, as he staggered around the deck like a little Frankenstein's monster, growling through his red mouthpiece as he held out his stiffened arms. Priscilla, then twelve, laughed as loudly as anyone. She looked radiant, too, sitting there on the bench flanking the barbecue with one leg folded underneath her pleated cheerleader's skirt. I'd picked her up from the sidelines of Harper Field earlier that day, and ever since she'd been half popping into her moves and silently mouthing the words to one of the chants that had inspired the seventh-grade football team to its 35–7 win: "W-I-N! South Battle Station, do it again!"

Betty, her hair and shoulders still as big as in the eighties, must have felt as delighted as I did, because after everyone had left and we were alone together in the backyard, she looped her arm around my side and turned us toward the western horizon, where the sinking sun was casting a red glow across the treetops of the state park.

"Isn't it lovely?" she said, and though she could have been speaking of the view (some days you could see all the way to the far-off fields of West Windsor Township, where Orson Welles's Martians had landed back in the 1930s), I'm sure she meant more than that.

"It is," I said. "It is."

And if I wasn't wrong to believe this, I now know I was foolish to think my situation would never change. But then I was like that oblivious beachgoer at the all-inclusive resort who goes kicking through the surf with his trouser legs rolled high. The eddies of my memory had stilled; I believed I was safe, that the troubles of my past were far behind me. Only I was wrong. Memory does not follow a predictable lunar pattern. It does not move in and out with all the regularity of the tides. It's more like a rogue wave, something that strikes without warning and pulls you struggling far from shore. I hadn't been walking away from my past all these years; I'd been circling round toward it, and soon, just a few years after this barbecue, in fact, I'd feel the sand rush out from beneath my toes and turn and see it on the horizon—a wall of water rising up to improbable heights, ready to engulf me in its shadow and drag me out tumbling round in the deep. Yes, a thundering tsunami rushing toward me, and on its leading wave, balanced there on the nose of a surfboard, I might as well place the bringer of all destruction, the one person who would perhaps cause my old friend Mr. Wilson to feel a warm flush of satisfaction, knowing he wasn't alone. My daughter, my very own daughter: Priscilla Reagan Leveraux. How dearly I love her, and yet still I sometimes can't help but wonder if I'd be writing this were it not for her.

PART TWO

JUST FILLING ORDERS

July 1998

IF I HAD BEEN BORN HENRY FORD, Priscilla, in her teenaged years, would have refused to drive. Had I invented the flush toilet, she would've grabbed the paper and gone outdoors. As I was a flavorist, that man in the white lab coat responsible for everything from the cherry in your can of soda pop to the savory sauce in your dog's dish of kibble, she reached for food as if it were a club with which she could strike me.

Maybe if I had been a man of greater faith, I could have more capably fended off her blows; or perhaps it was only that my faith was not great enough. You see, when my story picks back up, I was less prepared than ever to defend myself. The day where I'll begin was a Monday morning in the summer of 1998, and as I stood in the kitchen with the small of my back pushed into the counter, I read in my paper of the death of The World's Oldest Man. He was an Okinawan who'd lived with his children and their children and their children too, all in a house of rice paper nestled into the cliffs high above the East China Sea. For weeks I had eaten as he had eaten, drawing strength from the staples of his diet: a lot of octopus and squid (high in taurine, which lowers your cholesterol level and blood pressure) and, somewhat surprisingly, plenty of sweet potatoes. Now he was gone, though, and I was reading the profile of his successor, the first of my ersatz apostles to invoke the by-products of my own profession. Bedridden, all but deaf and essentially blind, childless and apparently alone, this man, one Alfred Livingstone Johnson III, claimed to have reached the age of 113 years and 204 days by cultivating a taste for vanilla cola, TV dinners, and a brand of cream-filled sponge cake famous for its longevity.

"I have not cooked," he was quoted as saying, "since cracking a can of corned beef in November of nineteen and forty-three."

It struck me as only the unexpected can, leaving me looking for connections and explanations, deeper meanings, a code. Part of me was thrilled. I wanted to photocopy this profile and push it off on anyone who might think "chemicals," rather than being the very alpha and omega of our lives, are only added to food in the lab. But this confidence was also short-lived. As the microwave beeped behind me, my mind circled round to more treasonous thoughts, those that said this article had been an editorial room jest, something that had slipped past the copy desk and onto page A22.

Could a man really live that long eating like this?

The questions that undermine our faith don't arrive through deep meditation and diligent study. They pop up like soldiers from a foxhole, ready to shoot you down before you even have the time to realize you're dead.

I tucked the paper under one arm, telling myself to concentrate on my work (the left leg, just focus on the left leg). This morning I had reached into the Deep-freeze for a breakfast sandwich that I'd selected on a recent ramble through my local Acme. (I liked to tour its aisles at least twice a month to stay abreast of all the latest flavor trends.) Sold as "The Manwich," this heat-and-serve meal weighed in at a hearty 790 calories and was comprised of one sausage patty, two eggs, a couple of slices of bacon, and a roof of American cheese as orange as a road cone. I was not eating it out of idle curiosity or owing to an extravagant appetite. It was my routine on Mondays to sit down to a long working breakfast, so in addition to my knife and fork, I had a legal pad and a pencil beside my plate, along with plans to break down and identify all the components of the flavors I could detect in The Manwich.

My meal's failures were apparent to me from the first bite: the bacon needed to be microwaved separately for optimum crispness, the "eggs" had been misquoted, if you will, and the savory flavorings used to prop up the processed meats and cheese were no more memorable than the propylene glycol that carried them. Usually, all of this would have given me no small amount of pleasure (FlavAmerica had not been invited to bid on the contract); but this morning I set my pencil down after scribbling only the most rudimentary of notes, then reached for my stomach, feeling the first pangs of gastrointestinal distress, if not the deft acceleration of things to come.

Pipes flushed overhead, hair dryers roared and fell silent, and then the kids came shuffling in with all the grace of the undead. Ernest, now twelve and dressed in blue satin shorts and a white youth soccer jersey, got the step-stool out and poured himself a bowl of cereal before joining me at the table. Priscilla, meanwhile, stood before the open mouth of the refrigerator long enough to affect the temperature in the room. Finally, she took a grapefruit half-veiled in Saran Wrap to the counter and began carving into it with a serrated spoon. Her first bite showed that while she was sixteen years old, there was nothing sweet about this age. Turning a sour face to me, she asked, "Is this in season?"

"Pardon?" I couldn't remember the last time I'd heard the question. "I don't think we have those anymore."

"What do you mean?"

I knew of vast warehouses where apples were kept in a state of suspended animation, the temperature and oxygen levels there so low that, with the right chemical spray and a good seal of wax, a Golden Delicious or a Granny Smith could be picked in August of one year and sold at your local grocery store in December of the next. I assumed the same was true for grapefruit, but suspected my daughter would not look upon this as evidence of progress and new ideas. She had taken that halved grapefruit into her hand and was staring down at it as if she were Hamlet up on stage with Yorick's skull.

"Try some sugar," I said.

She went into the cupboards and a few seconds later said that we were out.

"There's plenty of sweetener," Betty answered, as she came down the stairs drinking from a can of diet cola. "Should be with the tea," she said, blurring past us into the pantry, her skin giving off a warm glow thanks to the twenty-five minutes she'd spent on the elliptical.

Priscilla found the one hundred–count box of white packets that

Betty had purchased to make her rare cup of Lipton palatable, then shook the tiniest amount of white granules over her sour fruit.

Ernest sat across from me, reading a manual for a new computer game while he ate. His bowl of sugar cereal had transformed since it had come tumbling out of the box in the colors of our flag. Now, through some process of modern alchemy, the milk dribbled down my son's chin blue blue blue. He looked up from his bowl, feeling my attention upon him. I looked to the remains of the breakfast sandwich I'd pushed between us.

"Done?" he said.

I shrugged and nodded. He fell in on The Manwich with all the ferocity of a scavenger.

Churchill once spoke of Russia as a riddle wrapped in a mystery inside an enigma; if I were to speak of Ernest in a similar way, I might describe him as a corn dog wrapped in a slice of pizza stuffed inside a Hot Pocket. I couldn't explain it. The boy ate like a ravenous dog, but still he had been the smallest child in his most recent class photo, smaller even than Duc and Hung Jackson, the two roly-poly Vietnamese boys who'd been adopted by a black, gay Vietnam vet and profiled in the local paper. More than once I'd watched my son eat a bucket of fried chicken or a second frozen pizza, only to see him stand in his underwear on the scale in the bathroom and show the same weight as the previous month. *Was there something wrong with him?* I'd been asking the question since he'd been diagnosed at six months with what our pediatrician had called "failure to thrive" (and Betty had translated to mean "failure to mother," in part because she'd refused to breast-feed him after suffering through Priscilla's ministrations on her inverted nipple). I had tried to maintain a positive attitude about him through the years, but it had become harder and harder to keep that up as I sat with him in my lap and watched as one ham-fisted nurse after another drew a vial of blood from his arm. To date, we had ruled out celiac disease (three times), gluten sensitivity (twice), and even irritable bowel syndrome. Just a month or two previously, we had taken him to Children's Hospital in Battle Station, where the latest specialist had snaked a tube down his throat and come out into the recovery room to tell us it didn't look like he had a tumor or GERD or even a misshapen esophagus. We left that day knowing as much as we had known at six months, which was nothing in the form of a question. *Was there something wrong with him?*

As my son ate, I picked up the box that my breakfast sandwich had come in and read the list of ingredients on the side. Sure enough, on the third line, placed inside parentheses listing the components of the vegetable shortening, there it was: "beta carotene [color], Sweetness #9, and natural and artificial flavors."

Ernest turned the sandwich round in his hand and began eating at it from a new angle.

I heard a man's voice then — a strained and throaty rasp that sent my eyes over to Priscilla, who had pushed up on her toes to turn on the little yellow radio that sat on top of the fridge. The radio had belonged to Aspirina, but after our housekeeper died the previous summer (a bus accident that made the local news), we forgot to point it out to her nephews when they came over to claim her things. Now, when Priscilla wasn't forcing us to listen to "world music," she was spinning the tuner to the far left end of the AM dial, where so many of the talk show hosts, like this one, sounded as if they'd been handcuffed to a chair.

"You don't have to join the Widows of Sugar Hill or become a member of the Sweetness #9 Action Network," the man said. "You want to do something? Get to know a guy like Jack Thompson in Madison, Wisconsin, who farms organic on two urban acres. It's in seven thousand products, America! You think you're safe? Buy your vegetables from a guy like Go Sun Tiak in Houston, Texas. Do you even know a farmer like Go Sun Tiak?" He spat the name as if it were a poisonous venom. "Shame on you, America! If the answer's no, for shame!"

I sat there, my buttocks stiffened in my chair, thinking back on those days of happy jingles: *Pour a little cheer in your life!*

Betty reemerged from the pantry, stuffing two breakfast bars into her purse. Then she crossed to the fridge, stopping as she reached our daughter.

"Let me take you on a shopping spree," she said.

Each day this summer Priscilla had worn the same thing: a black hooded sweatshirt, tan Ben Davis work pants, and a pair of red flat-footed sneakers that were no more technologically advanced than those I'd worn as a teenager. The outfit was so formless and unbecoming, it so thoroughly denied the existence of her changing body, that I feared my daughter had been sexually molested or heaven forbid raped. Betty assured me I was just worrying ("A mother knows," she said) and dismissed the drabness of our daughter's new wardrobe by saying it was only further evidence of "Priscilla being Priscilla." Our daughter certainly was her own thing. She was a celebration of recessive genes—the one person in the family with freckles and attached ear-lobes, and with red hair that even Betty's parents hadn't been able to explain. The mystery was deepening, too. Ever since she'd quit the cheerleading squad the previous year and abandoned all of her old friends, I'd looked upon her with a mixture of fear and confusion, as if experiencing my first touch of Alzheimer's and having trouble connecting a familiar face to a name.

Priscilla gave her mother's outfit a quick once-over, saying she'd rather not look "like a first lady on parade." Betty turned to me, visibly wounded. Just a few years earlier, she never would have left the house in the pink skirt-jacket combination she wore this morning. But the culture was undergoing a sea change (celebrities had started to appear on the covers of her "stupid magazines," pushing strollers and holding babies against their hips), so she had reintroduced all the colors and styles that she'd embargoed during business school.

"You look wonderful," I told her. "Pink but powerful."

Thus fortified, she turned back to our daughter, reminding her that we still hadn't bought her anything for the upcoming school year. "Why don't you take my credit card and go to the mall?"

"I'd rather go to prison."

"You can't wear the same thing every day."

"Why not? I'm not cold. I'm not wet. I'm not naked."

"But, Priscilla, it's going to be in the high nineties today."

She shushed her and pointed up at the radio. My back stiffened. My chin lifted. I turned one ear in the direction of the noise.

"But let's not forget about the women, Mark." A second voice had begun to speak. Calmer than her co-host, she sounded as if she were leading a guided meditation. "The women are farming organic too," she said. "Are you out there, Ellen Mills? Are you joining us this morning on listener-supported 1640 AM in beautiful Eugene, Oregon? If so, save some of that red cabbage for me. Mark, you have to try this stuff. It melts in your mouth, people, really it does."

"Get to know a woman like Ellen Mills, America! She's our only hope! You think I'm kidding? Just last month in Moses Lake, Washington, a twenty-four year-old man walked down the soda aisle of an Albertson's supermarket and shot two nuns dead."

"Oh dear!"

"And do you know why?"

"Why's that, Mark?"

"He got very heavy into the diet soda."

"Oh no."

"And he snapped. For some people it takes a lifetime of use, but for others it's over with that first sip."

As if on cue, Betty rose from the bottom shelf of the fridge, cracking open her second can of diet cola that day.

"Mom!" Priscilla spat grapefruit into the sink. "Didn't you hear what they said?"

Betty shrugged, sipping from the can. "It's not exactly peer-reviewed." Then she turned in a slow circle, wondering, "Where did I leave my keys?"

Priscilla rinsed her mouth out at the sink, spitting loudly every few seconds.

I pointed up at the radio. "Your mother's right. These people, they're, you know, they're probably broadcasting from a van somewhere out west."

Ernest finished off The Manwich and reached for a glass of orange juice he'd dyed with a splash of red food coloring. A "Bloody Sunrise," he called it.

"They're probably wearing tin foil hats," I said, "and have underlined passages of Nostradamus at the ready." I tried a little chuckle. "Who'll bet me? Five dollars we hear Nostradamus's name before the top of the hour."

"Symptoms of Sweetness #9 poisoning include anxiety, apathy, a generalized dissatisfaction with life." The man was rattling at his handcuffs. "Aphasias and impotence, rage disorders, dyspepsia, a forgetfulness that verges on panic. Do you want me to go on?"

Priscilla was blotting a paper towel against her tongue. "I'm gonna die!" she said.

Betty came out of the pantry, shaking her keys up over one shoulder. "Here they are!"

"Didn't you hear him?" Priscilla said. "'A forgetfulness that verges on panic.'"

Betty opened the fridge and crouched down before it. "I may be forgetful, dear, but I'm nowhere near panicked. Besides, if anyone knows this stuff is safe, it's your father. He tested Sweetness #9 on rats and monkeys when he was just out of college."

Priscilla looked at me in disbelief.

The voice of the woman on the radio dropped to a whisper. "Sweetness #9 also disrupts the menstrual cycle, ladies, so if you're having female problems…"

"Okay, that's enough!" I jumped to my feet and twisted the radio's dial to off. "How come we can never listen to a little light jazz?"

"Is it safe?" Priscilla said.

I was all adrenaline and fear, a trapped animal intent on escape. Again I pointed at the radio. "They might as well be naming every ailment of the American Condition! Why not blame all these things on lack of exercise, or improved methods of detection? Social isolation," I said. "I can go on."

Betty rose from the fridge then, holding a small plastic container of pre-cut cantaloupe and a bag of shake-and-serve salad that came with a white plastic fork and a squeeze packet of low-fat Italian dressing that I knew must be sweetened by The Nine. Looking at her bar-coded lunch, staples she always insisted I pick up for her at the supermarket, I felt like an inflatable thing that had been popped with a pin, and could manage no more words in my defense. Were we really a country that couldn't even cut its own cantaloupe anymore?

At the beginning of my career, when the average kitchen in this country was half its current size and used twice as much, I'd believed my work was contributing to the liberation of the American housewife—and that mine was a patriotic and essential duty, too, for once women were set free from the demands of the daily meal, they too could contribute to the nation's economy and help lift our GDP, thereby showing to the world just how superior Capitalism was to Communism.

Even after Betty went off into the workforce and our schedules began to conflict—Betty and I with our careers and various professional organizations, Priscilla with a growing sense of volunteerism, and Ernest with the sporting life we inflicted upon him even after he'd discovered something he truly loved, a leadership position in the Young Druids Club of North and Central New Jersey—even after all of this, I didn't feel any great reservations about the changes I was helping to bring about. By then, we had Aspirina, who provided us with healthy, home-cooked meals to fuel our many endeavors. Working in consultation with each family member, our housekeeper stashed dozens of color-coded Tupperware dishes in the stand-alone freezer in the garage, allowing us to reach for and reheat them at our own convenience. Priscilla's had had red covers and been increasingly influenced by conscience (free-range chicken, grass-fed beef) more than good taste. Betty's containers had been green and governed by the fear of another name; there wasn't a diet too unethical or unscientific for her to try. Since kicking off all of her weight with the help of Jane Fonda, she'd counted points and done The Scarsdale, followed Jenny Craig, and lived for long stretches of time on little more than cabbage soup. Presently, she was refusing the potatoes, grains, and breads she'd sworn by in the eighties, and was eating a diet so heavy in protein you would've thought she was a bear preparing to sleep through the winter. Only Ernest had gone without. (The dietary habits of the world's oldest men and women had influenced the contents of my containers.) He had always loved the chicken enchiladas and soft tacos and wet burritos that Aspirina had made especially for him, but at some point he had come to love their commercially made counterparts no less, perhaps even more. So enamored was he of the products of my profession that he knew gas stations according to the quality of the frozen pizzas they sold and could speak of the complexities and nuances of a two-minute hamburger as if he were a Frenchman with his nose thrust into a glass of that season's first Bordeaux.

As Betty turned from the fridge, Priscilla pushed up on her toes to click the radio back on. The male co-host was describing The Nine's chemical composition (9 percent methanol) and telling us that our bodies couldn't metabolize its constituent parts (formaldehyde and formic acid).

"And to think that's why my thighs have been growing all these years," the woman said. "I haven't been getting fatter — I've been storing Corporate America's formaldehyde!"

Betty had gone to the counter to pack her things into an insulated lunch bag, but here she looked up at the radio. "It causes obesity? But that doesn't make any sense. It's a no-calorie sugar substitute."

"The FDA has gotten almost one hundred different complaints about this one little ol' sweetener," the man on the radio said, "and still you think it's safe?"

"There's even one listed here as 'cessation of breathing,' Mark. Isn't that the same thing as death?"

"Only if you're not holding your breath, Bonnie. Only if you're not holding your breath."

Priscilla wouldn't stop looking at me. I had retreated to the table by now, so I took cover behind my newspaper. It provided little relief. All I could see was the photo that ran alongside the profile of Alfred Livingstone Johnson III. It was a close shot of the old man in his gated nursing home bed. He lay there with his eyes closed and his mouth slightly parted, as if he were in the midst of releasing a horrible sound. A fluke and a farce, that's what he was. Not a rock on which you could build a church. He was like one of those lottery winners who appear on the evening news holding an oversized check. He didn't make you think you could do it if only you lived as he had; he reminded you of the long odds.

Betty clapped her hands. "You've got thirty seconds, E. Do you hear?"

Since Aspirina's death, we had been trying to occupy our son with as many activities as possible. Today it was a half day of soccer camp, something he tolerated because a friend of his from the Young Druids Club was joining him in his misery.

"Remember to drink plenty of water," I said, as he rose from the table. "It'll be a hot one today."

Nodding, he pushed a cream-filled dessert into his mouth. I have no idea where it came from. Then he was following his mother out through the utility room to the garage, grabbing his soccer cleats and shin guards from the floor before the door closed behind him.

I cleared the table after he left, listening to the radio station as it went to a commercial break. The second spot to play advertised *Sweetness #9 — What Is to Be Done?*, a report documenting all the peculiarities of the sweetener's approval process and the many hazards of its use.

"Completed after years of impartial research by a team of Albanian scientists far removed from the power brokers in Washington, this essential, two hundred and forty-three-page document can be yours for only $19.95. If you call in the next thirty minutes…"

I set my son's bowl in the sink. "The next thirty minutes."

"Shh!"

"That's 1-800," and now Priscilla was scribbling down the number.

"You can't be serious," I said.

"Can I use your credit card?"

"What could you possibly need it for?"

She returned her pencil and a reporter's notebook to the vast marsupial front pocket of her black hooded sweatshirt. This was what she'd retreated to after dropping her pom-poms — the high school paper. Even the summer recess hadn't stalled her new obsession. "The truth never sleeps," she'd told me.

"Does it matter?" she said now.

And I knew the answer as well as she did: no. When she was in the first grade and came home to ask for a pink phone, we got her one even though she didn't have anyone to call. Then there was her My Little Pony phase and all the Hello Kitty outfits and paraphernalia you could imagine—one thing after another we'd bought for her, never once stopping to consider the question of need or utility. Why should I expect that to change now?

"I could always ask Sarin's dad," she said. "You're not the only one with a credit card, you know."

And so it was pointless to resist. My one summer training to be a lifeguard had taught me that. You only tire yourself out going against the current. Better to let the riptide take you where it will, then pop up above the waterline and move in to shore without a struggle.

"If you give me the number," I said, "I'll place the order for you at work."

The first hint of a smile. "You will?"

I held out my hand—"though I still don't know what purpose it will serve"—and then she was tearing the sheet of paper from her notebook and giving it to me. "Thanks," she said, smiling freely now, though only for a moment—a honk came from outdoors. "Sarin!" she said. Just as quickly, as if she'd heard the first wail of an air-raid siren, she was running for the door.

"Will you be back for dinner?"

"I don't know! I've got my phone!"

As the front door slammed shut behind her, I was striding into the dining room to watch through the window as she ran down the lawn toward an ancient Volkswagen Bug covered in bumper stickers memorializing every failed liberal campaign since McGovern and the manatee. The driver was a wispy young thing with a pink scarf wound round through the base of her puffy little Afro. She'd transferred into South Battle Station High School the previous fall, after Priscilla's sophomore year had already begun. They met in journalism class and by February were crouching down together in the wilds of a nearby state park to count frogs for a local 501c. Ever since, they'd been inseparable, though because they preferred to "hang out" at Sarin's house (for reasons I chose not to dwell on), I'd met the girl in person only once before.

The one time Sarin had spent the night at our place, the girls had stayed up late in the great room, mocking romantic movies on the big screen. I came in at one point to offer them a bag of popcorn I'd seasoned with some white cheddar flavoring, but from the way they looked at me you would've thought I'd suggested they eat a bowl of anthrax.

"I'm a vegan," Sarin said, as if that were explanation enough.

I tried to tell her she had no reason to worry. "The cheese flavoring," I said, "was in no way derived from animal by-products. I should know. I made it myself."

"Well"—and she shared a conspiratorial look with my daughter— "I'm not one of those vegans who eats fake pepperoni or sausage. If meat is murder, why would anyone want to simulate it?"

I should've known to surrender (there is no arguing with a teenaged vegan), but I thought some jalapeño-flavored popcorn might appeal to them instead. I had three cases of flavored salts in the garage— caramel, sour cream and onion, a half-dozen varieties in all—the lot of it a thank-you gift from a client whose sales were up 24 percent since releasing the "new and improved flavors" that we at FlavAmerica had created.

"You don't get it," my daughter finally put in. It wasn't that jalapeños and popcorn didn't go well together; it was that she and Sarin believed it wrong to achieve this rarefied combination of flavors without first going to the bother of chopping up a jalapeño themselves. "Do we have any in the fridge?" she asked.

"Jalapeños? No. Only pickles, I think."

"We're fine, then."

I told her she was being ridiculous, but she only wondered how this was any different from my position on welfare. "If that money provides incentives for people to remain poor, how does eating something ready-made teach me to be self-reliant?"

I was starting to realize how unfair parenthood could be. You raised a child up right, or as right as you knew how, and then a woman died of breast cancer in Berkeley, California, catapulting her daughter clear to the other side of the country so she could spread an influence that otherwise might never have appeared.

I didn't like it. I wanted to go back to the glories of the Reagan Years, back before the crash of the Dow Jones Industrial Average and the flattening of the seltzer market. (The two events followed each other so closely that they have since become one in my mind: Black Cherry Monday.) But there was no going back, I was beginning to suspect. I was Humpty Dumpty, and not only had I fallen, I'd watched as my wall had come tumbling down on top of me.

As a young man, I had feared I would never have the pleasure of seeing it: East Berliners streaming into the west; and then when I did, I reacted with little more than a passing exhilaration. It was too much all at once. As the Soviet Union fractured and Russia began to be carved up by its rising class of oligarchs, I felt more and more like a Sovietologist pushed out into a world without global Communism. I had always been like that sailor of old who charts his course by the fixed glow of Polaris, only my guiding light had been the ruby red star flying high above the Kremlin. Everything had spun around it, my philosophy and ideals, my understanding of every point between bitter and sweet, and yet now here it was a generation after we'd answered Sputnik with Tang, and not only were Muscovites freely passing beneath their city's first Golden Arches, but my own daughter was demanding nothing less than organic fresh-squeezed and befriending a Californian vegan.

After watching the Volkswagen Bug sputter away, its black and gold California plates soon lost over the slope of our hill, I moved back into the kitchen, feeling a stabbing sensation in my side. I steadied myself at the island counter-top, suddenly very conscious of my breathing. Was it accelerated? My throat went dry, my scrotum twitched. I felt as if a hole in my skull had opened up, allowing everything that was inside it to seep up and out of me like so much inverted molasses. I sat on a stool, wondering if it was my breakfast. Then the sound of the radio had me sending one hand to the side of my neck to check my pulse.

"Hi. You're on the air with Mark and Bonnie. Welcome. We're listening. Do you have a story you'd like to share?"

Since the mid-nineties, when Ernst Eberhardt retreated into semiretirement and began catching the bus to work only two or three times each week, I had been performing those administrative duties that my mentor had once reserved for himself. "You're an honorary German," he'd joked, while first entrusting me with these responsibilities. "You think anyone else in this building would remember to keep the lights on?" I didn't mind that my new duties kept me out of the lab more often than not; I enjoyed losing myself in the minutiae of the business, and what's more, it allowed me to make a home for myself in Ernst Eberhardt's spacious corner office.

This morning, after speaking to a gum arabic supplier in the Sudan (at a cost of ninety-eight cents per minute) about a long-delayed shipment, I pushed my wrist out from beneath the cuff of my white lab coat — 9:23 — and saw that I had just enough time before the next item on my day's calendar to order the Albanian report. After looking to see that the door was closed, I reached into my pants pocket for the slip of paper that Priscilla had given me, then reached for the phone and dialed. Moments later, after navigating through a short automated messaging system, I was speaking with an operator who fielded my order and asked for my name.

"Pardon?"

"Your name," she said. "Who are we billing?"

I had pulled out my credit card, but only now, as I stared down at its raised letters, did I stop to consider how dangerous this might be. Did I really want the Albanians knowing who I was? And where I lived? Because if they *had* researched Sweetness #9 as extensively as they had claimed, they might have come across my name in some dark recess of the *Federal Register,* or been given my notebook — *I'd left it behind in the lab!* — by a disgruntled former employee of Goldstein, Olivetti, and Dark. I was no "Chen" or "Cohen," after all. No "Chavez" or "Romanov" or "Smith." I was a "Leveraux," and you'd find no great abundance of us in even the Paris phone book. So what would they do once they realized who they were dealing with? These were Albanians, you must remember. From Albania. A country that had split with the Soviet Union when Khrushchev started questioning the worst practices of Stalin. *More* Stalin, not less — this is what Albania had wanted. And things certainly hadn't improved since then. Why, just the previous year there had been rioting in the streets of Tirana. Armories had been looted, fires set, the United Nations called in, and all because the government had replaced its formerly controlled economy with a brand of capitalism built on pyramid schemes and incomprehensible systems of modern finance. A billion dollars had been lost, taking money from more than two-thirds of the population, and so what was extortion, blackmail, or mindless violence to a people such as that?

"Are you still there?" the operator said.

"Yes, yes," I told her, though I wouldn't be if I gave her my name. If I gave her my name, the Albanians would get together to plot and plan, and then some unshaven man named Darko or Vladislav would step out of the shadows one night saying my name in the form of a question. "David Leveraux?" It could be over like that. I'd nod, or my voice would betray me on instinct, and then he'd bring the gun blurring round from out of sight and fire from the hip, first one shot, then two more as he stood over me, just to be sure.

I cleared my throat. How could I not clear my throat? "Do you take money orders?" I said.

I had heard something about Las Cruces, New Mexico, in the commercial, but only with the help of the operator was I able to get the appropriate PO box number and Zip Code.

"Wonderful."

"Now, that *will* take three to four weeks longer to process," she said.

116

"Oh, yes, I know, that's fine, that's actually much better suited to my needs."

I hung up then and sprang to my feet, feeling an unexpected lightness. The grumbling of a diesel engine soon turned me to the office window, where I twisted open the blinds and watched as a school bus parked on the far side of the street and began flashing its red lights, the modest skyline of downtown Battle Station to its rear. The first two children to appear — boys younger than my son, no more than nine or ten — came shooting round the front tires like corks popped from bottles of champagne; a quickened step behind them was their chaperone, a pretty young thing fresh from Penn State or Bowling Green, some dimple-cheeked innocent whose face brought to mind ethyl vanillin, marshmallow, flavor #909. She grabbed the boys near the nose of the bus, then demonstrated, with broad gestures and a slow, deliberate speech, that they were supposed to stop, look both ways, and only then cross the street.

The next to appear was an older woman with a thick body and a stern, unforgiving face. She stopped at the side of the bus and held out a stiff arm to delay the approach of the boys and girls behind her, these the more obedient ones. She looked left, right, left, then swung her body out like a gate and drew tight circles in the air with her right hand. The children crossed before her. They came hand-in-hand-in-hand, a long procession of bodies that registered in my mind as a kind of binary code: fat, thin, thin, fat, thin, fat, fat, fat, thin.

I leaned into the blinds to watch the final few children move in beneath the tri-colored sign hanging over the front door. The last child was an Asian boy so obese he had fat folds on his neck and even in the middle of his forearms.

My building sighed: the central air kicking in, sensing a loss somewhere.

The brief feeling of euphoria that I had felt after hanging up the phone was gone. In its place were thoughts of something I never would have believed possible as a young man. A Fat Asia. How could you explain that to a boy raised on Mao?

* * *

"Ready?"

I turned to find Ernst Eberhardt standing at the door, dressed in his usual wools and tweed, but somehow lacking the sense of style I'd come to associate with him. He had no fewer than six different colors on display between his black shoes and his tan coat, and though he'd always been blessed with the ability to coordinate the many different aspects of his wardrobe, I'd been noticing of late that one detail was now always off. This morning he looked like a man who had forgotten the color of his socks (yellow) by the time he was buttoning up his vest (burgundy) and knotting his tie (green). Still, I couldn't identify what exactly I would change.

"Right behind you," I said.

As I stepped out of my office, the last of the kids were pushing in through the front door, their voices going in every direction as they sniffed at the air. "Bubble gum!" more than one said.

Eliza, a woman of fifty-some years who was fallen in every way, stood from behind the front desk and came over to Ernst to tighten his tie. "I told you the yellow one," she whispered, "or the green vest."

"I thought you said green tie."

"Green vest," she said, as Ernst, irritated, stepped away from her, clapping his hands together to gather the children's attention. "Welcome to FlavAmerica!" he said. "I can tell there are more than a few good noses here this morning." He moved through the crowd with all the confidence of a miracle maker in a Bible story. "We use hundreds of different chemical compounds to make our flavorings, but at the end of every day, no matter which ones we use, do you know what the office smells like? Yes, you do: bubble gum."

He extended his hand to the elder chaperon. "Ernst Eberhardt. A pleasure to have you with us."

He had been doing this for years. Believing field trips good for company morale, Ernst had made it a standing policy to open the doors of our labs and test kitchens to schools, youth groups, and science camps like the one visiting us today. His script never changed. He started by asking if anyone had heard of Brillat-Savarin, even though, at least for as long as I had been cast in the rôle of his sidekick, no student ever had.

"A shame!" he said this morning. "Such a brilliant fellow. Brillat-Savarin," he said, in that soft, hissing accent of his, "considered food a theological issue. God, he said, requires that we eat to live, so he invites us to the table with appetite, sustains us" — but here his face went blank and he paused with his finger in the air.

"With the pleasure of flavor," I said.

The circle of children swung their heads in unison toward me.

"Yes." Ernst nodded. "Sustains us with the *pleasure* of flavor and rewards us with the energy in our food." He bent over, shaking his head as he placed his hands on his thighs and looked into the face of a young boy. "You'll have to forgive me. I've grown older than my memories. Did you know you could grow that old? You can."

He stood and returned to his script. "But what of flavor chemists? Or flavorists, as we like to call ourselves. What do we do?" He turned toward the hallway, asking that we follow him into the test kitchen, "where we'll pass around the meatless sausage links we've been developing and see how Jews can enjoy the savory pleasures of pork" — his finger shot up over his shoulder — "without breaking kosher."

As the children followed him in through the door to the flavor application studio, I broke away from the group and hurried down to the break room, knowing I'd likely find our junior flavorist in there — Frederick Archibald Beekley — and hoping I could convince him to take my place. A three- to four-week delay on the Albanian report might have been to my liking, but I knew my daughter would soon grow suspicious, so I thought I should run to the post office and drop a money order in the mail. At least that way I could tell her I'd done everything I'd said I would.

"Ah, there he is! Just the man I wanted to see."

Beekley was lying on the sofa, with little more than his feet and his hair visible. I would have needed nothing more to identify him in a crowded room. His shoes, propped up on one arm of the sofa, were unlaced high-tops ("Air Jordans," he liked to remind me, whenever I spoke of the need to update the company dress code, "first-generation Air Jordans"), while his dense thicket of copper-red hair was styled in the likeness of a young Frederick Douglass or an old Albert Einstein. *Take me seriously,* his hair said. *I dare you.*

"Ernst asked for you," I said.

Beekley sat up, lowering a copy of *Food Product Design.*

"Didn't the school kids just get here?"

"Science campers, that's right. He thought you might like to help out."

He tossed his magazine onto the coffee table, giving me an incredulous look.

"You're serious?"

I held a smile, as if I could wait him out.

"He knows how I feel about kids," he said. "And to put it very bluntly, after what I was forced to endure last summer—"

"It was a cap gun, Beekley! Nothing more!" A boy had pulled it on him the one time he'd joined us on a tour of the premises. "If anyone could enjoy a prank, I thought it'd be you."

"The *fear* was real, David. That's what's important."

"And what if *I'm* scared? What if I need a moment alone?"

He reached for his magazine. "Fear's your natural habitat. Besides, The Kraut loves you. You two are like Sonny and Cher. You know, before the one became a Republican droog and the other a transvestite. I couldn't possibly replace you."

"And if we were to replace you? Hmm? Have you thought about that?"

He looked at me, eyes unblinking.

"That's right, Beekley." He had one of those names you wanted to repeat. I had to stop myself sometimes. "You think you could catch on somewhere else if we threw you out a couple of months before the end of your apprenticeship? Seven years gone just like that?"

"I don't work well when threatened."

"Sometimes I wonder if you work at all."

He lay back on the sofa, kicking his feet up onto the far armrest. "I'm like a writer. You should know that by now. Just because I'm lying on the sofa with one hand stuck in my pants doesn't mean I'm not working." He tapped the side of his head, his index finger disappearing into the jungle of his hair. "I'm very close to figuring out that cappuccino flavoring I've been having trouble with. I just have to distract myself long enough to allow it to appear."

While once I had gone through life with an affable half smile, now my most natural expression moved between the poles of disbelief and disdain. I didn't look at Beekley as if I'd accidentally swallowed a hard-boiled egg; that was a face I reserved for the most significant geopolitical events (the collapse of Communism) or the most unexpected and distressing news (the death of Princess Di). He did, however, inspire the same expression I adopted whenever I noticed someone leaving the men's room without first washing his hands. At least once a day I'd look at him like this, wishing I could fire him for a simple dress code violation or act of insubordination, even if I knew that doing so would bring no less harm on the company than it would him. Though technically still supervised by one other senior flavorist and myself, Beekley was already without question our best man, capable of dreaming up great fugues of flavor where others could imagine only a dour toot of the horn. When it came time for him to take his final test and be reviewed by the membership committee of the Society of Flavor Chemists later this year, there was no question he would pass. The only question was whether he would still be with us two years later, when his contract would allow him to field offers from other flavor houses.

"By the way"—he tossed his chin out toward a thirty-five-gallon garbage can to the side of the soda machine—"I hope you don't mind." A handwritten sign taped to it read Y2K: ARE YOU READY? "It's for cans and dry foods. An emergency pantry of sorts. I thought maybe you could mention it in one of those company memos you're always writing."

"Isn't this a little premature?"

"Premature? You do understand the magnitude of Y2K, don't you?"

He told me how the first generation of computer programmers had been like a young married couple in their first cramped apartment, looking to save space in every possible way. Computers had taken up entire basements, and a kilobyte of memory had cost as much as a Cadillac. So when they entered dates into any program, they used two digits instead of four, never once stopping to think of the confusion this would cause when we rolled into a new millennium and would need to tell the difference between the end of one century and the start of the next.

I nodded patiently for as long as I could, then finally broke in. "Yes, yes, I know, Beekley, I've read the same stories in *Time* and *Newsweek*."

"Then you'll know the smart ones have already built a bunker in Montana. We're not talking about a weekend trip to Atlantic City here. It's the end of the world as we know it. Takes a little planning, doesn't it?"

"Fine, of course, I'll mention it. I'll even bring in a can of pumpkin pie filling tomorrow *if* you'll first relieve me of this field trip today."

He made a face that told me his thinking on this matter hadn't changed.

I threw my finger out at him. "You need to start pulling your weight around here. Even da Vinci had busywork, you know."

He lay back, lifting his magazine over his head.

"And when you come in tomorrow, I expect to see that lab coat ironed. Do you hear? You're one splash of red food coloring away from looking like a Mexican butcher."

"Word of advice, David." He turned the page of his magazine. "Don't turn your back on those kids, and by all means — shoot first."

After turning out into the hall and hearing voices still coming from the test kitchen, I made my way toward the door of the flavor development studio, thinking to ask one of the other two flavorists on staff to cover for me.

My long-time colleague "Tennessee" Terrence Matthews was out of the question, for in addition to having five years of seniority on me and being a master of sweet-brown confectionery flavors (you've never tasted a better butterscotch), he was, as Beekley liked to say, "an old-school flavor chemist," uninterested in anything outside of the hard sciences. Just in the last year alone, with one eye on an adjunct teaching position in his retirement, Tennessee had returned from a five-month stay in Israel, where as a Fulbright Scholar he'd collected and synthesized the essential oils of the Biblical World—many endangered, some previously believed extinct. For this feat of exploration and taxonomy, *Perfumer & Flavorist* magazine had awarded him its cover (and we had given him a nickname, "Mr. May," which he had tolerated for all of one day). Yes, asking Tennessee to lead a field trip was out of the question. It would be like asking a leader of the women's movement to babysit your kids. Even if I knew the answer would be yes, I wouldn't be able to sit through the explication leading up to it.

My best hope was our newest hire, a Sri Lankan native who'd begun his studies in chemistry at the Technical University in Munich, continued them at Leeds in England, and finally ended up right here in the United States, pursuing a Ph.D. in food chemistry with a concentration in sensory evaluation at none other than Cornell. Those of us at FlavAmerica had tried to learn the most basic rhythms and intonations of this young man's native tongue, but we'd found all five of his given names incompatible with our ingrained speech patterns. Consequently, we'd shorn just a fragment off of one of those names (Kobalavithanage) and, in part because he had such an impressive mustache, took to calling him by Stalin's *nom de guerre:* Koba.

When I turned in to the flavor development studio, Koba was unbuttoning his lab coat so he could more freely fiddle with his fly. "Don't know where the bugger popped off," he said. "But I suppose I'd be off my trolley to question the craftsmanship of these trousers. I've put on more than one stone since coming to America." He looked to Tennessee, who stood at his work station using a spring clamp to hold a test tube in a pot of boiling water. "You wouldn't happen to have a hair grip, would you?" Getting no response, he turned to me. "How about you, David? I'd hate for Ernst to come in and see me with my John Thomas hanging out."

Tennessee was a good old boy with a high head of dyed black hair and a mouthful of new white teeth. "I reckon there were a half-dozen words in there I didn't un'erstand," he said. "Can you remind me again why we hired a man doesn't speak a lick of goddamn English?"

Koba had me to thank for that. Nine months previous to this, Ernst Eberhardt had given me a letter he had received from him requesting an informational interview. I agreed to meet Koba at a buffet restaurant on the other side of the Stupfer Bridge, thinking I'd do little more than split the check and point him in the right direction. But he was such a brave eater, I couldn't help but take notice. He combined pungent Asian sauces with Swedish meatballs, mixed his mashed potatoes with guacamole and yellow mustard, and ate no one part of his meal separate from another.

He smiled shyly when he noticed me observing this. "I tell my wife it's to broaden my palate and experience new taste sensations," he said, "but I'm afraid she still refuses to dine with me in public."

After watching him bite into a piece of sheet cake topped with a jalapeño pepper, I'd seen more than enough. "You just put yourself onto a very short list, young man." I reached for the check, waving off his efforts to split it. "A very short list indeed."

Later, I explained to Ernst that our needing him was not just a question of diversifying the workforce. "I know you'll take on any man, woman, or robot who can do the job. But you must ask yourself, with Thai, Indian, and other emerging cuisines becoming more prominent in the marketplace, how can we really be sure we understand what the average American wants to eat? Why, even Wendy's is serving a chipotle hamburger these days. And it's not the survival of the fittest, remember. It's he who can adapt."

With my mentor's approval, we brought Koba on board that winter and lifted his probationary status in the spring after some basic sensory testing had confirmed he had the mouth and the nose for the job. He was nothing if not professional. He never wore a distracting cologne or lotion, and he never complained about being the first one in each morning or the last one out at night. How many times had I stopped on my way to the parking lot and seen him sitting on his stool in the flavor development studio, flipping through Heath's *Source Book of Flavors* or Steffen Arctander's seminal study on the uses of essential oils? He wasn't one of these wild-haired young men drunk on theory. He studied our Bible, the book listing the ingredients of all our in-house flavorings, and understood it's sometimes wiser to carpool than to reinvent the wheel.

Most impressive was the marbled notebook in which he recorded his thoughts on the raw materials he encountered while standing across from me each day in the lab. After smelling one, he'd jot down his impressions of its odor, taste, strength, and lasting power on a blotter, then note its kosher status, cost, and supplier, as well as any peculiarities relating to its regulatory status both here and abroad. This is no small matter, for while there are but four basic tastes in this world (sweet, sour, salty, bitter), there are some four thousand different aromatic impressions (browned, fatty, rancid, pungent, to name just a handful associated with cooked beef) along with a host of trigeminal sensations — grainy, warm, soft, painful, etc. — that can further influence any flavor.* Only by encountering each of these aspects in the lab — and learning how to describe them in a language shared by your co-workers — can a flavorist build up the type of vocabulary needed to discuss the products of the profession, be it a flavor as simple as your basic six-note cherry or a more complex and elusive blend involving no fewer than one hundred volatile aromatic molecules.

If there was one problem with Koba, it was, as Tennessee was quick

---

* I could reference a fifth basic taste, *umami*, but not without inviting controversy. This much is irrefutable: In 1908, Japan's Dr. Kikunae Ikeda, Ph D, walked out into the Pacific with his trouser legs rolled high and pulled from between his pale white feet a simple piece of green sea tangle. If there is in the history of food science an act that rivals that of the lifting of Excalibur, this very well may be it, for it was from this slender curl of kombu seaweed that Dr. Ikeda extracted the salts of the naturally produced glutamic acid, thus isolating what he believed to be the fifth basic taste available in this world—"something common in the complicated taste of asparagus, tomatoes, cheese and meat," to use the words Dr. Ikeda himself spoke at the 8th International Congress of Applied Chemistry in Chicago in 1912.

Derived from the Japanese adjective *umai* (旨い), meaning "delicious" or "palatable," *umami* can be described as being meaty, brothy, or savory, and is especially prevalent in aged or fermented foods, like cheese and soy sauce. While some food scientists believe *umami* overlaps in some way with one or more of the four basic tastes, others are quick to dismiss it further and speak of it in derision, often by linking it to "Chinese Restaurant Syndrome," that condition, marked by dizziness, headaches, and chest pains, that troubles some people after eating food enriched by the flavor enhancer monosodium glutamate, which itself was first commercially produced as a direct result of Dr. Ikeda's pioneering work and then later brought to the United States after U.S. soldiers in Occupied Japan had fallen upon the abandoned field rations of the vanquished Imperial Army and learned why Hirohito's troops had found their food so delicious.

to remind me, his very foreignness. Since leaving his native Colombo at the age of seventeen, he had become more British or European than American. His sense of cultural drift didn't make him in any way unique at FlavAmerica. I had been raised in England, of course, and Beekley had circumnavigated the globe as an army brat. But we had assimilated, and Koba clearly had not, as we all could see the first time he looked at the sign above the door to the flavor development studio — ASK NOT WHAT YOUR COMPANY CAN DO FOR YOU, ASK WHAT YOU CAN DO FOR YOUR COMPANY — and didn't get the reference.

"Kennedy!" Tennessee roared that day. He counted it off on one hand. "A New Englander, a bootlegger, a papist! How you gonna succeed in this industry if you don't know a goddamn thing about John Fitzgerald Kennedy?"

His question, as I'd first learned at Greystone Park, wasn't an unreasonable one. Ten thousand new food products are released into the American marketplace each year, and of these, nine out of every ten will fail.

"And you wanna know why?" Tennessee asked.

"Is it the quality of the flavorings used?" Koba gamely answered, before suggesting that perhaps the size of one's advertising budget might play a part in it.

"Wrong!" Tennessee said. "Wrong again! Anticipation, that's the goddamn thing."

"Yes," I put in, eager to contain my colleague's passions. "Tennessee is absolutely right. A flavorist needs to be able to forecast where a culture will be so that he can know what it will want to taste when it gets there."

"You're goddamn right he does!"

"It does you no good to give a lemon-ginger chewing gum to a public raised up on wild strawberry. You may find success with that formula in Guangdong Province, but here in the United States you'll only suffer a humiliating defeat."

"You're goddamn right you will!"

It didn't matter that since Gorbachev had starred in a Pizza Hut commercial I could barely see my way through to the end of the day, to say nothing of the future. I was a senior flavorist, well versed in the theory of our trade, and it was my duty to share my knowledge with those coming along at my rear. We were like cultural anthropologists, I told Koba, and so in addition to having him read *Beverage World* and *Prepared Foods* and all the other expected trade journals, I stayed late with him at the office no less than twice a month so we could flip through collectible Sears, Roebuck catalogues or discuss the importance of Bat Boy or Bigfoot or some other recurring character from the *Weekly World News.* I felt somehow responsible for him, though perhaps subconsciously I was only trying to work through those memories of my own awkward transition into American life. Whatever the reason, I gave Koba regular assignments and tested him weekly. One Saturday I had him attend several Little League games in Toms River and write a brief report about what was selling well at the snack shack; the next I had him scout out the cereal aisle at the local Acme for so long that security was called in on the suspicion that he was a lurking pedophile.

Beekley, whose expertise on hip hop, extreme sports, and conspiracy theories of the post–Cold War era filled in the holes in my own scholarship, joined us on several occasions to offer a younger perspective. Once he had us follow him out to the parking lot, where we found an orange 1969 Dodge Charger parked and waiting for us. "Slide in through the windows," he instructed. "Not like that. Legs first." Koba was a gangly fellow, six foot four at least, all knees and elbows, and with thick-framed glasses that were quick to slide down the bridge of his nose. "Give him a little push then, David. There we go." Minutes later we were racing down the Turnpike and Beekley was lecturing Koba on the "General Lee," daisy dukes, and the late-career evangelism of John Schneider.

"Write that down," he'd say every few minutes. "That's important. Then get back to me next week with three thousand words on the mustache and its rôle in promoting or subverting traditional notions of masculinity in the nineteen seventies. Do not," he said, emphasizing this by giving a quick double toot of the horn, "forget to analyze the mustache as homosexual icon."

*   *   *

Before I could ask Koba to cover for me that morning, I heard Ernst's voice moving in from the test kitchen, and then saw him appear at the door with the children from science camp crowding in around him.

"This is where we put the pleasure in," he said. "That man there is 'Tennessee' Terrence Matthews, our longest-tenured senior flavorist." He barely nodded hello. "And this one here"—Koba gave a big smile as Ernst pointed him out—"is FlavAmerica's newest apprentice, Koba."

Koba came over to Ernst, holding a test tube in one hand and a glass pipette in the other. Earlier that morning I'd given him an assignment: to devise a bing cherry flavoring like the one he'd come up with the day before, only this time using chemicals that had a combined cost of 30 percent less.

"Price points," Koba said, after explaining his task to the group. "This is how one wins battles in the food and flavorings industry. Isn't that right, David? By making sure you can beat your competitor on price points."

With an approving nod from me, Koba stepped out amongst the children and passed the mouth of his test tube beneath their noses.

"Cherry!" one boy shrieked. "It smells just like a cherry!"

"Can I taste it?" the obese Asian boy asked, his flared feet spread wide beneath him.

"No, I'm afraid not," Koba smiled, lifting his thick Stalinist mustache and flashing his brilliant white teeth. "Excepting for the rare coffee flavoring, we don't taste much of what we make here, at least not at this early stage. The nose is more than enough."

"Mmm," Ernst agreed. "Your tongue's reputation is greater than its abilities. Seventy percent of flavor is perceived by the nose. The nose," he said.

"Just think back to the last time you were sick," Koba added, and I was glad to see him so eager to contribute. Such a dedicated worker! You could see it in the argyle socks that matched the sweater vest he wore beneath his starched white lab coat in the winter, and in the clean part of his hair that was present all year round. Business. That's what you thought of when you saw Koba: business. "Why, with a stuffed nose and swollen glands," he said, "I'm sure you couldn't have tasted much more than the salt in your chicken soup, now could you?"

"Though our thoughts on flavor shouldn't stop there," I said. "For how would fried chicken taste without its crunch? Or a peach without its fuzz?"

"Color is no less important," Ernst said, shaking a bony finger. "Who among you would eat a split pea soup if it were blue? Or red?"

The children laughed.

"You'd have to eat it blindfolded, no matter how delicious."

"Flavor is a most mysterious thing indeed," Koba concluded, "and yet in the end it is also very simple. Put something in your mouth and you don't have to think about it: you either spit or swallow."

It was an innocent mistake, but still one that left a precocious young boy shuffling a fist up beside his mouth while distending his far cheek with a poke of his tongue.

"Kevin!" the elder chaperone said, giving him a slap on the shoulder.

I coughed into my fist—"Yes, thank you, Koba"—and pushed out through the crowd into the hallway, already thinking of *Deep Throat* and *Behind the Green Door,* blue movies that would form the basis of my next cultural lecture, the title of which I'd announce to my apprentice in a memo later that day: "The Evolution of American Pornography from the 2¢ Postcard to the 10 GB Hard Drive."

"Just this way now," I said, throwing my hand out toward the double doors, "and we'll go out to the killing floor, where all of our orders are prepared in bulk."

I LEFT WORK EARLY THAT DAY, intending to buy a money order for the Albanians, but the line at the post office snaked so far out the door—and was comprised of people who looked so limp and defeated—that I immediately turned back for my car, trying to convince myself that Priscilla might no longer even want *Sweetness #9—What Is to Be Done?* Teenagers are a famously fickle bunch, after all. One minute it's The New Kids on the Block, the next The Backstreet Boys. Priscilla was no different, I knew, and so by the time she realized she didn't have the Albanian report, she might be on to something else. *Save the whales!* She still might get upset to learn I'd never ordered the report, but at that point I could always appease her by making a donation to Greenpeace or agreeing to buy dolphin-safe tuna from now on.

I was still sitting in the parking lot—key in the ignition, a satisfied look on my face—when my cell phone rang. It was Betty, asking about dinner.

"Are there any left-overs?" she said.

For much of the last year, we'd been coming home with cartons of Chinese or bags full of Indian; that, or been calling the pizzeria we both kept on speed dial. But while there might have been a few breaded nuggets of sweet and sour chicken rolling around in a Tupperware dish at the back of the fridge, or perhaps a couple of slices of pepperoni hidden away in a pouch of aluminum foil, I didn't think we'd be able to find enough food to feed a family of four. This prompted Betty to suggest we look to the Deep-freeze, but of late I'd started to find something unsatisfying about this, too. It wasn't that I didn't like the flavor of frozen food; I did, of course I did; it was only that I didn't like to eat it in the company of anyone else. Timing was the problem. If Ernest used the microwave first, he'd finish his meal before I could get mine fully cooked, and then when at last I was done, Betty would be poking her finger into the ice-cold center of her entrée and saying it could use another minute. It seemed we either needed to get rid of the microwave entirely or buy three more.

I started the car, asking Betty if she was up for McDonald's. She said she was, though only if we ate there.

"I don't want the smell to linger and remind me of what I've done," she said.

Betty's offices were located just across the river from FlavAmerica, in Battle Station's now fashionably redeveloped downtown. There, in a storied structure of vaulted brick and paned glass that had once housed the factory that produced the woolen blankets used by the U.S. Army during the two world wars, she was employed as a sort of interior designer writ large, an Albert Speer for the new age. Whenever a city, county, state, or region developed an interest in becoming more tourist-friendly, they contacted New Horizons, LLC, which in turn sent Betty out to drive around, get lost, look for something to eat, and take pictures of everything there was to compliment or complain about. A few weeks later she'd be back to give a PowerPoint presentation to a city council or board of chosen freeholders. "Do we really need these 'Under New Management' signs?" she might say, while stopping on a photo of a roadside café. "Because what do they really tell us? 'Keep going. Don't trust the soup. There's been trouble here.'"

After agreeing to carpool in to work the following morning, I crossed the Stupfer Bridge to pick up my wife, then called our daughter, even though I knew where she'd be: Sarin's house. Or not house but loft. Her father, a freelance photographer, was renting a cavernous space in an industrial district of South Battle Station, where life looked as grim and graffitied as downtown had been in the seventies. I didn't like my daughter spending so much time there, but the more I insisted she stay away, the more she insisted on going.

Priscilla was waiting for us outside when I pulled up, leaning back against the brick wall of the four-story modernist building that her friend called home. She didn't hurry to get into the car. She pushed off from the wall and walked over slowly, lowering her head to the window as her mother opened it.

"Where are we going?" she said.

"Get in." I glanced into my rear-view mirror, as if expecting to see flashing lights. "You keep talking to us like that and some policeman's bound to stop me on suspicion of solicitation."

"McDonald's," Betty said.

"You're kidding, right?" Priscilla's face was as firm and unforgiving as the side of a battleship.

"What? It's too hot to cook at home."

"Now come on," I told her. "We're losing the air conditioning."

She finally opened the passenger door and fell down into her seat, saying something I couldn't quite make out. This had been happening more and more of late. For at least a year now, Priscilla had spoken a language closer to German than English. Her words had a tendency to run together into a sort of linguistic gruel, forcing you to rely on the many shrugs and eye rolls and audible gasps with which she otherwise communicated.

I made a quick U-turn, asking my daughter to repeat herself. "I didn't quite hear you."

"I said I'm a *vee*-gan. You are familiar with the term, aren't you?"

"Yes." I found her in the rear-view mirror. "The people vegetarians call crazy. Is this Sarin's influence?"

Priscilla looked out her window.

Betty patted me on the thigh. "Let's just go. We've got to get E, remember."

Ernest had spent much of his summer with a boy named after one of the prophets of the Hebrew Bible. Jeremiah lived in a vast eighties-era apartment complex off Highway 1, a little more than a mile downhill from our house. I parked a few spaces over from the stairs that led up to his unit, then hurried out through the heat and humidity to his door.

A teenaged girl I'd never seen before answered my knock, but this was in no way a surprise. Jeremiah was one of a handful of foster children living here, all under the watchful eye of a woman in her forties who had agreed to let our son stay with her for a few hours each day after soccer camp if only we'd reciprocate by buying her foster children memberships to the Boys & Girls Club down the road.

This evening Jeremiah's mother, a plump, permed woman whom Betty called "The Saint," moved into the doorway behind the teenaged girl and said something I couldn't hear over the hum of her window air conditioning unit. She moved out beside me and closed the door behind her, asking if she could ask me a question.

I dislike no other question more. "Of course," I said.

"Your son," she said, "he doesn't use verbs, does he?"

I'd been out in the heat for less than a minute, but already beads of perspiration were making my arms feel swampy and the base of my shirt wet.

"I thought I was just imagining things," she said. "You understand how it is. With so many kids, I can't always give each one the full attention he deserves. But this morning I made a point to shadow them around, and if this isn't the truth, my name isn't Madeline Jones. He doesn't say verbs, not ever."

The sun hung in the sky over my shoulder; she squinted and smiled and held a hand up over her eyes as she talked. "I was just wondering if it was because he'd been diagnosed with something. I'm not prejudiced or anything—Jeremiah has ADD, no different than all my kids—I just thought I should know"—somehow her smile grew bigger—"you know, in case you wanted me to remind him to take his pills. Jeremiah's always forgetting," she said, "so when he's over at your house, by all means remind him." She slapped her mouth then, her eyes growing large and round. "Oh my Lord! I'm not telling you something you didn't know, am I?"

I'd imagined her question a moment before she'd asked it. Would it make me a bad parent? "We really should be running," I said. "We've got reservations for dinner."

While Ernest was still inside collecting his things, I hurried back to the car and told the others what I'd learned.

"No verbs?" Betty said.

"Had you noticed?"

She turned in her seat to question Priscilla. "Does this sound right to you?"

"Considering the junk he eats? It wouldn't surprise me if he's got Sweetness #9 poisoning."

Betty rolled her eyes. "Priscilla!"

"What?" She reached into the front pocket of her sweatshirt and flipped to a page in her notebook. "'Aphasias and impotence,'" she said, "'rage disorders, dyspepsia, a forgetfulness that verges on panic.'"

I spoke to her through the rear-view mirror. "You never would have said that until this morning."

"Whether I knew about Sweetness #9 poisoning before today is irrelevant. You don't have to believe in cancer to get it."

I shushed my daughter and motioned discreetly to the stairs. "He's coming."

"Do we tell him that we know?"

"What do we know?" I said. "That a woman who probably didn't graduate from high school has suspicions?"

These were the last hurried words we could share. Then Ernest placed a corn dog in between his teeth, opened the door, and in one fluid motion fell down into his seat while tossing his backpack in back. After he pulled his corn dog free, I dropped my head down to one side, noticing the curl of green ketchup that ran the length of his early-evening snack.

"What?" he said.

It wasn't just me; we were all staring.

"Nothing."

"Green ketchup?" Priscilla asked.

Her brother looked at her no less suspiciously than she looked at him; then he parroted the line I'd heard on television: "Same great flavor, new bold color."

Betty and I shared a look: six words, not a single verb.

I threw my arms across her seat and backed out, then turned the car north, in the direction we'd come from. As I sped toward McDonald's,

I remembered the dreams I'd had as a young man, before my stint at Greystone Park had put an end to such thinking. Back then, when not imagining a future in flavor, I'd often considered working for the CIA. I'd thought I could be the type of agent who can get the truth out of someone after only a few minutes in a closed room, and so here I put those dreams into action.

"Some weather we're having," I said, "isn't it?"

I looked for Ernest in the rear-view mirror, but he only bit into his corn dog and shrugged.

"Priscilla keeps telling me it's global warming."

"Because it is."

I sent my daughter a stern look over my shoulder. She had an over-sized personality, more like that of a president than a political adviser—the exact opposite of her brother, who played Atwater to Priscilla's Reagan, content never to take center stage. Understanding my purpose now, Priscilla nodded and sank back into her seat.

"It's certainly unusually warm," I continued. "It's not even August yet, and already we've had seven days this summer over ninety. What do you think, E?"

He turned his corn dog round on its stick. He was eating the dough off first. "Heat wave," he said.

Betty sighed. I gave her a reassuring nod.

"Yes, a heat wave. What have we had—two days in a row at or above ninety-four? And tomorrow it's only going to get hotter, they say."

"Ninety-nine."

"No! That high? What makes you say that?"

"The computer."

"When I looked this morning, my homepage said to expect a high of ninety-five."

Ernest looked for me in the mirror. "The temperature reading: ninety-five." He gestured with his corn dog. "But the 'feels like'? Ninety-seven."

I smiled at my wife. *Feels like!* But she was quicker with grammar than I was and had already determined the phrase had been used as an adjective to modify the reading of which he spoke. As she turned to look out her window, I pushed my foot down on the gas. "How do they even know what it feels like?"

Ernest was biting into the meat of his corn dog now. "Computers. Inputs. Variables. All very complex."

"But how does a computer determine a *feeling?* Can you tell me that?"

"Logarithms. Statistics." His voice betrayed his loss of interest. He looked around for a place to dispose of his now meatless stick. "Et cetera, et cetera."

"Well" — I let out a long breath — "all these years I thought I was leaving you a better world, but now it seems I may have been wrong. *Computers that feel.* You want my advice? Don't go west, go back. I'm not sure where we went wrong, but it has to be back there somewhere. Do you hear me?"

That evening at McDonald's, Ernest popped the lid off his drink and dropped a long burst of red food coloring inside. He was like a Texan who couldn't be separated from his Tabasco; he carried a little bottle of Red Dye No. 40 around with him wherever he went. Betty and I had disapproved at first, of course we had, but our son's attraction to the coloring ran deep, past frosted cakes and Shirley Temples to streaked glasses of milk and eggs he ordered "bloody-side up" from waitresses who didn't know how to react. *What could be the harm?* we had thought, because it was either this or struggle to get him to eat anything all. *And really,* we had said, *if you don't give it to them at home, they'll only find it somewhere else.*

After the dye had fallen into his soda, Priscilla said something to her brother in Spanish, causing him to answer her in kind. I had always been grateful to our housekeeper for teaching them the language. It gave you an edge in college and the business world. But as they rattled on in their Mayan-inflected tongue, with Priscilla saying ten words for each of her brother's flat, laconic replies, I began to have second thoughts. They were like peasants plotting a revolt.

"What were you two arguing about?" I asked, after Ernest had ended things by standing up from the table and going off for some more ketchup.

"I was telling him he shouldn't be using that stuff. It's gotta be dangerous," she said.

"The red dye?" Betty had been cutting into her Quarter Pounder with a plastic knife and fork (she'd read that you ate less if you cut your food into tiny pieces), but here she pulled her utensils away from her meal and gave me a concerned look. "Is it, David?"

"It's perfectly safe," I told her.

"Perfectly?" Priscilla said.

"Well, 'generally' might be the better word."

Now it was Betty who echoed me: *"Generally?"*

I glanced to the front of the restaurant, where a man at the register was pointing Ernest toward the stash of ketchup packets by the soda fountain. "That's the language the federal government uses when approving a new food additive for use," I said. "They say it's Generally Recognized As Safe."

"Have they ever been wrong?" Priscilla asked.

I snorted and looked to Betty, as if she might agree that this was no way to go through life, with such a depressingly negative attitude. But my wife sat there with her utensils suspended over her de-bunned Quarter Pounder, waiting for my answer no less anxiously than our daughter.

After sneaking another glance at Ernest—he was now coming toward us with a fistful of ketchup packets—I spoke in a hurried whisper. "Well, Red Dye No. 3 was pulled a few years ago when the FDA learned it caused tumors in the thyroids of male rats, but they were overly cautious, if you ask me. You could withstand a lifetime of exposure and the risk would still only be something like one in one hundred thousand. And that's for cancer," I told my daughter, "not verblessness."

Betty smiled brightly as Ernest sat down. "Found some?" she said.

He shrugged and nodded, then began biting off the corners of his packets and squirting ketchup into the bottom of his Big Mac container.

Priscilla slumped down in her chair, looking off toward the sprawling Playland connected to the restaurant. Ronald McDonald had appeared, to the delight of a small scrum of children. Priscilla shook her head. "What does it say that I learned about him before I'd ever heard about Jesus?"

Betty fixed her with one of the looks she'd learned in business school.

"What?" Priscilla said. "I can't talk about Jesus now?"

"You can talk about Jesus in the proper place and at the proper time. Right now we're at the dinner table."

"This is McDonald's."

"And we're eating dinner."

"Can you at least hurry up? It is fast food, isn't it?"

Ernest raised a finger to ask for our patience, then said, after he'd swallowed a mouthful of fries, "The average American family? Six minutes at the dinner table. Fact."

"Six?"

"How'd you learn that?"

"The *Times*."

"Speaking of counting," Priscilla said, "did you see the sign out front? 'Billions and billions served.' They used to keep track. It used to say 'Fifty billion served.' 'Seventy-five billion.' Now they're like, 'Why bother? We're just gonna kill 'em all anyway.' They should put up a sign saying how many are left. 'Seventy-five billion cows to go.' 'Fifty billion.' They could do the same with acres of the rain forest."

Betty glanced at her watch. "If we hurry, we just might be able to finish in five minutes." With this, she slashed at her burger with her plastic utensils, and Priscilla sank still lower in her chair, propelled by her ninety-ninth sigh of the day. Ernest burped. And so this is it, I thought. This is The Family Leveraux. The one in a constant battle with her weight, the other so generally dissatisfied with life, and the third so small and apparently verbless.

I sent my eyes out the picture window, watching as the man in garish yellow pantaloons performed in front of the kids like a demented Marcel Marceau. Maybe it was the fact that he was in a glass room surrounded by glass walls that brought to mind the communal glass tank in which I'd once placed my rats in Animal Testing; maybe it was the fact that we'd listened to those agitators on AM radio in the morning, or that Priscilla's thinking had started leading my own. I can't say for sure what did it, nor was I expansive about this in my pocket diary the following evening, when I jotted down only one line: *It's happening again, isn't it?* But as I looked back to my family, the tagline of a commercial years removed from the airwaves bubbled up to the forefront of my memory. *Now with Sweetness #9.* It was as unforgettable as my name or social security number. *Now with Sweetness #9.*

My hand jumped out, fluttering in the direction of Betty's cup of diet cola. "You know, sugar's flavor profile is much more well rounded than what you've got in there. It resembles a nicely designed bell curve, whereas that" — I cleared my throat — "that sugary artificial, it... it flattens your cola more than flavors it."

Betty reached for one of my fries (she'd insisted she didn't want her own order) and answered with a practiced smile. "I prefer the taste. You know that."

Priscilla reached into the front pocket of her hooded sweatshirt for her pencil and that reporter's notebook she never went without. "What's this all about?" she said. "Why are you championing the natural over the artificial?"

"What? Am I doing that?"

She flipped to a clean page and pushed the tip of her No. 2 into the paper. I heard a tiny snap. The tip? It might as well have been my life.

"What are you doing?" I said.

"Sarin and I spent the day planning out the editorial calendar for the fall. We're gonna do a think-piece on the cafeteria. Maybe a series."

"A think-piece?" Did the floor pull away beneath me, like sand running out with the tide? Did people stop and point to a big wave rolling in from the horizon, not yet understanding how tall and overpowering it would grow? "What do you mean?"

"Is Sweetness #9 dangerous?" she said. "Why else would you tell Mom to stop drinking her soda?"

I smiled as if this were an absurd scenario, and in many ways it was. I had once believed the *Washington Post* would expose all of my efforts at suppression and my many lies of omission; now I realized it was a call from the fact-checker at my daughter's high school's paper that I should fear.

I spoke to Betty instead of Priscilla. "I was only saying maybe we're at the age where we should give ourselves over to the joys of the sugar-cane. Mmm? We turned our backs on margarine, didn't we? Retreated to the saturated pleasures of the cow."

"What were the results of the tests you ran, Dad?"

It was Priscilla. She wouldn't let it go. Still, I kept my eyes on Betty. "Is it rude to turn down an interview request from your own daughter?"

Betty sipped from her straw. "Not at the dinner table, no."

"C'mon, Dad. Just answer the question."

My trunk stiffened. Priscilla, an instinctive journalist, fed me silence as if it were a length of rope with which I could hang myself.

"What makes you think I'm withholding something?"

"That twitch in your eye."

I reached for it.

"I'll find out one way or another," she said, "and as with every story, some people will come off sympathetically, while others" — she shrugged — "less so."

I held back a smile. A little Nixonian, no different from her father. "Are you at least willing to let me speak off the record?"

"Are you saying you know something?"

Betty reached for my chocolate shake.

"Because if you're willing to let me go on background —"

"You said 'off the record.'"

" — I'll give you what you want. But if you just want to run a fool out in between quotation marks, you'll have to get it in dribs and drabs like everyone else."

"What aren't you telling me?"

"I'm British. Doesn't she understand I'm British?"

"Stop playing with her, David."

"E, tell your sister the direct approach won't work with me." I sat back, bouncing one finger in the air. "Though I do like the idea of coming clean in the pages of *The Campus Crier*. Why didn't I think of this before? All the therapeutic value of confession, but with none of the public embarrassment. What's your circulation again?"

"He's joking," Betty said. "You know your father."

I motioned to her pad with my burger, telling her to take this down. "That man on the radio was right. Symptoms of prolonged Sweetness #9 exposure include anxiety, obesity, selective mutism in monkeys, and a generalized dissatisfaction with life."

She was writing with a just-playing-along look.

"Other possible side-effects include agenda journalism—"

She looked up.

"—Communism, the disparagement of Ronald McDonald."

"Very funny, Dad."

"Really, David."

"What?" I was like a Bond villain. Once I'd started in on the exposition, I couldn't stop. "This is a big story. Forget the high school paper, you may need to write a book. Have I told you about the monkeys?"

Ernest looked up from the last of his fries.

"It all begins with monkeys," I said.

Betty poured salt over what remained of her Quarter Pounder, then placed a paper napkin over the corpse of her dinner. "Let the regret begin."

Priscilla leaned back in her chair, her eyes not leaving mine. "So did you at least order the Albanian report?"

"I thought you would've forgotten about that by now."

"Thought or hoped?"

"You should trust your father. Why don't you trust your father?"

She pocketed her pencil and notebook, then stood and extended her hand. "Can I have the keys? It smells like a crematorium in here. I'd rather wait in the car."

ON THROUGH THE SIXTIES, before the second wave of feminism crashed ashore and swept this life away, Ernst Eberhardt had a long string of secretaries who performed shorthand for him on either side of his desk. One of the last of these young women remained with him longer than most. Her name: Eliza Abigail FitzGerald. They remained together for three years, until Eliza came to his row house one Sunday morning, planning to surprise him with warm croissants. The key she used to let herself in had been a recent victory for her in their relationship, or so she thought before she reached his bedroom upstairs. It was there that she found Ernst in bed with a busty young blonde he'd met while thumping melons at a roadside stand. Eliza grabbed Miss Melons by the roots of her dyed blonde hair and dragged her kicking and screaming into the street, cursing Ernst the whole while for being too cowardly to tell her any other way.

A month later Miss Melons had passed out of season, and Eliza was simply gone — off to Downey, California, where she'd land a job with the Post Office and deliver the mail on the street of a young Karen Carpenter. For parts of four decades she remained away, long enough to marry a man and celebrate a silver anniversary and see all of the equity in her home of twenty-some years disappear after her husband fought and lost a protracted battle with cancer.

When Eliza reappeared in our front lobby in the summer of 1995, looking for a fresh start (and, I thought, a little money), Ernst met her with an awkward hug that became a friendly if uncoordinated kiss. An early lunch followed, and this spilled over into a candle-lit dinner. The next morning I was asked to apologize to Soon Bok, our quiet, respectful, and preternaturally organized receptionist, and inform her of our generous severance package. Minutes later, Eliza was taking her place at the front desk as if nothing had changed since LBJ was in the White House.

I didn't like her—not the prunish looks she seemed to reserve for me, not the squeaky shoes and polyester slacks that she wore, not even the tiny wad of Kleenex she was constantly stashing up the sleeve of one of her many tiger-print blouses. But she made Ernst happy in his old age, and so in turn she lent me a sort of happiness as well.

It was because of Eliza that my dinner was interrupted at McDonald's. Just moments after Priscilla left for the car, my phone rang, and when I reached for it and saw the name flashing on its screen—*ERNST (Cell)*—I knew it must be serious. Eliza had purchased the phone for him at some point in the last year or two, but Ernst had never taken to it. When he wasn't forgetting it in his knick-knack drawer at home, he was puzzling over its unfamiliar buttons ("Why won't it stop ringing when I set it down?") or being reminded that it only worked if you first charged its battery.

I stepped away from our table to answer the call, but for a moment the conversation went nowhere, as Ernst and I struggled with a slight delay. When we weren't talking at the same time, we were apologizing for doing so and telling the other person to go ahead—and then hearing the same thing in return.

"Where are you?" I finally managed to get in. "Are you all right?"

"I'm embarrassed," he said. "That's where I am."

After dropping Betty and the kids at home, I drove out to the coast on Highway 18, wondering how Ernst could have gotten so far from his intended destination. He'd taken the bus to Edison after work, having decided to surprise Eliza with a new car. But after he pulled out of the lot in a blue Jetta GLX, the surprise was on him. He hadn't had a driver's license as long as I'd known him, and for every road he recognized from those years when he had owned a car, there were three or four new ones that got him turned around.

I finally found him near Edenville, parked in front of a wooden structure that had a crudely painted sign standing atop its slanted wood shingle roof. KEYS MADE, it read. PO BOXES.

I pulled in alongside him and stepped over to the driver's window. Ernst was asleep, his mouth hanging open to reveal a jumble of stained teeth. He'd been in his late fifties when we first met, not much older than I was now, but even if he had already walked with a cane back then, he'd done so jauntily, always leading the way whenever we went on a long walk. Now, though, he looked as old and exhausted as his wrinkled suit.

I knocked gently, and then hard enough to wake him. Ernst reacted with a start, looking at me in his window as if I were a shaded figure coming for him in a bad dream.

"It's David!" I said. "Open the door!"

His fear quickly transformed into confusion as he ran his hand down the door panel beneath the window. "There's no handle!"

"The button!" I pointed. "It's a button!"

He finally pushed one. The window lowered between us.

I reached in to pop the lock, and then he was stepping out, saying, "When did the world get taken over by buttons?" He didn't wait for an answer; he hurried inside to use the facilities, going in through the front door just after a man with a handlebar mustache had walked out holding a clump of mail close to his leather vest. This man avoided my gaze, leaving me to think of all the dubious figures who must transact their business inside: those with hidden bank accounts and deviant mail-order pornography habits, shut-ins seeking meek Filipina wives, and tenured professors in search of romance through the personals ads in the *New York Review of Books*. Then it occurred to me: What better place to receive the Albanian report?

Inside, I filled out a form at the front counter, providing my contact information and specifying the size of the box I required. The clerk was almost as old as Ernst, but fiercer looking, with a buzz cut and a body as lean as a strip of beef jerky. He picked up my form and read it, pausing on the name.

"Jürgen Mockus," he said. "Is that Swedish?"

I tried a smile. "Lithuanian, actually."

He had a toothpick in his mouth, one he moved this way and that with his tongue. "I knew a Swedish gal once. A socialist." He paused to judge my reaction. He looked like the type of person who could weaponize a ballpoint pen. "Can't say I've ever met a Lithuanian. You were Communist, weren't you?"

I tapped my chest: *Me?*

"With the Russians, I mean. The Soviets."

I shrugged, going for my wallet.

"Well, we get all types through here these days."

I laid a twenty on the counter and glanced in the direction of the restrooms.

The man made change from an old clanging register, then retreated behind a blue curtain and came back with a key.

"You're number nineteen seventeen." A smile as he set it down on the counter. "That should be easy enough for you to remember."

Though Battle Station had long been known as a textile town buoyed by fat government contracts and a workforce of dedicated Hungarian and German immigrants, the last of its great mills closed in 1961, eight years after the end of the Korean War made it impossible for the Weber Woolens Company to avoid bankruptcy. At that point the city's middle class scattered in all directions, and Battle Station's reputation fell as quickly as its tax base plummeted. Two of FlavAmerica's competitors relocated during these trying times, one all the way to Pleasanton, California. Ernst Eberhardt, however, never considered such a move; he insisted we dig in, and so we were able to watch, from our location on the banks of the Raritan River, as the embattled downtown rose like a phoenix on the far shore of the polluted waterfront.[*]

The city center's celebrated rebirth would never have happened had the Hilton Hotel and Conference Center, seeded by tax deductions and a gift of cheap public land, not sprung up across from us in the

---

[*] The river caught fire in 1971, but as this was two years after the Cuyahoga did the same, it only made the local and regional news.

mid-eighties. In the years that followed its opening, the city became a reference point in discussions about brownfields and the power of eminent domain, with first cafés and restaurants opening to serve the conference center's many visitors, and then several small theaters and a large multiplex taking over what had been Factory Row. When a supermarket opened its doors in 1997 (the first to serve the downtown area in more than forty years), I began urging Ernst to buy one of the condos that had been built atop it. It was just a short walk from there to the Stupfer Bridge, and then only another five or ten minutes to FlavAmerica on the other side of the river.

He wouldn't hear of it, though, even if the one thing Ernst preferred to taking the bus was a good long stroll. He insisted on living where he'd always lived, in an area of Battle Station where the urban decay was not yet fully realized. Here, almost two miles to the east of FlavAmerica, where even tattooed twenty-somethings didn't envision their next skateboard shop or cooperative café, a Dunkin' Donuts operated by an extended family of Thai immigrants occupied a street corner where once a German American sports club had stood. Ernst lived five lots up from it, in a spartan two-story brick row house dominated by green aluminum awnings that had been streaked white by the passing avian population. His neighbors, as relative newcomers to the area, if not the country, were both less fortunate and more honest; they had bars over their windows and bed-sheet curtains.

After I parked in front of Ernst's house the next morning (he had insisted on thanking me with breakfast), I ran into Eliza as she was coming down the front steps. She was wearing yet another tiger-print blouse, this one held in place by a thin black belt circling her belly, and had a smile on her face, even after she'd noticed me.

"Morning, David!"

"Aren't you feeling chipper," I said.

She fished her key chain out of her purse and pushed a button to unlock the doors of her new car. "A little present," she said.

As the Jetta responded with a beep, I turned to look up the street as if seeing the car for the first time.

"You have a very generous boyfriend," I told her.

Still smiling, she dropped down into the car, saying she'd see me at work.

The front door was unlocked, so as I pushed my way inside, I called out my mentor's name and said a few words about crime statistics. Ernst leaned his head out of the kitchen, fidgeting with one of his ears—probably turning his hearing aid on.

"Just fixing the coffee," he said.

I sat down at the bench in the hall to take off my shoes and put on the pair of house slippers he left out for guests; then I joined him in the kitchen, happy to see he looked as bright and fresh as his clothing: a crisp white half apron worn over his usual pair of green woolen pants and a starched blue dress shirt, the color of which matched his cashmere socks.

"You had better be hungry," he said.

I took my seat at the small table pushed up against the wall, eager to partake of the lavish spread. There were plates of imported cold cuts and a fan of European cheeses, a tin of Norwegian sardines and another of English kippers, two loaves of sliced bread in a basket—one dark, one white—a couple of hard-boiled eggs, a bowl of creamed butter, and a small dish of red caviar. This was in no way unusual. It was my mentor's custom to host such a breakfast for one or more of us from FlavAmerica every other week. (Tennessee liked to point out that I was rarely excluded—and that the house slippers didn't fit him.)

"So," he said, setting a cup of coffee down in front of me. "Tell me. How are your beautiful children? You never bring them around the office anymore."

I took a sip of my coffee, then carefully set the cup down in its saucer. "Your namesake—"

"In principle," he said, echoing the words I had given him when I'd first told him of my son's birth.

"Ernest is no longer using verbs."

Ernst was a wise man. He sat across from me, holding his tongue. What could he possibly say?

"Or at least we think he isn't. We only found out yesterday, and you know how Ernest is. Like his old man, keeps his cards close to his chest."

"What are you going to do?"

I shrugged and reached for a slice of black bread. "Nothing drastic just yet. We need to monitor the situation, maybe get our hands on a writing sample."

"It's only when he speaks?"

"We think so, yes. Spanish, too, I believe."

"I'm sure it's nothing." He put on a forced smile, as if thinking he'd turn us to a happier subject. "And your daughter?"

I sighed and sent my knife into the butter. "She's working on a think-piece about the cafeteria."

He repeated the phrase with all the caution of a non–native speaker. "Think-piece?"

"I should buy you a gift subscription to *The Campus Crier*. That way, if you see me doing a perp walk on the front page, you'll know why I haven't been coming round."

He let out an agreeable little huff. "You're blessed. Do you know that? You think I have anyone who'd care enough to investigate me?"

"Eliza."

He grunted. "I had my chances with her, but that was thirty years ago. Now I can only hope to make up for my mistakes."

"Give her a ring, not a German car. If it's marriage you want, trade in diamonds, not leather seats."

He shook his head, saying it was too late. "A man who marries for the first time at my age" — and here he reached for the little porcelain holder that held packets of sweetener on one side and sugar on the other — "he's a caricature. But you" — he grabbed a packet of Sweetness #9 and opened it over his coffee — "you have more than a past. You have a future. A family. Children. All things to grow into and be grateful for."

"Don't get me wrong," I said. "I'm grateful — I am. I've just started to think that instead of coming out into the waiting room to tell me 'It's a girl!' the nurse should've said, 'It's Woodward and Bernstein, I'm afraid. Do you have anything you'd like to say on the record?'"

He drank his coffee.

I pointed at his cup. "I thought you were a sugar man?"

He glanced at the design of his torn packet and only then realized what he'd done. "It's so easy to get them confused." He set a packet of sugar down beside the one he'd used. Both white, they looked almost identical. "Was so much easier when the contents were pink."

"Well, you should be more careful. As Priscilla's readers will soon know"—and my voice grew ominous here—"Sweetness #9 leads to obesity, apathy, anxiety, and a forgetfulness that verges on panic."

My intent was comic, but he seized on that last symptom, saying he felt the need to apologize again for requiring my help the previous day.

"I used to know how to drive to Edison." He shook his head. "But now...well, you'll have to be kind to me when I come down with Alzheimer's."

"Don't talk such nonsense. You got turned around, is all."

"Let's hope. I had a friend who came down with the disease. Died a couple of years ago."

"Alzheimer's?"

He nodded. "Man couldn't remember what he'd had for breakfast, but he'd talk about the distant past as if it were happening before his eyes." He spoke down into his cup, smiling at the memory. "He crashed my car in the late sixties, one weekend when his own was in the shop. "This was not long after Eliza left me," he said. "It was one of the last great Cadillacs. If Noah had driven, he would've driven this car. I only bought it so I could go through the Holland Tunnel on the weekends." He looked up, telling me American women won't date a man who insists on public transportation. "At least that was the case when I still worried about such things."

He chewed on a piece of bread and cheese, then continued. "That car couldn't have had more than two thousand miles on it when he drove it into a tree. He was coming back from a romantic rendezvous on the Jersey Shore. Said a deer ran out in front of him."

He swatted at the air. "Years passed. I all but forgot. Then I sit down at his bedside near the end and he starts telling me the story again, this time with a different ending. There was no deer. There was an Italian woman with her head in his lap and a pothole that made her bite." He chuckled. "When they tumbled out, bloody and embarrassed, he was lucky it was only the car that was totaled."

The cuckoo clock over the door chimed the hour. He waited for it to finish before doing so himself. "Can you think of anything worse? Cancer may slowly kill you, but only Alzheimer's has the power to reveal all of your lies."

We ate for another ten or fifteen minutes after that, but our conversation had stalled. We both seemed to be elsewhere, our minds adrift. Finally, I looked at my watch and asked him if he was coming into the office.

"No, maybe tomorrow," he said.

"Well, I had better get going. Leave Beekley alone too long and he's liable to burn the place down, isn't he?"

A LITTLE BEFORE LUNCH THAT DAY, Beekley appeared in the doorway to the flavor development studio. He didn't enter the lab, though; he just stood there, tapping a rolled-up copy of *Food Technology* magazine against his leg.

Knowing he wanted our attention, I did my best to ignore him. "Now, after you've done that," I told Koba, who stood across from me at his work station, "I want you to find two chemicals that occur naturally in and characterize the flavor of apples, then locate those chemicals that could make them riper, sweeter, and juicier."

Koba jotted all of this down in his notebook, though without his usual powers of concentration. His eyes kept flitting over to the door.

Like so many men of his generation, Beekley threw all of his loose change at the Salvation Army, dressing not to show people who he was but rather who he wasn't. Today he looked like he worked in a video store: a pair of coarse khakis, a white A-frame undershirt ("a wife-beater," he insisted on calling it), and a short-sleeve button-up paisley shirt whose flared collars could've poked an eye out.

"All right," I said. "What is it? An earthquake drill?"

"Everyone needs to come with me," he announced.

"Where to?" Koba said.

Beekley shook his head. "Can't say. Just come. I have something very important to show you."

I wasn't about to follow him anywhere, and not only because I feared he might want to drive us in the orange van he'd bought earlier in the year—a vehicle that had come complete with a tinted bubble window and now, after several costly "improvements," boasted floor-to-ceiling carpeting and a bed in back. No, it wasn't just the journey I wanted to avoid, it was the destination. Beekley was our resident collector of obsolete technology. He had a reel-to-reel high-fidelity system at home, a rotary phone, and plans for a dark-room; he even boasted of getting all his pornographic needs met by nudist magazines of the early 1950s. In short, he'd done this sort of thing before, and just as often as not, he had nothing more significant to show us than a stack of *Nude Living* magazines he'd found at the Goodwill or a *Star Wars* figure still in its box.

"I'll bite," Tennessee said, as Beekley turned out the door.

"You can't be serious?" I said. Koba was looking to me for direction.

"C'mon, David." Tennessee slapped me on the back as he passed. "You took the morning off. The least we can do is give this gentle fool a few minutes of our time."

If the redevelopment process in downtown Battle Station began when Mayor Higgins sank a golden shovel into the plot of dirt now occupied by the Hilton, its logical conclusion came in 1994, when the Stupfer Bridge, the now celebrated Stupfer Bridge, had one of its three lanes of traffic closed off to automobiles—a very controversial decision at the time—so that the "historic city centre" (as the signs read) could appear more pedestrian-friendly.

Almost immediately, scores of local residents were flocking to the bridge on the weekends to jog or stroll or show their civic pride in Spandex shorts and a pair of Rollerblades. I, too, often traversed this span, if not to meet Betty for lunch, then simply so I could pop into a bookstore to buy a grande cappuccino or browse the latest Stephen King. That all of this could be done on a corner where once you could have bought (or so it is said) a rock of crack cocaine never ceased to thrill me, at least until that summer of 1998, when a farmer's market appeared beneath the shadows of the bridge. Then, feeling as you do when you arrive at a party and realize you're the oldest one there, I found myself driving on my lunch hour into those parts of the city that my daughter considered "more authentic," where the Chinese restaurants had paper tablecloths and napkins, and you could walk into a corner liquor store and find cigarettes sold at the front counter for a quarter apiece. I'm not sure I was even conscious of what I was resisting, but I do know when it was that I toured the farmer's market stalls for the first time: that day when Beekley led us out of the office, saying there was something we had to see.

"You can't tell us where we're going?" Koba said, after we had moved up onto the Stupfer Bridge and heard Beekley remind us of just that. "Why can't you say where we're going?"

"If I told you," Beekley said, "I might as well tell you. Now just bear with me. You'll understand soon enough."

"It's the farmer's market," I said to the others. "He thinks he's going to tell us something we don't know about America by pointing out the crooked carrots and the overpriced tomatoes. It's a craze, I know. Sweeping the nation. Everyone wants to talk to the farmer who grew their potatoes and make sure he's got dirt beneath his fingernails."

Beekley walked on, willfully ignoring me until Tennessee and Koba had fallen a few paces behind us; then he told me he thought I should know that he'd gotten an email from Priscilla the previous night. "Asked if I knew anything about Sweetness #9," he said.

"Christ." His stride wasn't longer than mine, but it was quicker. I struggled to keep up. "So you know she's investigating me?"

He glanced over his shoulder. "She said it was for a think-piece."

"Yes, and I doubt she'll be happy until she finds a way to bring me down."

"She's a comer, David. What do you expect? That's what comers do. They come for you."

A moment, and then: "You're not helping her, are you?"

Again, he glanced at me.

"Because if I open the paper one day and see something attributed to 'a source inside FlavAmerica,' I will know who it is, and I will act accordingly."

He smirked, shaking his head. "I don't know what to say, David. If I were a mole, I wouldn't tell you. And if I told you that I wasn't, there'd be no way for you to know if I wasn't simply covering for the fact that I was."

A man on a unicycle passed us, going the other way.

"I hope you have children one day," I told Beekley.

We moved down off the bridge then and out amongst the stalls of the farmer's market, which lined both sides of the riverfront walkway.

Tennessee stopped at a table to study a basket of heirloom tomatoes. "They're neither uniform in size or color," he said, "and this one"—he turned it over, then passed it on to Koba—"has dirt adhered to its burst seams."

One of the two farmers tending this stall, a bearded man in a tie-dyed Grateful Dead T-shirt, smiled as if we were there to play some elaborate joke on him. We'd rushed out of the lab so quickly that Koba, Tennessee, and I were still wearing our lab coats.

"We're local," he said, apropos of nothing.

"So are we," Tennessee answered.

Beekley led us away from the table, saying that while the tomato might be somewhat revealing, it said only so much all by itself. "Multiple data points, that's what we need if we're to understand the American consumer. When you put one thing next to another, *that's* when you know you have something dense and meaningful."

Koba smiled giddily. "This is exciting. I can't wait to find out where we're going."

"It is nearby, I hope." We were passing the last stall now and leaving the farmer's market. "We do have work back in the lab, you know."

Beekley pointed to a building at the far end of the street.

"Is that a museum?" Koba said.

The building was still half-covered in scaffolding. An unlit neon sign jutted out over its front door. "MUSEUM," it read, quotation marks and all.

"It's not even officially open yet," Beekley said. "Today's a free preview."

Refusing to elaborate, he ushered us in and encouraged us to go on before him, saying he'd already been there twice that morning. Koba and Tennessee drifted up to the second floor, lured by an arrow promising the work of a Dutch master. I toured the main floor, which was devoted to contemporary artists: Dalí, Edward Hopper, too much Warhol and too little Picasso, then Lichtenstein and a couple of Jackson Pollocks.

As I stepped away from one of Pollock's masterworks, Beekley said, "Three seconds. Ten years ago, people spent an average of ten seconds in front of a painting. Now we're down to three."

"How'd all this art get here?" I said. "To Battle Station, I mean. Shouldn't it be in New York? Is it on tour?"

"Seven seconds gone in ten years, David. If I had told you our life expectancy had fallen seventy percent, you'd agree it was a monumental shift in the human experience. But it's seconds and not years, so you think it's no big deal."

"I don't care about stop-watches; I want to know about the art. Did some billionaire move to town? One of these young Internet men rich on porn or offshore gambling?"

"Soon, they'll combine museums with gyms. The Guggenheim is already designed for it. You'll run around an indoor track, building up a sweat as you fly past the works of art. Then you'll arrive in the room with all the nudes, where you'll take the opportunity to lather up and have a shower."

"Tell me, Beekley. How is this here?"

"It's fake."

I pointed at the painting in front of me. "The Pollock?"

"All of them," he said. "Every painting in here was once believed to be real but later discovered to be a fake. Go up to the second floor. You'll find a woman renting headphones. You can double back around, listening to a guided tour and learning about all the deceit you've taken in." He grinned as if there were nothing better. "Don't you understand the significance of this?"

I looked at a young artist who'd set up her easel before the famous Hopper depicting a handful of lonely souls at a late-night diner. She was halfway through her studied reproduction of the studied reproduction.

"What do we do, David? We tell people, 'This is what a strawberry tastes like,' and eventually that's what they come to believe: *this is what a strawberry tastes like.*"

I turned back to the Pollock. "But it's all splatterings and drips. You can't fake a Pollock."

"You think it's any less difficult than faking a strawberry? Some guy in Oregon uses computers and fractal geometry, pattern analysis and machines. Hell, once you've got the real thing to study, it's easier than painting the original. This particular piece hung for seven years in Pittsburgh."

I looked at it anew, my chin floating out to one side. When I moved on to the next, Beekley said, "Ten seconds."

Koba caught up to us a few minutes later. "Rembrandts!" he said. "The second floor is filthy with them! You have to come see, David."

Beekley pointed to the ceiling. "One painting up there hung in a Portuguese museum for twenty-five years. Hundreds of thousands of people saw it. Can you imagine? Fathers took their sons, and then those sons grew up to take their own sons. Then last year its paint was tested and the truth revealed: the pigments were unlike any Rembrandt could have known."

"A reproduction?" Koba said.

A couple walked by hand in hand, both of them wearing headphones. I hadn't noticed it before, but every second or third person had a pair on.

"Do you mean to say there are reproductions on the second floor?" Koba said.

"It shouldn't change the experience," Beekley continued. "They thought they saw a Rembrandt, and if you can't tell the difference, why not just enjoy it? But once you learn of the real thing, that's a whole new ballgame. It's no different than when someone tastes a wild strawberry for the first time, or one of those heirloom tomatoes we saw out there. Have you tried one? They're like heroin. You'll be chasing that first taste your whole life."

"What is he saying?" Koba asked.

"Don't you get it, David? Once people realize they've been eating only the *idea* of a strawberry, or the idea of a tomato — don't you see what will happen?"

I looked at him. He scared me at times like this. He was a young man in full control of his powers, not unmoored by the collapse of global Communism. He had a powerful nose.

"You've got to tell me." Koba looked ready to grab me by the lapels. "Are they fakes? The Rembrandts up there?"

Tennessee was standing behind me, I realized; I don't know how long he'd been there. I only noticed when he reached into the pocket of his lab coat for a flask.

"In a few days," Beekley finished, taking in all of us now, "after word gets out and the newspapers do their write-ups, this won't be a museum anymore, or even a place friends recommend to one another saying, 'Just go. I don't want to spoil it.' It'll be a place people come to knowingly, to show each other a smirk. They won't be able to enjoy the pure experience of the inauthentic anymore. They will realize the distance between themselves and the truth, and knowing this they will grow mad, angry, perhaps even violent. Don't you see? We've been discovered," he said. "Our days are numbered. We might as well be making horse-drawn buggies, or trading in hydrogen futures on the strength of the zeppelin industry's forward prospects. We're doomed," he said. "This museum, like that market out there—it is our gravestone."

WHEN I GOT HOME THAT NIGHT, I followed the sound of Moroccan music into my son's room and found the boys bathed in artificial light. Jeremiah sat on the foot of the bed, half-hidden from me between two tall ferns that belonged in the study. The television sat on top of the dresser facing him, playing an episode of *Xena: Warrior Princess.* Ernest sat at his desk in the corner, immersed in a computer game. "Prepare for battle," it said. Chin lifted, eyes vacant, fingers tapping away at the keyboard—my son didn't register my presence until I'd crossed to the windows and opened the blinds, and then he did so with only a groan.

I wanted to tear the plug from the wall—all of them. As a child, I hadn't spent my every waking hour stuck to a screen. I'd scraped my knees on the playground and run just to feel the fluttering of my school's blue and gold tie over my shoulder. Ernest, though—he was beginning to remind me of a shackled prisoner being transported to trial. If you took away soccer camp and Little League and all the other activities he embarked upon with nothing more than great reluctance, he only visited the outdoors in transit, and never with any pleasure. Whenever stepping free of a car, bus, or minivan, he'd squint up at the horrors of the high-hanging sun and move quickly to the nearest door, eager to return to the comforts of the box.

I looked down at his laundry hamper. He'd laid his soccer uniform on top of it, ready for the next day. The shorts, as always, were clean; he never came home dirty. "I'm starting to think you're afraid to slide," I said.

This, too, elicited little response. After shrugging, he turned back to his computer — "My liege," it said, "how may I assist you?" — and began clicking away at its keys. Was it my fault? Had I failed him in some way? I thought of Aspirina, who had fed him countless fried plantains all those years and helped him fall asleep as a baby by singing Spanish lullabies. Was I supposed to learn Spanish?

I put the shorts down on top of the hamper, hearing the Moroccan music on the television build. Pagans had gathered in a natural rock amphitheater, assembling before a bald black man who stood high above them on an overhanging ledge. Tattooed from skull to foot, he thrust a python into the air with both hands, flashing his white teeth as he roared. The crowd erupted in glee. The spectators danced and spun and made sounds like elated Muslim women.

Jeremiah dropped his forearms down onto his knees, allowing his face to push out from between the two ferns. It was only then that I noticed he was drooling — a strand of saliva stretched from his plump lower lip to his lap.

"Are you all right, Jeremiah?" I stepped toward him, sending a hand to his forehead as he sat up, moving back between the two ferns. "You don't feel warm." I pushed aside one of the leafy fronds between us. "Have you taken your medicine?" He looked back at me with a faint look of recognition in his eyes, just a flash of life, like the squiggle of a fish at the bottom of a stream. I let the branch swing back into place. "What have you two been up to?"

Ernest half turned round in his chair, holding a Bloody Sunrise in one hand. "That demands coins of the realm," the computer said. My son's face gave off the glow of a dim light bulb. He shrugged and said, "Nothing."

Jeremiah was still wearing his soccer shorts, but instead of the V-neck jersey that was supposed to accompany it, he had on a faded blue sweatshirt that bore the lapsed logo of a non-regional football franchise which had a storied history of loss. "Does your mother know you're here?"

Jeremiah looked to the television. A commercial had started to play. A child no older than Ernest stood in the bathroom, wearing a shaving-foam beard as he applied deodorant to his armpits. "Be a Big Man!" the voice-over said. "Use Big Man deodorant!"

"Well, maybe I'll just get your mother," I told my son.

Seconds later Betty was following me down the stairs, wearing a synthetic track suit that made a swishing sound as she walked. The colors were somehow wrong on her, I thought. The outfit reminded me of the flag of a newly decolonized African nation.

"Do you know how long they've been here?" I asked.

"They were home when I got home."

"Do you think maybe they spent the day sniffing things pulled out from under the sink?"

We were nearing our son's door now. Betty raised a finger to her lips to silence me, then led the way inside and did exactly as I'd done before her — push through the ferns like a latter-day Livingstone, then reach for Jeremiah's forehead.

"You don't feel warm," she said. "Does your stomach hurt?"

Ernest finished his glass of dyed juice and set it down beside his keyboard.

"Get your friend a glass of water," Betty said.

He looked to me, as if to confirm the merits of this command.

I wasn't about to challenge my wife's authority — not here, at least. I nodded. Ernest got up and rushed out of the room.

A minute later Betty and I were retracing our steps upstairs, and I was whispering what I had not dared say until now.

"It just seems a bit like you're reloading the child. Maybe some dry bread would've been best."

"Dry bread?" She stopped at the base of the stairs, turning to me so suddenly I almost bumped into her. "If you wanted to give him bread, why didn't you do it yourself?"

"I was just thinking—"

"What? That I should know what to do? What do you expect? You drag me in there as if I'm some kind of witch doctor. 'There's a boy in back drooling. Can you do something?'" She started up the stairs, but stopped again after only a step. "I'm a tourism development consultant, David. Have you forgotten? I deal with blight, not drool."

As I followed her up the stairs, taking one step for her every three, I realized how right she was. I had hoped that some form of innate motherly wisdom would take over, that she'd be able to call upon something that had been passed down to her over the generations, like a family recipe for Thanksgiving gravy. *And if the boy ever drools, feed him two spoonfuls of molasses and a half cup of dry oatmeal, then be sure to sit him in a chair facing west.*

Betty turned into the great room. I continued on to our bedroom and moved into the walk-in closet, meaning to change into my house pants. But before I could do anything, I noticed something new on the wall. A split photo frame had been hung between Betty's side of the closet and mine. The photo on the left was a Polaroid I had taken myself while we were on vacation in Hawaii, back when doctors were still advising us to adopt. Betty stood on the balcony of our hotel room with her arms hanging down at her sides like dead things dangling in a deli window. She was forty pounds heavier than she'd ever been, and dressed in a flower-print muumuu. "I look terrible," she'd said right before I snapped the picture. But I'd insisted on taking it, saying we needed some evidence we'd been on holiday. It was a mistake. It looked like a ransom photo.

The picture beside it had been taken several years later, after Betty had lost all her weight. It was a candid shot of her leading an aerobics class at the studio where she'd worked part-time for a year after regaining her figure. In the photo she wears leg warmers, black tights, a pink-and-black-striped leotard, and a smile as bright as her neon headband.

"It's motivation," Betty said, when I stepped into the doorway of the great room to ask her about what I'd found. "I can't go back."

"But you look wonderful. I don't know what you're worried about."

She didn't respond; she had her back to me and was exercising along to a tape in the VCR. A black man's face filled the TV screen. It was bald and dotted with perspiration.

"Who's this?" I said.

"Cher's personal trainer."

I watched from the door as the man in the black and purple wrestler's singlet ran in place. "Jab, kick, knee punch!" he said. Behind him, standing in staggered formation, two beautiful women who had body fat only in the breasts and buttocks performed the same exercises. "Body blow, body blow, body blow!"

I watched Betty as she exercised, but no matter how hard I tried to picture her in that leotard I'd come to know so well in the early eighties, I found I'd developed a peculiar double vision. I couldn't help but see the "Before" photograph superimposed over the "After."

I looked past her to the box of cookies on top of the cable box. It was an American brand so popular in the Middle East that a supermarket chain in Abu Dhabi had asked us to replicate its flavor for its line of in-store generics.

"Did you try the others?" I said.

I'd left a Ziploc bag holding our first attempt from the lab in the cupboard downstairs, thinking I'd perform an impromptu taste panel one night after dinner.

Betty glanced to where I was looking, then swept the floor with one leg—"Finished them last night!"—and sprang up delivering a high kick in my direction. "You've got to stop bringing your work home with you!" She moved toward me, flinging sweat, a flurry of flying fists and feet: *jab, kick, knee punch!* "Promise! I can't control myself!"

"Okay," the black man continued, as the pace of the electronic music backing him accelerated. "It's time for the two-minute hate! Remember to keep those knees high!"

Images of fat people flashed across the screen, much like they do on the evening news whenever there's a report about the rising obesity rate. Everyone was shown from the torso down.

"Kick that fat, kick that fat! Uppercut! Uppercut!"

I was glad to hear the doorbell, even if I hadn't changed into my house clothes yet. I rushed down the stairs to answer it and was met by two Mormon missionaries on the front step. They asked if I was interested in learning more about the writings of Joseph Smith, but I barely heard a word. They were both of them fat, the one with a button missing from the belly of his white shirt, the other so large he probably couldn't see that his fly was open.

"Do you think we can use your phone?" the one said. "It just stopped on us."

It was only then that I saw the black Buick sedan parked in front of the Ikeda house across the street. Steam rose up from under its popped hood.

"I thought you boys rode bicycles," I said.

Their cheeks plumped up around their smiles, and then they were pinching at their ill-fitting grey trousers and trying to explain. The bikes had been stolen, and a member of the local ward who owned a Buick dealership had offered them the use of a loaner.

The one whose black name tag read ELDER PETERSON said, "I told you not to keep driving when that light started blinking."

"We need to call the Auto Club," the other told me.

I noticed one of the Ikedas standing at the window of their dining room, watching all of this through a part in the curtains. "I'll just get the cordless," I said.

Forty minutes later, our street was as busy as it had been all day. First, a moving truck pulled away from the driveway next door (the Wilsons had divorced earlier in the year, and neither had wanted to keep the house), and then, going in the other direction, the tow-truck carrying the Mormons. I waved from the end of the driveway, with the phone tucked into my back pocket, then turned for home, only to stop again when I saw Sarin pull up and park.

As she got out of her Bug and circled round to my daughter's side of the car, I marveled at how different the two girls looked. In the last year, Priscilla had grown four inches in height and no less in the chest. Her steps were heavy and flat-footed. Even on a level surface, she walked as if she were falling down the stairs. Sarin, by comparison, was all straight lines and arrested dimensions, but even so she was somehow infinitely more feminine and graceful. She sashayed. She threw out her narrow hips as she walked and answered them with a rhythmic bounce of her shoulders. She dressed like a girl, too — wore studs in her ears and rings on her fingers, and coordinated her make-up with the scarf she wound round through her hair. If her politics and California cooking were going to rub off on Priscilla, I hoped her low heels might eventually catch on as well.

"You're late," I said.

"We got hung up at McDonald's."

"Ah! Finally gave up on this vegan farce, then, did you?"

Priscilla stopped midway up the lawn and waited for me to catch up. "We were interviewing people at the drive-through."

"For your think-piece?"

She nodded, asking again if I'd ordered the Albanian report.

"Of course," I said. And it was true: I'd dropped a money order in the mail that afternoon.

Priscilla continued for the door. "Why were you out here in the first place? Were you waiting for me?"

I shook my head, telling her about the missionaries. "They broke down and needed a tow."

Priscilla stopped on the front step. "Did you invite them in?"

The expression on my face made the answer to this question perfectly clear.

"This is so like him." Priscilla spoke to her friend as if I weren't there. "Last month it was the Jehovah's Witnesses."

"They have great buffets," Sarin said.

"He wouldn't even accept their literature."

"My dad's a Rosicrucian," Sarin told me.

"You don't say."

"What am I supposed to do?" Priscilla continued. "Just wake up one morning and decide to become a Hindu?"

"That would kill your mother."

"I'm serious."

"Well, look around you then. Take the Ikedas." I pointed. "They're Southern Baptists, aren't they? And Jon and Ken next door" — both associate professors at the nearby university — "they go in for something Eastern, I believe. Knock on their door, you'll smell the incense."

Sarin headed inside, whispering about a need "to go."

"They don't have bathrooms at McDonald's?"

"She's principled. She wouldn't pee there if you paid her."

I followed my daughter inside, telling her then that if she did feel the need to follow a religious impulse, I hoped she'd at least have the good sense to stay away from the ben Israels. They were the black family three doors down, always dressed in white. "Lost Tribe of Judah — lost for a reason, if you ask me. Did you know their church has a PO box in Chicago and a leader in the federal penitentiary in Joliet?"

As we turned into the kitchen, Betty came down the stairs, red in the face and short of breath. "Has everyone already eaten?" she asked.

I returned the phone to its cradle on the wall, telling her Priscilla had stopped at McDonald's.

"I thought you hated McDonald's."

Our daughter was crouched down before the crisper drawer, rummaging around for something to eat. "We were interviewing people!"

Betty reached in over her for a diet cola, then turned back toward the hallway at the sound of Sarin's voice. "I'll call you," she said to Priscilla, before heading out the door.

Betty exited to the garage then, saying she'd investigate the freezer, while Priscilla rose from the crisper drawer, holding a cucumber that had a plastic seam running down its side.

"So what were they like anyway?" she said.

I took her place in front of the fridge, not sure if I wanted a snack or a meal. I'd had a late lunch. "The missionaries? Fat," I said. "Obese even."

She said something in response, but I could barely hear it over the sound of her chopping off the ends of the cucumber.

"I hardly think you can call me a fascist simply for pointing out the truth."

"A *FA T*ist," she said. "I said you're such a *fatist*. You are familiar with the term, aren't you?"

"Not exactly, no." Ernest and Jeremiah entered from the hallway. "But I am glad to hear you didn't align me with the politics of National Socialism. We take what we can get, I suppose."

"What does their weight have to do with anything? That's all I'm saying. Maybe it's genetic."

"Oh, please." I closed the refrigerator door and crossed into the pantry for something salty. "Is this the conversation stopper they're teaching you in school these days? Because tell me, why has the obesity rate been on the rise only these last ten years? Have aliens come down and fiddled with our DNA? Given us all newer, fatter genes? No."

I stepped out with a bag of potato chips and spoke as if addressing the missionaries. "What happened was we won the Cold War and got soft. That's the truth of it. To celebrate our victory, we gorged ourselves on sweets and junk food. Lost any sense of discipline. Don't scoff. We'd be better off facing the truth than letting it fester. You only encourage more of the same if you do."

"You are so blind," Priscilla said.

"If anything, I should've told those boys what I'm telling you. They won't convert the former Eastern Bloc looking like that. Or tell me, would you have trusted this Jesus chap if he were morbidly obese?"

Ernest and Jeremiah stood in front of the microwave, watching something inside spin round and round. Here, my son looked back at me over his shoulder.

"That's right," I said. "If he were four hundred and twenty-three pounds and sweating in the midday sun? You know the type. Sweat shorts and a pair of flip-flops, always breathing through his mouth." I lifted my arms at the elbows, and did it for effect. Jeremiah grinned, no longer drooling.

"You are so juvenile," Priscilla said.

"Yes, the guy who fills up his Super Big Gulp at the fountain and then has a quick sip and tops it off again? This is your spiritual superstar? No. If you really wanted to help, you'd say enough with the water into wine and all the fish you can eat, there's something to be said for moderation and a good run around the block. Do some knee bends, why don't you. Yes?"

Priscilla swept a mound of cucumber coins onto a plate and turned, pointing her knife at me. "If I were you, I wouldn't feel so comfortable. You're the one making all the flavors these Mormons can't resist."

"Me? I'm not holding them down. I'm not telling them to drive a Buick instead of getting on a bike. Personal responsibility. I may have wandered politically over the years, may have fallen for those who use a good pie chart and whatnot, but I still believe in personal responsibility."

"Then tell me"—she quartered a tomato with two efficient *thwaps*—"what are the most popular flavors for snack foods?"

I'd been struggling to open my bag of chips—pulling at them, drying my hands, trying again—but here I tossed them onto the counter, saying they should store nuclear waste in these things.

"C'mon, Dad. I know you know this."

I looked at her. "What?" Had she been reading one of the trade magazines I left in the bathroom downstairs?

"Let me remind you, then. Those that overwhelm the taste buds and disappear almost immediately. Sounds a little like the digestive equivalent of crack, doesn't it?"

"Priscilla." I grabbed the chips. "Priscilla, I know this is not the era of *Father Knows Best,* but did you just compare me to a drug dealer?"

"Crunch all you want, we'll make more!"

"And what would you have us do? Return to the days of the Commissar of the Commissary?"

"When the revolution comes—"

"Oh, please!"

"—what are you going to say? I was only filling orders?"

Betty came back from the garage holding a box of Lean Cuisine. "Salmon!" she said, hoisting the entrée high over her head in both hands, as if she were the archbishop of Canterbury approaching the pulpit with The Word of God.

I bumped out past her, muttering as I moved through the utility room.

"Only filling orders!" I said.

At my workbench, I grabbed a screwdriver from the pegboard organizer and stabbed at my bag of chips. *Tsssssh!* Such a wonderful sound, that rushing release of air, but fleeting, too, the pleasure all too fleeting.

I sat on my stool and stuffed my mouth, chewing, muttering, unable to leave this behind me. When I'd calmed down some, I reached for a small metal figurine and pulled a mounted magnifying glass round toward me. I had my paints, brushes, and a little dish of water nearby, right where I'd left them the night before. Modeling. I'd first lost myself in the hobby when I was living in England and my father would return from the office in London with one of the kits then popular with young boys: RAF bombers and German Panzer divisions, Aston Martins and Rovers and the *Queen Mary*. I must have pieced together and painted nearly every plastic part they sold, but none with the same all-consuming passion that I'd give a diorama the summer that my father moved us to New Jersey. Then, at the onset of puberty, in a new country without the comfort or companionship of a friend or foe, I escaped my longing to be back in my mother's England by re-creating the Normandy Invasion on my bedroom floor. I focused on Utah Beach, though with a slightly ahistorical eye. Along with the barges spilling their troops and the planes hanging from overhead wires, I placed one more group of Allied soldiers beneath the threat of the Germans in their pillboxes above: the 3032nd Mobile Baking Division, with whom my father landed on this beach on D-Day+24. The Fighting Quarter-masters hunkered down behind their mobile kitchen, eager to move on toward Berlin and start pumping out sixty thousand pounds of battle-field bread each day.

Following that diorama, I built still more: "Winter at Valley Forge," "The Retreat (1812)," and "Victory at Yankee Stadium," commemorat-ing the Baltimore Colts' stunning world championship of 1958. But in college I gave it all up after my roommate looked at me strangely when I told him I was thinking of doing the Lincoln-Douglas debates. I had only returned to the hobby this summer, but already I had completed a small Cro-Magnon scene ("The Discovery of Fire") and another that paid tribute to one of Genghis Khan's brave warriors, that unknown man who, after riding for hours across the lonely steppe, had over-turned his shield on the coals of his company's fire and created, first to the amusement and then the delight of his fellows, the world's first Mongolian barbecue.

This evening I was working on the scene of Nicolas Appert's moment of triumph, when he stood in his food-splattered kitchen in the French countryside, sinking a glass bottle of partridge, vegetables, and gravy into a tub of scalding-hot water. He lived during the Age of Revolu-tions, when military conflicts were so frequent and so large that you could no longer hope to feed your troops with food culled from the surrounding villages. "An army marches on its stomach," Napoleon had famously said, before offering a prize of twelve thousand francs to anyone who could devise a method of food preservation that'd allow his soldiers to eat fresh rations no matter how far from Paris his ambitions carried them. Appert — a brewer, a baker, and a pickle maker — was the one to lay claim to this money. He did not understand how his bottled foods kept scurvy, malnutrition, and starvation at bay; we'd have to wait for Pasteur to explain all of that. But his intuitive leap was no less remarkable, as from it grew the modern canning industry, a development that drew a distinct line between the rot and rancid days of the Middle Ages and the prolonged life and improved health of the modern world.

I leaned into my lit magnifying glass and painted food specks onto his half apron, but I couldn't concentrate. I'd laid a piece of newspaper down on the workbench to absorb any stray splashes of paint, and the article facing me said the consumption of fresh fruits and vegetables had plummeted in the last ten years. Apples were down 72 percent, cabbages 65, and fresh potatoes a distressing 74 points. *Seventy-four?* Was that even possible? I half wished I subscribed to *Pravda* instead of the *Times.* At least then I could expect something more promising than the truth. *Teen suicide is down 30 percent since 1980.... Sugar has stopped accounting for 23 percent of a teenager's calories.... More than one-third of all meals are no longer consumed away from the home.*

I pushed the magnifying glass away and set my metal figurine down, unable to forget what Priscilla had told me. Could I really be responsible for the weight of those missionaries? When I'd started on as a flavorist, there had been seven thousand products on the shelves of the average supermarket — ten times the number that could have been found in the dry goods store that employed a young Abraham Lincoln, but not even half of what you could find today. We'd come so far! I'd thought. But now I wasn't so sure that all of the distance between the past and the present represented progress alone.

I reached into my bag of potato chips, though they weren't exactly potato chips, at least not to my mind. They were pepperoni pizza–flavored potato chips, chips that left you with no memory of the potato.

Flavor chemists no longer pursued the Platonic Ideal, the perfect potato chip, the one chip that could unite us all. Now we developed an endless variety of flavorings—Sweet Maui Onion, Dill Pickle, Chesapeake Crab—so that everyone would be able to find that one chip developed just for them, an essentially American promise.

I ate slowly, quietly, softening each chip with the moisture of my saliva, thinking again of what I'd said to my daughter about Communism. Communism had always been the bulwark that had pushed back against our excesses, but since Gorbachev had given way to Yeltsin and Yeltsin had given way to too much drink, there were no more proxy wars in Africa, Asia, or Central America, no more grand global efforts to challenge our methods and suggest a better way. Now, the only turf battles were between PepsiCo and Coca-Cola, and even KFC and Long John Silver's had joined forces together under one roof. It was just us now, and were we rising toward our greatest potential or sinking under the weight of our worst inclinations?

I pictured those Mormons walking through the supermarket and turning down an aisle lined by an infinite variety of potato chips. There was Barbecue and St. Louis Barbecue and Baby Back Ribs, there was Sour Cream and Onion and Salt and Vinegar, Cheddar Cheese and White Cheddar, and chips that were popped and baked and made out of sweet potatoes and beets. Did you blame a man for blowing himself up while crossing a minefield? Because isn't that what the supermarket had become? A minefield? Down every aisle those Mormons would find a flavor engineered just for them, a temptation as undeniable as it was artful. So of course they were amongst the growing class of the obese. It wasn't just the fall of Communism that had done it. We were all of us human and weak, born to succumb to our impulses and desires, and what if not desire had we been perfecting for the last ten years or more?

When I went back indoors that night, I found Ernest brushing his teeth in the bathroom off the hallway.

"Jeremiah gone?"

He nodded, moving his toothbrush from one side of his mouth to another.

I checked my watch—just after eight o'clock. "Little early to be brushing your teeth, isn't it?"

He shrugged, a pink foam building up at the corners of his mouth. When I was a child, I'd used baking soda or a colorless toothpaste with nothing more than fluoride added to it. My life had been so bland by comparison. Breakfast had been beans and toast, a bowl of shredded wheat, or maybe the viscous yellow of a soft-boiled egg. Lunch was prepared at school beneath a canopy of steam, and dinner—a reliably narrow band of colors served up at home: green vegetable, pink meat, white potato, all chased with a glass of thick milk.

I looked to the tub and shower behind him. The curtain was pulled back to expose the blue bar of soap and the bottle of red shampoo. My son's world was a world of bold primary colors, always enthusiastic, never in doubt. If Ernest got sick, he drank a pink liquid as thick as motor oil that tasted of bubble gum or candy apple, not one of the wincing spoonfuls of bitter goo that my mother had delivered to me.

I watched him spit a foamy pink streak into the sink, rinse and spit again, then gulp some water and apply a second telegenic curl of toothpaste to his brush.

"Another go? Dr. Levinson's going to love this."

He spoke around the brush in his mouth. "Good flavor."

He was quicker this time—sucking on the brush, letting the paste wash across his tongue; then he was spitting, rinsing, and putting his neck gear into place. I stopped him at the door and gave him a kiss on top of his head; then he sauntered off toward his room. After his bedroom door had closed behind him, I reached for his tube of toothpaste and held the list of ingredients up toward the light. Fourth over from the left, alongside Red Dye No. 40, there it was: Sweetness #9.

Only filling orders. Was I really no better than a Nazi?

I lay awake considering the question long after Betty had fallen asleep beside me. Then I walked downstairs and opened my son's door, just to watch him sleep. I'd done this hundreds of times before, though rarely since he'd entered grade school. Tonight he was curled up on his side in a ninja pose, his arms and legs scissored out in front of him, the sheets kicked free.

I stepped into the room and picked up the glass from his computer desk. There was a little juice left at the bottom, the red dye visible, a thick and bloody residue. I set the glass down, wondering if it really was as simple as my grandmother had claimed: *You are what you eat.* Food enters your stomach, after all, and moves into the digestive tract, where the nutrients it provides are absorbed through the walls of your intestines; then everything's flushed round through the bloodstream and on up to your head, where only the permeable blood-brain barrier separates what you've ingested from the 100 billion or so neurons that control your endocrine and nervous systems. It's here, in the 100 trillion synaptic connections that bridge these neurons, that chemical signals fire in the dark, forming all of your perceptions and thoughts, the very driving agents of our shadowy lives. And are these perceptions and thoughts stable? Can we ever say *this* is who I am, *this* is my character, *this* is Ernest Leveraux? Or does it change every day, hour, or minute, depending on your diet and whatever happens to pass through your bloodstream?

I brushed my son's hair from his face and watched his eyelids flutter as he dreamed. Such an innocent, good-looking boy, the type of child I could imagine in the Sunday paper, modeling a Mickey Mouse T-shirt for a local department store; and yet no matter how familiar he looked, I feared I'd already let him drift away, that I'd never truly know him as I had when he was a toddler. What would happen next? I wondered. Could he lose his pronouns, and then his most dearly held nouns? *Daddy, I love you.* When was the last time I'd heard him say that? What had happened? What had I done?

"I'm sorry." I kissed his forehead. "I'm so very, very sorry," I said.

And no matter how long I stood there, I couldn't do it that night, I couldn't convince myself anymore it was just the American Condition. I had let go of the left leg, and now, if only in the quiet of this darkness, I saw the whole prisoner before me, his body strapped down on the gurney, his arms splayed out at his sides, and the poison dribbling down through the IV, drip drip drip.

PART THREE

BLACK CHERRY MONDAY

August–September 1998

THIS WAS THE SUMMER the supermarket introduced its fleet of motorized carts. There were six in all, plugged into chargers at the front of the store. I never knew which was worse, walking behind one and reading the bumper sticker applied to the back of its padded black driver's seat (RIDER WEIGHT NOT TO EXCEED 400 POUNDS) or feeling the presence of one too late and scrambling to get out of the way.

A few weeks after ordering the Albanian report, I walked aimlessly up and down the aisles of my local Acme, wanting only to avoid the relentless grilling I knew I could expect to face at home. ("What do you mean it's still not here? You did order it, didn't you?") The supermarket had always been my refuge. I liked to study the corner displays to see who was paying for the most valuable real estate, or take in the boasts *(Now with 25 percent more iron! New, improved flavor!)* emblazoned on the bright packaging. Sometimes an old woman would even ask me to reach for a box on a high shelf, and I'd see I was going for a product flavored by my own hand.* How couldn't I enjoy the fellowship of this place? The supermarket was our church, the last place where we all still congregated and mixed. You couldn't take communion there, but if you timed your visit just right, you might find a smiling divorcée in a red apron, ready to offer you a sample of something savory on the end of a colored toothpick.

---

* Flavor chemists are not like the winemakers of the Napa Valley. We do not slap our name on every bottle that we touch. If we did, our clients would be unable to promote their products as "home-made" or place a grandmother's face on the box and promise the taste of another time. At Goldstein, Olivetti, and Dark, this commitment to anonymity was so great that it even followed us out onto the softball field, where we trotted into position while wearing grey leggings without stripes and navy blue shirts made fancy only by the word *Team.*

But then the Mart Carts were introduced and everything took on a new appearance, even something as simple and eternal as the eggs. Priscilla preferred brown. Brown eggs, brown rice, brown sugar, brown bread. The color white didn't represent purity to her, as it had to the children of my generation. To her mind the color was evidence of a great deceit, so she insisted that we avoid it even when selecting our coffee filters.

I turned down the soft drink aisle and stood before the wall of two-liter bottles, studying the abundance of diet cola until I heard a faint electric whir coming toward me: a Mart Cart, this one driven by a morbidly obese woman who couldn't have been more than forty years old. She was so large that her upper arms were held out at her sides, balanced on little ledges of fat, but it wasn't this that left me flat-footed. It was her face, the doughy features of which were framed by limp, shoulder-length dirty-blonde hair. She wore such a fierce and pointed expression that I thought she must be driving her cart with the same fixed determination of a kamikaze pilot. I was almost too late. Just before she barreled into me, I threw myself into the display of soda, and it was then that I saw the first of the labels that so troubled me that evening. *No preservatives or colorings,* it read. One beneath it promised *Absolutely nothing artificial,* while even the half gallon of milk in my basket spoke to me with the language of a contrite lover: *Our farmers would* never *use bovine growth hormones!* When had we started selling an absence? An apology?

"Excuse me," the woman said.

I turned to see her Mart Cart parked parallel to the cases of diet cola. She pointed to a twenty-pack of cans on the lowest shelf.

"Would you mind?"

I stepped toward her, hearing her say she couldn't reach. But then I stopped short, as if refusing to be implicated in a crime.

"You know what's good?" I said. "A little fizzy water with a splash of cranberry." I'd heard this recommended on the radio just the other day, while listening to Mark and Bonnie talk to a pilot who'd suffered a seizure over Missoula after drinking a powdered pink lemonade in Cheyenne. Eighty-four people had almost lost their lives, and all for a few measly calories. "It's got that fizziness I like so much," I said, echoing Bonnie's words, "and it even prevents urinary tract infections."

The driver of the Mart Cart turned slowly in her seat, throwing first one leg down onto the floor and then the other. "You think because I carry a few extra pounds you can tell me what to eat?" She bent over and picked up the case by herself. "Asshole," she said.

It wasn't the year to be facing down a confession. Clinton was in office, and after his acknowledgment in mid-August that he'd had a "not appropriate" relationship with Monica Lewinsky, the pundits on TV and the columnists in the papers raised a hue and cry unlike any I'd heard since the early seventies. Clinton, Nixon — what did it matter who it was? It all came out in the end, and it was only bloodier if you dared delay it.

I first tried telling Betty about my past a couple of hours after I'd had a root canal. "There's something I should say," I told her, but I was drooling and drugged, my cheeks puffy, my mouth swollen. I might as well have been Khrushchev banging on a table with his shoe.

"Did you say you need to pay?"

Strangely, the urge to unburden myself only waned when I was around the one person who was most interested in hearing the truth: Priscilla. But then she made me feel so tense that I couldn't help but be on the defensive around her.

"It's been more than a month already, Dad. And still it's not here? Did you really order it?" She wanted me to show her my credit card bill. "Trust but verify," she said. "Isn't that what you always tell me?"

Sarin didn't make matters any easier. She had started spending more time at our house in order to teach my daughter how to make seitan and tempeh and live on little more than beans and grains. One evening while cooking, she tired of my routine deflections and told Priscilla they could always start their series with a think-piece on artificial colorings. Sarin had done some research, it seemed, and so she knew that Red Dye No. 3 wasn't the only one to have been pulled from the market. No. 2 had also had its GRAS designation revoked.

"Russian studies in the early seventies linked it to increased rates of cancer in female rats," she said.

"Why are you telling me this?" I asked.

"Do you have any comment?"

Priscilla had her notebook out.

"If you want to know the truth," I told them, "I blame the Soviets. What better way to send jitters through the American marketplace than to question the safety of the dye that colors our lipsticks and hot dog casings? The Canadians are still using Red No. 2 today. You should write that down, Priscilla. Now, that's all I'll say on the matter. Communism will kill you quicker than a maraschino cherry ever will."

At a certain stage in my life, work would have provided me all the shelter I needed. But in recent years the newspaper had started to publish articles about a rare and sometimes fatal form of fixed obstructive lung disease ("microwave popcorn lung," they were calling it), and so now whenever I stepped into the lab and tinkered with my buttery artificial (every flavorist needs a pet project, something to occupy himself between contracts), it was as if that golden stick of butter I'd been chasing since my youth had been left out on a plate in the sun. I had no reason to fear the diacetyl (2,3-butanedione) that I mixed in my test tube; it only posed a threat to those workers at the factory who handled the chemical in bulk. But even so, even so.

I was sure I would feel better if only Ernest would start using verbs again. I knew he had it in him. The previous Thanksgiving he'd said, "Pass the gravy" — I was certain of it. And two Christmases ago, while we were sitting around the tree opening presents, he'd asked me, "Should I get another?" This was indisputable. I had videotaped evidence of it, evidence that I played for myself and Betty on more than one occasion that summer.

For some reason, I thought he must have fallen silent because we'd stopped spending enough quality time together. But this only raised the question: How much time is time enough? To investigate, I called friends who had children and asked them how much time they spent with their kids. "Let's define that as having the child within your visual range," I said. No one was free with information. Our conversations were polite but strained. More than one person joked, "You're not taping me, are you?"

A good friend from college bristled when I grew too persistent. "You're going to pin me down? Okay, I spend between two and eight hours a day with my daughter. All right?"

I had the phone squeezed between my chin and shoulder so I could take notes. "And is two for weekdays and eight the weekends?"

"What is this for again?"

"I just don't understand what I'm supposed to do with a six-hour range. You might as well be telling me you either neglect your child or love her very much."

Though Jason hung up on me (and if you're reading this, Jason, please accept my apologies; these were difficult days for The Family Leveraux), I viewed the first number he gave me as a good baseline, one I subsequently pursued.

The first day I carried a stop-watch in my pocket, I camped out in the downstairs living room, hoping to catch sight of my son on one of his trips between his room and the refrigerator. Near ten, I spotted him one last time, when he came out to put a plate and an empty glass in the sink. I followed him into the bathroom, small-talking as he brushed his teeth, then gave him a kiss on the top of his head and watched him walk away. As his bedroom door closed behind him, I fished my stop-watch out of my pocket and saw how much visual contact we'd had since breakfast: fifty-nine minutes and forty-one seconds.

I couldn't leave it at that. The one-hour mark, though far short of my initial goal, was like a new thousand-point threshold for the Dow Jones Industrial Average, an all too important psychological plateau. So I knocked at my son's door and pushed inside, and then I stood there silently like a man at the mall who's taken a wrong turn and finds himself lost amidst a field of pink lingerie. I didn't say a word, nor did he, but when I knew I had my hour, I nodded at him as if we'd agreed on something and stepped back out into the hall.

I wasn't the only one who believed he had an answer to The Ernest Question.

Working on the belief that verbs were like so much bad cholesterol, something that could be flushed from your system if only you'd get your heart rate up and exercise a little more, Betty enrolled our son in a prestigious fencing school in Princeton. I joined her at his first match, secretly hoping I'd hear our son bark out a full-throated "En garde!" Instead, while his opponent fell into a dynamic pose across from him, with his foil angled up and held at the ready, Ernest stood there flare-footed and slouching, with the tip of his own weapon pushed down into the padded blue mat.

I cupped my hands around my mouth and yelled from the sidelines, "C'mon, E! You know how it's done!"

Priscilla showcased her own reform effort later that same evening when we stopped at a pizzeria for dinner.

"When Sarin lived in California," she said, "her father went out to the prison once a month and taught the men there how to eat the Rosicrucian way."

Our pie had just been delivered to our table. Priscilla was reverse-engineering her first slice: taking off the cheese and pepperoni, eating only the crust and sauce.

"Rosicrucian?" I said.

"It's basically macrobiotics, no sugars, a lot of raw vegetables. To eat well, he says you've just got to learn to get out of the way.

"He had a food co-op donate all the groceries," she continued, "and after six months even the warden was singing the program's praises. The prisoners became more tranquil, their interpersonal relationships improved. Some of the African-American prisoners started learning Spanish, even though they didn't need a foreign language to get their GED, and a former high-ranking member of the Aryan Nation made a great show of reading *The Autobiography of Malcolm X.*

"Newspapers started to write all about it after this one guy on death row used his last words to promote the program. Maybe you read about his last meal in the *Times.*"

"What'd he have?"

"Deep-fried seitan steaks with a mushroom and basil gravy, a broiled millet squash loaf, collard greens, and a dried fruit compote."

"Nothing to drink?"

"Fresh carrot juice," she said. "Six ounces. He was from Compton and known as Lady Killer, apparently without irony. They posthumously made him an honorary citizen of a village in the south of France."

The TV caught our attention then; it was hanging in the corner, broadcasting a car chase or the news of a celebrity's death — I forget which. The point is, it was only later, as we were finishing up our dinner, that Priscilla returned to the subject she'd introduced earlier.

"Why don't we give it a try?" she said. "Macrobiotics, I mean."

Her brother looked at her as he had when she'd first pulled off the cheese from her pizza.

"I'll do all the cooking," she said, looking now at her mother. "You won't have to lift a finger."

"Is that what you think I want?" Betty looked at me, her whole face collapsed. "So much for winning the Mother of the Year Award."

Priscilla looked squarely at me, desperate for a show of support, a co-sponsor who'd help carry her bill. "What do you say?" she said. But these were difficult political times, when I knew not where to cast my allegiances; so I stuffed the pizza into my mouth and chewed while my wife took the floor.

"It sounds nice, really it does," she said. "It's just" — and she grabbed a piece of pepperoni that Priscilla had peeled free and abandoned on her plate — "well, we've all got our own tastes, for one, to say nothing of our different schedules and activities. Besides which, I just think it's too much work for you. Do you know what it takes to feed a family of four?"

By the end of August, I was driving out to my rented mailbox each lunch, as slowly as a man driving to his own funeral. Each day it was the same thing: no Albanian report, again and again. However much I dreaded receiving it, I hated anticipating it just as much. My performance as both a flavorist and an administrator was suffering — so much so that I feared even Ernst must have noticed. I had become a born-again doodler, a man enthralled by open windows and spiders crawling up the wall. I was sure everyone could see it. My coffee breaks had become more numerous, my "working" lunches more lingering, and if I wasn't coming in late one morning, I was cleaning out my test tubes and driving home early that same evening.

When Ernst called to invite me to breakfast on the first Friday in September, I was sure it was so he could push aside his coffee cup and lapse into German while pounding at the table and venting his spleen. "Tennessee tells me you're barely there," I thought he'd say, "and that when you are in the lab you're still no more present. You think I hired you for this? This is how you repay me!?"

That morning, after only five or ten minutes of strained conversation, I couldn't take the anticipation any longer, and I think that's why I said, "Why'd you hire me?" Just like that, like a streaker breaking onto the field. "At Greystone Park of all places, I mean."

He had been speaking about the subtlety of flavors found in a new microwaveable jambalaya, but here he paused for a long moment and reached for a slice of cheese. "You were a scholar of American culture," he said.

I smiled weakly, and he must have seen that I couldn't believe it anymore, so he started again.

"We're very similar," he said. "Do you know that?"

"Are you saying you too once summered at a state hospital?"

He bit into a piece of dark bread, telling me he didn't know what good a state hospital would have done when the entire continent of Europe had gone mad. "I went into a factory," he said. "This was after they finally let me into this country. I was no displaced person, you know. Certainly not a Jew. I was a German who had been in the bunker. It didn't matter that I was only a flavorist; I had to fight for that stamp in my passport. Fight," he said.

He looked up to the cuckoo clock over the door as it chimed the quarter hour.

"When at last they did let me in, I didn't care for anything anymore. My sisters were gone, my friends, and a girl I knew, the most beautiful girl. I had nothing, not even the desire to work. For the first time in my life," he said, "flavor meant nothing. So I went into a factory and asked for a job. Manual labor. The simple life. This is what I thought would save me."

He sipped his coffee and spoke to the center of the table.

"If I can surround myself with so many moving parts, if I can join an assembly line, I can become a machine." He smiled at the memory. "To stop thinking. To forget. This is what I was after, but I might as well have tried to commune with the saints."

He looked up and found my eyes. "In that factory we were making fertilizer. From ammonium nitrate." He laughed shortly. "The same ammonium nitrate this same factory had used to make bombs during the war. 'There's a growing Communist Menace,' the foreman said. 'The government needs us to remain vigilant.' So we planted our bombs in the fields in case we needed to drop them again from the skies." He looked away, off to his silent cuckoo. "I wasn't yet even thirty, and all of my blond hair—it had gone white."

He brought his cup to his mouth, but set it down before drinking.

"There's no escaping life, so I quit that factory and used my savings to rent out a floor above a Jewish dress-maker in the Garment District. You know the rest. I almost failed until I talked to that reporter about Hitler and became an overnight success. I moved FlavAmerica to New

Jersey. Even remembered my love of the female form. Then one night at the Holiday Inn a friend from Goldstein, Olivetti, and Dark" — he glanced at me — "they're not all so bad over there, you know. He tells me about your troubles."

I looked to the edge of the table nearest the wall, where the porcelain sugar holder stood bookended by the salt and pepper shakers.

"He talked about you as if you were crazy, but if you were, I thought I must be too. So you saw a few things you wished you hadn't, or stood for a moment in the shadow of something larger than you cared to know. And for this you should lose your dreams? Your life?" He shook his head. "You stayed in my thoughts. I never had children. Maybe I was reaching the age where I stopped always thinking of myself. I began to ask around." He smiled. "To park outside the Japanese like you did, to lay on the horn and honk. It spoke well of your determination, your spirit. So when I learned you had taken a job at a gas station, I called your wife — I had an old résumé of yours on file — and she told me it was worse than I believed. My information was already outdated. You had moved on to Greystone Park."

Again he looked at me. "You were no crazier than I was after the war. I knew it even before you had the presence of mind to tell me Gordon Lightfoot was a Canadian. So I gave you a second chance. Is that so wrong? It's what America gave me. It's what America promises. And what are we supposed to do on this planet if not give back what we have already received?"

I sat there like a man in the confessional — eyes averted, hands busy — wanting nothing more than to be out of there, but only after everything had been said. "So you know?"

"I know what I know," he said. "What good does talking about it do?"

He poured from the French press, freshening my cup and then his own.

"And how come you never told me before?"

"You needed to forget."

He reached for a packet of sweetener and poured it into his coffee. I pointed. "You're doing it again," I said. "How can you be doing it again after everything you just said?"

He raised his voice — "It's Eliza!" — and swatted at the air over his cup, saying he wouldn't get confused if it wasn't for Eliza. "She prefers this sweet stuff. I only buy it because of her."

"Well, you should tell her to stop."

"She's a fifty-nine-year-old woman."

"There's no reason for the confusion," I said, reaching for and laying out two packets on the table: one sugar, one Sweetness #9. "The Nine has this little pink bar," I said, pointing to it on the packet's lower right-hand corner. "You just need to arrange them" — and now I dumped all the packets on the table and began doing just that — "so the pink bar is visible."

Ernst smiled as I returned the packets to the porcelain holder, now all neatly organized.

"I appreciate your help," he said, "but I'm an old man. At my age, what danger can danger possibly pose anymore?"

When I came home that evening, I parked in the garage and stepped out to my workbench, over which I'd pinned a piece of graph paper that I kept hidden beneath a map of the world that I'd received with an issue of *National Geographic*. Usually I exposed it only after everyone else had gone to bed, or when I knew I was alone. But this evening I couldn't wait, or I didn't care.

On that piece of graph paper, I'd charted the amount of time I'd kept my son within visual range since the end of July. The dates ran along the bottom of the sheet of paper; the minutes and hours went up the side. The first couple of weeks of my study had been quite promising; the black line rose and fell as if charting the progress of a bull market. But things had become more bearish of late, ever since the end of a James Bond marathon on TNT. Sadly, I suspected our numbers would only grow worse now that school had started up again.

After turning indoors, I found Betty in the great room, with her legs curled in beneath her and a bowl of ice cream balanced on one knee. I sat down beside her, not saying a word, just thinking of all that charted silence, and worrying that the sins of the father were in fact visited upon the son.

"I know, I know," Betty said. My ghostly look was like a vacuum; Betty had filled it with her own anxieties. "I shouldn't be eating this." She licked her spoon. "I've gained five pounds since summer, when usually I lose that much — if only so I can gain it back over the holidays. But it was just so hot today."

I gave my wife's thigh a quick rub, telling her she shouldn't worry so much about her weight. "You look wonderful."

"I don't need your rote encouragement."

"There's nothing rote about it."

"You haven't looked at me in years," she said.

I looked at her. "Don't be ridiculous."

"What did I wear to work this morning?" She sat there in her house clothes, a pair of khaki shorts and an orange top. "You don't know, do you?"

"That pantsuit. The baby blue one Priscilla says reminds her of Hillary."

"It was Casual Friday."

My voice cracked. "Was it?"

"If my body were South America, your eyes would be a ship going around Cape Horn."

I decided to go for a run. I didn't have a destination or a route; I ran just to feel the breeze in my face, both that evening and the following two nights as well. It felt good, certainly it did, but I also couldn't help but think I looked foolish doing it. I wasn't one of these runners whose ankles and knees and elbows work together, seemingly expressing some graceful law of physics; I ran like a hoodlum fleeing a botched crime, and so by Sunday I had slowed my pace and begun race-walking, thinking this might be something I could continue to do at my age — at least until a carful of heckling teenagers pelted me with cans of Keystone Light on the side of the road.

I barely slept that night, though this was nothing new. A handful of times in the last week or two, I had pushed up on my elbows in bed and found myself transfixed by the same red numbers glowing on the face of my alarm clock: 3:21. Like a countdown: 3-2-1. A countdown to my own day of reckoning, the crash of all my most high-flying lies. It was just a matter of time, I knew, just a matter of days or hours, and then there it'd be, my very own Black Cherry Monday.

I got out of bed and went into the closet for a small brown bottle I left hidden beneath a stack of sweaters each night. It contained peppermint oil, and though the smell was meant to be as cool and reviving as a brisk run through a foggy forest, its full power had been lost on me by now. This was the cruelest part of the aging process: my olfactory epithelium was shrinking. Each night that I awoke sleepless and reached for that little brown bottle as another man might reach for a pack of cigarettes, I unscrewed its black cap and breathed in deeply, smelling less and less of the reviving scent.

I had known all along that my olfactory epithelium, the only part of the brain that protrudes from the skull, would at some point recede from inside my nasal cavity and leave me with fewer sensory receptors with which to meet the world. But only now that I could smell less did I understand more. I wasn't just growing older. I was dying, wasn't I? What else is death but a slow retreat of the senses? Yes, I was dying, and if I could be completely honest with myself just this one time, what could I say I had made of my life? Such a simple question, as ordinary as a shopping list, and yet as I got back into bed and closed my eyes against it in the dark, I felt like a man who's had a black bag thrown over his head. Had I been a good father when it was no longer enough to simply be a proud one? A loving husband when the romance was gone? Had I bravely confronted all that life had put before me, or had I shrunk away, too fearful and full of pride to test myself against the obstacles; shrunk away again and again?

I had been there when Priscilla was born, and I'd cheered Ernest on as he took his first steps. But a second child, as anyone with children knows, is a demythologizing of the first. At some point after I'd grown certain my son had all his fingers and toes and could chew his own food, I had drifted away, gotten lost in my work, even hired a housekeeper, for Christ's sake, if only so Betty and I could be sure there was nothing else that was expected of us.

Oh, ladies and gentlemen of the blogosphere, members of the Twitterati, hear my dolorous sigh. I had awoken in the middle of the night at the age of forty-nine, wondering what I could do about my wasted, ill-spent life. I wanted to go back and correct whatever error had grown so exponentially large and grotesque over the years, because I feared what would happen if we continued on without change. Sleep thankfully took me, but I kept tossing and turning out of it, like a fish struggling to find a hole in a vast commercial net. Then at last I fell into the right position, though the peace of mind this afforded me was all too brief. What seemed like seconds later I heard what I thought were Canada geese and felt Betty shaking me at the shoulder. "Didn't you hear the alarm? You're going to be late."

It was a Monday — and more important, the day the Albanian report arrived.

AFTER RACING BACK from my mailbox, I dropped the manila envelope on my desk and stood over it for a long moment. The envelope looked as if it had been dragged by a mule from one end of Albania to the other, then thrown onto a ship that was taking on water. Dirtied and torn, water-stained in one corner and taped together in another, it bore the blurry stamps of postal and customs organizations in Tirana, Paris, and Washington, D.C. When I sent my hands into it, the skin of the envelope gave like an over-ripe fig.

Still too anxious to sit down, I flipped through the report's many pages as quickly as I'd worked through my first issue of *Playboy* as a teenager. There were charts and studies, pages of written analysis by the Albanian authors, translations of findings originally made in Russian and Bulgarian, and slanted mimeographs and photocopied photocopies of photocopies marked *Confidential*. There was this and so much more, but nothing — nothing, so far as I could see — that had been torn from my own marbled notebook. I could give it to my daughter with a clear conscience. She might use it as ammunition in her war against "processed food," but there was no way she could turn it against me, at least not directly.

Feeling a rush of endorphins and adrenaline, I dropped into my chair and flipped through the report once more, more slowly this time, working my way from back to front. And then there it was, a recognizable flash of letters that left me feeling as if someone had reached into my mouth and pulled out my stomach: *Charles Hithenbottom*.

"It is being important to remember," this typewritten page began, "that companii Goldstein, Olivetti, and Dark was being allowed to

189

present to FDA in its application for approval of Sweetness #9 only documents to be choosing to be including, not all many documents being created. Former FDA toxicologist, Robert Handley, in quitting his position of authority after The Nine was being approved for dry goods despite his many angry protests, says: 'This is like allowing a murderer or rapist to coordinate and rule over his own parole hearing or trial, and it's all done in the name of protecting proprietary information.'"

The Albanian-penned commentary went on to say that even though Goldstein, Olivetti, and Dark withheld certain information from the FDA, and falsified information in certain reports documenting its animal studies, the dangers of Sweetness #9 could still be detected "in the inconsistencies of the 48-page Summary of Chronic Toxicity Test, filed by CHARLES HITHENBOTTOM, animal testing analyst at Goldstein, Olivetti, and Dark. His writing shows one laboratory rat to be living on page 7, dying on 23, and resurrecting again in his body on page 44."

Two shadowy snippets of text, both photocopies torn from Hickey's original report, appeared beneath the Albanian commentary. The first read:

On day 124, E3CL9 refused its water bottle and rodent chow, and exhibited violent behavior when submitted to a forced feeding. Aberrant behavior remained on display throughout that week, after attempts to force-feed the test subject were abandoned owing to the risk to lab-worker safety. On day 128, E3CL9 was discovered dead in its holding tank, with its nose buried in the sawdust. An autopsy revealed the cause of death to be possible self-asphyxiation, though dehydration and long-term mental degradation, as a result of the formation of holes in the subject's brain, cannot be ignored as contributing factors.

The next snippet spoke of E3CL9 as being alive and in good spirits and showing no signs of obesity at the conclusion of the study, but this cheerier entry held no sway over me. I knew the truth now: my Louie was dead; my Louie had most certainly killed himself.

It was at this moment that Beekley stepped into my office. The lights flickered behind him, casting strange shadows across his face as he stopped just inside the door. He held a shotgun diagonally across his chest. *A shotgun?* I half rose from my chair, wondering if I had been so absorbed in my reading that I'd failed to hear the blasts in back. Was there a pile of bodies in the lab? Koba still twitching underneath his desk, his last words lost in a gurgle of blood at the back of his throat? I opened my mouth and let out a quiet croak of protest, but that was it, that was all, because then, like Louie's, my whole world went dark.

When I came to, I was lying on the sofa in the break room, Koba's face just inches from my own. "He's all right," he said. "He's back."

I sat up, slowly, and saw Eliza turn away from me into the hallway. A handful of others remained: Koba, Tennessee, and Beekley, and then our team of food scientists — Anthony, Amaka, and Uche.

"David, I'm so sorry," Beekley said. He pointed to the shotgun, leaning against the wall next to the refrigerator. I could see a price tag dangling from its trigger casing. "I only wanted to talk to you about my new plans for Y2K. I thought we should put together a company armory."

I drank from a cup of water Tennessee handed me, then looked to Beekley with a pained expression.

"I was just telling the others," he said. "Everything's computerized, and every computer's connected. Don't tell me this is a minor matter of ones and zeroes that can be fixed by a couple of ambitious computer programmers. Nothing will be spared when the system shuts down at the stroke of midnight. Come the first day of the new millennium, the lights will go dark and prison doors will slide open, spilling rapists and murderers into our streets. People will panic, David. It will be unlike anything we've seen since the Black Plague."

My neck felt buttery, my pulse was all a-rumble. I could only manage to say, "A shotgun, Beekley?"

"Think about it. Have you thought about it? The great industrial system of food production will grind to a halt, and when people have finished the last frozen entrées they've kept stashed in the cold of a stream, what do you think will happen? The common man won't know what to do with bruised fruit and soft potatoes, with lettuce half devoured by aphids and the stringy meat of wild game. Forget *Mad Max*. When people are cut off from their natural papaya flavoring and essence of lobster, that movie will look as welcoming as a Disney cartoon. Men, women, and children will give up the pleasures of their bodies for a hoarded can of Campbell's soup. They will realize the power of their food additives only when they are forced to endure a diet of gruel and colorless pastes, when what's for dinner is a soft carrot as rotten as their souls or another helping of tree bark soup."

He knelt before me, while the others stood at his rear, as rapt and silent as disciples.

"When people learn who we are and what we can do with all the chemicals we store in bulk, they will come for us." He stood, going for his shotgun. "They will come, David" — again, he held it diagonally across his chest — "and there will be blood. The only question we have to ask is, Will we be masters or will we be slaves?"

I felt a tickle in my nose and began to cough. Betty. I looked to the door, sure it must be her — the smell was that unmistakable, like a rain cloud moving low over a lush forest as a musky creature ran about through the shadows below. The scent was so different from the one I'd known as a newlywed. Back then, I had plunged my nose into the hollows of her collarbone and lingered like a man in an opium den, breathing in the sultry and exotic perfume she'd daubed against her skin. Ever since business school, however, Betty had been embarrassed by the bold Oriental scents she'd once worn. Now she bought her fragrances in the same department that sold men's ties, and the memories of the most passionate encounters of our youth were lost to me unless I happened to run into some woman just up from one of the developing patriarchies of the third world. A year or two back, when I'd gone to the national meeting of the Society of Flavor Chemists in Anaheim, California, my nose had alerted on this lost scent one afternoon when I stepped into an elevator at the Doubletree Inn where I was staying. A Spanish-speaking woman in a baby blue housekeeping outfit was already in there, and when the doors of the elevator closed, sealing us off from the distractions of the world, her perfume, my god — I wanted to hit the red button and bring our carriage to a jarring stop, to turn and tear at her uniform and lift her leg up toward my hip, and then do it, plunge my nose deep down into the swales of her neck and breath in that glorious fragrance.

The sound of my wife's heels grew louder. Then their clickety-click was turning in to the break room and she was coming straight for me. "David? What happened? Eliza called and said you fainted?"

I covered my nose as she drew near. I held the top of my head and moaned softly.

She glanced at Beekley—then the shotgun—and reached for my hand, pulling me up to my feet. "C'mon, Dr. White's agreed to see you."

While fighting traffic on Highway 1, Betty asked if I was having an affair.

I had been breathing into a brown bag that I'd found on the floor. It smelled of peanut butter and jelly.

Betty pointed at the glove box. I popped it open and found a crumpled supermarket receipt inside.

"I found it while doing the wash," she said. "Has it been going on long?"

I turned it over and saw what I'd written. *Jezebel. The Holiday Inn. A blue dress.*

"I'd rather know the truth than be left guessing. The truth I can handle, David. But lies and guessing…"

It was too shameful to say to her face, so I turned to tell it out my window.

"They're talking points," I said.

"What?"

I told her about the stop-watch, and the piece of graph paper I'd hidden away in the garage beneath the map of the world.

"You thought Ernest would get better if you'd spend more time with him?"

I nodded. "But every time I stepped in front of him, I didn't know what to say. When did we all become such strangers?"

Betty stopped at a red light. She didn't look at me.

"So I started jotting down notes," I said. "Something would come to me in the shower, or I'd pull over on the side of the road and scribble a few words down. They're talking points," I said. "I'm no better than Nixon; my fatal flaw's a need to record. The blue dress is Lewinsky's. The rest"—I set the receipt on the dash—"I don't know. I thought I could speak to him about fidelity and commitment. I was building up this whole speech in my mind."

Betty looked at me, then pulled away with the green light.

"I'm sorry I wasn't the mother you'd hoped I'd be," she said.

It was only then that I realized I wasn't the only one implicated by my confession.

"If I'd been a better mother, I'm sure we would've been a better family. It's always a bad mother storyline, isn't it?" Her body jumped from a little hiccup of a laugh. "And to think I wanted it so badly when I was young. If the police brought that woman to our house tonight, bleeding and desperate for a glass of water, I'd turn her away—I'd tell the police I didn't have the slightest idea who she was."

I sat in silence, breathing into my paper bag until I couldn't resist the need to check. I pinched my wrist. My pulse was high, very high, higher than it should be.

"Are you okay?"

"Mmm."

"You look a little pale."

I released my seat-belt to relieve the pressure it placed on my heart and carotid artery, then breathed in deeply, free of the bag, detecting again the smell of my wife's perfume. I opened the window.

"David, I've got the air conditioning going."

"Your perfume. It makes my nose itch."

I held my nose up to the crack in the window. Like a dog. Twenty-five years of marriage and here I was, a dog.

"They wouldn't take me seriously if I wore that stuff you like."

"It was good enough for you when we were dating."

"So was the same amount of work for half the pay." Betty turned off the A/C. "You sure there's nothing you'd like to tell me?"

It wasn't the time for further confession. I could barely breathe. It took everything for me to say, "There's no Jezebel. I'm not sleeping with some Spanish woman in a budget hotel."

"Because the last time you fainted…"

I grabbed the side of my neck.

"You're not gay, are you?"

I moaned.

"What? It happens. People wake up one day and realize it, or they admit it's not going away. I'm okay if that's the case."

"You're okay?"

"I just want to know the truth. Tell me the truth, David."

"My wife of twenty-five years is *okay* if I'm gay?"

She spoke to the road. "It's not like we're the most amorous couple in the world."

"And how could we be? I don't buy you lingerie anymore, because everything I like you find insulting. The last time I bought a bottle of perfume, you sprayed it into the air and said, 'Smells like cheap whore.' I've only got so many senses, you know, and you don't exactly access my heart through the stomach."

"Don't get so excitable."

"Excitable?! Twenty-five years of marriage, two kids, a beautiful house in South Battle Station Township, and you're asking me, 'Are you gay?'" I pinched my wrist, holding my arm high up on my chest. I groaned—my pulse couldn't be that high—and yanked the lever at my side, falling back into a flat position.

"Hold on," Betty said, snatching a CD from the floor. "We're almost there."

She pushed the disc into the stereo. The sounds of the rain forest played. We drove the rest of the way in a sort of Amazonian silence. I counted the number of times the monkey cried.

WE'D LEFT FLAVAMERICA in such a hurry that I'd forgotten to change out of my lab coat. This caused a minor scene in Dr. White's waiting room when I came in from the street with one arm thrown around my wife for support. People looked up from their magazines and exchanged nervous glances, as if I were a symbol of the failures of modern medicine.

Betty argued the urgency of my case at the front counter, and then I was being waved through and shown to a windowless room in back.

I sat in isolation on a strip of sanitary paper. All about me, educational posters were crowded with the warning signs of disease and death. One showed a cutaway of the stomach that revealed a gastric and duodenal ulcer; another showed the yellow plaque buildup inside an unhealthy artery. I was standing and reading a poster's sidebar about lung disease when Dr. White stepped through the door holding an aluminum clipboard. I must have jumped at the sound of him.

"Sorry about that." He was a deep-voiced man with a torso like the trunk of a redwood tree. There was no fatness to his girth. He was all solid strength. "Didn't mean to startle you."

"You didn't startle me." Years ago, when the kids were still little more than so much promise and I was riding high on a swell of optimism in the Reagan Years, Dr. White and I, along with an attorney he knew, had been members of the same threesome, traveling to courses all around the tri-state area on the weekends like the manifestation of an old joke: an atheist, a black man, and a Jew. I never did understand what my friends so loved about the game (it is a beer-fueled inefficiency, if you ask me), but since forging a bond on the greens and fairways, I had felt free to speak my mind around him.

"It's natural to jump at the unexpected," I said. "The fight-or-flight instinct, isn't it?"

"Something wrong with your neck?"

I was clutching it with one hand. It felt better this way.

"Well." He flipped open the cover of his clipboard and spoke while making a quick notation in my file. "I think you might benefit from a regime of anti-anxiety medication."

My voice rose like a flock of scattering birds. "Christ! You leave me in here surrounded by posters detailing diseases of the heart, liver, and lung, and then you storm in without so much as a knock and have the gall to suggest I've got anxiety? Just like that? I know talk therapy has fallen out of favor, but really."

He set his clipboard down and went to the sink to wash his hands, telling me if it was a little time on the couch I wanted, he couldn't help. "With what little the government pays anymore and the rising cost of malpractice insurance, to say nothing of all the forms they've got me filling out, it's seven minutes per patient or I don't meet my monthly nut." He reached for a paper towel and dried his hands. "But that doesn't change the fact that your wife tells me you fainted at work."

"One of our employees came into my office holding a shotgun," I said.

He turned to me, pushing one hand into a pair of latex gloves. "Anxiety is a physical reaction to a misappraisal of the facts. It is both fear-based and irrational."

"He had a shotgun!"

He snapped the second glove on.

"What are you doing?" I said.

He was applying lubricant to two fingers now.

"You refused the prostate exam last time." He motioned for me to spin around. "There's no reason we can't kill two birds with one stone."

"Are you serious?"

"It's called multitasking, and a man your age can't afford to refuse a doctor twice. Now drop those pants."

I stood, reaching for my zipper, and turned to lean in over the examining table. He moved behind me. "Betty says this happened once before?"

I glanced back over my shoulder.

He inserted two fingers. "She's worried about you, David."

I dropped my face into the strip of sanitary paper and grunted.

"Easy now."

I squeezed the sides of the padded table. Tears pushed up into my eyes.

"Yes," I said. "Yes."

Dr. White snapped his gloves off into a upright canister marked HAZARDOUS WASTE. I turned round slowly and accepted a wad of Kleenex, ready to tell him everything.

"That's not for your eyes." He smiled and handed me another.

As I cleaned up, he sat in a chair against the wall and wrote a few more notes in my file. "I'll send you to get a CAT scan, just to eliminate the possibility of a tumor."

"You think I have a tumor?"

"I'm ninety-nine percent certain you don't, but you fainted, so we'd better be sure. I'd like you to start taking something now, though."

"A pill?"

"Do you some good." He stood and went to a supply closet, then came over to me with a trifold booklet that contained two rows of foil-backed pills. "That's enough for ten days. If you find yourself having a reaction—"

"What kind of reaction?"

"Some people experience increased anxiety."

"Isn't that what this is supposed to treat?"

He nodded. "It's only for the first seven days. Then it's clear sailing. Just let me know if you're feeling out of sorts. We can always adjust the dose."

"But maybe I have a reason to feel the way I do."

"That sounds like a question for a poet, not a doctor. Now here." He handed me a second trial pack of pills.

"I don't need these."

They were blue. "Of course you don't, no one does. But if you find you don't need some more when you're done with them, let me know and we'll get you on a prescription." He smiled. "Think about someone else for once. Betty took care of you today. When's the last time you took care of her? Has it been a while? If it has, you wouldn't be alone."

It was overwhelming. I'd come in here thinking he'd prescribe me a sedative for the night, and now my hands were full. "But Viagra," I said.

"We all can use a little help every now and then. Don't be such a ma-cho man."

I wasn't in a position to argue. I was still weak from the prostate exam. My zipper hung open.

"One last thing. If you get into a panic before the pills start to perco-late down and take effect, I want you to find the nearest wall and slide down to the floor into a sitting position." He held up the flat of one hand to show me he wasn't joking. "I'd rather your pride take a hit than your head. And, oh yes." He scribbled out a prescription, saying I could take one of these if things got especially bad.

I tried to read his writing. "Lor…"

"…azepam. They'll make you not care about anything. But be warned. Habit-forming. So don't let them replace your evening glass of wine." He checked his watch. "Six minutes." And smiled as he reached for the door: "Make an appointment before you leave. Need to see you again in ten days."

It was almost two o'clock by the time I came out to my wife in the wait-ing room, so I told her I planned on calling it a day. Betty didn't think I should drive, but after I told her the doctor had diagnosed me with nothing more serious than a panic attack, she dropped me at my car, saying she'd meet me at home.

I stopped at the Acme on the way and filled my prescription for the lorazepam — the only pills I had told Betty about. I don't know why I didn't say anything about the others; maybe it was simply that I didn't feel I needed them, or didn't want her to think that I did. Whatever the case, I kept those trial packs stashed in my jacket pocket when I came into the kitchen and found her cracking an egg into a bowl.

199

"Snickerdoodles," she said. "I thought I'd surprise the kids."

I filled a glass at the sink and shook out one of my pills, telling her I was going to relax upstairs. Minutes later I was doing just that in the great room, flipping through the channels until I heard the words of a man in pressed blue jeans and a western shirt.

"You continue to lie because you are fearful and full of pride," he was saying. "Afraid that if you tell the truth, bad things will happen, and full of pride because you care too much what others think. The one shows a lack of faith, the other forgets that God sees all."

He paced back and forth across the stage of some evangelical church with blue stadium seating, stopping every now and then to direct his words to another section of the audience. "Look to your Bible!" he said. "Allow yourself the blessing of a new life!"

I set the remote down beside me, the pill already making me feel like some shelled creature who'd been opened up on the table.

"The Book of Revelation," he said, flipping open the black Bible he carried, "tells us he who overcometh shall be the Lord's son. That's the good news; the bad is: the fearful, the unbelieving, the abominable, the murderers and whoremongers and sorcerers of this world—"

"Sorcerers?" I said, my voice gone gauzy.

"The idolators," he continued, "and *all the liars,* shall have their part in the lake which burneth with fire and brimstone."

The words seemed to vibrate in my ears; the colors on the screen had grown brighter, the imagery softer. I sat there with my jaw hanging open, feeling so relaxed and content.

"Now, some of you already know this, but I only got but the one thumb."

He stopped and held his right hand up. It was the one without a thumb.

"I was alone when that buzz saw tore through me, but it didn't matter—I thought I was enough. Me! I was a surgeon, remember, a surgeon before I got the call, and I thought I could sew myself up."

The crowd answered with delighted laughter.

"That's right. Didn't work out so well. All I did was poke myself with a pin. So I drove to the hospital, and about halfway there I realized how empty my life was. Empty!" he said. "My wife had left me, my kids didn't care to take my calls, and my friends wouldn't play poker with me on account of the fact that I was a known cheat.

"I finally pulled over, thinking I might as well bleed out. I was a member of the Church of Dan and didn't no one want to come see me on Sunday, least of all myself.

"I'm told I passed out. When I woke up in the hospital, a nurse was wheeling me into the operating room on a gurney, saying a Good Samaritan in a Ford truck had stopped and picked me up. Then those doors were banging open and I was pushed in beneath a bright light. Now, the unbelievers out there will say it was the drugs they were pumping into me that made me think this, but you gotta listen here. As I moved in beneath those operating room lights, I heard a voice as clear as that nurse's say to me, 'You gotta let me give you a hand, Dan. Let your good buddy Jesus help you out.'

"I sat up on my elbows and looked at the Ziploc bag they had sitting on my chest. It was packed full of ice, most of it melted by now, and my thumb was swimming around inside it. That thumb was my everything—the entire future I'd once imagined for myself. Who'd trust a surgeon without a thumb? But you know what? I knew I'd be better off without it. I'd been called to tell people you can't do it alone. So when that surgeon came in, I told him, 'You can keep that thumb; all I need's the Hand of God.' Now, if this had been San Francisco, or New York City, I think you know what would have happened. But I was in the Great State of Texas, so that surgeon looked at me and said—"

Betty entered the room then, holding a plate of snickerdoodles. "We thought you'd like a cookie!"

The kids followed her in as I stabbed at the remote and flipped over to one of the news channels.

"How do you feel?" Betty asked, and the way she and the kids looked at me, you would've thought I was a dog at the pound they knew they couldn't take home.

"Wonderful," I said, and I did. It wasn't just the drugs moving through my system, either; I truly felt great. Because I didn't need to take any anti-anxiety medication; I only needed to confess. All great religions spoke to the need for this act, and yet my own brand of faith provided nothing more than a menu card.

So I ceded the sofa to them and crossed to the big screen, on which news about Hurricane Igor was playing. This category two storm was still out in the Atlantic, not far from the coast of Virginia. I muted the set and put the remote on top of the cable box, then turned round to face my family as a radar picture of the storm appeared on the big screen, its ghostly tendrils spinning round and round behind me while the meteorologist traced its likely path to land.

I felt my family's anticipation as the president must feel the anticipation of the country before starting his annual State of the Union address. *Mr. Speaker, Mr. Vice President, Members of the One hundred and fifth Congress, distinguished guests, my fellow Americans...*

"Betty, Priscilla, Ernest," I began. "There's something I've been meaning to tell you."

PART FOUR

A SINGLE PACKET OF SWEETNESS #9

September 1998

HURRICANE IGOR PUSHED ASHORE shortly after we fell asleep, but rather than plowing through Chesapeake Bay as expected, he turned up the coast and moved back out to sea, where he soon encountered a cold front and absorbed enough dry air to lose much of his power.

My confession was in many ways equally anti-climactic. Betty sat through it with a patient smile, as if she were watching one of her children playing chopsticks at a school recital. Ernest, meanwhile, seemed more enthused to be in my company than he had been in months.

"Dead monkeys?" he said. "Rat suicides?"

"Well, this is what your father *thinks* he saw," Betty said. "Isn't that right?"

"Yes. It's all subjective, I suppose, but I thought you should at least know this much."

By now the lorazepam's effect was waning, and I was beginning to think Priscilla might reach for the crystal candy dish on the coffee table and throw it at my head. But instead, she sucked in a long breath and got to her feet.

"Can I be excused?" she said.

It was the most threatening thing she'd said to me all night.

"Is that all you want to say? You haven't even asked if I brought the Albanian report home."

She started for the door, telling me she didn't need it anymore. "Sarin ordered a copy."

"What? When? Does she already have it?"

"For a couple of days now."

"And you didn't say anything?"

Priscilla looked back at me from the doorway as if this were a question I no longer had the right to ask.

"Well!" Betty popped up, clapping her hands and looking down at Ernest. "What do you say we make a pizza?"

We had two ready-made shells in the fridge, and so we all went down and decorated our own individual half of one pie.

"You have to promise to never do this again," Betty said, while scattering olives over her side. "I know you were only trying to protect us, and that's nice of you, it is, but you just hurt yourself in the end. You've been eating yourself up with worry all this time."

I raised my hand in the style of a Boy Scout, amazed that so much fear and anticipation could be reduced to this. "I pledge a new policy of total transparency," I said. "I promise."

Priscilla leaned into the grater as she moved a block of vegan cheese up and down against it. She wouldn't look at me. I wondered if she saw her hand in this. I never would have grown so anxious, after all, if it weren't for the threat posed by the Albanian report. But it was also possible that she'd simply heard enough and was now retreating deeper inside herself, farther and farther away from me. She was so quiet, and how else does estrangement begin if not with language?

"Listen," Betty said, perhaps sensing this herself, "don't look so gloomy, okay?" She grabbed Priscilla's hand and gave it a little shake. "I know you might be scared, but this is the Age of Negotiation. If something takes away five years of your life, you take a pill that gives you back ten. Do you hear? And, really, we can't lose faith in the American supermarket, because do you know what?" She looked between Priscilla and Ernest. "Through the abundance of it and the miracles of modern medicine the average life-expectancy in this country has increased, what? Ten years? Fifteen? Twenty?" I was nodding to show her that I'd go that high. "That's in this last century alone, and do you know what's happened? Along the way my father grew to stand two inches taller than his father, and your uncle Peter grew to stand two inches taller than him. That's right. We'll be fine," she said. "Everything in moderation, that's all we need to remember. Because, really, regardless of what your father said, I think we're threatened by nothing more serious here than the American Condition, just like that man Hickey said. Or can someone show me where those fat monkeys are buried?" She managed a little laugh. I tried to echo it. And then she smiled at me, the smile of Napoleon Hill and Ronald Reagan, a smile of strength and support that made me feel a love for her unlike any I'd felt in years.

I never once stopped to think it was only an act put on for the benefit of the kids.

THE OUTER BANDS OF WHAT had been Hurricane Igor began passing over northern New Jersey the following morning, flooding basements in low-lying areas and causing cars to stall out at the most problematic intersections. When the worst of it was over us, I sat behind the desk in my mentor's office, going through the day's mail. I knew not to expect Ernst that day, and not only because he wouldn't dare take the bus in such weather. He'd need to preserve his energy for the annual meeting of the Society of Flavor Chemists, one of the most important and exhausting industry events of any calendar year. Scheduled for that weekend, it promised to be especially memorable for those of us at FlavAmerica, because in addition to introducing Koba to the Society as our new trainee, we were going to see Beekley certified as a member with full voting rights (if he passed his oral defense, as expected) and our leader honored with the Golden Beaker Award, commemorating a lifetime of achievement in the flavor sciences.

Finding an envelope addressed to Ernst, I opened it and read:

Dear Mr. Eberhardt, I am writing on behalf of the Board of Directors of Better Health and Flavorings to make a proposal for a business combination of Better Health and Flavorings and FlavAmerica. I spun round in my studded leather chair. The wind lashed at the window, throwing against it great sheets of rain. *As you may remember, last summer I received a letter from you indicating that "now is not the right time" to enter into discussions regarding an acquisition transaction. I have chosen to follow up with you today to inquire if that sentiment remains unchanged.* My hands shook as I skimmed through to the end. ... *Better Health and Flavorings would acquire all outstanding private shares in FlavAmer-*

*ica for a per share consideration of…promises to be a compelling value
realization…I hope you share our enthusiasm, and I look forward to receiving your prompt and favorable reply.*

I shot up from my chair—"A prompt and favorable reply!"—and
paced the room, frothing like Lear out on the heath ("Spit, fire! Spout,
rain!"). The thought of working for them was inconceivable, for as devoted readers of the *Wall Street Journal* should know, Better Health
and Flavorings and Goldstein, Olivetti, and Dark were essentially the
same company. A few years after my departure from Animal Testing,
Goldstein, Olivetti, and Dark had become known as Goldstein, Olivetti,
and Dark–Fuchs AG, to reflect its short-lived merger with the German
manufacturer of electronics and farm equipment. When the Germans
soured on the flavorings industry, they sold their holdings, at a con-
siderable loss, to Avantage Capital, SARL, a French private equity firm.
Less than a year later, scientists in Japan announced that Sweetness
#9, once run through a centrifugal separator, provided all the same
benefits to commercial food production as high-fructose corn syrup,
and almost as quickly the FDA expanded its approval of the sweetener
to include baked goods and processed foods, as well as pharmaceuticals, candies, frozen desserts, and coffee beverages. Avantage was in
the picture for less than four years, but it made such a killing flipping
Goldstein, Olivetti, and Dark that one of its founders later purchased
a club in England's Premier League. The company it sold out to, a
U.S.-based multinational agricultural biotechnology firm with head-
quarters in Moscow, Idaho, assigned the rights to Sweetness #9 to a
newly formed subsidiary, the Sugar Hill Group, and unloaded what
remained of the original Goldstein, Olivetti, and Dark to the world's
third-largest producer of fragrances and flavorings. At the time, this
company was known as American Food & Chemical, but it has since
been rebranded as Better Health and Flavorings.

I collapsed into my chair, wondering if my rage was misdirected.
After all, Better Health and Flavorings had nothing to do with Sweetness #9 anymore; only the Sugar Hill Group did. But Hickey and many
of the administrators under whom I'd once worked weren't with the latter; they had stayed on with the former. Strangely, I felt most venomous

toward Goldstein, Olivetti, and Dark, a company that technically no longer existed, but directing my animus toward it made about as much sense as sending my prayers up to the acronym cobbled together from its name. In the end, I felt a great pang of envy for the Palestinians and the Jews. At least their hatred could be passed down through the generations.

I reached for the letter again, realizing now that it was wishful thinking to believe I'd be able to retain my job. Beekley they'd keep, and Koba, too, perhaps (he was so much unmolded clay). But me? Like Tennessee, I didn't have youth on my side. As soon as I'd shown them where we kept our client lists and the bible containing all the recipes for our proprietary blends, they'd kick me to the curb with a twenty-dollar gift card to Starbucks as severance pay. It didn't matter that after twenty-odd years I had a fair amount of stock and could expect a "compelling value realization" as a result of any sale. As soon as the money ran out, and it would, where would I be?

"Justice," I said, as the storm howled outside. Was this justice? My wife and kids had let me off easy, but now here it was, ready to come ashore like a slow-moving storm: Hurricane Better Health and Flavorings. Would this be the thing to bring about my undoing?

Later that morning, unable to wait for an invitation, I drove to Ernst Eberhardt's place, almost stalling out as I turned off of University Avenue onto his street. The road was flooded at the intersection, with water clear up into the sandbags protecting the door to the Dunkin' Donuts.

After parking, I stepped out into a puddle, then hopped away from it, shaking my foot as I opened my umbrella against the rain. The wind immediately caught it, turning the umbrella inside out and pulling me across the road. I ran up to my mentor's door and pounded on it, then crashed through, shaking myself dry like a dog, after he'd opened it.

"What are you doing?" he asked. He wore a blue cardigan over a white T-shirt that had lost the elastic in its collar. A trail of contrasting condiments stained one leg of his khaki pants. "Are we having breakfast?"

"It's an unscheduled visit," I said, as I set my umbrella down in the stand, then hung up my raincoat and sat on the bench to peel off my wet sock. "I'm sorry about this, but I just had to show you something." I stepped into a pair of slippers and reached into the pocket of my sport coat for the letter.

Ernst read it as he led the way into the kitchen, but he barely gave it any consideration at all. As soon as we reached the table, he set it beneath the porcelain sweetener holder that was pushed up against the wall and told me they were like the newspaper. "They'll call you every day if you let them, just to see if you've changed your mind. How many times do I have to say I don't want the paper unless it's written in German?"

"So you're not selling?"

"Let's have some coffee. Can we at least have some coffee?"

I sat at the table, watching as he gathered two cups and measured out the crystals from a jar of instant. The refrigerator started up with an asthmatic rumble. The wallpaper above it — a hunting motif marked by pheasants and thickets of trees — had peeled away in one place. The whole kitchen appeared shabbier than I remembered it. A shingle was missing from the roof of the cuckoo clock over the door, the linoleum curled up in places and was so old I didn't think it could ever look clean, and the dark wooden cabinets were no more updated than the chipped Formica counter-tops. Smelling something, I looked to the sink and saw a tower of dirty dishes. It was enough for me to release a breath that sounded as strained as the refrigerator.

"Eliza doesn't help out around here anymore?" I said.

"She's a liberated woman."

"What does that mean? She's as filthy as a man? Look at your pants, Ernst." He wiped at the condiment stains. "Is this how you dress when you don't come in to work?"

He crossed his arms, staring down at the kettle. I sighed again, no longer sure if it was right to have come here with the hope of convincing him to keep the company.

"Maybe you should sell," I said. "If not to them, then someone else.

I don't know how you persist in living here like you do. You're a capitalist. You should be celebrating your successes, not living in a German neighborhood that doesn't have any Germans anymore."

"What am I?"

"Alone. The beer garden we used to frequent sells pupusas and chalupas now. If you stand on a street corner and say 'schnitzel' too loud, you're bound to get knifed by a black man who thinks you're a Jew with a funny curse. What kind of home is this?"

"Mine."

"Yours. Your home was in Dresden before the war. You're in America now. We move and keep moving. Go to Florida," I said. "Arizona. Sun City. *Sun City.*"

The kettle went to a boil. He brought it to the table and poured the steaming water into our cups.

"You'd think this was Communist Russia," I said. "That you didn't know we have freedom of movement."

He went into the fridge for a glass jar in which several long hot dogs were suspended in cloudy water. As he twisted off the lid, more than just the smell of smoked meat was released.

"I was working on a line of deli meat flavorings when we met. The whole week I'd had it wrong." He fished out a hot dog and took a bite, showing no pleasure on his face. "The after-notes lingered like the taste of cold metal. But then I went to a matinee at the Phoenix" — he pointed toward a movie theater that had been demolished more than twenty years ago — "and I saw her. She dropped her keys in front of the box office and bent over to pick them up."

"This isn't Eliza you're talking about, is it?"

"Beneath the fabric of her skirt, her flesh shifted like the pistons in a great machine." Ernst placed the hot dog in his mouth like a cigar so his hands were free to play with the memory. "I caught a glimpse of that zipper only women wear. On the side? The fabric pulled away from it as she bent over; it sparkled in the sun. Is there anything more arousing than this reminder of a woman's carnality? Of what lies beneath?" He pulled the wiener from his mouth and reconsidered its pink, reconstituted flesh. "This is why women in Muslim countries

212

wear veils. Their men are more honest. They acknowledge how easily they are undone."

When he looked up again, he was smiling in a way I hadn't seen in years. "I offered her a job before I even saw her face. 'Work for me,' I said. 'I need you to work for me.'" His smile somehow grew larger. "We made love three times that night."

"Dear Christ, Ernst. I really don't think I need to hear this. You know how I feel about that woman."

"I was a young man again, my balls as heavy as military-grade steel." His voice was like light sent from a dying star. It pulsed outward, full of an improbable vitality. "And when I awoke the following day?" He pointed upstairs. "I sat at my desk and wrote out the formulas for almost the entire line of flavorings I was working on. I could taste them in the back of my throat. The chemical names came to me one after the other, still vivid from my dreams. I plucked them from the air like ornaments from a Christmas tree."

It was his "Kubla Khan," a month's worth of work performed in a frozen moment. But as he looked at the last rounded bite of his hot dog, he shook his head with all the sadness of Coleridge over his own noble fragment.

"Eliza awoke before I could finish. She called out to me, urging me back to bed. And I would have been a fool to have resisted. Or worse, an old man." He swallowed the last of his hot dog as if it were medicine. "The taste," he said, "it has never satisfied. But it is a martyr to love."

"And so this is why you insist on my losing my hubcaps every time I visit?"

"I purchased a condominium for her last month. In that new mixed-use development downtown."

"Over the Acme?"

He nodded. "She doesn't come around here anymore. She thinks she can starve me out. That I'll come to my senses and join her over there in that well-decorated box. But I won't do it. If life is a process of losing the things we love, I'll not go somewhere where it's easier for me to lose my memories of them. This is my home. You can haul me out of here when I'm dead or no longer sure I'm alive."

I nodded, letting my eyes drift back to the letter pinned beneath the sugar holder. Ernst noticed and reached for it.

"I'm to be honored at the Society meeting this weekend," he said. "They'll have me up there like a man lying in a coffin, listening to his own eulogy." He handed me the letter. "I'll make my intentions known then," he said, while reaching into the sugar holder for something to sweeten his coffee: a packet of Sweetness #9.

"What did I tell you about organizing?" I turned over the porcelain holder, spilling its contents across the table. But this time none of the packets that came tumbling out had a tiny pink bar on one corner of the packaging; there was no sugar, only Sweetness #9.

"We must be out," Ernst said, when I looked up from this mess.

"What do you mean 'we'? You said Eliza doesn't come around anymore."

He drank his coffee. He looked up at the cuckoo clock.

"Ernst," I said.

And then he stood and took his cup and saucer to the sink. "I'm sure I can't explain," he told me.

As I was driving into the parking lot, I got a call on my cell phone that I answered while fumbling out of the Volvo. "Yes, yes, I hear you," I said. "Beekley, you say? Oh well, that is distressing." I hurried in through the rain to the back door, trying to make the client know that the problem would certainly be addressed.

"A top priority," I said, while marching across the production room floor. "We'll have a new sample out to you by the end of the week, if not sooner, I promise you that."

Moments later I was turning in to the flavor development lab, where Koba stood alone at one of the work stations, performing some general compounding.

"Where's Beekley?"

"Popped out for coffee, I think. Problem?"

I crossed to Beekley's desk in the far corner of the room and found the notebook in which he scribbled all of his formulas, including those for flavorings in progress. After flipping through a couple of pages, I found what I was looking for, then went to the shelf that ran the length of one wall and collected a dozen or so amber bottles while consulting an open page.

When I had everything I needed, I reached for a glass pipette and began to transfer the appropriate amount of each chemical compound into a test tube. Beekley came in sipping from a cup of Starbucks as I was running the finished mixture through the mass spectrometer.

"Do you *ever* work?" I said.

"I assure you I've been working all morning." He reached in beneath the back of his lab coat and pulled out a folded copy of *Guns 'n' Ammo* from his back pocket. "You think anyone else would read this if I didn't? What do you know about guns, David? About violence? There's a whole segment of the population out there that hangs an embroidered copy of the Second Amendment over its headboard at night, and if you don't know what they like to snack on, or what they're having for dinner, just who is going to train Koba here? Can you tell me that?"

Koba looked up from his notebook, smiling nervously at our attention. I smoothed down the front of my lab coat and took a step toward Beekley.

"I got a phone call a short while ago. From Terry Butler."

"Oh?" He set his magazine down.

"Yes, and do you know what he said? That the wild cherry you sent over was a little off-putting."

This was one of three flavorings that had been requested by a multinational pharmaceutical company that was readying to launch a new line of liquid anti-psychotics and serotonin reuptake inhibitors for children. Our standard bubble gum and candy apple had already been approved for use, but three iterations of wild cherry, a flavor our test panels suggested cut across ethnic lines, had been rejected, the most recent one more vigorously than any prior to it.

"I had to admit I didn't sign off on it. 'Beekley's my best man,' I said. 'I don't need to second-guess him.' But after hearing the urgency in his voice —"

Beekley looked at the mass spectrometer. "You second-guessed me?"

"That's right." I thrust my nose into the mass spectrometer's open chamber, then pulled away from it, pinching at one nostril and inhaling deeply. "Now stop me if I'm wrong," I said, "but the 'burnt' and 'fecal' top notes I detect suggest you were going for something far wilder than our customary wild cherry."

Beekley set his coffee down and folded his arms across his chest. "The sample I sent over before this one was perfectly good. They had no reason to reject it."

"He said he couldn't be sure, but he thought it tasted a little like — and this is his word — *shit*."

Koba put his pen down and closed his notebook, then started for the door, unbuttoning his lab coat. "I think I'll just grab an early lunch."

Beekley leaned back against the counter, shaking his head. "There's no way he could've known that."

He knew what I was accusing him of. Just as a cartoonist might slip a single pornographic frame into an animated feature, knowing the audience would never realize it, a flavorist might drop an off note into a flavoring just for fun, certain that it would never be detected by even the most discerning human nose. Most people can identify no more than three components in any odor or flavoring; even a talented flavorist might only be able to name another three or four more.

"There's still time for me to withdraw my sponsorship of you in the Society, you know. And then who would want you, hmm? You'd be no better than a stateless person."

Beekley sighed and crossed before me to his work station. "I just don't know if we should be doing this," he said.

"What?"

"Making it like candy."

"Children's medicine? So this is political, is it?"

Now, I understand what this was all about; he had no fewer qualms about the present than I had about the past. But I wasn't ready for his discomfort. I had left the early seventies behind only a short time before, so it'd be a while still before I could catch up to him and enter the present day.

"What if kids start trading them on the playground?" he said.

"'Give you my bubble gum anti-psychotic for your candy apple anti-depressant.'"

"This is why we have nurses, Beekley. To dispense medicine. Or are you for sick children now? Hardly a platform I can support."

"All right, all right. You'll have a new formulation by the end of the day. But when I'm called before Congress to explain how America's children came to be like fatted calves, standing there ready and compliant for the next Rasputin or Richard Milhous Nixon, it's your name I'll say while leaning into the microphone."

AFTER BETTY HAD FALLEN ASLEEP that night (she rarely made it through Leno's opening monologue), I tired of lying sleepless in the dark and went downstairs, thinking I'd go out into the garage and tinker with my latest diorama. ("The Birdseye Express," I was calling it: a scene that showcased Clarence Birdseye's first insulated railroad car, which provided his frozen food a nationwide system of distribution and assured his company's success.) As I reached the bottom of the stairs, however, I saw the light on beneath Priscilla's door. It was a school night, so I turned toward it, then knocked twice and pushed my head inside.

"Lights out," I said. "It's past midnight."

Priscilla was sitting on her bed, reading the Albanian report. She didn't look up. She just grunted and turned the page.

I came over and sat down beside her. She was surrounded by a half circle of literature. In addition to the Albanian report in her lap, there was a Timothy Leary biography that showed the guru in all his wild-eyed glory on its cover, a history of social protest movements, and a copy of *The Campus Crier,* above the front fold of which was the headline SCHOOL DISTRICT PROFITS WHILE STUDENTS SUFFER. I skimmed through the first few paragraphs of the article, learning of a contract the school district had recently entered into with a national pizza chain. "Co-opting the cafeteria," the article called it. Not a word about tax relief.

"Is this the first installment of your think-piece?" I said.

Priscilla shrugged. "It came out last week."

She'd tied her hair back with rubber bands and applied a thick white cream to her face. I went to brush a lock from her forehead—it had fallen down into the cream—but she snapped her head away from me.

"What is it?" I said. A candy heart covered Timothy Leary's third eye. *Be Mine*, it read. "Is it a boy?"

"Please."

"What then? You've barely spoken to me since last night."

She kept her eyes on the Albanian report. Dozens of transparent sticky notes stuck out from its pages. SIGN HERE, they read, the words held inside a hollow red arrow.

I looked over to the bookshelf beside her computer desk. Its top- and bottom-most shelves were given over to books documenting her increasing skepticism of food, politics, and culture, but in between was the anachronistic bric-a-brac of a childhood already gone by: a teddy bear that wore a pink bow around its neck, a framed picture of Priscilla as a cheerleader, her baby book, and a snow globe I'd given her after attending a conference in Montreal.

"Are you angry?" I said. "I'd understand it if you were."

Finally, she looked up. "Why should I be?" she said. "You're obviously suffering from prolonged exposure to Sweetness #9. You're sick, Dad. The anxiety and the apathy. You need help."

Though I didn't believe this, it touched me all the same. She was like a little girl again, if only for a moment. Worrying about her father!

"I'll be fine," I told her. "You watch. When I get my CAT scan next week, they'll just tell me to drink more water or take a multi-vitamin." I gave her knee a reassuring shake.

"And E? He just needs more water? How many weeks now without a verb? How many weeks before we finally do something?"

I looked down at the Albanian report. Someone had already gone over it with a blue highlighter. Priscilla held a pink one at the ready.

"Everything will be fine," I said.

She snorted. I looked back to her bookcase, wishing I could tell her what she needed to hear, but knowing I couldn't. This wasn't cancer we were talking about, some dark mass that a doctor could point to on a back-lit x-ray while plotting a plan of attack. What was troubling my son was more like Epstein-Barr, a new and perhaps still unnamed condition as mysterious as the human soul. *No verbs?* I would have thrown a kidney at it if it would have helped, but what could I do?

"Listen. An old college friend of mine is working on the Human Genome Project. I'll give him a call and see what he has to say, and then maybe take your brother to see Dr. White. We'll get it figured out, okay? We'll get him an EEG, an EKG, a PET, a CT, an MRI — we'll fight this thing with information, do you hear? You just have to think positive. Can you do that?"

"He needs to be detoxed," she said, as if she hadn't heard any of this. "All the chemicals have built up in his brain, blocking the connections. You need to make him go on the Rosicrucian diet with me. We all should do it."

"Priscilla, do you really believe your brother would go along with that?"

"He'll learn. We have to lead by example."

I was shaking my head. "If he took a brown bag of macrobiotic treats to school each day, he'd trade it — at a loss — on the playground, then sneak something at a friend's house, or refuse to eat anything at all. Is that what you want?"

"He's not the only one who needs it. Mom's been sleep-eating."

"What? What do you mean?"

I listened in disbelief as she said she'd come out into the kitchen no fewer than three times in the last couple of months and seen Betty with her hand in the breadbox.

"Carbs? Your mother's been eating carbs?"

"I tried to stop her one night, but it only embarrassed her. She woke up and pretended to sleepwalk upstairs. It's all in here," she said, tapping at a highlighted section of the Albanian report: "'Sweetness #9 obstructs the carbohydrate-induced synthesis of serotonin, which is needed to regulate cravings and normalize the body's intake of food.' Don't you get it? It triggers the primitive desire to eat."

Her green eyes were like vast suicide windows she'd flung open before me. I sat before them transfixed.

"We've all OD'd," she said. "Sleep-eating, obesity, a rise in certain aphasias, anxiety."

"I'm not anxious anymore," I said. "I feel much better now."

"Your eye still twitches."

I reached for it, wondering if Botox was the answer. "And so what about you?" I said. I figured we might as well have it out. "What does the Albanian report say about you?"

I expected a spirited defense. I expected her to tell me she was the only healthy one, protected by the umbrella of a vegan diet. Instead, she sat there like a woman on a park bench in the rain.

"I'm depressed," she said.

And the simplicity of that message — it pierced my heart like a well-driven nail.

I sat there silently for longer than I would have liked, and when I did speak, I wasn't satisfied by what I'd settled on saying. "Just concentrate on your work." What else could I say or do? "Write the best think-piece you can. Nail me to the wall if you'd like."

This got a smile out of her, but then she wiped at the tears that were cutting channels in her white facial cream and told me she'd quit.

"*What?* The paper? When?"

"Yesterday. Me and Sarin."

"But why?"

"Some parent," she said, and then amidst the sobs and mumbling it came out. A man who worked for ConAgra or Sysco or Monsanto hadn't appreciated the story he'd seen in his son's high school paper. He'd asked the principal about fact-checking, and he'd used the word libel, and after saying he'd be reading the following installments with great interest, the principal called the girls into his office, along with their journalism teacher, and said they'd need to clear everything through legal from now on.

"Our adviser suggested we switch to the sports page. So we quit."

"Is this why you were so quiet?"

She shrugged. "It doesn't really matter. People only believe what they want to believe anyway."

I reached for her knee again. I'd never heard this from her before; she sounded so adult-like, so cynical. "It'll be okay," I said.

But she shrank away from me, pulling her legs up into her chest.

"Will you stop saying that? It'll only be okay if we do something. How can you allow Sweetness #9 to stay in this house?"

I envied her certainty, her quickness to isolate an enemy and formulate a plan of attack. Get rid of it and we'll be better! She viewed life as a Hollywood producer does, as a thing with three acts and the truth. But I'd lived with the problem long enough to wonder what good it would do to raise your pitchfork and go running off after Frankenstein's monster if there'd always be another monster waiting for you in the shadows at home.

"And what about Red Dye No. 40?" I said.

"We should get rid of that too."

"And then what? Who's to say there's not something else we don't even know about? That there's not another father out there talking to his daughter this very minute about some other food additive we've never once stopped to question? Where does the purge end?"

I told her about the Delaney Clause, saying that when it was passed, outlawing any food additive that caused cancer, we had only been able to see the disease in parts per million. "This was in the sixties," I said, "and now we can see cancer in parts per billion — even parts per trillion. And do you know what we discovered? Even broccoli causes cancer. But should we stop eating it? No. The threat is very, very small."

I tried to reason with her. I spoke of war-time England and how scientists there had determined that a diet of green leafy vegetables, fresh milk, and whole-grain bread would give you all the nutrients you'd ever need. "But Churchill never made this the focus of his rationing program, not even during the worst of the Blitz. He knew what you and I know: that the inhabitants of an advanced country won't tolerate such bland fare day after day. We need the savory and the sweet," I said, "even if it means risking a night of German bombing to get it. So either we go back to living a life not far removed from the hunter-gatherers or we do what your mother says we do and accept a little risk. You ask me, it's a simple choice. Right? Priscilla," I said. "Will you look at me?"

And though she did, it wasn't with the nod and the look of understanding that I had hoped to see. Wiping at the cream beneath her eyes, she said, "So if there's nothing we can do, why did you tell us anything in the first place?" And then, "To make yourself feel better?" And then, "To let yourself off the hook?"

I sat there a moment longer, allowing her to look at me as if I were Public Enemy No. 1; then I rose from the bed and turned for the door. "Lights out," I said. "I mean it."

A COUPLE OF MORNINGS LATER, the rumble of a moving truck sent us hurrying into the dining room, through the window of which we were able to observe the arrival of our new neighbor. He was a white man of about forty years who must have been at least one hundred pounds overweight, and as he stepped out of a massive SUV, he held in the cup of his hands a tiny potted bonsai tree. While the movers opened up the rear of the truck, the fat man unlocked his front door and took that tree inside.

I didn't see him again until the following evening, when I spied him through our bedroom window after coming in from work. He stood in his backyard, wearing what looked like a pair of white silk pajamas, as he moved through one slow pose after another, practicing tai chi.

Betty came up behind me as I was undoing my tie, saying she'd spoken to him out on the driveway that morning.

"You'll never guess what he does for a living."

I looked at her. She was drinking a glass of cranberry juice and sparkling water. I couldn't remember the last time I'd seen her drink a diet cola.

"He's a life coach and nutrition expert," she said.

"You've got to be joking. He must weigh three hundred pounds."

She gave me a sidelong look and asked what that had to do with anything. "Can Joe Torre hit a hundred-mile-per-hour fastball? It's not what you can do that's important but what you know." She continued by telling me he guaranteed his customers would lose no less than 15 percent of their body weight in no more than a year. "And that's a money-back guarantee," she said. "You don't have to buy a bunch of fancy food, either, or attend a whole slew of classes or follow-up sessions. You just meet with him that one time and you're set."

"How much?" I asked.

She wouldn't answer at first. As she moved into the walk-in closet, she said he required his clients to sign a non-disclosure form and promise not to enter into a competing business. "He must've really figured something out," she said.

"How much, Betty?"

She began to undress, stepping out of her black pants.

"Ten thousand dollars," she said.

I snorted. "To have a fat man tell you what to eat? You can't be serious."

"That's very offensive, David. His name is Neal."

"Well, I'm sorry, I didn't mean to offend *Neal,* but the thought of giving him ten thousand dollars — I hope you're not considering this."

As she unbuttoned her blouse, she looked down at her body, as if imagining which parts of it would melt away after she knew our neighbor's secret. "It is a lot of money," she acknowledged, but when she looked up, her face said something else. I'd seen that expression before, back when she'd decided to give herself over to the Scarsdale Diet or the Jane Fonda Workout. It was the look you see at Lourdes or down at the drunk tank whenever the alcoholic is swearing off the sauce for good. The look of a new believer.

She stepped over to me, reaching for my belt.

"What are you doing?"

She smiled. "Maybe I'd look like a sorority girl again."

"You know I don't need that."

"There's got to be something you need."

She pulled down my zipper.

"The kids," I said.

"Priscilla's at the bookstore," she whispered, "and E won't hear a thing. He's off slaying dragons. Don't you want to?"

She touched me. I threw my eyes out to the far wall, where I found her "before" and "after" pictures staring back at me. I looked down at her. She looked up at me. And the expression on my face — it was as if she'd asked me to name the capital of South Dakota.

She let go of me, knowing I didn't want to. "If it's not Jezebel," she said, "it must be me."

"Betty."

Usually she was quick to change, but this evening, after grabbing the pants of her tracksuit, she turned to face me wearing only her underwear and bra. The elastic bands of her underthings cut into her flesh, making her appear like one of those stone fertility figures that archaeologists dig up in the field.

"I want to," I said. "Just give me a moment."

I went out to the en suite bathroom, and reached into the drawer on my side for the Viagra I'd left there. By the time Betty was stepping up behind me, now wearing the bottoms of her tracksuit, I was pushing a blue pill through its foil backing.

"Is that what I think it is?" she said.

I leaned in beneath the faucet and swallowed the pill down with a quick drink of water.

"We just have to wait thirty minutes," I told her.

She reached for the package of pills I'd set down on the counter. "How long have you had these?"

"Just a few days." I tried to bring her into my arms, but she turned away from me, going back into the walk-in. I followed, telling her that Dr. White had given them to me.

"And you didn't say anything?" She reached for her tracksuit top now and zipped it up. "What happened to your new policy of total transparency?"

Later, I'd think it unfair that she had expected me to tell her. I'd been given the pills *before* initiating that policy, so if anything my silence on them should have been grandfathered in. At the moment, though, I only managed to release a pained little gasp in my defense.

"Where does it end?" she said. "How many secrets do you have?" She bumped out past me and crossed to our window, moving more for the sake of motion than purpose. "Should I look for track marks up your arm, or maybe take a flashlight into the garage and search for a box filled with Swedish movies?"

"Betty, I don't know why you're reacting like this."

"What? Maybe you've got a whole other family down in the piney woods, or a homosexual lover named Randy living in upstate New York."

"We're back to the homosexual question, are we?"

She extended a stiff arm toward the bathroom. "You've had the fountain of youth at your disposal all week and you've had *no* desire to sleep with me?"

"I was waiting for the right time."

"And when's that, nineteen seventy-three?"

"I thought it was now."

She lifted her tracksuit top and pinched at the flesh bunched up around her waist. "Is it because of this? Don't look away, David. You're always looking away. Is it all my formaldehyde that turns you off?"

"I thought you said you didn't believe any of that."

"I was talking for the benefit of our kids! You scared Priscilla half to death. I'd be surprised if she ever ate again. Do you know she photocopies pages from that Albanian report and leaves them under my windshield wiper each morning?"

"Just get it out of your system. I deserve it."

"What, you think I'll be done with you in one evening? That it's that easy?"

"I'm not the only one with secrets, you know. What about you? Have you been sleep-eating?"

She pointed to the door. "You're on the sofa tonight!"

"Or how about Greystone Park? When did you decide to come back to me? After Ernst assured you I'd be adequately employed? When you knew I'd be able to support you if you went back to school?"

"You expect me to tell you on your terms? Is that it? When all these years you never once thought about me? I'll tell you when I'm ready, David. And it won't be tonight."

She turned to face the window. I stood there, not certain what I was supposed to do. It was only six o'clock.

"You're sure you don't want me to come back in thirty minutes?"

"Go see a movie," she suggested.

So I started out, getting as far as the door. Then I remembered something: the Society dinner was the following night.

"Should I leave your ticket on the kitchen table?" I asked. She'd not only promised to join me, she'd already paid her forty-five dollars and checked the box for steak. "Betty?"

"I think," she said, and it was as if she were channeling these words from an extra-terrestrial being several star systems away, "you should go." And here she turned to face me. "Alone."

THE 360TH MEETING of the Society of Flavor Chemists, Inc., was held at the Sheraton Newark Airport Hotel, located at Exit 14 of the New Jersey Turnpike. It began with a mid-morning board meeting, continued through lunch with a Chemical Sources Association roundtable, and ended in the evening with cocktails and a dinner of chicken, beef, fish, or vegetarian. Before moving into the main banquet hall for the last of these events, we gathered on the mezzanine level for cocktails and hors d'oeuvres. I grabbed a glass of pinot grigio from the cash bar and moved over to the long table holding a dozen or so heated silver trays, where I found the outgoing board president moving down the buffet line alongside a young man in blue jeans I didn't recognize.

"The future's limitless," the outgoing president was saying. "Do you know the cost of producing protein from waste effluent? Down near three cents a pound. That's a third the cost of animal- and agriculturally-derived proteins."

The man at his side was a journalist, I took it. As I grabbed a wonton, he scribbled in a pocket notebook. "A third the cost, you say?"

The outgoing president pointed a stick of satay chicken at him. "Write this down verbatim. We can feed the world today. We have all the flavorings we need to get the job done. We only lack the political courage to do it."

I continued around them, forgoing the stuffed mushrooms I'd had my eye on, but soon found my path blocked again, this time by a chemical salesman that FlavAmerica had dealt with for many years. He stood before a large iced bowl, piling shrimp onto his plate.

"David," he said, looking up with a boozy smile. "Just the man I wanted to see. What's this I hear about Better Health and Flavorings? Making a full-court press, are they?"

I reached for the ladle in the communal bowl of cocktail sauce, telling him I was sure I didn't know. "I'm just a cog in the machine, Larry. I'm sure you know as much as I do."

He leaned into me like a ski jumper in mid-flight, pointing a finger out from around the side of his rocks glass. "They want NoNilla®, don't they?" His breath was sour and overpowering, his bulbous nose a starburst of broken capillaries. "You don't have to tell me. Couldn't be anything else."

I chuckled and reminded him that this product generated but a small fraction of our total annual sales, which the previous year had surpassed $14 million for the first time. He didn't care to hear it, though. He shook his rocks glass in my face and told me to look into the future.

"You think the boys at Better Health and Flavorings don't know what they're doing? They've got more analysts than the Department of Defense." He drank from his glass and made a face. "And, hell, with China coming on board and India and all the rest of the developing world too, there won't be enough to go around here soon, and that counts double for vanilla."

He turned uneasily then and looked off toward a knot of flavor chemists from Better Health and Flavorings, who stood at a table chatting with the Japanese. "There's a tyranny to high-volume orders, David." He slurred his words like a latter-day Willy Loman. "If they even take my calls anymore, it's to ask that I sell at a humiliating price. Well, listen." He turned back around, his finger bouncing out again from the side of his glass. "Those bastards want to turn capitalism into a blood sport, fine, so be it. But you tell the Kraut to do the same. Whatever they offer, demand a million more. They've got it. They've been keeping plenty from me all these years." He looked down into his glass. "Empty," he said.

I dipped a shrimp in cocktail sauce and chewed, as behind me the outgoing president and the journalist stepped closer.

"I just want to make sure I have this right," the journalist said. "What you said earlier, do you mean 'shit'? That there's a future in flavoring protein farmed from shit?"

I gave Larry a big smile. "Well, don't be a stranger." Then I made a beeline for a high-top cocktail table opening up near the railing, and I stood there looking around for my co-workers. Tennessee was downstairs, drinking alone at the better-stocked bar in the lobby. Ernst and Eliza, meanwhile, were on the far side of the mezzanine level, sitting at a low table and talking with two of my mentor's contemporaries, both past recipients of the Golden Beaker Award. Ernst tapped the floor with his cane, no doubt in the midst of one of his stories. Eliza laughed and primped her hair. She'd had it done earlier that day in New York City, a perm job dyed one of those unfortunate catalogue colors between pomegranate and pimento.

I felt a pang of envy. My mentor had weathered difficult times with Eliza, overcoming even his biggest mistake. And how had he done it? Had it been as simple as writing a check for ten thousand dollars? I realized I should have thought about the rewards, not the costs. For this and so many other things: the rewards, not the costs.

Koba and Beekley joined me a few moments later, speaking of the rumored take-over. Talk of it was everywhere that night; the subject was almost as prominent as chatter about Monica Lewinsky or the surging New York Yankees.

"I know," Beekley was saying, and his hair stood so tall this evening that he reminded me of a troll doll. "If he sells to Better Health and Flavorings, he'll donate his millions to Oklahoma State and demand they put his name on a new football stadium. Or, no, he'll buy a large tract of land in Kansas and build a huge ark made out of plastic. With his remaining money, he'll fill it with two of every animal known to man—or better yet, only those indigenous to Germany."

"I think he'll turn FlavAmerica into an employee-run cooperative," Koba answered. "He's got no family of his own, so why wouldn't he leave it to us? He clearly has no need or fondness for money. The man lives like a monk."

Beekley appeared deeply aggrieved by this, even though his own politics were aligned with such thinking. "Ridiculous," he said. "The scenarios are supposed to be *ridiculous.*"

"Well, I'm sorry," Koba said. "I don't drink 'ironic' beers and understand your whole theory of 'the ridiculous.'"

"What do you mean?" Beekley set down his bottle of Miller High Life. "You're being ridiculous right now."

"I'll tell you what'll happen," I broke in. "If Ernst cashes out, he'll give his money away, you're right about that, but it won't be to you or me or anyone else in America, save for a few dollars to Eliza." I had their attention now, but here the doors to the banquet room opened, turning heads and sending the crowd into motion. I grabbed my drink and led the way. "The money will go to Germany," I said, before reminding my co-workers that our leader had traveled there with Eliza the previous summer and visited his childhood home of Dresden for the first time since the war. When he returned, he spoke at length about the church in which he'd been baptized, a grand baroque structure that had once dominated Dresden's skyline but now lay in ruins as both a reminder of the folly of war and a testament to the lack of development in the Communist East.

"There's been talk in the German-American community of rebuilding it." I sat down at a table that had a plain white card sticking up from a vase of flowers: *FlavAmerica,* it read, above the Society's logo. "That's where his money will go, to Dresden. You think he lacks motive?" They looked with me to the doors, through which Ernst was now walking with Eliza. "That man didn't just serve during the war," I said. "He served Hitler his dinner."

IT WAS A STORY EVERY FLAVORIST knew, if not from casual conversation, then one of the many mentions of it in the Society newsletter. "The Hitler Detail," Ernst called it, a story that began in 1940, just weeks after Paris had fallen like a drunk woman in the street.[*] It was then that Hitler, still manic from his brief visit to the occupied French capital, left Paris for a whistle-stop tour of World War I battle sites — more a tourist at this stage of the war than the commander of the army that had already swallowed half of Europe.

Hitler's train eventually brought him into the Frankfurt Rhine-Main area, where, in the waning years of the nineteenth century, Pavel Pabst (not to be confused with his piano-playing contemporary, the native of Königsberg who taught at the Moscow Conservatory) had unlocked the secrets of the conifer tree and produced the world's first chemically

---

[*] My account of my mentor's story is deeply indebted to *How Great Thou Taste: A Corporate History of FlavAmerica,* which I discovered while cleaning out Ernst Eberhardt's house following his death. The manuscript was then unknown to me, but its clean prose and lack of idiosyncrasies (Ernst was always capitalizing words he shouldn't have, a carry-over from his native tongue) told me it had been ghostwritten. As to the authorship of the book, I can only hazard a guess: an editor at *Food Product News* who never turned down an invitation to the beer garden that Ernst and I once frequented. Sadly, these suspicions can neither be confirmed nor denied, because the editor was murdered in 1989 after being discovered in bed with his lover. The account of this crime that ran in *Food Product News* suggests there wasn't a struggle between the two men so much as there was a struggle to escape. While the husband went to the dresser for his pistol, the editor pleaded for his life and fled out the window, wearing only a watch and a bedsheet. He was shot while racing down the steps of the fire escape, and fell to the sidewalk below as the wind caught the bedsheet and pulled it away. By the time the police arrived, the suspect was sitting on the curb in front of the body, wearing the dead man's watch. All of which is to say, *How Great Thou Taste* was left incomplete—and for good reason, you might be allowed to think, if you were to say, as I so often do, that my mentor's story is most logically completed by my own.

synthesized dose of vanillin. Hitler insisted that they stop at his Wiesbaden lab to pay their respects, and it didn't matter that the consensus ran against this (a tour of a flavor production facility during the war!); Hitler could not be denied.

Ernst Eberhardt, then just a trainee of not quite twenty years, saw nothing strange in Hitler's visit, but then it hardly seemed to him that Germany was at war at all. He lived in one of the country's most renowned spa towns, and as he whiled away the hours on the weekend at a sidewalk café, he delighted in the lingering looks he drew from young women. It was no different for his sisters in Köln and Frankfurt, the younger a painter, the elder already a mother. Whenever he visited them, he'd attend art gallery openings or drive off into the country for a picnic.

Hitler entered the laboratory shortly before noon, surrounded by his publisher, Gerhardt Bloch; his photographer, Heinrich Hoffmann; an unknown SS escort; and Lukas Schmidt, the Pabst, Pfaff & Pfeiffer executive who had jumped apoplectic from behind his desk when his secretary told him whose sedan had just parked at the top of the building's circular drive.

Perhaps it was Ernst's youthful good looks and stunning blond hair that drew Hitler to him. What is known is that the Führer stopped at his side and looked down at the beaker in his hand.

"And what are you working on?" he asked.

Ernst looked at the beaker and tried to keep his hand from shaking. "Something sweet, mein Führer. For a hard candy."

He offered it up for inspection, and Hitler dipped his nose into the mouth of the glass tube, nodding as he pulled away from the clear colorless liquid inside.

"Orange," he said. "It's orange."

Ernst smiled and nodded—"Yes, that is right!"—as did the publisher Gerhardt Bloch. *Orange! Wonderful!* Hitler's photographer knew a good moment when he saw one. He stepped forward and captured the smiles with a flash, after which the SS officer accompanying them leaned into the Führer's ear, no doubt to whisper his fears of an attack that would begin with a chemical splash.

Four years would pass before Ernst would see his country's leader again. By then his favorite cafés had closed, the art galleries had gone dark, and Pabst, Pfaff & Pfeiffer had been shuttered so its scientists could be reassigned throughout the war-time economy.

Ernst was sent to a research facility on the Baltic coast, a little more than a year before the British bombed it in the early morning hours of 18 August 1943. The dormitories housing the scientists were targeted during that raid, killing three of Ernst Eberhardt's closest friends. He was saved from the explosions and the fires that followed them only because of the schnitzel he'd eaten at dinner. It hadn't agreed with him, and so he'd awoken in the dark and followed the beam of his flashlight to the outhouse, where in his prolonged discomfort he'd fallen asleep. He awoke on the run to the sound of bombing, so scared that his legs kicked free of his boxer shorts as he stumbled and fell naked toward the line of trees.

The following month, the production of the V-2 rocket was moved underground, taking Ernst with it deep inside a mountain near the village of Niedersachswerfen. It was there that he thought he would sit out the war. But then in February of 1945 he was notified of a second, more important subterranean assignment, this one in Berlin.*

His first two days in the *Führerbunker*, no one would describe his duties to him. Each time Ernst dared approach someone to ask, he was told to return to his bunk and await further instructions. He saw Hitler only once, in passing, while coming back from the toilet. Pausing at the head of the stairs, Ernst heard his voice growing louder as it moved up from the bunker's lowest level. Dr. Morell was at Hitler's side, and though Ernst wasn't able to stand there long enough to make sense of their whole conversation — a bodyguard led the way and hurried Ernst on with a questioning look — he heard enough to know Hitler was talking about the use and effects of cyanide. How much? How long? How painful?

Hours later, Ernst awoke from a frantic dream and looked for a win-

---

* Ernst later informed me that he entered Hitler's bunker much sooner than this, but I have allowed the date to stand uncorrected here as a record of what he included in his memoirs.

dow, trying to determine the time by the presence of dark or light. But this was a world without a sun or a moon, some fifty feet belowground, lower even than the corpses. He turned lazily onto one side, hearing the breathing of three other men, and reached to the side of his bed for the flashlight he'd brought with him from Peenemünde. He flicked it on and held it over his wristwatch, seeing the time was not quite three o'clock. He brought the watch up to his ear and listened, first making sure the timepiece was working, then pleased by the sound that it made. He felt reassured by the slow *tick-tick, tick-tick* of the second hand. It brought to mind the rise-then-fall of a pickaxe, allowing him to see the future as a brick wall, something methodically being chipped away by the present. *Tick-tick, tick-tick.* Only a tiny hole needed to be cleared; then he could punch through and make his escape.

Ernst sat up in bed shivering from the cold and swung his legs round to the floor. He hunched forward, his arms draped down across his thighs, and rubbed his palms together. The imagery of his dream still haunted him: Hitler had come for him down a darkened hallway, pulled by the force of a leashed Alsatian. He cornered Ernst, and then Fräulein Braun appeared to pry open his mouth and drop a capsule of cyanide inside. "Do tell me how it tastes, Ernst," Hitler said, the only words Ernst remembered from the dream. "Do tell me how it tastes" — and then the dog's barking had awoken him.

Ernst swallowed dryly. A brandy, that's what he needed. Whenever he'd cried as a child, his mother had rubbed some on his lips and sung "Sonny Boy." He lay back down and closed his eyes, eager to retreat farther into the warmth of this memory, but then he felt a hand shaking his shoulder and he sat up, banging his head into the mesh wiring of the bunk above his. A soldier stood before him, the same one he'd seen earlier with Hitler. "Come," he said.

He had no choice, so he stepped into his slippers and threw on his robe and made his way down the concrete stairwell to the sitting room on the bottommost floor. It was there that he met Hitler's personal secretary, Martin Bormann, the man who had reassigned Ernst to Berlin and only now saw fit to give him his orders. Bormann turned from the bar trolley when Ernst appeared and handed him a brandy.

"You are to provide the Führer with meals full of zest and mouthfeel and exuberant high notes," he said. "Food is scarce, even here. But Our Leader"—and he pointed to the door through which Hitler slept— "cannot know. Do not ask me if we can win the war. I only know that you are to deliver flavor, regardless of what ingredients are on hand. If the cook prepares eggplant, you will make it taste like Beluga caviar. Am I understood?"

More than fifty years later, while he stood at the podium in the main ballroom of the Sheraton Newark Airport Hotel, Ernst shook his head at the memory of it.

"Understood. What was understood was 'this is not the place for me.'"

Those of us attending the Society dinner sat before him, with the last of our chicken, beef, fish, or vegetarian going cold on our plates.

"The ventilation in that kitchen was so poor, I wished I was in a submarine choking on the diesel fumes." He shielded his eyes against the overhead lights, looking for something behind the glare. Ten seconds passed, long enough for the silence to make a roomful of people uncomfortable, not least of all me. He'd once been such a raconteur; now I wasn't sure what he'd say next—or if even he knew.

Koba, never one for conflict, cupped his hands around his mouth and cried out, "You're the Gorilla of Vanilla, Ernst!"

I tapped my fork into the side of my water glass. "Hear, hear! Hear, hear!"

Then others joined in, and Ernst was holding up the flats of his hands, begging for our silence. "Please. I may not have a wooden tongue, but I'm no better than any of you. If I hadn't made NoNilla®, someone else would have." He spoke slowly and with an accent that hadn't softened through the years. He pinched off the ends of certain words with a soft hiss. "Clifton perhaps." He pointed to a contemporary of his, also a recipient of the Golden Beaker Award, and then the woman sitting next to him. "Or Vanessa there. You look lovely, Vanessa. They can tell you. Your first great work of art catches the world off-guard; the second—yourself."

Waiters in red coats and black bow ties circled the room, collecting plates and silverware. Ernst shook his head, stuck on some thought or memory; then he noticed Eliza as she stood from her chair on the dais, and he waved her back down.

"I'm sorry," he said. "When I get to thinking about that war, it's as if it's thinking of me. Just another reason to hand the company over to David. He'll keep it in good hands."

I was then pushing a piece of chicken across my plate, trying to sop up the butter that had rushed out when I'd cut into it. I looked to Beekley to see if I had heard this correctly—his shocked smile told me I had—then placed my knife and fork down and stood, coughing into my cloth napkin.

Everyone in the audience had turned to show me their deranged smiles.

Eliza whispered into Ernst's ear.

"Oh, dear." He fiddled with the flexible neck of his microphone. "Now she reminds me what I forgot to do before coming down. David, you're taking over FlavAmerica!" The audience found this greatly amusing, but as Ernst spoke between them and me, I felt a weakness in my legs that dropped me back down to my seat. "They were playing that damn war again on the TV. I meant to tell you before we came down for drinks. They should call it the Hitler Channel. Every time I turn it on, those damned Soviets are moving through the streets to get me. I'm no Nazi, mind you. I've never been anything more than a flavorist. But can you imagine working under Stalin? The man was a non-taster. Wouldn't know sweet from sour if you scraped it across his tongue."

Eliza half stood from her chair and said something few could hear. Again, Ernst waved her down, saying, "I know, I know, I'm rambling."

"The Gorilla of Vanilla!" Koba yelled, but this time no one joined in.

"I wasn't about to be spirited away to the Kremlin," Ernst said. "That's all I mean to tell you. There's a reason I'm standing here today." He shook his head, silent for a moment, then seemed to regain his senses when he spotted something on the table below him. "Is that chocolate pudding?" The waiters had started moving through with dessert.

"I may not have learned much in my life, but I do know you never talk over dessert." He lifted one hand above his shoulder. *"Also sprach Zarathustra."*

And with that, he turned from the podium to a spontaneous burst of applause and a few loud whistles. At my table, this show of appreciation quickly turned toward me. Koba clapped like a victorious footballer facing the crowd after a match. "Bravo," he said. "Bravo, David. I'm so happy for you."

Beekley cackled with delight. "You're just another made man in New Jersey now!"

Only Tennessee was less than effusive. Showing a renewed interest in his steak—he was trying to cut a sliver of meat away from a thick vein of fat—he nodded and shook his head before setting his utensils down and offering me the smile of a stroke victim. "What can I say? You're the best man for the job. I'm very happy for you."

It was a parody of congratulations, and for good reason, too. I was no Fulbrighter. I wasn't the man the International Federation of Essential Oils and Trades would soon recognize with its third-ever Distinguished Service Medal. I was a has-been flavorist, a man who was capable of paying the bills on time and little else.

"I can't explain it," I said with a nervous chuckle.

"What's to explain?" And then Tennessee gave me a big smile that was more sure of itself. "Our happiness on this earth is like one of the phantom flavors I build into every one of my butterscotches. It has but one purpose: to deliver a cruel aftertaste that makes you desire more of what you no longer have."

I was still puzzling over his meaning when his hand shot into the air and he snapped his fingers. "Waiter! Double Old Grand-Dad!" His eyes found mine. "Anything for you, David? Make it a round for the table," he shouted. "We need to celebrate."

I didn't want to be rude, so when the drinks came, I lifted mine to my lips and sat at the ready as he gave a brief toast he'd learned from a family of Russian-Israeli Jews while living in Tel Aviv. *"Za vas!"* My stomach closed around the shot like a fist. I stood from my chair, knocking it over behind me.

Koba put his glass down, having taken only a sip. "Everything all right, David?" I looked at his dessert—chocolate pudding topped with a curl of ketchup and a sprig of parsley—and turned for the door, reaching for my stomach. The carpet was a dizzying pattern of geometric shapes, chosen for its ability to hide stains. I tucked my chin into my chest and turned out toward the men's room—but it couldn't wait. I fell to a knee as the back of my throat opened, and then I was crouching there on the floor like a wild animal, panting over a slick of orange vomit.

As I recovered my breathing, I wiped my forehead with the back of my tie and looked up to see a man in a red coat and a black bow tie pushing a room service cart toward me. With a small flourish, he removed a metal cover from one of his plates and set it down on top of my mess. *Voila!* He smiled like a magician who's just made the Statue of Liberty disappear.

I stood, apologizing and reaching for my wallet, but he wouldn't hear of accepting a tip, so I gave him something more valuable still: the truth. "I don't deserve this," I said.

His smile began to falter.

I hurried into the bathroom, propelled by a return of my gag reflex. To be silent all these years, to only now tell my family and be rewarded for this—I tried to vomit into the sink, but I managed only a sick-sounding cough that sent a man out of a bathroom stall, still buttoning his fly. As he left, I turned on the water and rinsed my mouth, wondering if maybe I was wrong—maybe I did deserve this or shouldn't think of the question of merit at all. Because had I deserved what I'd received in Animal Testing? Or on that day in Texas when my parents had lost their lives? I splashed my face and rubbed water round to the back of my neck. Maybe this was simply how the Wheel of Fortune spun. You were pinned to it at birth and sent rolling away into your life. There was no profit to be had in trying to line up where you were with what you had done. You got dunked in the waters when you should be lifted up high, then raised toward the sun when your every action said you should be hidden in a low, dark place.

Someone came in whistling then, so I turned the water on and splashed my face a second time. It was an older gentleman in a navy blue double-breasted suit who had perfectly groomed silver hair. He addressed me while turning to the urinals.

"Congratulations, you little devil."

"Pardon?"

"I said, 'Congratulations, you loyal fellow.'"

I made a show of drying my face and fixing the knot of my tie. "Oh, thank you. Who are you with?"

"Better Health and Flavorings. I'm one of the suits, mind you. Not a creative."

"Didn't think there'd be anything of interest to you here."

"Came to talk with Ernst. Sent him a letter earlier this week. Maybe you read it?" He flushed and dipped his knees while zipping up. "It must have been good to flee the madhouse."

"What?"

"I said, 'It must've been good to see him stay in-house.'"

He joined me at the sinks to wash his hands.

"Ernst has always done the right thing," I said.

"You don't know it."

"What do you mean?"

He shut the water off and flicked his hands dry. "I said, 'Don't you know it.' Are you all right? You look a little peaked."

"I'm fine. Thank you."

"We should talk. I'd like to present you our best offer."

He gave me his card, then leaned into the mirror and pulled his lips back to look for food between his teeth.

"That's my direct line," he said, gesturing to the card. "When you're ready, give me a call, and I promise: next time" — with a glance he took in our surroundings — "I'll take you somewhere fancier, buy you a proper lunch. How's that sound?" He gave me a slap on the shoulder, then started for the door. "Again, you have my heartfelt congratulations."

Or at least that's what I told myself he must have said, because it was either that or "my heartfelt strangulations."

* * *

When I reemerged from the bathroom, the doors to the banquet hall were open and everyone was streaming out toward the bar. I wanted to retreat to my hotel room, but I was like a piece of flotsam caught up in the current. "David! Let's get a drink. We'll celebrate the good news!" I felt like a politician, glad-handing my way through the crowd with a frozen smile, and laughing at jokes whose punchlines didn't merit much more than a chuckle. ("Why did the tofu cross the road? Because nobody wanted him!")

I ordered Ernst and Eliza a round of schnapps, and listened with averted eyes as Koba toasted me as if he owed me his life. But as the drinking continued and the crowd thinned out, it seemed only those intent on misery-making remained. Tennessee pulled me close in a bear hug and slapped me hard on the back before leaving. "Why do the slippers fit you?" he said. "Five years' seniority I've got on you, the respect of my peers, and still whenever Ernst deigns to invite me over for breakfast, I've got to squeeze my feet into slippers that fit you and not me."

When he had left, there was only one person sitting on my side of the bar, the outgoing Society president. He downed the last of the red wine in his glass, then came over to shake my hand and say we should have lunch. "There's a lot we need to talk about."

I told him I looked forward to the opportunity, but it was one of those lies we all so easily tell. After he too had gone, I stared down into my glass of diluted scotch, imagining myself as the captain of a great seagoing vessel, a man in command of one of those massive tankers that transport oil or a fleet of new cars. My cargo was something else, though, the future of an industry that I now found so questionable: flavored effluent. Enough to feed the whole world.

I set my drink down and looked to the other side of the bar as a man stood from a stool, tilting back his head to empty his bottle of beer. It was then that I recognized him, a man I hadn't seen in twenty years, but a face I'd never forget.

"Hickey?" I said.

He turned away from me while setting his empty bottle on the bar, showing no sign that he'd heard me. I started round toward him, calling for him again. "Charles Hithenbottom!" He walked with an uneven gait, but as I dropped my head down to one side to look for the play of his pants against a prosthetic limb, I hit my forehead against a bistro table and fell to one knee. When I looked up, holding the side of my head, a black woman in a tight-fitting sparkly blue dress stood over me. "Are you all right, sugar?"

"Fine, yes." I stood, but did so uncertainly enough for her to point me to a love seat by the fireplace.

"Maybe you'd better sit down."

As she walked me over there, I looked round her for Hickey, but saw him nowhere. Had I only imagined it?

"Are you here with your wife?" she asked.

The question was as sobering as a whiff of smelling salts. "I'm fine, thank you," I said, and the steeliness of my voice must have convinced her to go.

I sank into the love seat, looking down at the low table that stood before me. On it rested an ashtray, a red bulb candle, and a white porcelain sweetener caddy, with the sugar organized neatly on one side and the sweetener on the other. A row of pink bars ran along the tops of the packets of Sweetness #9, and looking at them, I couldn't help but think about how far I'd come. *Look at me now, Ma! Top of the world!*

I know what happened next, but not when: I fell asleep, and then was awoken by a security guard who shook my shoulder and asked if I had a room.

I stood, apologizing, and sent my hands into my trousers. When I pulled them out, I held a key card in one hand and a packet of Sweetness #9 in the other. My possession of the former convinced the security guard to leave, while the sight of the latter kept me rooted in place like a tree. How had it gotten there? My eye twitched, my shoulders jumped—I reacted as if I had been splattered with paint. My anxieties were no less vivid and incomplete. Instinctively, my mind called up an image from earlier that day—the leader of Better Health and Flavorings pulling back his lips to look for food in between his teeth—and then I heard a sound, a hard knocking sound like that of a pirate walking on a wooden leg, and I spun round looking for Hickey.

But no, it was the security guard chatting with the man who worked at the front desk. He had his baton out and was tapping it down against the counter, emphasizing some point he was trying to make.

Laughter came from the elevators, where a young couple stood waiting for the doors to open, their bodies intertwined. I looked down at the table in front of the love seat, seeing again the porcelain holder with all of the sweetener on one side. Had I grabbed a packet myself? And then blacked out? I'd never done so before, but I'd had more than enough to drink. I told myself that must be it. And so when I stepped into the elevator a few moments later and pushed the button for the ninth floor, I was smiling as I watched the numbers light up over the door. Everything was fine; there was nothing to fear. It had only been my anxiety talking, and knowing that — that the threat was self-made — was as calming and therapeutic as any drug.

The doors opened with a *ding,* and then I reached into my pocket for my key card and moved out into the hall, already thinking nothing of this, just as I would continue to do until November, when I'd receive a second packet of Sweetness #9 and all of my thinking would change.

PART FIVE

SEVEN DAYS IN NOVEMBER

November 1998

Day 1: Friday

IT WAS WAITING FOR ME on my desk when I turned in to my office from the flavor development studio. A plain white envelope. No stamp or postmark, no return or mailing address.

I sat down in my chair and pulled at the beaded brass chain of my shaded green desk lamp, then held the envelope up to the light. The silhouette of a small rectangular object appeared. I tore the envelope in half and dumped its contents onto my desk.

Just as I suspected: a single packet of Sweetness #9.

It shouldn't have had the power to shock. I'd seen these packets in restaurants and alongside the free coffee in the lobby of every hotel—even in my own kitchen cupboards. Still, I looked down at it as if I were a young boy again, attempting telekinesis for the first time.

The packet gave off a warm pink glow from inside, meaning it had either been harbored in these United States for at least four long years or been sent to me from Mexico, where the granules of The Nine were still bathed in a bright pink dye during production.

I sprang from my chair and popped my head out of my office.

"Where'd this come from?" I said. "This envelope you left for me?"

Eliza sat at the front desk, working on the computer. She offered me a cool reptilian stare over the rims of her bifocals, then said she'd found it beneath the mail slot when she'd come in.

"I wasn't about to touch it, either," she said. "I worked for the Post Office when the Unabomber was still doing his thing. Did you open it already?"

I nodded.

"Then consider it a good day. You live."

As she returned to her typing, I went back to my desk, closing the door behind me. It was as if an accelerant had been released into my bloodstream, quickening my thoughts. Had the Albanians found me, perhaps because Priscilla had ordered the report using her name? Or were Mexicans to blame? Why else the pink granules? I blew into the mouth of the torn envelope, first the one half, then the other, thinking there must be a note inside, something making threats against my person or demands upon my bank account, maybe a map describing where and when to meet. But no, empty, so I turned in my chair to face the window, remembering now that night of the Society meeting. Hickey! Why after all these years had I seen Hickey—and then awoken a short time later with a packet of sweetener in my pocket?

I pulled open my pencil drawer; the orange bottle of lorazepam rolled toward me. I grabbed it and closed the drawer, then slid it open it again and felt around until I'd found something else: the trial pack of anti-anxiety medication.

Dr. White had said it would make me feel more anxious the first seven days I used it, and that, along with the belief that I didn't have a problem requiring daily medication, had been enough to keep me away from it until now. But (and if every unhappy person is different, their story of obsession is somehow the same) I didn't want to feel like this anymore. I was always pushing down at the top of my skull or pawing at the side of my neck, conscious of the beating of my carotid artery. Some mornings I stood over the toilet studying the shape, consistency, and color of my stool as if it were a work of modern art; other days, I'd have Betty take Polaroids of all my most suspicious moles so we could compare them with those she'd taken three, five, or ten years ago. I saw death, disease, and degeneration in everything that I faced, and I thought so much about what I should've done and couldn't do that the immediacy of the present all but disappeared.

Dr. White was right. We all could use a little help every now and then. So I pushed the first pill through its foil backing and laid it on my tongue, telling myself not to think of the anxiety that might swell and surge over the coming seven days. It was like being in a burning building. You had to throw yourself through a wall of fire to escape. And besides, I thought, as that pill dissolved like a Communion wafer on my tongue, what better time to do this than now? In seven days, at the end of my most anxious period, I'd sit down to a plump Thanksgiving turkey, thankful for my new, worry-free life.

I had gained no new responsibilities as a result of my promotion, but I had been given a new title (Chief Creative Flavorist, Director of Flavor Development, and Chief Financial Officer) and a few additional perks, the foremost of which was an increased ownership stake in the company. I suspect Beekley and Tennessee wouldn't have agreed on which of these was the least deserved, but one thing is certain: they had responded to the transfer of power about as well as the Romanovs had responded to the transition to Communism.

Tennessee was more reserved in my company these days, though also more voluble in the men's room. I learned this one morning while he was chatting away at the urinals and didn't realize I was behind the door of the second stall. Beekley, on the other hand, never said a word against me in public, preferring to wage a more covert form of warfare.

Shortly after swallowing my first anti-anxiety pill, I went into the break room and found him and Koba bargaining over a tube of summer sausage that had arrived in a gift basket delivered by Federal Express. I was so focused on their conversation ("Would I lie to you, Koba? Americans consider the summer sausage far more valuable than chocolate") that it was only as I reached for the kettle that I realized what Beekley had done.

"Oh dear god," I said. "Your hair, what on earth did you do to your hair?"

He'd shaved it down to the skull in a fashion he described as a "fade" and said was very popular in the late-eighties hip hop community.

"Do you like it?" Before I could answer, he'd turned back to Koba to give him a new homework assignment. "Listen to Kid 'n Play and Kris Kross, then interview no less than five people of color about hair, reversed blue jeans, and the placement of the other in white culture."

Koba was taking this down in a tiny notebook he carried with him every day in his breast pocket. "Did you say reversible blue jeans?"

"Reversed," Beekley said. "As in worn backwards."

For a moment, Koba looked no less stupefied than I did. "I don't understand," he said.

"Of course you don't," Beekley answered. "That's why you need to do your homework."

"Is this because of the new dress code?" I asked him.

I had announced it a couple of days earlier, saying in a memo that all hair should "be trimmed and neat, suggesting one word above all: Business." Beekley, though, as only a small child or an egotist could, had taken this all too literally. He'd had his barber etch a variant of that word into the side of his skull: *Bidness*.

"It's one thing after another with you, isn't it?" I said.

"I'm sure I don't know what you mean."

"Just as you didn't know you were parking in the Kraut's old space this morning?"

"Oh, I'm sorry, David, I didn't realize that type of thing meant so much to you. Perhaps you could send out another one of your memos. How does that new color-coding system work? Is it orange that's below red in terms of urgency, or is that yellow?"

"I believe yellow requires a response," Koba said, before seeing my expression and returning his notebook to his breast pocket. "I think I'll just take my summer sausage and go."

When he had turned out into the hallway, I filled the kettle and put it to a boil, telling Beekley if this was a game of chicken, I wasn't the one who'd be driving off the cliff. "You're only hurting yourself, you know. Or tell me: You think you'll ever go on a third date looking like that?"

It wasn't just his hair that made me say this. Today he wore burnt-red polyester pants, a seasick green button-up dress shirt whose collars stuck out over the shoulders of his unbuttoned lab coat, and a mustard-yellow tie so wide it could have doubled as an apron.

"A Mormon missionary wouldn't wear that tie," I said, swatting at the thing. "A teenaged boy from Provo, Utah, would rather sin before the Angel Moroni than walk the streets of Mongolia looking like that."

"'All flavorists and food scientists,'" he said, quoting from the dress code, "'should wear business casual clothing, with women's outfits not too revealing and men expected to wear ties.'"

"You've read the words, but you don't understand a thing."

He snatched a card out of the gift basket then, saying there was one thing he did know. He cleared his throat and read: "'As our new line of children's medicine debuts in the marketplace, I wanted to send your team this small token of our appreciation. By the way, our test panels were especially enthusiastic about the wild cherry! I'm so glad we stuck it out until finding the right one.'"

Beekley handed me the card. "'With gratitude,'" he finished, "'your Corporate Overlord, etcetera, etcetera, P.S. Do give Beekley a raise.'"

Eliza popped her head in then, saying I had "a Mrs. Goldfarb" on three.

I didn't recognize the name, so I asked her to take a message. But Eliza said she'd already tried to do that and been told it was important. "She's the vice principal of your son's school."

I marched into my office and grabbed the receiver while punching the flashing button marked *Line 3*. "David Leveraux," I said.

Mrs. Goldfarb got right to it. After acknowledging how valuable my time must be and saying she'd try not to waste it, she told me she was only calling because "it seems your son has stopped using verbs. Were you aware of this?"

I sat stiffly in my chair, as if a sniper had me in his sights. "Yes. Yes, I was," I said. "May I ask how you found out?"

"We administer routine testing to ensure our students are being properly served. Now"—I imagined her flipping through a folder at her desk—"your son did quite well on the written portion of his exam, but his scores on the oral portion..."

I stood. "Did you say 'oral'?"

"...were not exactly up to standards."

"Of course not. He doesn't use verbs."

"Yes, we're aware of that now, but it's not what *causes* the score that's important, it's what we can do to bring it up to the state-mandated level."

She spoke in a steady, precise manner, as if being deposed by the legal offices of Jackson, Dean, and Hershowitz.

"It's the student we must look out for, you understand, and so to ensure that he receives the help he needs, we've reassigned him to a classroom for students with language-based learning difficulties."

"Pardon?"

"A letter saying the same will go out in the mail today, but I thought it important that I call you and let you know."

I had walked as far as the phone's cord would allow. "Do you mean to say he's in ESL?"

She laughed. "Oh, we don't call it that anymore. It's English for Speakers of *Other* Languages."

"Other languages?" I imagined a room in the basement with low overhanging pipes, condensation on the walls, and Jeremiah sitting in the back row, holding a thick pencil in one hand and drooling freely. "But Ernest doesn't — *you don't think he's a foreigner, do you?*"

She seemed amused by the question. "We don't investigate the immigration status of our students, Mr. Leveraux."

"Well, maybe you should! He's an American! Born in Battle Station!"

Her voice tightened. "I think you should know, your son has become something of a distraction. Just last week he was humming during an exam. He got up and started pacing."

"Was this an essay test?"

"I'm sorry?"

I sank down in my chair, still holding the card from the gift basket, I realized. "Perhaps he was composing his thoughts," I said. "Ambulation — it's well known to aid the writing process."

She spoke as if not having heard me. "We believe your son would be best served if he were placed on Ritalin."

"What?" I flung the card across the room. "You think you're going to put him on drugs? Have you talked to our doctor about this?"

"We have our own specialists."

"As did Hitler, but that's no reason —"

"Mr. Leveraux!"

" — to put my child on Ritalin!"

"I lost many relatives to the Holocaust!"

"And my father was a member of the 4032nd Mobile Baking Division! He stormed the beaches of Normandy and passed out the first loaves of bread at Buchenwald!"

Our emotions got away from us. We had to settle down with some heavy breathing and a few conciliatory remarks. As we recovered, I opened my desk drawer and reached for the bottle of lorazepam, telling Mrs. Goldfarb as I unscrewed its cap that we'd spent the last several weeks visiting many, many specialists.

"Our son's fine," I said. "His brain checks out fine, his vocal cords aren't tangled or damaged, he's not allergic to the eight most common food allergens" — I popped the pill into my mouth and dry-swallowed it — "and his chromosomes and genetic material show not the first sign of a known abnormality. He's just a quiet, verbless boy, that's all."

"I'm very glad to hear that, Mr. Leveraux, but the fact remains that Ernest does exhibit 'stimming.' The humming and walking in class, I mean. It's very common among children with Attention Deficit Disorder."

"ADD? My son and I sat through an entire James Bond marathon this summer, and you're going to tell me he has ADD?"

"The situation requires our attention."

"The boy can play the same computer game for seventy-two hours."

"And Ritalin has been proven to be quite effective — "

"Mrs. Goldfarb."

"*Golden*farb."

"Everything's proven! That's the last thing you learn as a scientist and the first thing they teach you in business school. 'Don't worry, we'll prove it.'"

"Ernest fidgets. He won't look his teacher in the eye."

"We can't all be salesmen."

"He mumbles."

"As did Gould, Glenn Gould. The man wouldn't even stop for a recording session."

"Are you suggesting your son sit at a piano instead of a desk?"

"Are you telling me music is no longer part of the public school curriculum?"

"Mr. Leveraux, if you don't like the idea of Ritalin, there are plenty of other drugs we can try."

"Not with my son."

"Wellbutrin. Effexor."

"You'll see I'm quite firm on this matter."

"Dextrostat. Desipramine."

"You're wasting your breath, Mrs. Goldenfarb."

"Or Prozac," she said. "Because I should warn you, if he persists in his behavior—and *you* persist in yours—this could be considered a matter of parental neglect."

"Neglect?" I stood so quickly my chair flew out behind me. "Are you threatening me?"

"I am merely making a recommendation."

"And why are we having this conversation on the phone? Shouldn't we be speaking in person? What are you, afraid of confrontation?"

"This conversation is over, Mr. Leveraux."

"I should go before the school board and say *you* need a pill!"

But I was already talking to a dial tone.

Betty and I descended on the school that same afternoon to demand that our son be returned to his proper classroom. We spoke of lawsuits and bad publicity, of friendships with state senators (a lie) and forthcoming letters to the editor in the local, regional, and national papers (true). But it wasn't as simple as escorting Ernest out through one door and in through another, as Mrs. Goldenfarb herself told us. Our son had already been reclassified in databases available to the district, county, and state.

"We can't just hit a few buttons on the keyboard and make it all go away," she said.

"And why is that?" I asked her. "Because you've already hit a few buttons on the keyboard and made it all happen?"

She smiled firmly, sitting back in her chair. "There's a protocol to follow. So unless your son retakes the test and passes, we'll just have to let it play out."

*　*　*

As Betty drove us home (she had met me at FlavAmerica and gone with me to the school from there, saying we could carpool the next day), she suggested we just go ahead and do it.

"Medicate him?" I said. "But why?"

"It could be *aphasia voluntaria*."

Before our insurance carrier had sent us its first letter denying the dubious and explaining its policy on the experimental, we had met with a specialist who had said just that.

"You think he's faking it?"

"It's not that he's not talking on purpose; it's that something's holding him back." These too had been the doctor's exact words. "It could be Social Anxiety Disorder."

"And it could be demonic possession, but that's no reason for us to rush out to one of Aspirina's old *botánicas* and a buy a black candle and a smudge stick of sage."

Betty gave me a steady, unblinking look, then turned off the highway toward home.

"What is Social Anxiety Disorder anyway?" I said. "A few years ago none of us had heard of it, and now we're not even allowed to doubt its legitimacy? You watch. Here, soon they'll be warning us about Social Adaptability Disorder. 'Do you enjoy speaking in public? Do you make friends quickly when you move to a new town or place of work? You may have Social Adaptability Disorder.'"

"David, our son is in ESL. We have to do something."

"How about military school?"

"You can't be serious?" She saw that I was. "Well, why don't we just beat the verbs out of him? Have you thought of that? It'd save us some money."

As she turned onto our street, I told her he could probably use a little discipline. "I'm starting to think I've been lax as a father."

Betty shook her head, then told me that she'd gone online after getting my call and done a little research. "And apparently there's this girl in Wyoming who didn't speak at all until the second grade. Then they gave her liquid Prozac and now she's talking a mile a minute."

"Well maybe we shouldn't be putting words into her mouth," I said.

"Are we going to guarantee her a job on one of these cable news channels?"

"What's gotten into you? You used to be perfectly sensible. You could even say morbidly sensible."

"Morbidly sensible?"

"But now you're no different from Priscilla, afraid of progress and new ideas. Why don't we at least try it? He's in ESL, David!"

She hit the button on the clicker and drove the car into the garage, in beneath the tennis ball hanging from a string.

"It's English for speakers of *other* languages," I said.

She didn't answer; just sat there listening to the hot oil dripping into the collecting pan beneath us.

I took a deep breath, then told her that I too had gone online and done a little research. "And do you know what I learned? The pharmaceutical industry spends eight billion dollars per year on gifts to American physicians. That's eight *billion* with a 'b,' Betty. And we're not just talking pens and coffee mugs and memo pads either. They're shelling out for trips to ski resorts and Honolulu. Honolulu, Betty! And yet still you don't think Big Pharma exerts an undue influence over our lives?"

"Big Pharma?" She got out of the car and moved in through the utility room. "Since when do you call it Big Pharma?"

"I'm not saying this medicine doesn't do what they say. I'm only saying maybe they're giving it out too freely. It's as much crowd control as it is therapy."

"And so you're sure there's nothing wrong with our son? And what if you're wrong?"

"Betty. Betty, listen." We were moving up the stairs to the second floor, speaking in strained whispers. "The adolescent brain is very plastic." These had been the words of a more optimistic specialist. "If one part can't do its job, another will adapt to pick up the slack. So if Ernest really is suffering from some condition we haven't yet uncovered, we probably just have to give him time to heal."

She chuckled as she moved into the walk-in closet to change. "And to think it's you who's saying this!"

"What?"

"A plastic brain? That's a biological Communism! 'Do what you can, take what you need.'" She took off her blouse. "And this from the man who campaigned for Nixon?"

"Patience, that's all I'm saying. Just have a little patience."

"And that's it? That's the full extent of your plan?" She stepped into her tracksuit. "Because if it is, can you tell me one thing? Just one thing. When does patience turn into doing nothing at all?"

I didn't answer her, not even after she'd said it again.

"When, David? Tell me."

When she saw that I wouldn't speak, she moved out past me and went into the great room, from which I soon heard the militant cries of Cher's personal trainer: "Jab, kick, knee punch! Body blow, body blow, body blow!"

Dinner that evening had the feeling of an intervention. It began normally enough, with our complimenting Priscilla on the pasta she'd cooked, but soon thereafter we'd exhausted this small talk and were looking round the table like poker players trying to intuit the bluff. Finally I set my knife down and wiped my mouth with my napkin and looked directly at our son, telling him that we needed to have a talk.

"Your mother and I are very worried," I said. "We all are," I added, taking in Priscilla with a look. "Obviously you know you've been assigned to a new classroom."

He nodded. "Me and Jeremiah."

"Is that right? Yes, well, what you may not understand is that the school is asking us to start giving you some medicine."

"Like Jeremiah," he said.

"Yes, like Jeremiah. But the thing is, while he may need it, I'm not sure you do."

"It's poison," Priscilla said, before her mother could shush her.

"It's certainly nothing to mess around with," I agreed. "So if by chance you've been faking it all this time, the not using verbs, I mean, I need you to tell me now so we can tell the school, and you can go back to your old classroom. Do you understand?"

He nodded. I took in a slow breath.

"So what do you have to say, Ernest? There is something you'd like to tell me, isn't there?"

He stared down at his mound of spaghetti so long I thought he might have forgotten the question. Everyone looked at him, and then me, and then him. Then at last Ernest looked up and shrugged, and he said to me, he said, "Salt." Just like that, just the one word. "Salt."

I picked up my fork and twirled some pasta on it, then just as quickly set the fork down and reached for my napkin. "*What* salt?" I said.

The shaker was nearest my plate. Ernest sat across from me, looking between me and it.

"*That* salt?" he said.

"*What what* salt?" I said.

He looked to his mother. She looked no less nervously to me.

"*What what* salt?" I repeated.

"Please?"

"*What what salt?*"

He tried parroting me. "What what salt?"

I threw my napkin onto my plate. "*Pass* the salt!" I stood from the table. "Pass it! I know you can say it! Now c'mon! Pass the salt! It's not that hard!"

When I realized everyone was looking at me and not him, I knew I'd gone too far. "I'm sorry," I said. I started for the stairs. "I'm sorry."

Betty came into our room a few minutes later and sat down beside me on the foot of the bed.

"It's been a stressful day," she said.

She didn't know the half of it, though, so I told her about what I'd received in the mail that morning and showed her a piece of paper I'd scribbled on minutes after opening that anonymous envelope.

"Is this an enemies list?" she said.

I hadn't titled the page, but I understood how she could make that interpretation.

"You've got Priscilla listed here."

"At number five," I said in my defense. "I was trying to be exhaustive.

And you have to admit, she is something of a fundamentalist when it comes to food."

Beekley was at number four, if not because I feared he'd been turned by his knowledge of one of the conspiracies of the post–Cold War age, then because he'd brought a shotgun to work.

"And Hickey?" Betty said. "The man from Animal Testing?"

At number three, right behind the Albanians. "I thought I saw him that night of the Society meeting," I told her. "I drank too much and fell asleep in the lobby—"

"David!"

"—we were fighting, I wasn't at my best. Anyway, when I woke up, I had a packet of Sweetness #9 in my pocket."

I could no more explain its meaning than I could provide a reason for placing "Mexicans" at the top of my list, above even the Albanians.

"I suppose it's wrong to think it must be one or more Mexican nationals," I said. "It occurs to me now that it could be someone who bought the packet off eBay. You know, to emphasize my connection to Sweetness #9's early days. But for the time being"—I shrugged—"we'll just leave it at that: Mexicans."

Betty gave the list back to me, sighing loudly.

"Should we tell the kids?" I asked.

"*What?* No! Why?"

"Transparency."

"And what would you say? That you got a vaguely menacing letter in the mail this morning? That you're not sure what'll happen next, but if a man with a wooden leg isn't involved, it could be a rogue Albanian or a group of radical Mexicans?"

I nodded. "You're right. Not presidential."

She reached for my leg, then, and gave it a little rub. "Are you feeling okay? Because you've looked a little jumpy today."

I realized only then that I hadn't told her about the anti-anxiety medication I'd begun that morning.

"When did you get a prescription for that?" she said.

"I should schedule a daily press briefing," I told her. "Dr. White gave it to me, but I didn't think to say anything before now because I didn't think I'd ever use it. Anyway, apparently the first seven days you're on it, you can feel increased anxiety."

"Well, maybe you shouldn't be taking it right now. Do you really think this is the best time?"

"It's always going to be something, isn't it? And besides"—I fished an orange medicine bottle out of my pants pocket—"I've got the lorazepam to even me out. Took another one just a few minutes ago, in fact. I feel great."

Betty couldn't help but smile.

"What?" I said.

"Nothing."

"No, what is it?" I said.

"It's just you don't want Ernest to take anything, and yet you seem to have a full pharmacy at your disposal."

I suppose I could have answered her by speaking of Sweetness #9 and my experiences with it. If The Nine had been deemed safe for public consumption, after all, what did it matter if the medicine they wanted to give our son had also been approved for use? But none of that came to me in the moment. My answer was far simpler, even reflexive. "We always want better for our kids," I said. "Don't we?"

Now, I can't help but wonder what might have happened if I had answered differently and agreed that the Ritalin or Prozac was something we should try. It wouldn't have made the medicine any better or worse for our son, but it would have brought Betty and me together. It would have been a decision we'd both made as parents, placing the burden of its consequences between us, not only with her. But I'm getting ahead of myself here. For now, let it be enough to know that it's yet another moment I wish I had back.

Even after everything I'd taken that day, I couldn't sleep, so when the microwave beeped a little after midnight—just once, someone there to open it before it could make another sound—I popped up from bed and went downstairs, thinking I'd need to tell Ernest to get off the computer and remind him it was a school night.

The hallway was thick with the smell of cooked meat, but its trail

260

didn't end at my son's bedroom door—it carried me on to Priscilla's. The floor creaked beneath me as I stepped up to it. I heard a thump from inside, and then racing footsteps.

"What are you doing?" I said, pushing into her room.

She stood alone at the window, struggling to open it while holding a plate in one hand. On it was a half-eaten microwaveable hamburger.

Priscilla returned slowly to her bed and set the plate down on top of her green comforter.

"I couldn't help myself," she said. "My cravings, they're so strong."

I sat down beside her, telling her not to worry about it. "It's been a hard day. We all deserve a little treat."

She looked up then, her eyes already moist. "You won't tell Sarin, will you?"

She took in a jagged breath. "She's been a vegetarian her whole life."

"Let her be her and you be you."

She reached for her burger and began to cry, saying she wanted Sarin to like her.

"Just be yourself." Parenthood, it seems, is advising others to do what you can't do yourself. "You can't go through life living a lie, trying to please others."

She took a bite of her burger, considering this; and maybe by some law of probability I had finally said the right thing, because it was then, while chewing thoughtfully, that she told me, "I'm in love with her, Dad. I love Sarin."

I'd never suspected it, not even for a moment, but as soon as I heard those words it made perfect sense. *Be mine!* the little candy heart had said.

"Do you hate me now?" she asked. She was dressed in a pair of grey sweatpants and that black hooded sweatshirt she never went without.

"Why would I hate you?" If anything, I felt as if I'd won the lottery, because it was only here, now, that I knew I wasn't the type of parent to throw his child's baby book into the trash. I'd never imagined this scenario before, but once I was in the midst of it, I knew it as clearly as I knew my own name: I only wanted her to be happy.

"You need to tell her," I said. "Because do you know what the other option is? Winding up like me. Sitting on a lie half your life. Will you listen? I know. It'll eat you up and spit you out and you won't even recognize yourself in the end."

Priscilla's chest jumped to take in a sudden gulp of air. She unhinged her jaw and widened her eyes to hold back another hot rush of tears.

"So you won't tell her? About the hamburger, I mean?"

"Your secret's safe with me," I said. "I'll even tell you one of my own. Just don't tell your mother. Even she's never heard this."

Priscilla waited patiently, all eyes.

"It's about your great-great-great-grandfather. In his later years, he traveled the eastern seaboard putting on puppet shows denouncing God and the free market."

"Stop!"

"Now you know why your mother doesn't know. If this got out, her reputation at the Chamber of Commerce would be ruined. He was a union man," I said, "an agitator in the coal mines of Pennsylvania when he wasn't much older than you are now."

"Maybe he had red hair, too."

"I wouldn't doubt it, I wouldn't doubt it. Anyway, this is the story my grandfather told me. He said they had been using dynamite to open up the shafts to get the coal out, but their methods were needlessly careless, costing a handful of workers their lives. Your great-great-great-grandfather wanted to change all that, and so he stole a stick of dynamite and used it to request better wages and improved working conditions."

My face grew serious. I gestured with a stiff finger. "No one was hurt. He staged his protest after hours, and only the executive offices were targeted. He simply wanted to make a point: so long as our workplace is dangerous, yours will be too."

Priscilla was smiling.

"This was a company town—nothing there but its workers, its store, its housing development—and so when the dynamite went off, everyone spilled out of their beds and onto their front porches to see what had happened. There was a full moon that night—much was made of this in the opposition press—but still no one saw anyone walking away from the mine on the single road that ran from it through town. The company was sure it had to be your great-great-great-grandfather. He'd always been the squeaky wheel, and he didn't pipe down much afterward, either. But no one would speak against him in court. I'm sure they were threatened with the loss of their livelihood, probably offered money and promotions, but no one would speak against him when they were called in for questioning."

We both smiled.

"He probably stopped to shake hands. Probably kissed babies and stepped inside for a slice of pie. That was your great-great-great-grandfather Jürgen."

We sat there for a long time, considering this man we only knew through a story. Then we stood and walked together to the door, where Priscilla did something I'll never forget. She gave me a hug and squeezed me a second time as if she wouldn't ever let go. This is the moment where I wish my story could end, right there in her hold. But we had to break away, and I had to tell her what may have been the biggest whopper of all.

"Everything will be fine," I said. "Do you hear? Everything will be just fine."

Day 2: Saturday

WHEN I WOKE UP the following morning, it was as if my anxiety was waiting for me at the foot of my bed, holding my slippers. *Had another packet of Sweetness #9 been delivered to the office?* No matter how many times I tried to push away the question, it kept rushing back, making it impossible for me to concentrate on anything else. I forgot to put water in the coffee machine before turning it on, then corrected this mistake only to realize I hadn't filled the cone with any grounds. For breakfast I had an egg that seemed somehow naked; when I finished, I remembered the bread I'd left in the toaster.

Near ten, I told Betty I was going to run to the office and see about some paperwork. She didn't mind. She'd felt slighted to learn about Priscilla from me. ("Apparently, a mother doesn't know," she'd said.) So she made plans to spend the day with our daughter, cooking bread and making barbecue tempeh.

When I got to the office, it was just as I'd feared—another plain white business envelope lying beneath the brass slot of the front door. Hearing music, loud and with a sharp percussive beat, I took it into the back, where I found Koba and Beekley. They'd pushed the sofa away from the soda machine and placed a large piece of cardboard on the floor. Beekley was spinning on top of it, his legs awhirl above him.

"David!" Koba was dressed in casual clothing: a pair of khakis and a long-sleeve Madras shirt. "Look at what I can do!" He began moving his limbs stiffly, popping and locking his torso and arms into place, a wave of motion moving out from one wrist to the other. "It's called The Robot. Isn't it wonderful? I'm doing The Robot!"

Beekley jumped to his feet and pushed a button on his boom box to silence it. "Something wrong?" he said. "Your eye is twitching."

I handed him the envelope, telling him it was the second one I'd received in as many days.

He shook its contents, then held it up to the light. "Is this a packet of Sweetness #9?"

I nodded, telling him my first job out of college was at Goldstein, Olivetti, and Dark. "In Animal Testing," I said.

"That's so old school. As is this." He looked more closely at the contents of the envelope, remarking on its color. "Is this Mexican Nine? Why would someone send you a packet of Mexican Sweetness #9?"

I saw no reason to withhold this information anymore. "I conducted a chronic toxicity test on it prior to its bid for FDA approval."

He handed the envelope back to me. "I guess you know where all the dead bodies are buried, then, don't you?"

"Why would you say that, Beekley?"

He just gave me a look.

"What are you?" I said. "A member of the Sweetness #9 Action Network? One of the Widows of Sugar Hill?"

"The Widows of Sugar Hill? David, I'm a life-long bachelor, you know that."

"What do you expect me to think, Beekley?" I pointed at the face of the envelope. "It's blank, meaning it was hand-delivered. It's here, you're here. The only way it could more obviously be your work is if you called me up to whisper, 'It's coming from inside the house.'"

"*When a Stranger Calls*," Beekley said with an appreciative smile.

Koba looked between us, confused.

"The movie," Beekley explained.

"Is that the one with Dustin Hoffman? About divorce?"

"It's about a babysitter who receives threatening phone calls from a crazed killer," I said, still looking directly at Beekley. "The police trace the calls to inside the same house."

"Oh my. That's terrifying," Koba said.

Beekley nodded, suddenly very excited. "The horror genre in many ways defined life in the nineteen seventies. You have to understand:

after Vietnam and Watergate, we were a country horrified by what we had become, so we washed ourselves in the blood of *The Texas Chainsaw Massacre* and *Halloween* and *Friday the 13th,* needing to feel the catharsis of these on-screen atrocities before we could be reborn into the feel-good movies of the Reagan Years. *Porky's, Weird Science, Stripes.* Have you seen *Weird Science*? Write that down. If you rent five movies for five nights, it's only five bucks."

I stood there like a ghost, my voice barely a whisper. "So did you? You have to tell me, Beekley. Are you behind this?"

He only then remembered the envelope in my hand. "What? No! You think someone's stalking you because of what you know or did? That maybe this is the prelude to extortion or violence?"

It was so terrifying to hear these thoughts coming from outside my own head. I nodded.

Beekley went into the fridge for a canister of pressurized orange cheese and spoke while sending bursts of it into his mouth. "You ask me, it could be the work of the GLF."

"The GLF?"

"The Gastrophilic Liberation Front," he said, before his voice became more nasal. "Le Front de Libération Gastrophilic. They're slow-fooders based out of Quebec, active since nineteen eighty-seven, and most recently linked to attacks on food production facilities in two provinces and three states. Vicious group, absolutely brutal. I've even heard chatter online that suggests they're assembling a children's martyrs' brigade."

"You've got to be joking."

"Joking? Do you also want to tell me the organic food movement doesn't have a paramilitary wing? Who's the one being naïve here, David?" He squirted more cheese into his mouth. "You could be one of a dozen or more flavorists getting these packets of sweetener in the mail. The Nine doesn't have the best reputation, you know. I've got friends who rate it just a cut above Agent Orange." He pointed to the front of the building. "Dreadlocked men could burst through these doors at any minute, holding semi-automatic weapons they've cleaned with organic vegetable oil."

He rattled on like some excitable professor, speaking of abortion doctors stalked by pro-lifers and animal research facilities that had been ransacked by masked activists. He knew of a nuclear physicist who'd been blinded by battery acid, and a scientist with the CDC whose work with measles, mumps, and rubella vaccines had so enraged the mothers of autistic children that the government had offered him the use of a new name.

"And you think this could be something like that?"

He squirted more cheese into his mouth, nodding.

I wanted to take a knee. "So what should I do? Call the postmaster general?"

"Please. A man who deals in lost mail?"

"What, then?"

He put the cheese back into the fridge, telling me it wasn't too late for us to buy a gun safe. He pointed to the space beside the soda machine. "There's plenty of room."

Koba smiled hopefully. "I'm sure it's probably nothing."

Then Beekley reached into a drawer and came over to me with a Ziploc bag. "You better put that in here," he said. "You don't want to tamper with the evidence any more than you already have."

I took the side streets home, wanting to remain in motion, my destination forever deferred. Then as I was driving through South Battle Station I saw two large words—SECURITY CAMERAS—painted in red on the side of a white windowless building, and I made a U-turn and parked alongside the door.

A tired-eyed man stood at the front counter, scratching at his side. He wore faded blue jeans and a black T-shirt that didn't quite cover all of his belly. Slump-shouldered, and with thinning hair and a two-day beard, he'd probably looked forty-three since he was seventeen.

"How can I help you?" he said, with breath that would've announced his presence to a blind man.

"I'm a local business owner," I told him, this story springing from me fully formed, "and in the last week I've become the target of vandals. Graffiti and the like. The worst vulgarities."

"Kids," he said. "They got no moral compass anymore."

"That's right. But I thought if I had a camera fixed to the side of my building"—already he was nodding—"I'd scare them away or at least be able to take some hard evidence to the police."

The man held up a finger, then stepped over to a neighboring display unit and slid open its back panel and reached inside for a box.

"This is The Eagle Eye." He set it down between us. The cover of the box had a photo of a sleek CCTV camera on it. "Top of the line, unrivaled functionality, tamper proof. It'll pan, tilt, zoom, give you night vision technology, you name it. If I were Saddam Hussein, this is the one I'd buy."

"And the cost?"

"Seventeen forty-nine."

"Seventeen dollars?"

"Seventeen hundred."

A moment, then, "Do you have anything else?"

The next one he showed me came in a larger box.

"This is The Hawk," he said. "She'll give you six hundred lines of resolution at distances of up to two hundred feet, one hundred at night. Tamper proof; you don't worry about the wind and the rain. I sell a lot of these."

"It looks bulky."

"Bulk scares the bad guys."

I told him I might have misspoken. "I'm more interested in catching someone in the act."

"I like your style." He stepped away again, then returned with a third box, on the cover of which was a picture of a halved orb made of darkened glass. "This is The Invisible Eyeball."

"That's quite a name."

"It's quite a system. Sleek, doesn't mar the sight lines. You just pop her up there on the wall and people think it's a motion-sensitive light. It's a bargain at three hundred bucks."

"Does that include installation?"

"Installation is extra. As is a power source and recording equipment."

"I've got a spare VCR. Would that be sufficient?"

"Only if you want to replace the tape every six hours. This one here"—he walked me over to a neighboring display unit, where a massive black VCR-like machine sat on the top shelf—"this is the T1-60. You can slide a tape in there, go to the Bahamas for forty days, have a mai tai, look at the pretty girls, then come back and you don't miss a thing. That'll get you nine hundred hours of full-day real-time results on a single cassette. I wouldn't even try to sell you anything else."

"Okay," I said. "Out the door, ready to go, just press play, what does it cost to get this all in today?"

"Today? A rush job will run you more. As will a weekend install."

"By nightfall," I said. "Today."

He looked at me as if trying to guess the number that was five dollars below as high as I was willing to go. He must have read me right, too, because a few seconds later we were shaking hands and he was telling me I wouldn't regret it.

Later that afternoon my cell phone rang while I lay on the couch in the great room, watching a college football game. The screen of my little Nokia flashed *Unknown Caller*. I muted the television and answered it.

"David!" the voice on the other end said. "Joseph Willingham!"

I answered with silence.

"Of Better Health and Flavorings?" he went on. "We spoke the night of the Society meeting. In the bathroom?"

"Oh yes!" I was excited, if only to learn it wasn't a Mexican or an Albanian.

"Hope you don't mind my calling on a Saturday, but I'm off to Shanghai tomorrow and I wanted to see if I could have a word with you before I left. Is this a bad time?"

"No, no." I walked out of the great room and turned in to my bedroom. "I'm just curious how you got this number."

"The Society roster," he said. I'd been obligated to provide my contact information when I'd served as the chair of the Bylaws Committee. "Hope you don't mind my not being shy about using it?"

I walked into the closet and shut the door behind me, then reached into the pocket of the jacket I'd worn that morning for the Ziploc bag that Beekley had given me. It held that day's envelope inside it, still un-opened. "It's just funny timing, I suppose."

"I'm sorry, I couldn't hear that. You're breaking up."

I moved out toward the window. "Is this better?"

"There you go, yes. Well here's the thing. I sensed from our initial conversation that you weren't too excited about selling FlavAmerica. But I've been in this game long enough to know everything is subject to change, so I thought I'd call and see how life in upper management is treating you. Do you enjoy having the buck stop on your desk?"

Our neighbor was doing tai chi again. I turned away from him to-ward the door when I heard Betty coming in, wearing her tracksuit from the gym.

Mr. Willingham laughed, mistaking my silence for something it was not. "A tough negotiator, I like that. Never say more than you need to. Well, listen, as a goodwill gesture, let me open up to you a little bit. I think FlavAmerica's got something very special there in NoNilla®, and with China opening up, a company could make a fortune if it posi-tioned itself right. It's a very tricky market over there, though. Entirely based on who you know and, let's be honest, how much you'll pay. We're almost set up in Beijing now, and we could use a good man to be our Director of East Asian Affairs. How'd you like me to tee that up for you? A little exotica in late middle age? Hmm? Do a man some good, I'd think. Provide more than a little money, too. Well, I've said enough. But if any of this interests you, you contact my secretary and have her set up a time for us to sit down and push some numbers back and forth. Sound good? Or you still not ready to change your mind?"

I'm not sure I said more than five words between hello and good-bye. But as Betty stepped out of the walk-in closet, dressed now in her house clothes, it became clear to me what they were doing. "Those bastards!" I said. It was a negotiating tactic!

Betty followed me down to the computer in the study, hearing me whisper of the day's events. By the time I'd told her about the security system I'd purchased for FlavAmerica, she was standing at my back and watching as I moved my cursor to the search bar on our Yahoo home page. *Charles Hithenbottom,* I typed, and sure enough, there he was, referenced in an article in the *Journal of the American Association of Laboratory Animal Science.* "Testing and Efficacy Analyst at Better Health and Flavorings," it read. "Jupiter Park, New Jersey."

"Just as I suspected." I leaned back in my chair, smiling like a detective at the conclusion of a case. "Don't you see? The Cosa Nostra or the KGB would come at you with all the power of the fist and the boot, but Better Health and Flavorings—they're more sophisticated than that. They want to intimidate me without my even realizing that's what they're doing. First Hickey plants that packet in my pocket at the Society meeting, and now I get another in the mail just before this Willingham character calls. It's obvious, isn't it?"

Betty stood there, looking down at the Ziploc bag in her hand.

"They think if they scare me, I'll open up and be more willing to make a deal."

"Maybe we should go to the police," Betty said.

I shook my head, reaching for the phone book. "No crime's been done yet, unless you consider this tampering with the mail. And what's the postmaster general going to do? Nothing. Here we are." I'd flipped open to the white pages and found Hickey's address listed alongside his telephone number. I wrote it down on the face of an envelope, affixed a US flag stamp to it, then led the way into the kitchen.

"What are you doing?" Betty said.

I reached into the cupboard for the box of Sweetness #9. "Two can play at this game," I said. I sealed the packet of sweetener inside the envelope, gave it a lick to seal it, then wrote across its back: *You can stop now. We're onto you. And it's not working.*

Priscilla came in from the garage then, holding a big black Glad bag. As I stuck the envelope into my back pocket, she reached between us for the box of Sweetness #9 and dropped it into her garbage bag.

"What are you doing?"

Just as quickly, she moved on to the refrigerator.

"Cleaning up," she said. She grabbed a squeeze bottle of barbecue sauce, glanced at its list of ingredients, then dropped it into her bag and reached for the sweet and sour.

"That's still half-full," Betty said.

Priscilla worked in silence now, grabbing tubs of yogurt and jars of jam, bottles of salad dressing and tubes of crescent rolls. When she moved on to the freezer, grabbing first the tri-colored popsicles and then all of our frozen entrées, Betty asked the question again:

"What are you doing?"

Priscilla closed the freezer and gave a firm look while passing between us to the rear of the house. "Someone has to be the parent," she said.

We followed. "What are you talking about?"

"I'm not going to let him do it anymore. Have anything with Red Dye No. 40 or Sweetness #9."

Betty and I looked at each other as our daughter turned in to the bathroom.

"You can ground me," she said, "you can lock me in my room, but if you do, the historical record will show that you first had to rip this bag out of my hands."

Maybe it was imagining her failings that did it, or the threat of what I'd received in the mail these last two days, I don't know, but without another word Betty moved away from me and joined our daughter in the bathroom. And what could I do then? A family is nothing if not a grand coalition, an entity that cannot survive if fractious.

"Here, let me hold the bag," I said.

And so I stood there as they reached for the expired decongestants and a medley of flavored cough syrups, stood there pointing out the vitamins modeled on the characters of a Stone Age cartoon and the soaps and shampoos that were every color of the rainbow. It didn't matter if I believed this would help or not; it felt good to be doing something, to be united in action. So we continued into the bathroom upstairs, then doubled back down through the pantry and out to the stand-alone freezer in the garage. By then our bag was bulging, and we were sated like cavemen after the kill.

"I still can't believe the crescent rolls have red dye in them," Betty said, holding the twist-to-open cylinder up before her eyes so she could read its list of ingredients.

I didn't need to repeat myself: I'd already told her that Yellow No. 5 was combined with the red food coloring to give the cooked dough a golden, just-from-the-oven appearance.

"And the Sweetness #9 holds it all together," Priscilla said.

"Get the lid," I told her.

She held the garbage can open, and then I emptied the bag into it and we stood for a moment over the detritus of our sweet and colorful past.

When we returned indoors, Ernest was sitting at the kitchen table, drinking a bloodied orange juice. He wouldn't look at us. Instead, he reached for the little bottle of red food coloring that sat on the table beside him, then added another couple of drops into his glass.

I nodded to Betty and Priscilla, asking for a moment alone. Then, when it was just me and my son, I sat down across from him and placed my hands on the table where he could see them.

"Ernest," I said. "You understand why we're doing this, don't you?"

And that puckered look he gave me—so intense, somehow already soured to the world—it was the same one I'd seen when I first held him in my arms at the hospital and knew in a rush of love and sadness that he was my son. Ernest, I'd call him. I knew the only name I could give him was Ernest.

Day 3: Sunday

There had been a time when having breakfast with my mentor was the highlight of my week. We'd sit and read the trades or discuss the merits of the latest Flexible Package Achievement Award winner, or sometimes chat with a visiting scholar or chemist passing through town. My mentor's row house was like a celebrated salon. Hours would pass without my realizing it as we broke down the scent or flavor of some beloved brand like Old Spice or Coca-Cola, both of which are built on the same strong pillars of lemon, orange, cinnamon, ginger, and vanilla. I never felt like anything less than a captain of industry in his company, a man who'd risen high enough to tell the world when his day would begin and end.

But since I had been promoted to Chief Flavorist, our visits had changed. I kept wanting to check my watch when I was with him, and I only refrained from doing so because his generosity made me feel so ashamed. The first Thursday after that Society meeting, Ernst told me just what my promotion entailed, but he didn't speak extemporaneously; he consulted a series of index cards, his entire morning's conversation seemingly rehearsed and scripted. When he finished with one topic, he moved one card to the end of the pack and read from the next. The following week I sent Tennessee over in my place, both in an effort to placate my colleague (though I think this visit only reminded him of the heights he had not attained) and because I'd had to take my son at the last minute to a specialist in Manhattan to see about his verblessness. So many more doctor's appointments followed in the coming weeks that I went a month without seeing Ernst. Then when I did return to his table, I only did so in the company of Koba or Beekley or Tennessee, because I found it so difficult to sit there alone with him anymore and think of how diminished he now seemed.

Owing to this, I reacted with equal parts shame and fear when I got a text from Eliza that Sunday telling me that Ernst would like to have me over for lunch. I was so certain that he had taken notice of my absenteeism that I rehearsed an apology on the drive over.

When I got there and heard no response to my knock, I reached for the spare key above the lamp and stepped inside calling out for Ernst and then Eliza.

My mentor emerged from the kitchen, but almost as soon as I saw him I averted my eyes and moved toward the bench in the hall, busying myself with my coat and my shoes.

"Sorry I've been such a stranger," I said. "There's just been so much going on with the family, and then everything at work."

He stood there tight with fear, as if not recognizing me. He was bare-footed as well, and dressed in pajama bottoms and a plain white T-shirt.

"Aren't you cold?" I said. "At least put your house shoes on. Winter's here."

He did as I instructed, then followed me into the kitchen, where I saw the sink was once again filthy. A tower of dishes rose from it, with nubs of bread and coffee grounds floating in the stagnant water trapped on each level.

"You should hire someone if Eliza insists on keeping house like this."

"Eliza," he said.

I turned round, as if expecting to see her come in from the hall, then noticed that nothing had been prepared. I crossed to the oven and asked if he'd like me to cook. "How's pizza sound?" I turned on the oven, then found a ready-made shell and a packet of shredded cheese in the fridge, along with a can of olives and a jar of sauce in the cabinet. Ernst sat and watched as I spooned the marinara into place and sprinkled the cheese over it, and then I handed him the can of olives, asking if he'd like to split the bottle of Dunkle Weisse I'd seen in the fridge.

He grunted his assent, so I went for the bottle and an opener, and as I reached into the cupboards for two glasses, I noticed what he was doing at the table—putting all of the olives in one place. He'd piled them as high as my fist.

"Ernst." An acrid odor turned me round from him to the oven. Tendrils of black smoke rushed up from its door. "My god!" I pulled it open, sending a rush of smoke to the ceiling and causing the fire alarm to sound. I grabbed a pair of metal tongs and reached inside for the offending item, then flung it down into the sink. It landed with a hiss. I turned the water on over it. A few scraps of burnt wool, some charred leather buttons, a curled elbow patch. His sweater.

"Why would you put your sweater in the oven?" I said, and he looked at me with no less confusion than I showed him.

"I was cold," he said.

The alarm continued to bleat.

"Oh, Ernst."

"I was cold."

I didn't pack a suitcase for him. I thought I'd only need to drop him at Eliza's condo. But when I got there, I found a letter waiting for us, taped to the door and addressed to me.

You don't know what it's like, she wrote. *He lives in the past more than the present, and while that may have been fine when he'd at least reminisce about our good times in the sixties, now it's like he doesn't even know me anymore, like I haven't even been born yet. This morning he told me about his "one true love," some Magda he knew during the war. "I'll never feel like that again," he said. He couldn't understand why I was crying.*

She worried I'd turn her into a villain, and as if to overcome this she mentioned that she didn't plan to keep the condo. She only wanted to know that I wouldn't come searching for her. *I was away twenty-five years,* she wrote, *and now I'm supposed to be his caretaker? We've been together less than five years across five decades; we don't have enough memories in the bank for that. And I've already done this once before, with Luther*—her first husband. *It's your turn now. Your turn to learn more than you ever wanted to know.*

*   *   *

The first time Beekley showed me his orange van, he spoke of it like a blue-blood gushing over a cherished yacht. I didn't understand it. "Men in vans don't marry," I'd told him. "They have their photographs stapled to telephone poles." This morning, though, I was glad to be able to call on it. With it, Beekley collected all of the many things from my mentor's home that I thought might make Ernst feel more comfortable with me at home: a suitcase full of clothes, his favorite armchair, the cuckoo clock, a handful of framed photographs, and some familiar dishes and food from his kitchen, including a box of Sweetness #9 that Koba had grabbed from the cupboard.

Betty knew all that Ernst had done for me, so she didn't protest when she got home and saw him camped out in his armchair in the living room. No, rather than question why I hadn't at least consulted her, she called her brother Peter, who had no obligations in New Hampshire other than those imposed upon him by his sponsor (go to meetings, be of service).

"He'll fly down tomorrow," she said, after we had gotten Ernst to bed in the study once occupied by Aspirina.

An hour or two later, after we had gone up to our room and gotten in beneath the covers, she said something else. "What do you think Eliza meant when she wrote 'Now it's your turn to learn more than you ever wanted to know'?"

We sat side-by-side in the bed, up against the headboard, the remote down in the valley of the covers between us. I wasn't sure what to say, but hearing in Betty's voice the same thing that I had felt when I'd first read those words, I thought it only right to offer. "Would you like a lorazepam?" I said.

Day 4: Monday

There are those amongst you who will say that the health of one individual is not connected to the health of his country. I wish nothing more than to agree with you, but after my "illness," as I spoke of it in court, I have come to accept that while the healthy may be able to disregard the state of the nation, the infirm have no such luxury. The American Condition is real, I am saying. It can trigger in you a response as wild as any new regime of medication. For this reason, I must ask for your patience while I introduce one last movement into this seven-day symphony, if only because in the end it plays such an important part.

I first became aware of it on Monday morning, while driving in to work. The news station on the radio said an explosion had gone off at a Save-a-Lot supermarket in Ewing Township. Not a big one, but powerful enough that a woman was badly burned and blinded in one eye when she opened the fogged doors on the frozen food aisle and reached inside for a box of blueberry waffles. I didn't think anything more of this until an hour or so later, when I came out of my office to find Beekley going into the supply closet for the old Zenith television set that we only hauled out for that rare natural disaster or moment of geopolitical import.

"Is it Clinton?" I quickened my pace down the hall. "Did they finally come for Clinton?"

Beekley turned in to the break room, trailing the cord. When I got in there after him, Koba was already down on his hands and knees, plugging the set into the outlet behind the emergency Y2K pantry, which by now was half filled with everyone's least favorite canned goods. When

Koba stood, slapping his hands clean, Beekley reached for the rabbit ears and began working at them like a dowser searching for water.

"There!" I threw my hand out as the image of a supermarket rolled into place.

Beekley stepped away from the set as if from a house of cards. A young Asian-American woman stood in the foreground of the store, backed by a line of yellow police tape. She spoke in that voice newscasters reserve for airplanes that have fallen out of the sky.

"On the heels of attacks this morning in Ewing Township and Poughkeepsie — "

"What happened in Poughkeepsie?"

" — violence came to the Acme supermarket in Doylestown a little after nine a.m."

"Was it another explosion?"

"This time the explosive device rang out on not one aisle but three, each evenly spaced throughout the store."

Panic ensued, the reporter said. With Thanksgiving shoppers clogging the aisles, the strong trampled the weak, the young pushed aside the old, and the uncoordinated and sickly threw themselves over the glut of shopping carts that had piled up at the front doors.

"Forget your worst day at Costco," Beekley said, as the camera panned live across the scene. "This is a modern-day Gettysburg."

In the parking lot, men and women, both young and old, were sitting on overturned shopping carts and the bumpers of fire trucks; some lay with their heads in the laps of strangers as they were treated for broken arms, fainting spells, and minor cardiac events; others stood alone like stoics, staring off into a future they couldn't comprehend or didn't wish to join. Seventeen people in all had been injured, four seriously.

The reporter pointed to a boxy red truck that had *Bomb Squad* emblazoned on its side in large reflective print. "At the moment," she said, "a robot the size of a riding lawnmower is moving up and down the aisles inside, looking for any evidence of additional danger. The robot has four cameras attached to it, including one at the end of an extendable arm that can rise to a height of ten feet. Only when it's determined that it's safe will officers from the Bomb Squad" — again she glanced at the truck—"move in. But even after they do, many people here in Bucks County, if not the entire tri-state area, may think twice the next time they do their shopping. Reporting live for WKLA News in Doylestown, Pennsylvania, this is Sandra Wu."

I called Betty that day to see if she'd like to have lunch at the English pub on the ground floor of her building. It was a time to be with friends and family, those you loved. But she was in a small town on the out-skirts of Amish Country, speaking with the mayor about the prospects of her company's proposed consulting contract. Hearing she wouldn't be back for another couple of hours, I drove home to watch the news in the living room.

Priscilla hadn't gone to school that morning so she could care for Ernst. She sat alongside me on the sofa, the television tuned to one of the news channels. The FBI, the ATF, and a special investigator from the FDA had gotten involved. Tips were coming in by the hundreds to a 1-800 number that had been flashing across the screen for the better part of the morning. As I ate a roast beef sandwich over a plate I bal-anced on my knees, a former mercenary who'd been a part of armed conflicts in seven countries on four continents described the type of "small-scale explosive device" that might have been used at each of the attacks and how the person or persons involved might have ac-quired the necessary materials and expertise. His words washed over us like a Latin mass. Nitrogen, organic peroxide. Heat, friction, shock. Very unstable. Detonated by cell phone or timer, maybe packed in dry ice.

"You'd be surprised," he said. "These types of explosives may be initi-ated by a complex chemical reaction, but you can find instructions for them online. It doesn't take a very smart man. I could leave right now and have a box of Cheerios blowing up in your hands by early evening."

News of another school-yard shooting would have run off me like water down a duck's back, but this was something else. We weren't talking about the open market of Gdansk or Kharkov, where butchers hacked into the joints of freshly killed beasts, and a pig's head hung for sale on a swaying metal hook. This was the American supermarket, a brightly lit place that took double coupons. Who could bring violence to a place like that? And why?

On the drive in to the airport that afternoon, I hit one of the preset buttons on my radio and heard two familiar voices.

"There's this religious nut out there saying this is God's punishment for our cultural degradation."

"Gays, Mark. He says it's because we're not roasting gays on the spit. At least that seemed to be the gist of it."

"That's right, Bonnie. But you know what? It's not God who's angry, it's our bodies. Poison in, poison out. It's that simple, America. These attacks are just the fall-out of a food system run amok."

"You know what everyone needs to do, Mark?"

"What's that, Bonnie?"

"Plant a victory garden. Take back control of your food."

"Get a little dirt under your fingernails, America. It won't hurt you, but not doing it will."

After picking up Peter at the curb, I flipped over to a station that looked at the day's events through an economic lens. Here, a man whose smooth voice brought to mind cuff links and silk ties told us that stock prices had fallen for all the major supermarket chains, while commodities such as wheat, sugar, and corn had also taken a hit. He sighed dramatically, as if he'd lost tens of thousands of dollars since breakfast. "I hate to say this," he said. "but I don't think it's going to get any better. I think these prices are only going to continue to fall. This is supposed to be the busiest week of the year in America's supermarkets, but when people go home tonight, I think they'll be looking into their fridges and freezers and wondering if they can make do without a trip to the store."

Betty was doing just that when I got back from the airport with her brother. As the garage door lifted and I drove the Volvo inside, my headlights caught her in front of the stand-alone freezer, holding the lid open. From the way she was staring down into it, you would have thought she was at a funeral, standing over an open casket.

"I can't believe this was full just two days ago," she said as we stepped out of the car.

On the drive down, I had told Peter about our purge of Sweetness #9 and Red Dye No. 40.

"I hope you like your steak with a little freezer burn," I said, as Betty hugged her brother. "I'm not sure we have much else."

"We'll be fine," Peter said. Like many alcoholics on the mend, he looked for happiness in the mere absence of all the many private horrors he had once known. "It'll give us an opportunity to realize how grateful we should be. In many parts of the world, kids live on a spoonful of rice cooked in dirty water each day."

"Well, it's not as bad as that around here just yet," Betty said.

"In fact," I told him, carrying his bag indoors, "I think we still have a jar of wasabi mayonnaise in the fridge."

After Betty had made a bed for Peter on the sofa in the great room, she closed the door behind her in our bedroom and went into the dresser for a Ziploc bag.

"It was on the kitchen table when I came in," she said. "There with the rest of the day's mail."

The Ziploc bag held a plain white envelope, still sealed, with a packet of Sweetness #9 inside. This much was obvious when I pinched the shadowy center and felt the granular texture.

"It's not the one from work?" I asked.

I had reached for the remote earlier and turned on the television. Betty had me hold the envelope up to the light of the screen. Its contents weren't pink; that much was certain. The light shined through the packet, clear and true.

I handed the envelope back to her, and as I did, I saw the banner on the bottom of the TV screen: AMERICA'S SUPERMARKETS UNDER ATTACK.

"I think we should get a security system installed outside," I said.

Day 5: Tuesday

Early the next morning, a high school baseball coach lost two fingers while reaching for a box of energy bars at a Foodtown supermarket in Toms River.

Fear spread quickly, as if from word of an Indian attack.

After the news went out on the television, college students and inner-city kids, as well as drug addicts and the hopelessly unemployed, began gathering outside supermarkets throughout the region. Mostly young to middle-aged, and almost entirely male, these people promised to take your shopping list into the store and bring your groceries out to your car for a price. Such entrepreneurs, trading on their risk and daring, charged wildly different fees, based on the number of goods you required and their or your level of desperation. Some profited from their suburban good looks, a commodity many shoppers were quick to seek out after the news stations gave a lot of play to one story of a woman who said she'd given a young black man $150 and a shopping list, never to see either again.

What could you do? There was nowhere else to turn. There had been a run on the nine-dollar-per-gallon milk sold at every 7-Eleven and gas station mini-mart between Maryland and Boston, and though there were reports of some people driving as far away as West Virginia or Ohio to do their Thanksgiving shopping, there were just as many stories about price gouging and people left without a choice because they didn't own a car. Fearing they might lose business to the restaurant trade, several enterprising supermarkets announced new delivery services that would ensure people could continue the "essential tradition" of a home-cooked Thanksgiving meal without fear. But when

283

someone shot out the front tire of one of these delivery vans, causing it to spin out of control and its driver to suffer massive injuries, courtesy clerks were no longer so eager to leave the store and get behind the wheel.

I had a call scheduled with a salesman in the field late that morning, but we barely spoke of his new contacts or our hopes of extending our reach in the Pacific Northwest. He had the television playing in the background of his Boise hotel room as he spoke of expecting something bigger and bolder, something still more spectacular to come. He lived out west, far from the danger; he could allow his mind to imagine a hundred bodies piled up in the aisles of an Acme, the shoppers victims of a poison gas attack and sealed doors; he could tell me of the thousands who could be poisoned by eating apples or pears injected with potassium cyanide or strychnine at a single compromised distribution center in California's Central Valley.

"It's a wonder it hasn't happened before," he said. "It's a wonder anyone goes to the store at all."

After an explosion in Jupiter Park killed a man early that afternoon (remarkably, the first fatality since this spree began), I turned in to the break room and found Beekley standing before a large map of the United States that he'd pinned to the wall.

"Can you feel it?" he said. "I can feel it in the roots of my teeth."

As he turned to me, I saw he'd been to the barber. His fade and the words carved into it were gone, replaced by a more severe and uniform hairstyle, one that gave him a militant look, the haircut of a sharpshooter or a sniper. That wasn't all: he was wearing a black arm-band over his lab coat, one that flashed out before me as he stepped closer to the map and crossed his arms against his chest.

"Violence is like a virus, and I think right now we're seeing it jump carriers from the schools to the supermarkets."

He'd pushed pins, each with a bulbous red head, through those cities on the map that had already been targeted: Doylestown, Levittown, and Ewing Township to the west and southwest, Toms River and Jupiter

Park out on the coast, and then Paterson and Poughkeepsie to the north. It was only once my eyes had strayed across the state line into New York that I noticed the other pin way out west.

"Moses Lake, Washington?" The cable channels hadn't said anything about it.

"A shooting in July," Beekley said. "Two nuns were gunned down in an Albertson's. The diet soda aisle, just like Poughkeepsie."

"How'd you hear about that?"

"I'm a professional, David. It's my job to know."

As he took out a black Sharpie and started drawing lines between the affected cities, my eyes strayed to our old Zenith, where the news was showing the senior yearbook portrait (late seventies, ruffled shirt and baby blue tux) of the Hispanic man who'd been fatally injured in Jupiter Park. He was a thirty-eight-year-old bachelor who'd recently been laid off from his job at the mall selling funny T-shirts; homeless off and on for much of his life, this one-time navy cook had found himself working as a "mercenary shopper" at the Pathmark on Jupiter Park's east side. His luck ended on his fifth or sixth trip of the day, when he went into the grocery store on behalf of a diabetic and reached for a sugar-free frozen dessert. He pulled it out close to his belly, the chief of police said at a news conference. "His spleen ruptured, and he died in emergency surgery." The chief then ceded the podium to the diabetic man who'd hired the victim, an elderly fellow who wore red suspenders and stood with the help of a walker. He wept openly, urging the public not to employ professional shoppers. "I'll never forgive myself," he said. "I'll never be able to look at food in the same way again."

Beekley had connected several of the cities on the map with a circle; now he drew a triangle that connected all the others, ending at the point of Moses Lake out west.

"What does it mean?" I said.

He stepped back, cocking his head to one side as he studied the geometric patterns on the map. "Just give me time, David. Every crime wants to sing for you. You only need to put it up on stage and wait."

I told him to take as much time as he needed.

*   *   *

That evening, trying to be a good host, I cooked Ernst and Peter the best meal I could cobble together: the last of the spaghetti, meat sauce from a jar that had gone moldy underneath its cap, and a bit of limp white onion I'd found wrapped in a paper towel in the crisper drawer. Betty finished a tub cottage of cheese over which she'd sprinkled a handful of mandarin oranges she'd found in a rusty can. While she prayed against botulism, our son, relishing the opportunity to reacquaint himself with the taste of frozen food, laid claim to a small frozen pizza I'd brought back from his namesake's freezer. He was so excited, he put it into the oven without knocking off the ice crystals that had gathered along its top. Then, because it had been removed from its packaging long ago and was therefore a mystery, he watched through the oven door as the ice melted, calling out his wishes as a craps player might call out the numbers he desired. "Canadian bacon and pineapple. Hawaiian pizza. Hawaiian." Finally, florets of broccoli appeared against a floor of orange, white, and blue cheese, and the smell became unmistakable.

"Gorgonzola," I said, as I pulled it out.

"Gross. Absolutely gross."

Priscilla dined on toasted white bread with a thin wasabi mayonnaise spread, and ate a side of edamame beans that had been seasoned with rock salt and toasted in a pan. When I told her this sounded quite delicious, she said the mayo didn't taste off but was past its "Best By" date and therefore difficult to enjoy, while the beans were too soft after sitting in the back of the fridge uneaten for more than a week.

At some point we turned on the TV and learned that what had been a rumor in the late afternoon was now a confirmed fact: a boy no older than Ernest had been arrested in Rockaway after he'd reached into his backpack and attempted to transfer a box of ramen to a grocery store shelf, only to have the jerry-rigged contraption detonate in his hands. One of the talking heads on cable was quick to label this a copy-cat attack. The explosive he'd used was barely stronger than a firecracker, and besides, he didn't even have a driver's license, so how could he have targeted so many supermarkets in so many different cities and states? Another commentator wasn't so sure. He said a group of children might be responsible for these attacks, teenagers communicating via the Internet. "There could be an army of them out there," he said. "Decentralized, asynchronous, irregular — a threat unlike any we've known since the Viet Cong."

When my mentor reached for the remote and clicked over to *World War II in Color,* no one argued. We'd all had enough.

"What are we going to do about Thanksgiving?" Priscilla said. It was two days away, and with the many hours required to thaw a frozen bird, and the difficulty of finding one that was fresh, we were running out of time to get a turkey.

Betty wondered why a vegan would be worried about any of this, but Priscilla, without looking at me, spoke of giving herself a "special dispensation to eat meat," calling it a "cultural rite" and tradition. "Besides, there's still sweet potatoes and stuffing to think about," she said.

"And pie," said Ernest, looking up from the last of his gorgonzola pizza.

"That's right," Priscilla said. "We need a pie. How can we have Thanksgiving without a pumpkin pie?"

"Let's just have a little patience," I said. "Let the police do their thing, question this boy, see what's really going on."

"Your father's right. They might crack this case tonight, and then tomorrow evening we can go shopping without any fear."

By bedtime, the cable channels were replaying the same footage over and over again, showing the boy's parents in Rockaway running from their modest house to their pick-up truck, off to see their son in custody. The man covered his face with his denim jacket, the mother with her Le Sac purse. But the woman made a mistake. Just before stepping up and into the truck, she lowered her purse and glanced back at the camera crews set up on the street. It was all the news channels needed. They froze on that image and blew it up until it was pixelated and fuzzy, like some disputed snapshot of Bigfoot.

In bed, I clicked away from CNN to Fox, where a famous evangelical was saying the child's involvement wasn't a surprise. "We've got kids being raised up by microwave ovens and big-screen TVs, and still you think we're living in The City on a Hill?" He shared the split screen with a short-haired woman who vigorously shook her head each time he smiled. "I wouldn't be surprised if there were an army of children behind these bombings, all of them protesting the meals their working mothers are feeding them. We need to get back to good, old-fashioned family values again."

Betty groaned as she reached to her lap for the control dial of the FaceLift Mask™ she was wearing. She'd bought the device from one of the shopping channels, and though she'd come to accept that it didn't make her look any younger, she liked how the short electrical impulses felt while they clenched and unclenched the muscles in her cheeks. I'd tried it once myself, in private. She was right; it did feel good.

"Of course," she said. "A bad mother storyline. It's always a bad mother storyline. 'If only she'd been waiting for him at home with a glass of milk and a plate of warm cookies...'"

I flipped over to MSNBC, where a correspondent in Rockaway was demonstrating the type of store-supplied reacher now in wide use across the tri-state area. It had a thirty-inch aluminum arm that ended in a pincher controlled by a four-finger grip. The newsman used it to grab a box of Stove Top Stuffing that had been set out on a table before him.

"You'd think he was handling plutonium," I said.

Betty's thoughts were somewhere else, though. "You don't think E could do something like this, do you?"

I hit the mute button and looked at her. "Ernest? No. God, Betty. Why?"

"What if he's suicidal? You don't think he's suicidal, do you?"

I hit the power button and set the remote down. "Because he doesn't use any verbs?"

"How could we know?" She looked like the Phantom of the Opera. "He says one word for every hundred we hear from Priscilla."

"But suicide. How could you even say it?"

"Good parents talk, don't they? I thought good parents talk."

I looked to the black screen, not sure what to say. She was right. How could we know? We'd only learn the truth after the fact. Suicides are at least kind in that regard. If murderers are like modernists, writers of dense impenetrable prose, their incomprehensible screeds and manifestos jumping off of rolls of dried vellum and continuing at a slant across the walls, then suicides are minimalists, their sentences plain and unadorned, like the final memos of frustrated bureaucrats. *We need to simplify the tax code...limit the power of the credit-reporting agencies...teach people that true love requires true love.*

"I talked to Dr. White this afternoon," Betty said. "The prescription's ready for us in the system. I just have to go to the pharmacy and get it filled."

I sat up a little higher in bed. "You did this without talking to me?"

"I'm telling you now."

"But for what, Betty? A prescription for what?"

"For what he needs, David. It's obvious he needs something."

"I just think we should be very careful. This isn't a new breakfast cereal we're talking about, you know. It's a mind-altering drug, a drug that has but one purpose, to *alter* our son's mind. And yet you're perfectly willing to throw the dice?"

"Throw the dice? I'm not saying let's dose our son with brown acid and blow smoke in his face. These are federally regulated drugs we're talking about."

A sound escaped me: *Hooo!* "Federally regulated? And who do you think sets these regulations? The same people who're regulated by them."

"Clearly your medication is making you anxious."

She turned out the light and rolled away from me.

"Just tell me this," I said. "Did you talk to Dr. White before or after learning about this boy in Rockaway?"

"Good night, David."

"Is it a kind of self-defense, this medicine?"

"Go to sleep."

"What if this boy in Rockaway's on the same thing? Have you considered that? Maybe it's causing him to act this way, not helping him.

Maybe we're all just clamoring for these drugs because the commercials are so convincing they can't help but boost sales by twenty-four percent."

Betty sprang up, throwing her pillow down across my chest. "Will you stop it? You're so sure of yourself, aren't you? But what about this? What if something truly is wrong with him? What if we can't know? Doesn't a scientist—and that's what you are, right?—doesn't a scientist believe in the process of trial and error, the scientific method? What happened to that? Can you tell me what happened to that?"

She fell away from me, not bothering to take her pillow. I looked down my nose at it, unable to move.

"All right," I said. "All right. But can we at least get through the Thanksgiving weekend?" I had an awful picture in my mind of everyone sitting at the dining room table. There was the turkey and the stuffing, the cranberry sauce and the brussels sprouts, and then beside everyone's plate, in line with the silver and the cloth napkins, a pill or two, each a different shape and color, corresponding with the diner's psychotropic needs. "Can we at least do that and talk about this afterwards?" I said.

Day 6: Wednesday

When I came home that afternoon after working a half day, I found a man standing on a ladder in front of my garage, installing an Invisible Eyeball up over the door (this was the soonest I could get him over; on top of everything else, he was getting holiday pay). I parked on the street and walked in through the front door, finding everyone downstairs watching TV in the living room. There had been another attack that morning, this one very close to us in South Plainfield. Currently, however, the station was broadcasting footage from CCTV cameras inside supermarkets across the East Coast. It was supposed to be the busiest shopping day of the year, but the aisles were practically empty. In one clip, a man ran into the frame, stopped before a display of canned goods, and extended his store-supplied reacher while shrinking into himself, as if bracing for a blast. Another clip showed a bulkier male, this one shaved bald. He wore construction boots and just a T-shirt despite the cold, and he walked slowly and deliberately, as if to make a statement. He snatched items off the shelves as if they'd insulted him.

"Maybe we should just order a pizza," Betty said.

"For lunch or Thanksgiving?"

"Both."

"Right," Priscilla said. "Just like the pilgrims did when they sat down with the Native Americans. Do you even realize how pathetic that sounds?"

"Priscilla's got a point," I said. "If it were Columbus Day, that'd be one thing. But we've got to cook our own turkey, don't we?"

"We?" Betty said. "Who's this 'we'? I'm the one who cooks it every year. You watch football and only come in to turn on the light in the oven. I'm the one who cuts her fingers peeling the potatoes."

Priscilla stood from the sofa. "I'll cook," she said.

"You?" Betty gave her a far too honest look. "Do you know how much work it is?"

She shrugged. "Someone just needs to drive with me to the store."

"Oh no," Betty said. "There's no need to be a hero at a time like this."

"Your mother's right."

I suggested we drive out of state, but how far was far enough? Harrisburg? Pittsburgh? Indianola, Indiana? And could we even get back in time to have the turkey ready by tomorrow afternoon, or would we have to spark a fire and roast it on the side of the road?

Ernest had been lying face down on the floor throughout our discussion, but here he sat up and turned round to face us. "Costco," he said.

Priscilla howled with disapproval, but I seized on the idea.

"No, no, your brother's got a point. No Costcos have been hit," I said, and when she countered by saying the same could be said for co-ops and natural food stores, I told her it was only at Costco that we could buy in bulk and bunker down until all this madness had passed us by.

Ernest was up on his feet and nodding. "One trip. In, out, over like that. Enough food for three weeks, maybe four. Genius. Pizza, too," he said. "For lunch. Today."

"That's right, they sell pizza and hot dogs, so we won't have to worry about anything till dinner."

"Everything they sell there is processed," Priscilla said. "Do you even remember what we did the other day?"

"Priscilla," I said, "this is like a time of war. Sacrifices must be made."

"Your father's right."

"Now you all stay here and I'll be back in about an hour."

"Oh, no, if we're doing this, I'm going, too," she said.

"Priscilla!"

"What, Mom? I need to make sure he buys something decent."

Betty threw up her hands. "Well, if she's going, I'm going too. What could I say if my daughter died buying me a pumpkin pie?"

Peter sat at the end of the sofa, nursing a cup of cold coffee. "Can you stay here?" I asked. Ernst Eberhardt sat in his armchair, off to our side by the fireplace. "I need you to watch Ernst and Ernest."

Peter said he'd be glad to be of service, but my son resisted. To prove his worth, he ran into the garage and came back with a metal garbage can lid and the 3-iron from my bag of golf clubs. "Like this," he said. He held the lid as if it were a shield, then extended his long iron and tapped a box of Ritz crackers that sat on the coffee table. Seeing that it was safe, he lowered his shield and grabbed the box.

"Excellent," I said. "Did everyone see that? Lift, tap, approach." I clapped my hands together. "All right, then, let's gather our supplies and move out!"

We were like a Special Forces unit dropped behind enemy lines. After I showed my card at the door, we scattered in four directions, wanting to be as quick and efficient as possible. The store felt spacious that afternoon, roomier than I could ever remember seeing it. The news had scared so many people away from shopping that Priscilla, Betty, and I had each grabbed a massive cart and pushed off toward our assignments. Betty went in search of pie and stuffing, Priscilla moved off into the cold room to stock up on crates of fruits and vegetables, while Ernest, who'd changed into a pair of camouflage pants and a bomber jacket, ran back and forth between me and my cart, accepting one assignment after another.

"Milk," I said. "The four-gallon box. Over there! I'll just grab the turkey!"

No one stopped for samples, and I paused needlessly only once, after reaching into the open-trough freezer for a thawed twenty-pound Butterball. As I turned to drop the turkey into our cart, I saw the corner display of Sweetness #9 facing me. They were selling two five hundred–count boxes for $8.99, the shrink-wrapped packages stacked twelve high and twelve across and just as many deep. I tried calculating the number of packages in all, but then I saw the two unpacked crates, both still wrapped in cellophane, that were stacked on the shelves high over the product on the floor. How many now? A million? Two?

Ernest hurried toward me like a man with a bum leg. He carried a large white bucket by the handle, but he struggled with its weight. I rushed to his side after seeing him drop his golf club and almost fall.

"What's this? Where's the milk? We need it for the mashed potatoes."

He picked up his long iron and pointed it down at the bucket. "For emergencies," he said.

I dropped to a knee and read the label: *Family Emergency Kit.*

"Ninety servings of dehydrated food." He counted it off by tapping the golf club against the bucket. "Western stew. Potato soup. Oatmeal. Cacciatore." He was out of breath. "Good for everyone, too."

"Vegan?"

"Not sure. Vegetarian, though. Kosher, too."

"Excellent."

He smiled proudly. "Last one."

"You got the last one? Excellent job, young man."

He continued tapping against the bucket. "Nylon ropes, waterproof matches, a compass, safety masks."

"That's all in here?"

"Even a crank flashlight/radio/cell phone charger."

"You'll get a medal for this." I heaved the bucket up into our cart, then tousled his hair. "Let's not forget that milk now, okay? Two percent!"

I found Betty a couple of aisles over, studying a crate of boil-and-ready Indian dinners across from the oversized bottles of salsa and the economy-sized cans of matzo ball soup. A sudden swelling panic swept through me. Because if a xenophobe was to bring violence to this store, some man desperate to call attention to a hopeless cause in Palestine, Chiapas, or Kashmir, this would be the first place he'd strike. Ethnic Foods.

"Betty!" I waved her away from there. "Let's go, let's go, let's go! We've already been here too long!"

She started toward me the same moment a voice turned me round.

"David!"

The man looked like Benjamin Franklin gone to seed: bald on top but with long greying hair around the sides, a landslide belly pushing out beneath a lurid Hawaiian shirt, and a pair of khaki shorts that gave a clear view of his prosthetic leg.

"David Leveraux?" he said.

I reacted like the fencer I wished my son had become, pulling my garbage can lid close to my chest and holding my 5-iron out as if it were a foil. "What do you want, Hickey?"

He took a step back, raising his hands. "Whoa there, tiger!" In one hand he held a jug of Canadian whiskey. "I just came here for a little drinky-poo and a tub of mayonnaise."

"Likely story," I said, still at the ready.

"Are you on drugs?" he asked.

I lunged at him, causing him to recoil with something like genuine fear.

"You can tell your handlers it won't work," I said.

"Let me rephrase my question: *Which* drugs are you on?"

"Play dumb all you want, Hickey. I know it's you. I don't see you for twenty years, and now twice in a matter of months?"

I lunged at him again, going for his shoulder. He shielded himself with his jug of whiskey and laughed as he spun away.

"Christ, David, that must be some good shit you're on. Why don't you share a little with your old friend? I'll give you a taste of the hooch."

Betty stepped up behind me then, holding her own garbage can lid out in front of her.

"Your wife, I take it." Hickey backed away from us, keeping one hand in the air. "I'm feeling a little outnumbered," he said, "so I hope you won't mind if I just play through."

Only after he had turned the corner of an aisle and was gone did Betty stand at ease.

"I'd like one of those lorazepams about now," she said.

That evening Betty came down into the kitchen, yawning and saying she craved "something mushy" for dinner. We still had to prepare the turkey, so I made an executive decision to open the Family Emergency bucket. After we had all reached inside it for the pouch of our choosing, we went into the dining room to eat, and Betty walked around the table to pour boiling water from the kettle.

Only Priscilla refused to grab a packet of dehydrated soup. While everyone else commented on the flavor of the Western Stew or Potato Soup, she drank from a glass of water and ate a slice of brown bread.

"Can I spend the night at Sarin's?" she said.

"Of course not," Betty answered. "Tomorrow's Thanksgiving."

"And besides, I don't think you should be spending the night over there anymore."

A whole conversation passed between us with only a look.

"Why's that?" she said.

"I think you know. It's just not appropriate anymore."

"Can I have Ryan Johnson over then?"

"Who's Ryan Johnson?"

"The sports editor for *The Campus Crier*. He's a real peach."

I spooned soup into my mouth. "You're too old for sleep-overs. Now eat your bread and water like a good prisoner of conscience."

Ernst could sit silently for hours at a time; sometimes whole days would pass and he barely said a thing. But every now and then his eyes would brighten and his whole body would radiate with a new spirit. This was just such a moment. "I once served a very important man that same meal," he told Priscilla. "Bread and water. Did your father ever tell you?"

He set his napkin down, and then his voice was sending us back, all the way to Berlin in April of 1945.

It started after midnight, when a guard shook him awake in the room he shared with four others. "Herr Bormann?" Ernst asked, thinking or hoping he was about to be given new orders. But the guard shook his head no, then commanded Ernst to follow him down a narrow concrete stairway to the bunker's bottommost floor. Here a lounge had been set up outside the door to Hitler's personal quarters. When the guard left him, no one stood between Ernst and it.

He feared he'd spoken in his sleep. He feared he'd said something about what had happened earlier in the day, when Speer had visited him and tried to convince him to do what Von Stauffenberg had already attempted—but not with a bomb this time; with a clear colorless liquid. "You could mix it in with the Führer's food or drink," Speer had said. "You could be far away from here before it ever took effect." It didn't matter that Ernst had refused any involvement in this plan. Just being asked was treasonous enough.

Ernst tightened the belt of his bathrobe, then stiffened as Hitler entered from his bedroom with his dog Blondi following at his heels. Hitler sank into a chair, holding his lame arm tight against his chest. "A drink," he said, and because Ernst wasn't sure if it was a question or a command, he nodded eagerly and crossed to the bar trolley, where he fixed a soda water for Hitler and a brandy for himself.

When they were thus fortified, Ernst settled down onto a black leather divan beneath a Manet that had been hung on the wall.

"Fräulein Braun," Hitler said, as Ernst looked up over his shoulder to inspect the painting. "Such a merry homemaker, even here."

Ernst looked to the painting facing him now, a sentimental portrait of a mill house that he knew Hitler had completed in his youth. He complimented its use of color and artistry, then was relieved to have Hitler carry the conversation from there. His mind drifted this way and that, fluttering about like a bird in its cage. First he addressed his betrayals and his legacy, then he moved on to the Jews and the Norwegians, before at last saying something about suicide.

"Excuse me, mein Führer?" Ernst had been looking down in his lap as if puzzling over a knot, but here he couldn't help but lift his eyes and notice Hitler's smile.

"I said have you ever considered suicide?"

Ernst Eberhardt curled his toes inside his slippers and brought his snifter of brandy up to his nose. Such subtle woody notes of flavor. Would this be the last taste he experienced? He swallowed, but the drink went down wrong—had he already been poisoned?—and so for a moment he coughed violently and sat there beating on his chest.

"Excuse me, mein Führer. Suicide, you say? Well, yes, I have considered it. But really"—he rose from the divan, conscious of the weight in his knees—"who hasn't? It is human nature, is it not?" He crossed to the bar trolley and set his glass down, convinced now that he'd at least live to experience another taste. Taste, after all, could not be confined to what you had on your plate or held in a glass, for what was frozen in the grim pucker of every death mask but the bitterness of our own mortality?

Ernst checked his watch—its face blurred—and nodded as if he could read it. "May I be excused?" he said. "I must prepare you a satis-fying breakfast in but a few hours."

Hitler nodded lazily, and then Ernst turned and walked up the stairs. The following morning, he decided the argument that had long since replaced his evening prayers. If he should be so lucky as to live, he would do so in America. Ernst had always vilified the Americans' mouths, considering their palates crass and vulgar, given over to peanut butter and Coca-Cola, to say nothing of the country's unrivaled ob-session with vanilla. But it'd be better than a life amongst the Soviets. Stalin, it was rumored, was a non-taster, a man whose tongue was equipped with as few as eleven taste buds per square centimeter—or one hundred times fewer than the most well-endowed tongue. Ernst couldn't imagine living beneath a man who was unable to register the subtle differences between sweet and sour. He'd eat a million hot dogs and withstand as many false smiles before that.

After dressing, Ernst went above-ground, where he found a heap of charred flesh steaming at the entrance to the bunker. Two soft-bellied soldiers stood over it, one with his uniform half-buttoned, each with hair the color of original sin. They spat on the carcass, causing it to hiss. Ernst looked up and asked a question with only the weight in his eyes.

"Blondi," the first soldier said, scratching at his chest.

"A controlled experiment," said the other. "Cyanide."

Ernst moved away from them, glancing up at the sky. Enemy planes could no longer be seen or heard at any hour of the day, but there was little relief to be found in this: it meant only that their troops were close enough to advance beneath the power of their own artillery. He looked to the eastern horizon, hearing the muffled thud of the Soviet approach. How far now? Twenty kilometers? Ten?

He entered the orangery and pushed through the trees to the back of the room, where he'd cleared some space for his seedlings. As he leaned in over them, he found the first tiny shoots of lettuce and cabbage wilted. His pots of herbs and cherished potato starts were no better. He looked up, knowing what he'd find even before he saw it: several panes of broken glass letting in the cold. He cursed softly, wondering if the enemy's bombs were to blame or if the guards had been making a sport of target practice again. Whatever the answer, he no longer felt as he had in Wiesbaden. This was war, all right. No place for a man, let alone a potato.

Back in the bunker, he helped prepare the night's bleak meal: bruised root vegetables, carrots so pale as to be almost translucent, and meat (for Hitler did fancy himself the occasional slab of ham, despite the rumors of his vegetarianism) to which Ernst added an ample dose of red dye. While this coloring made the main course far more presentable, his best work was reserved for dessert, a yellow gelatinous substance identified on the meal's tiny menu card as "vanilla custard." The quotation marks were appropriate, Ernst thought, because the custard's tell-tale consistency relied almost exclusively on the ground hooves of a dead horse (supplies were that scarce), while its flavor had been made tolerable only after he'd reached for the bottle marked *Geschmack Drei*.

Normally, Ernst stood ready in the kitchen, there to flavor an additional course if the Führer's appetite was good or face the inevitable punishment if ever he thought to poison a meal. This evening, however, Ernst appeared in the dining room as the Führer was still stuffing his mouth with the reddened meat.

"I am sorry to trouble you," he said. "But I wonder if I might be excused?"

Hitler looked up from his meal with one cheek puffed out by a mouthful of meat.

"I thought I'd take a quick constitutional, is all. To return the color to my face."

The Führer wiped the savory juices from his chin, perhaps thinking the subterfuge of this request a final effort on Ernst's part to be polite. No one would have faulted him if he had been more direct. After all, just the previous evening Hitler had told his secretaries to leave, warning them of what the Soviets would do when they arrived.

Hitler gave a wave of his hand. "Yes," he said. "That would be fine. Thank you, Ernst. You've been very good to me."

After emerging from the bunker with only a flashlight and a slip of paper folded in his shoe, he followed the dying path of the sun to the west. He wanted to find an American and surrender, but he knew the dangers of this plan. If he got too close to the sound of approaching artillery, he might come upon a retreating Wehrmacht unit and be pressed into action. Soldiers were dying quickly, and if he didn't meet a similar fate, he could be promoted in the field, forced to the top of the chain of command by a unit of boys and pensioners—and how would he emigrate then? Of course, straying too far from the sounds of combat was no safer. Then he would likely meet the fear and suspicion of bombed-out families, the survivors of total war, and seeing his full cheeks and well-fed belly, they might set upon him, suspecting he had something they hadn't had in their mouths in months. So Ernst walked in a kind of daze, listening for the rhythms in a system that held no order. He walked hungry and tired and refused the call of sleep until he staggered into a barn and took refuge in its hayloft.

At dawn he awoke to the sounds of a mechanical rumbling in the distance, then hurried down the ladder from where he'd slept, stopping when he saw a German soldier hanging from the rafters. Ernst jumped to the floor and ran the rest of the way out of the barn, seeing an American tank cresting a far hill.

He ran toward it, calling out, "Hallo! America! Hallo!"

Hearing this, three soldiers riding on the top of the tank jumped down with their rifles at the ready. One shouted, *"Halt! Halt, oder wir schießen!"*

"Don't shoot!" Ernst answered, and now the tank stopped and its barrel swung round in his direction. "I cook!" He lifted his arms high in the air. "I'm no soldier. I love America, I cook, Mae West!"

The German-speaking soldier stepped toward him with his rifle lifted to his shoulder. *"Zeigt mir deine Unterhosen!"*

Ernst's first thought was that this American spoke German rather well. His second was, Why does he want to see my underwear?

"Deine Unterhosen!"

The tank's barrel clicked into place, its overwhelming threat pointing directly at him. The soldier thrust a hand into Ernst's pants, sending the two into a spinning dance. It was only now that Ernst thought he had chosen the wrong direction. He should have joined the Soviets, for if their world was lifeless and grey, at least it wasn't a degenerate society, ready to fall like Rome.

The soldier pulled Ernst's underwear up into view — pleased to see it was neither military issue nor entirely absent, the latter of which would have suggested Ernst was a major or a colonel trying to hide his identity.

"You say you're a cook?" the soldier said.

Ernst accepted a cigarette from him. "In the bunker, yes. I was Hitler's personal flavor chemist."

The two other soldiers, who'd hung back to have a smoke, stepped forward now, lifting their rifles into position. "Did he say Hitler?" Even the tank seemed to have heard. The hatch popped open and a GI stuck his head out. "What's going on?"

Like that Ernst became a prize, promising these men a quick promotion or at least a few days away from the front. Within minutes they were headed back in the direction they'd come from, away from the end of the war and toward something safer. The whole time, their new addition sat atop their tank like a beauty queen on parade. First, Ernst was debriefed by a colonel in the field, then shuttled back farther still, until finally he was dining with de Gaulle in Paris. "The Manet," Ernst told him in more than passable French, "was regrettably hung lower than Hitler's own juvenile work."

After that, it was on to London and then Washington, where Ernst dined with more generals and dignitaries, more exiled leaders and men from lapsed states. Everyone wanted to hear the story. "Tell me about Hitler," they'd say, and so Ernst would entertain them in one of three languages, telling them he had but one regret. "I wish I hadn't left the bunker so soon. I should have been there when Hitler reached the end of his meal. Because to see him when he tried the custard I had prepared — he would have bitten his spoon clean in half, that or flown into one of his rages, jumped to his feet and overturned the table, and ordered the flavorist detained, detained and shot!"

"You see," Ernst said to us that night at the dinner table, "the custard's taste was not vanilla as advertised. It tasted" — and here he smiled at Priscilla — "like bread and water."

He had hoarded the necessary ingredients for weeks, doing his best to obtain the flavors through various crude processes of distillation and extraction, the whole primitive endeavor harking back to Pavel Pabst's pioneering work with the cambial sap of conifer trees. "I know what you're thinking: I should have done more. But" — and here he looked at me — "I was never the type for heroic action. Speer needed a soldier; I was a flavorist. I could sweeten Hitler's linseed mush for breakfast and give him that final taste of bread and water at dinner."

He smiled. "It was my first work of art. Bread may not be so difficult to replicate, but to follow it with a hint of water...your father can tell you the difficulty of that. Water has no taste, or rather only the taste of its impurities. And the flavor was undeniable. Central Berlin aquifer."

Priscilla sat stiffly in her chair, glancing between my twitching eyelid and Ernst. *"Geschmack Drei?"* she said.

It was what had sweetened the custard, but the question confused my mentor. He was adrift again, lost in time, so I spoke on his behalf, having picked up at least enough German to know this.

"It means Flavor Number Three," I said.

Day 7: Thursday

On the morning of Thanksgiving, Betty and I awoke to news of another supermarket attack, this one the ninth overall and closer than any that had preceded it.

"Is that our Acme?" I said.

On the television, a reporter stood in the supermarket parking lot, saying someone had been injured minutes ago while reaching for a package of donuts.

"That's our Acme," I said.

Betty grabbed the remote and turned the TV off. I looked at her, my eye twitching, then hurried into the bathroom for my pills. The trial pack of anti-anxiety medication looked like a ransacked Advent calendar. After pushing out the seventh pill through its foil backing, I tossed the packaging back into its drawer, then grabbed the orange bottle of lorazepam and struggled to uncap it.

"Go downstairs and get the paper," Betty said, after I'd finally gotten it open and dipped my head down to the tap. "Read the sports page. It'll take your mind off things."

I stashed the rest of the pills in my robe pocket and did as she said, or tried to. When I opened the front door, I found a manila envelope on the welcome mat. I picked it up and turned it over, not finding an address or a stamp on either side. Finally, I shook it tentatively. It made a sound like a maraca.

Forgetting about the paper, I took the package upstairs, opening it as I moved into the bedroom.

"What is it?" Betty said.

I dumped the contents onto the bed beside her: a dozen or more

303

packets of sweetener, maybe twenty in all, none of them Mexican. Betty and I both reached for one, noticing that something had been written in black ink along the crimped edge.

"Swastikas," Betty said. "Why would someone send us swastikas? We're not even Jewish."

I hurried down the stairs and into the garage, then returned with the VHS tape from our security deck. The system we'd had installed the previous day used stop-motion photography to capture an image every five seconds. I inserted the tape into our VCR, then rewound it to sunset and fast-forwarded through the events from there. Nothing suspicious appeared until just after sunrise, when a Trans Am parked across the street — and just as quickly drove away.

The tape ended in a burst of static. I rewound it to the Trans Am, paused, and hit a button on my remote to zoom in on the image. The driver appeared behind the window, his face a black blur, a splotch, a spectral presence.

"He must've seen the Invisible Eyeball," I said. "He must've circled round and parked down the street, then snuck up to our door on foot. There must be a blind spot. Look!" I had returned the image to a standard perspective. The mailbox was in the center of the shot, the Trans Am behind it. "You can't see the far corner of our lawn. He must've parked in front of Jon and Ken's house and walked up to our door. There's a blind spot!" I said, pointing. "Don't you see, Betty?"

And then it came to me. "Hickey!"

"What?"

"I'm not about to stand around and wait to see what he does next!"

I turned for the door, tossing the remote onto the bed.

"But, David, what are you going to do?"

I was still wearing my pajamas and slippers. Betty ran down the stairs after me.

"It stops now," I said, grabbing my coat from the closet in the hall and hurrying out to the garage through the kitchen.

Betty stepped into the garage as I was starting the engine of the Volvo.

"Are you sure this is a good idea?" she said. And then, as I backed out nodding my head: "I was thinking we'd eat around two!"

I drove to Jupiter Park in short time, stopping only at a pay phone to remind myself of Hickey's address. He was no longer living in a house; his life had taken a bad turn, throwing him into an apartment complex not much unlike the one Betty and I had once known.

I parked in a spot reserved for guests and walked into the interior courtyard, then up the concrete stairs to his unit on the second floor overlooking the pool. I knocked, he opened the door, and then my fist flew out toward him. Hickey dodged the punch, but my second one landed—a glancing blow that he responded to by locking me up in his arms and dropping me hard down onto the floor just inside the doorway.

I wheezed, reaching for my side. "I think you cracked my ribs."

"*I* cracked your ribs!?!" He bounced on top of me—"What the fuck?"—then did it again, asking if I was on drugs. "I mean it!" he said. "Tell me this time!"

"Nothing illegal," I managed, my breath short, my voice strained. "Anxiety medication, prescribed. Can you please—" He rolled off of me. "I might be having a reaction," I said. "The first week you're on them…" I pushed myself up into a sitting position. "They can make you more anxious," I said.

He closed the door—"The fuck!"—and walked into the kitchen.

"Do you have any Advil?" I asked.

"Seagram's," he said, coming back with two plastic cups. "It works better than anything I've got in the bathroom."

I sat up to accept my drink and took a seat in a rattan papasan chair that was so big I couldn't keep my legs on the floor. After my first sip on an empty stomach, I felt like I was sitting in a giant's cupped hand.

Hickey sat across from me in a massive high-backed wicker chair, the type I'd always associated with Huey Newton and the Black Panther Party.

"Now, how about you tell me what this is all about?" he said.

And so I told him about the packets of Sweetness #9 I'd been receiving, and the take-over offer, and my suspicions that Better Health and Flavorings was trying to intimidate me.

"So you're the one who sent me that packet of sweetener in the mail?" he said.

"I thought you were their muscle. The bad cop to Willingham's good."

"Christ, did you even think to check if I was still working for them?"

I mentioned my research online, but he just snorted and said he'd been let go — "for cause, they say" — more than a year ago.

"I was coming up on my thirty-year anniversary," he said, "and they wanted to keep me from getting all the benefits that would entail. My package had been grandfathered in, you know, back when we split from Goldstein, Olivetti, and Dark. A much sweeter deal than what they're offering today. Anyway, then some asshole calls me into his cramped, windowless office and says I'm downloading porn on my company computer, and sure, some of what they find on my hard drive is mine, but what the hell, David? I'm a single man. I gotta buy a separate computer just so I can masturbate? There's an environmental principle at stake, you know?" He drank some more. "And that shit they tried to pin on me? Blondes with big tits? What am I, fifteen years old? My tastes are more refined. I've lived a life. You think I still get off on blondes with big tits?"

He finished his drink and went into the kitchen for another, speaking to me over the counter that separated it from the living room. He'd been treating his house as a cash machine, he said. "I finally had to declare bankruptcy last January, about the time I moved here and started pissing off my neighbors by playing Iron Butterfly at four in the morning. Now I'm so piss poor I can't afford my monthly prostitute, let alone a proper doctor." He poured plenty of Seagram's 7 and added a splash of lemon-lime soda. "My mother tells me I'm an alcoholic, my father would like to bury my other leg in the backyard, and my dog — Christ, I'm like a country song — he died this summer, as fat as a cow. You think your life's bad?" He sat in his Huey Newton chair, sad and impervious. "Look in my freezer and you'll find a Swanson's frozen dinner that they make especially for sad fucks like me on Thanksgiving Day.

People have been afraid to shop? I been going three, four times a day, just to feel the rush. Been picking up every box in the store—tampons, dog biscuits, you name it—just trying to find a winner. Here." He reached down past the cushion of his chair and tossed something to me, a black blur that caused me to spill my drink as I went to catch it. A gun.

"This is a gun, Hickey!" My lap was moist from my spilled drink; I held the thing in two hands, not trusting my finger near the trigger.

"Put me out of my misery," he said. "Go ahead, I won't mind."

"God, no! Hickey!" I thought to put the gun on the table, but it was too cluttered with beer cans and takeout food. "Is this because of Sweetness #9?"

"What?"

"Your guilt. Because you were there at its inception. Some people would say we have blood on our hands."

He laughed. "Weren't you listening to me? My life is for shit. Look over there." I followed his gaze to a large open brown box on the floor. "Inside, you'll find a month's worth of ready-made food. My doctor said I should get it on account of the diabetes. But I couldn't stomach it for more than a few days. Not because of the flavor; the food was fine. But the eating out of a box. Delivered in the mail." He shook his head. "I'm like a stray dog, eating just to survive."

He took another sip of his drink, then smiled. "So if you've always thought of yourself as a metaphorical killer?" He motioned to the gun in my lap. "Pull the trigger and feel what it's like to be the real thing. You'd be doing me a favor. Really."

I put the gun down on the floor. "You're just sad. It's the holidays." I thought to invite him to my place, but didn't know what Betty would say. I tried a kind of hopeful smile. "You know the holidays."

I stood then, thinking I shouldn't leave, but not wanting to stay. "I'll just see about that Advil," I said, going into the bathroom after he told me to help myself. I found another gun in there (he had seven in all, I'd learn in the papers), this one on the shelf over the toilet, next to a scented candle. It was a six-shooter, big and silver, like something from a cowboy movie. I reached for it and couldn't resist doing a pantomime in the mirror. The Quick-Draw Artist. The second time I did this the shot rang out, and though I looked to my gun and then the mirror, believing it must have come from me, I saw neither a wisp of smoke nor a shattered reflection.

I rushed out to find Hickey flung back in his chair like that man in the old Memorex ad. The gun was down in his lap, blown there by the force of the shot, and when I stepped around to the backside of his chair, I saw the hole in the wicker ribbing, and then, more memorably, the raw one, like some molten soup, in the back of his head.

At that very moment, neighbors must've been looking away from their television sets or up from their breakfasts. *Did you hear that?* I ran on instinct, a primitive bodily flight, and was halfway down the stairs before I realized I was still holding the six-shooter. I thought to toss it into the deep end of the pool, but I was afraid of fingerprints, thinking mine must be on file somewhere as a result of my stay at Greystone Park. A door slammed closed behind me, and then I remembered I'd handled the gun that Hickey had used. But there was no time to go back, so I hurried out through the courtyard and then was pulling at the door of my car as I heard a voice cry out behind me, a voice that might as well have been my conscience rising up against me after all these years: "Stop him! He's getting away!"

What can be said of what follows? A comedy of errors. I hit not one but two cars trying to get out of the parking lot, then sped through the first stop sign, narrowly missing a bicyclist.

For several blocks I drove without knowing where I was or where I was going. Then, as I neared a four-way stop, I saw a policeman driving toward me. He sped through his stop sign, siren blasting and lights all a-twirl, and parked at an angle in front of me, blocking off my escape. There had been a report of shots fired, a speeding Volvo fleeing the scene, a man in pajamas and a bathrobe with a gun. As he tumbled out of his car, drawing his weapon, I scrambled to open my bottle of lorazepam. "Hands in the air!" he said, and so I threw my fists into the roof, spilling pills everywhere — on my lap, and around the gun I only now remembered I'd dropped on the passenger seat.

"I can explain!" I said.

The policeman pulled me out roughly and down to the street (I chipped my front tooth), then threw a knee in between my shoulders as he yanked my wrists up behind my back.

I turned my face to one side, my cheek pressed down into the cold pebbly blacktop. A man stood on the lawn of the corner house facing me. He leaned into a rake behind a pile of leaves, not moving when the wind picked up and began to undo all of his hard work. I imagine this was when the officer was reading me my rights. I don't remember it. At some point I closed my eyes and wished—wished so strongly—that I could just fall asleep.

Because of the holiday weekend, I wasn't formally arraigned until Monday morning. It was then that I was charged with two counts of misdemeanor hit-and-run, driving while under the influence (the lorazepam), and something called "depraved indifference." My attorney made much of my "unreasonable detention," reminding the court of my legal right to be seen by a judge within seventy-two hours, and the way he argued you would've thought I'd been held in a secret prison for twelve years. In truth, I hadn't minded the delay. It had kept me from having to explain myself to Betty or the kids until after the judge had refused to dismiss my case for what she called "a harmless error" and set a date for my preliminary hearing.

"Basically," I told my family that evening, after I'd posted bail and we were sitting around the kitchen table eating Chinese, "they say I stood by and did nothing while Hickey took his life. They say I may even have assisted him."

"And did you?" Priscilla said.

"No. God no. It was all a mistake. He wasn't even the one sending me those packets of sweetener."

Betty had picked me up from the jail and driven me home, but she'd said little more on the way than this: "I don't want to argue. I want to believe you. I just need to hear the truth." Now, as she fiddled with her chopsticks, she said she could've told me it wasn't Hickey if only I'd left the house with my phone that day.

When I looked at her for an explanation, she sent my eyes on to my mentor, who sat there silently in his chair, as still as a forgotten memory.

"He woke up after you left and asked for coffee," she said. "He refused the sugar, so I looked for the Sweetness #9 in the cupboards. There wasn't any. It was all upstairs on our bed."

I followed her eyes to the ceiling, then looked back down to the table when I understood.

Ernest smirked, shaking his head. "Swastikas," he said. "Jesus."

"But why?" I asked.

Betty had had plenty of time to think about it. She reminded me that I'd only started receiving the packets at home after Ernst had moved in with us. "He must've awoken in the night and put the package together." He was sleeping in the study, after all, the same room where we had a desk and kept the office supplies. Before that, she said, he could've dropped the envelopes at the office on one of his long walks through the neighborhood.

"He made that walk for years," she reminded me. "The wires in his brain must have crossed up."

"But why?"

The phone rang, interrupting us. I rose to get it and heard the voice of a foreign man on the other end.

"You are David Leveraux?" he said.

My attention became more focused. "Yes." Was he Albanian?

"Great-great-grandson of Jürgen Mockus?"

I was nodding now. "Yes," I told him, "yes I am," and then he was speaking to me excitedly, asking if he could arrange to visit when he came to New York City the following month.

"Who was it?" Betty asked when I'd hung up.

"A cousin," I said, still standing by the phone.

"What? I thought you didn't have any relatives."

"Long-lost, apparently."

"Well, that's great. Where's he from?"

I spoke the word as if it were the name of a newly discovered planet. "Lithuania."

Priscilla looked up from her tea. "We still have family in Lithuania?"

Betty looked at her. "What do you mean 'still?'"

"He's a bureaucrat of some kind," I said. "The Mormons came through Vilnius last month, asking for access to their records. One thing led to another and he found me."

"But I thought you were French-English," Betty said.

"As it so happens, I'm half-Lithuanian. "

"How am I only now hearing this?"

I came over to the table and sat down. "My grandfather changed his name from Mockus to improve business. Said 'Leveraux's Fine Footwear' had a better ring to it than 'Mockus's Shoes.' You know the French brand: very reliable. Anyway, my father was always threatening to change the name back, but he never got around to it. For me, with everything my grandfather did, it was never a question."

Betty got up and started walking circles. "This is unbelievable," she said. "My husband has a slave name."

Ernst Eberhardt came alive then, lifting his eyes as if the distant past had just come into view. "I knew a Lithuanian once," he said. "A homosexual like the man from Munich."

His eyes were clear, his voice strong and steady. It was as if he'd been conserving his energy these last few hours in anticipation of telling me this, a story I'd heard before, though a different version, one that contained all of the parts that he, as a good German, had previously skipped.

"This was in Peenemünde," he said, "where they had us working on special projects before I got reassigned to the Hitler Detail."

After England had defended itself in the skies and the United States had entered the conflict to truly make it a world war, Pabst, Pfaff & Pfeiffer was shuttered and Ernst was given a simple choice: the Eastern Front or the Baltic coast. He chose the latter, having been told that once there, he could expect to enjoy the company of Heisenberg, Stark, Lenard, and of course Werner von Braun, the man behind Hitler's V-2 rocket.

When Ernst arrived in 1942, he saw this claim was perhaps overstated. He was one of five thousand souls working there, and while

Heisenberg, Stark, and Lenard often strolled the grounds at the side of the great man himself, Ernst was far away from the center of power and authority, assigned to a small unit of flavor chemists who had been given only the vaguest instructions to develop a *Wunderwaffe* that would deprive the enemy of its will to win.

This chemical weapon should not be developed to destroy the enemy, they were told. If it was annihilation they were after, they would have already showered London and St. Petersburg with anthrax and unleashed all of the colorful gasses of the First World War. "Someone will still have to drive the buses when we get there," Hitler had reportedly said, and so Ernst had gone to work each day trying to create a wonder weapon that the Führer could deliver on the tip of a silent V-2 rocket.

The request intrigued Ernst more than the implications of it troubled him. He considered it while eating, while dreaming, even while performing his calisthenics in the morning. A militarized flavor — such an intellectual challenge! What would it taste like? How could it be deployed to make a citizenry compliant and weak? He emptied and filled his test tube each day, trying out one fearful idea after another. But who was he kidding? Hitler had asked for a weapon of mass deception, and all he could deliver was a better butterscotch.

After the British bombing raid of '43, in that listless week or two before the scientists were sent inside a mountain to continue production of the V-2, Ernst was joined in a makeshift lab every day by the only other surviving flavor chemists: a tall and lanky Lithuanian and a sallow-faced young man from Munich who wore spectacles and was always grinning at some private thought.

Even though the war had begun to turn in favor of the Allied Powers, the talk in the cafeteria each afternoon was still dominated by those who spoke of the next wave of rockets that would obliterate London and even New York City. Only the Lithuanian and the man from Munich showed no outward signs of patriotism. They seemed to look forward to nothing so much as the film screened in the recreation hall each Wednesday night. (Give them a good song and dance number and they'd have something to talk about for days.)

Their work habits were no more commendable. They arrived late to the lab each morning, forgot to stopper the brown bottles they removed from the flavor library, and even blew Ernst a kiss before leaving early. It was the kiss that infuriated him the most. These men never washed their hands, and so who could say what chemicals they'd handled that day and what risk it might bring to their mouths? Bad science, that was what it was, and that's what Ernst couldn't stand—more than being a bad German, being a bad scientist.

One afternoon, when they didn't return from a long lunch, Ernst strode out to the tent they'd been given after the bombing raid and pulled at the flap, expecting to find them lounging half-naked inside. When he saw they weren't there, he continued to the showers at the edge of the woods, wishing von Braun were at his side. "Do you see what I'm left with? Their commitment?"

There was only one man in the bathroom, a porcine fellow from the jet propulsion lab who sat on a bench in his robe reading the latest news about Stalingrad. They shared a glum look and a slow nod hello, and then Ernst started back for the lab, spying them in the distance. They were walking out of the woods, the Lithuanian holding a picnic basket as the man from Munich laughed, carrying a bottle of wine.

Rather than confront them, Ernst briskly returned to the lab. He wanted to get all of the details right for his report, so he went straight to their workbench and made a note of the papers littered everywhere, the half-eaten strudel from breakfast, and then—and this disturbed him more than anything else—a partially filled test tube left leaning at an angle atop a scruffy pink eraser. Ernst snatched it. He picked it up, ready to dump its contents into the sink, but before he could, his nose passed over the test tube's mouth and he smelled something sweet. Something warm. Something light and somehow pink. He breathed it in a second time, drawing the odor deep down into his lungs, and it was so divine, a sensation so vibrant and alive, that he imagined he might float up out of his boots. He kissed his fingertips. He couldn't help himself. He kissed his fingertips to compliment the work, and it was then that he tasted it—something sweet, something far sweeter than sugar, something unlike anything nature could possibly hold.

He rushed to the other side of the room and poured the contents of the test tube into his cold cup of coffee. The sweetness overtook the bitter taste. It was inspired, and so he returned to their work station in great haste, bringing with him a scrap of paper and a pencil, and while glancing between their notes and the door, he jotted down the formula and even the name they had already given it: *Geschmack Drei*.

"They were captured by the Soviets after the war," Ernst told us, "but I don't think they lived long enough to share their secrets. Even if they had, such sweetness could not have survived in Soviet Russia. And so when I left Hitler's bunker, I took with me only a flashlight and their formula, which was written on a piece of paper that I kept folded in my shoe."

This morning Ernst told us he had been reassigned to Berlin in late August of 1944, not February of 1945 as he had told everyone since being profiled by *Food & Flavor* magazine a few years after the war. I didn't dare stop him to question the date, as to do so would be akin to rousing a man from a waking dream. I sat there like the others, listening.

"When I arrived," he said, "Hitler was even more hypnotic than I remembered. He spoke of Frederick the Great and a miracle that'd save us from defeat. I believed his every word and secretly feared I'd failed him. I was a German. I wanted to win. What did I know? It was my side. That simple. And so I did what I could. I sweetened his linseed mush and muesli for breakfast, and I made more lively the vegetable juice he drank throughout the day. When he grew depressed, I increased the dose, believing *Geschmack Drei* would lift his spirits. But by March of '45, after more than a half year of use, he was speaking of suicide and admitting defeat. Such pitiful words I could have understood coming from the mouth of the Lithuanian or that man from Munich, but Hitler? I didn't know how to explain it. By April, when he was sending even his secretaries away, I no longer recognized him.

"I was among the last to leave," he said. "I was still there the morning Goebbels shot himself after watching his lovely wife feed their six sleeping children capsules of cyanide. I had sweetened their coffee. For months I had done this. Like always, that final morning they marveled at the taste."

He could remember the details and occupants of the bunker with greater force of clarity than he could recall the events leading up to his moving in with us. He spoke of SS-Obersturmbannführer Peter Hogel, of General Hans Krebs and Officer Burgdorf. He recalled mornings in the bunker's kitchen with Magda Goebbels and Eva Braun, and conversations about Native Americans with Dr. Ernst-Robert Grawitz. The last of these figures sat down one evening at the dinner table with his wife and two children and pulled the pin of a grenade while they ate. Grawitz's suicide was not a solitary act. He and all the others Ernst had named took their own lives, just as he and all the others had been amongst the most gushing fans and dedicated users of *Geschmack Drei*.

"Some took it in large doses over several weeks. Others had little more than a sip of sweetened coffee on the day they chose to die.

"After the war, I shared my concerns with the Americans who processed me. I made connections and spoke of unwanted side-effects. And they—what did they do? They took the formula, saying it might have a military use. What could I say?" he asked, looking directly at me. "I was glad to be done with it. I had a passport in exchange. A ticket to New York City.

"Years passed," he said. "I forgot, or stopped thinking about it, and then a friend from Goldstein, Olivetti, and Dark has breakfast with me at my house one morning and insists I put something in my coffee." His face brightened. He chuckled. "I recognized it right away. It had been reformulated—six times, I suppose—but even if it was weaker, it still registered on the tongue like a burst of sunlight."

He looked to me again, his mind having reached a time in which I existed, and like that it all came to a stop. His eyes grew clouded, his body fell into itself, and he looked away as if he'd been unplugged.

It didn't matter. His story didn't have an end any more than time did; it continued in me, just as the past carried over into the present, the one shaping the other as much as the other shaped the one, our lives as malleable as Silly Putty.

Ernest got up from the table first, and then Priscilla and Betty. I stayed there for another ten or twenty minutes, though, staring no less blankly into the future than my mentor. If the others saw his failures revealed through this story, I found my empathy. Because what *could* he have done to protest the use of Sweetness #9? Spoken out against the very government that had let him into the country in exchange for *Geschmack Drei*? He would have had his green card revoked, or been deported like that former guard at Treblinka who'd been discovered living in Cleveland. What's more, and this thought was almost exhilarating and certainly freeing, if The Nine was but a watered-down version of *Geschmack Drei,* that meant my refusal to do anything all these years could be but a symptom of Sweetness #9 poisoning. Priscilla was right. I was sick, no different from everyone else. For what is apathy if not a watered-down version of suicide?

When I got up from the table and led Ernst into his room, I felt strangely calm, but then I was only thinking of myself; now, years later, as I spend yet another day in this work shed banging away at the keys of my old IBM Selectric, I can see how my mentor's story must have shaken my family. I had warned them about Sweetness #9, however belatedly, but even that had not prepared them for this. Who was to say what would come next? They must have walked away from the table as if from a terrible car crash. After marveling at their escape from danger, they must have felt as fearless as those who've survived a near-death experience. I say this because like those who have escaped death, they soon decided there was no reason to hold back.

PART SIX

Small-Batch Organic Sauerkraut
1998–2012

AFTER PUTTING ERNST TO BED that night, I went upstairs and joined Betty in the great room, where she was mindlessly flipping through the channels. She got up and walked out almost as soon as I arrived, then went down and wrote a check on the kitchen table. I watched from the top of the stairs as she left through the front door with it, knowing where she was going and what she was going to do. After hearing the truth about Sweetness #9, she needed to believe she could have control over her body again, even if that meant paying the exorbitant fee demanded by the fat man next door.

When I got down to the table, I picked up her checkbook and confirmed my suspicions by reading the carbon. *Pay to the order of: Neal Sunderland. $10,000. For: A new life!*

Betty stayed away for several hours, long enough for me to wonder if she was planning an affair as well. When I finally did hear the front door open, and then her keying in the security code to lock up for the night, I was already in bed. She came in quietly, as if not to disturb me. I closed my eyes and pretended to sleep.

I had no right to question her use of the money. She earned plenty of it herself, and if she believed that the fat man's teachings might reverse what Sweetness #9 had or had not done to her all these years, I wasn't going to stand in her way. But that didn't mean I didn't want to know what she had learned, so the next morning at breakfast I found myself studying her actions before work. There was nothing to see. She grabbed a breakfast bar from the pantry as always and some pre-cut honeydew from the fridge, and then she corralled our son and went out through the utility room to her car.

Dinner promised to be no different, as she came in from work and suggested we finish up the leftovers from the previous night. I didn't know what to make of it. I had expected to see her eat a new animal, mineral, or vegetable product, or to have her refuse one she had heretofore regularly consumed. So finally I asked, "What's the secret?"

She had set her purse down on the island counter-top and was now reaching into it for a small white bag.

"If you're talking about last night," she said, "I can't tell you."

"Are you worried about a lawsuit? Did you sign a non-disclosure form?"

"I can't tell you," she repeated, pulling first a medicine dropper out of the white bag and then a red bottle with a white cap.

"Is it like a mantra?" I said, still not understanding what she was about to do. "Did he give you a mantra?"

"Ernest!" she called, uncapping the bottle. "Time for your medicine!"

He had been in the living room, watching television alongside his uncle and his namesake and his sister, but here he sprang up, ready and eager, as if they had discussed this on the drive in to school that morning.

"What's going on?" Priscilla said, following her brother over.

Ernest stood before his mother and opened his mouth like a baby bird. Betty fed him with the medicine dropper, one drop, two drops, three, and then, as she turned to the fridge to put the bottle away, Ernest smacked his lips, the delight clear in his eyes. "Wild cherry," he said.

Though I had never known Priscilla to need such motivation, I couldn't help but think her mother's decision played a part in her actions the following morning. It was then that Priscilla and Sarin led a protest against Station Zero, a private broadcast network whose owners had donated a fleet of new computers and televisions to the district in exchange for the right to broadcast thirty minutes of educational programming each day. Many viewed this as a boon to area tax-payers, but the girls did not, if only because the programming included three minutes of commercial advertising. The first time she was subjected to a spot promoting genetically modified foods, Priscilla asked to be excused to the bathroom. But the teacher didn't allow her to leave; she said students were contractually bound to watch.

So on the morning after Ernest was first medicated, Priscilla and Sarin waited for the commercial break, and then they and twelve other students across four classrooms raised their hands and asked to go to the bathroom. The response was just as expected: "School's about more than learning how to read and write; you'll just have to wait." But they refused to do as they'd been told. One after the other, to the shock and delight of their classmates and the horror of their teachers, the students relieved themselves in their chairs.

The principal responded like a general roused from sleep with news of a sneak attack. He had the school security guards pull all the suspects out into the hallway, and then (and you may have read about this in the papers) he had them strip down to their underwear—he said so that they could be searched for illicit narcotics. One sandwich bag filled with a dusting of marijuana was found, but not on the person of my daughter or Sarin. Something else was discovered there, if only by Priscilla. As my daughter stood beside her friend, she saw that while Sarin was wearing panties like her, she was also wearing a pair of control-top panties beneath them, cut down to the thigh. Nothing else could be seen; Sarin went to great pains each morning to make sure no bulge was visible. But once they were dressed and able to speak freely together outside, the truth emerged. Sitting in her car, Sarin confessed to being a boy who believed herself a girl. If there had been one good thing about her mother's death, she said, it had been the chance to move to a new town where no one knew the "truth."

Priscilla told her mother and me just like that: by making quotation marks in the air with her hands. Then she refused to talk about it anymore, telling us not to let Sarin in when she knocked on the door about an hour later. It didn't matter that Sarin had been meaning to tell her, I suppose; teenagers have a hard enough time arriving at their own identity without having to also question whether their incipient homosexuality is confirmed or denied by such a muddled same-sex crush.

I supposed it was just too much for her in the end. After learning the true history of Sweetness #9 and seeing her father charged with depraved indifference, Priscilla crept out of her window in the middle of the night. A runaway. Taking only a toothbrush and all of the money in her mother's purse, and leaving behind nothing but blowing curtains for a note.

"I don't know," Sarin said, when we called to ask if she knew where she might have gone. "Maybe some organic farm out west?"

At my preliminary hearing, I went against the advice of my attorney and read from a prepared statement. I told the judge that while I was deeply saddened by the death of Charles Hithenbottom, and certainly regretted my involvement in those events that preceded his suicide, I was a victim of circumstance. Yes, I had quarreled with him at Costco "like a knight of old" (to use the prosecuting attorney's words), but this was more a symptom of our nation's sickness than any evidence of a "long-standing blood feud going back to [our] days at Goldstein, Olivetti, and Dark" (again, not my words).

"If the supermarket attacks hadn't so thoroughly terrified the tri-state area" — they had concluded by now, but remained unsolved, much like the murders attributed to the Tylenol Killer — "I'm sure none of this would have happened. That it did while I was experiencing a sharp spike of anxiety as a result of a lawfully prescribed medication made this an even more unfortunate case of timing, as the pills certainly contributed to my acting so wholly out of character."

The judge was a somber woman of sixty-five or more years; her face was all sharp angles and bone. I told her that I had already been punished enough. Not only would I have to carry with me the traumatic memory of witnessing my former co-worker's death, but I would have to deal with the fall-out from the coverage of my arrest in both the *Battle Station Bugler* and the newsletter for the Society of Flavor Chemists.

"As a consequence of this, my reputation and that of my company has suffered terribly, and my daughter, no doubt embarrassed and ashamed of what I've done, has run away, fled without explanation, leaving me with a sadness I cannot begin to describe."

322

I turned to those in the front row of the audience who had come to show their support for me. There was Ernest in the same ill-fitting dark suit he'd worn to his grandfather's funeral; his uncle Peter, dressed in jeans and a flannel shirt; my glassy-eyed mentor, Ernst Eberhardt; Betty, in her best first lady outfit; and even my distant cousin from Lithuania, who had arrived just two days previous, looking remarkably like me, save for the red hair.

"In conclusion, I would like to add that I have not seen a dentist about my chipped tooth. In fact, I plan to keep it this way to serve as a reminder of the part I played in this unfortunate drama. I will, it should also be noted, not pursue any legal action—again, contrary to the advice of my attorney—against the city of Jupiter Park in response to how I was handled by Officer Landers, whose commitment to public service I commend."

When it was time for the judge to speak, she addressed the facts of the case. She said it couldn't be denied that my fingerprints had been found on the gun used by the deceased, and she acknowledged that I could therefore have shown the victim how to hold this weapon and where to place it. "As the state suggests, he could even have sat across from Charles Hithenbottom, using his own gun to force the victim to pull the trigger. But however much the state would like to see Mr. Leveraux prosecuted for the most serious charge against him, that of 'depraved indifference,' I wonder why the prosecuting attorney"—and here she looked squarely at him—"would believe this charge could be tried on the strength of conjecture alone. If Mr. Leveraux is a murderer"—and here her eyes swung toward mine—"he knows it in his heart. But I'm not certain anyone else can be led to believe such a thing beyond a reasonable doubt, especially given the fact that the victim appears to have lived, to put it kindly, a conflicted and troubled life." If she didn't reach for her gavel, it's how I remember it now in my mind. "I'm dismissing all charges but two counts of vehicular hit-and-run."

Though the judge's ruling was a great relief, it was hardly cause for celebration. Nothing had been since Ernst Eberhardt had told us his story and Priscilla had run away in the night.

Instead of going out to dinner, we stopped at the supermarket on the way home as if it were just any other day. Peter grabbed the cart and moved through the store with precision and purpose, slowing only to direct Ernst, who puttered around behind him in a motorized Mart Cart. Betty lingered before the display of diet cola, refusing to cave in to her desires and grab a case for herself, while at the same time unwilling to turn her back and walk away.

"She blames me, doesn't she?" she said.

"Who? Priscilla? Why?"

She spoke of her leaving so soon after she'd started medicating Ernest. "It's just another bad mother storyline," she said. "She must think I'm a monster."

I wrapped my arm around her and led her off in search of our son and my cousin, the latter of whom I found shaking a box of crackers to see if it was filled with anything more than empty air. "There is no smell," he said, with a wide-ranging look that took in all of the store's bright abundance. "All this food," he said, "and no smell!"

The way he smiled, I couldn't tell if he was remarking on a feat of wonder or if he'd found the error in our ways.

When we got home, I ate a microwaveable shepherd's pie alone in the kitchen and allowed myself a private hope where for so many years I had had none. As I pushed my fork through the top layer of cheese and mashed potatoes, just as I'd done countless times as a youth, I hoped my mother might rise up before me as clearly as a hologram when I breathed in the savory sauce of the beef. But my meal was stillborn; she remained as lost to me now as she had been since that terrible day in Texas.

I set my fork down and looked to the television in the living room. It was playing a documentary about the death of Princess Diana, and as a computer re-creation showed her black Mercedes entering the Pont d'Alma tunnel and slamming into the thirteenth concrete pillar, I started to cry, not so much because I'd never allowed myself a moment to grieve Lady Di's passing, but because I could hear the same show playing on the television in the great room above (Betty's brother and my cousin), as well as from my bedroom (Betty) and the study down the hall (Ernst).

I picked at my food, wondering if Ernest would remember Aspirina every time he ate a fried plantain or felt a burst of chili pepper. I feared I'd trigger memories in him only if he continued to eat frozen food — and only if that food remained profitable enough to stay on the market.

I went out into the garage before anyone could see me crying and sat at my workbench, where I put the finishing touches on the last diorama in my series on food history. I had started it after my release from jail. It showed our house from above, with the roof off and everyone — Betty, Priscilla, Ernest, and me — locked away in his or her own room, eating from a plate of food and watching television. This evening, I worked on the kitchen. This evening, I painted the microwave.

As he found he enjoyed caring for Ernst, Betty's brother stayed on with us. His help was both appreciated and needed, because my mentor's health quickly deteriorated. Ernst Eberhardt came down with pneumonia that same winter, and died in our home on 13 January 1999, after waking in the middle of the night with a piercing scream that caused me to jump from the chair next to his bed. He grabbed my hand and pulled me close with the strength of the look in his eyes. It was a mystical moment. My skin went electric. I felt so light and free. I thought he might reveal to me the secret of life. But his last words weren't words at all. He only told me a name. "Magda!"

The weekend after the funeral, Ernest helped me clean out his namesake's row house and discovered a stash of old pictures, including one black-and-white print of the young woman Ernst had loved before the war. In it, Magda sat on a large rock in a forest clearing, smiling at something the photographer had just said. Her name was written on the back and underlined in red, and below that was a block of text in German. I knew I had to have it translated. I felt as if it was this task that Ernst had meant to give me when he shot up in bed and attempted to share his final thoughts. So I took the photo to Koba, who was excited to say it was a recipe for Magda's mother's sauerkraut. "Should we give it a try?"

Our other big find at my mentor's house was Ernst Eberhardt's half-finished ghost-written memoir, *How Great Thou Taste,* which I discovered in his closet along with a case of old packets of Sweetness #9, their contents as pink as those packets I'd received anonymously while Ernst was still living in this house. I read his book in a single sitting. I kept thinking I'd come upon a chapter describing the reason he'd kept quiet about *Geschmack Drei,* or a passage telling me why he would use Sweetness #9 after realizing it had its origins in Hitler's war machine. But his was a corporate memoir, containing as many abridged stories as it had missing parts. If anything, reading it left me with more questions, not fewer. Did he spend his final years ingesting Sweetness #9 out of guilt, as a kind of slow suicide? Or was he conducting an experiment on himself to see if The Nine's threat was true? For some it takes a lifetime of use; for others it's over with that first taste. I like to think the packets of Sweetness #9 that he delivered to me were his way of announcing the results—that even in his declining state he had tried to let me know why he was slipping, or at the very least to direct my thinking toward it. But everything is conjecture. I can speak no more certainly of this than I can, in the end, of the verifiable effects of Sweetness #9.

Because Ernest had not started using verbs by the end of winter break, Betty and I decided together to add Ritalin to the mix, and remarkably this did work. Our son started speaking in complete sentences again, and though we didn't always like what we heard— slamming doors and whining, saying he could do something by himself—we were glad he was able to retake his test and transfer back into his regular classroom.

Like most high schools in northern New Jersey, the one my son attended wasn't without its fair share of connections to the horrors of 9/11. To honor those who died, an assembly was held out on the playground, and many somber speeches were delivered against a backdrop of fluttering flags and soaring patriotic songs. I didn't attend, but I was one of the parents called after a group of children fell in the heat and dropped into convulsions on the blacktop. Maybe you read the story that went out over the AP wire. The convulsions had been triggered by an overdose of pharmaceuticals. The children, including Jeremiah and my son, had hoarded them and started taking them in higher and higher doses.

Jeremiah's inclusion in this group led to greater scrutiny of his foster mother, who, it was discovered, had in her care only children with ADD — though most of these kids hadn't been so diagnosed before they'd gotten to her. Suspecting she'd started them on the pills because it meant up to two hundred dollars more of monthly support for each affected child, the state removed all of her children from her custody, including my son's good friend, who stopped drooling once he was off the Ritalin — and then disappeared from our lives entirely.

Betty took some pleasure in knowing "The Saint" wasn't as saintly as she'd imagined, but even so, the ordeal proved too much for her. We didn't renew Ernest's prescription after this, and though he didn't retreat to verblessness as a consequence, he didn't speak much in our presence either. Betty never forgave herself. She wouldn't listen to me when I told her he'd probably been getting pills from Jeremiah even before we'd ever gotten him a prescription ourselves; she'd only blame herself, saying she was the one who'd suggested we put him on the medication in the first place. "It's just another bad mother storyline," she'd say, again and again.

A few weeks after 9/11, while bombs were falling in Afghanistan and leaked bin Laden videos were still being played in full on the news, Betty left and didn't come back. Ernest was in school when it happened; I was at work. He came home first, but I was the one to find the note on her pillow. I didn't have the heart to read it through to the end. I brought it down to my son's bedroom and gave it to him. He stared at it for the longest time, and then he took in a deep breath and began.

You should know I love you all very dearly, her note began. *But I'm 197 pounds, heavier than I've ever been, and if I'm going to be any good to myself or you I need to be alone for at least one year to put Neal's secret to the test. I can tell you this much: I've left for Ukraine. Please know that I will be thinking of you every day. With much love, Betty.*

He stood there not moving after he'd finished, as if waiting for me to excuse him. I wouldn't, though. Not yet.

"Why'd you do it?" I said. "Lose the verbs. Make us think something was wrong with you. We took you to how many doctors, pricked you with a needle how many times? Why'd you do it?" I said. "Was it the drugs?"

For a moment he just looked at me as if full of rage, as if wondering how I could be so stupid as to ask. Then he said, he said to me, "Do you really want to know?" and if there was one question that could have made me want to avoid the truth, that was it.

The following month, I sold my mentor's row house and the condominium he'd bought for Eliza, and I contacted the CEO of Better Health and Flavorings and asked if he was still interested in meeting for lunch. We didn't have to push numbers back and forth across the table. I was satisfied with the first figure that I saw.

I was sad to leave my co-workers, but I knew they would prosper and that we had been diminished for some time anyway. Tennessee had taken early retirement not long after Ernst Eberhardt had died. Meanwhile, Koba found secure employment with a flavor house in Paterson and has since become a fully certified member of the Society of Flavor Chemists. He lives in South Battle Station Township, I'm told, and recently became the father of twin girls.

Beekley would have been kept on by Better Health and Flavorings, but his heart was no longer in the work. The supermarket attacks had convinced him there was no future in it, and when Y2K failed to reinvent our lives as he'd once imagined it would, he became as lost as I had been after the fall of Communism. All that changed on 9/11. Like so many young men about to run down to the military recruiter, he stood before the TV, saying he had to do something. A few days later he showed up at work with a U.S. flag pin on the lapel of his lab coat. "I just wanted to say good-bye," he said. "I won't be coming back. I'm gonna do my part to keep this country safe."

"You joined the army?" I said.

"Not exactly."

"The marines? Don't tell me you joined the marines."

"I won't be fighting with a gun, David. Where I'm going, I'll have something a little more powerful than that."

He told me he couldn't say anything more, that he'd already said too much, but my desire to know must have weighed on him, or if not that, his need to tell me must have been great, because a couple of months later he called from a pay phone and risked losing his security clearance.

He sounded drunk and clearly exhilarated, speaking of an elite team of flavor chemists that had been recruited by the Defense Advanced Research Projects Agency and brought together at a secret lab in the mountains of northern New Jersey. It was like the Manhattan Project, he said. "We're working on a weaponized odor, the mother of all stink bombs." Osama bin Laden was believed to be in the mountains of Tora Bora. "And it's gonna get him. They'll deliver it on a bomb that'll pierce down through all that rock and drive him out into the open. I wish you could smell it, David. Even with all the gear I have to wear, the goggles and the Hazmat suit, I still have to burn my underwear when I get home each evening. It smells so bad it makes you proud to be an American. Can you imagine it, David? Can you imagine the smell?"

I didn't hear from him again after that, but I recently learned via email from an old flavor friend that he died under mysterious circumstances in a brothel in Algeria, shortly after the invasion of Iraq. Fare thee well, Frederick Archibald Beekley. Fare thee well, young man. You will be missed.

Betty sent us her first postcard in December of 2001. It didn't include a return address, only a postmark from Kiev, Ukraine, to which she said she'd traveled to celebrate the holidays. She didn't offer much else, and in the coming months her infrequent communications were no more enlightening. In them she spoke of the hardships of her new life (she had been robbed one morning while jogging, her foreignness revealed by the bright tracksuit she'd worn) and begged for our patience while she "learn[ed] how to live life again."

On the first day of the new year, I went through the house, collecting everything that included Sweetness #9 and Red Dye No. 40 and telling Ernest that this time we were staying on the diet for good. For several months we barely spoke about anything other than a military school in Virginia, which I assured him had a cafeteria offering a wider range of food than he could expect in our house. He stayed, however reluctantly, and our life in South Battle Station Township was as silent and as empty as ever.

If only to have something to do, I began writing members of Congress and newspaper reporters — anyone who might like to hear the story I could tell about Sweetness #9. If you look online, you'll find a few articles from that time mentioning me by name. If you were to do a little more research, you'll even discover that in the spring of 2002 I went before the House Energy and Commerce Subcommittee on Health to speak about the dangers of Sweetness #9. My timing was off, though: the congressmen I spoke with were only interested in the vulnerabilities of our food delivery system that might be most easily exploited by terrorists.

"Real threats," the chairperson of this committee told me, "not fanciful stories about Nazis and mind-control pills."

I'm not sure my writing this will do any more good than my visit to Washington. It won't undo the damage I inflicted on my family or myself, and if experience is the only thing that teaches us anything, it won't keep anyone from doing anything they shouldn't. It will help me understand what I have and have not done, though (or what I believe I have and have not done), and I suppose that is a small good thing: to acknowledge one's life, not just to oneself but to others.

Late in the summer of 2002, I flew with Ernest to San Diego and there rented a car and followed a meandering route north to Seattle. I was sure Priscilla had started a new life out west, and so we went from one farmer's market to the next, hoping to see her peddling heirloom tomatoes or summer squash. The search proved fruitless (even after stops at Burning Man and the Rainbow Gathering), but all the same it was transformative. At some point I adopted what I came to call the Churchill Diet (nothing but greens and fresh milk and bread) and began dreaming of my own life here on the other coast. I had Magda's photo in my wallet and all the money I'd come into as a result of selling FlavAmerica, and I wondered why I didn't start over as a producer of small-batch organic sauerkraut.

Betty had said she'd be away for at least a year, but when we got back from our road trip we found she hadn't written with news of an impending return. When three more months passed without any word, I sold our home and relocated with Ernest to an eighty-six-year-old farmhouse on a forty-acre plot of land in Potter Valley, more than three hours north of San Francisco.

For two years it was just the two of us and a few hired hands struggling to coax something edible up out of the dirt. Ernest flourished even as our crops floundered. I can't say it was going back to the land that did it; there was no control group in this experiment. But in those two years he grew more than he had in the past ten. By the fall of 2005, when he was leaving for UC Davis without any firm academic plans, he didn't just look like a man; he looked like a new person.

By then I had two goats that I kept tied to a series of iron poles across the property. They're still here, and in addition to keeping the grass down, they provide all the milk I could ever need. The bread that I eat I bake myself, using a slow-rise method I learned about in the *New York Times*. (Some habits I'll never give up; the paper, which I now read online, is one of them.) The rest of the food comes from the fields in back: a rotating crop of green leafy vegetables, most of which I sell at farmer's markets in Ukiah, Kelseyville, and Willits. My most popular item is "Priscilla's Famous Organic Sauerkraut," which follows Magda's recipe and can now be purchased at Whole Foods and several smaller natural food stores.

It was through this sauerkraut (or rather the website promoting it; we ship jars as far away as Japan and Beirut) that Betty, now using her maiden name, returned to me. She drove up one day in a rental car and walked out into the fields until I looked up and saw it was her. She was so incredibly thin. Even before I could cross the distance between us, a head of cabbage falling from the hold of my hand, I knew she must be sick.

It was cancer, and it was terminal, and she'd come back to learn about Priscilla. "Say she's here," she said. "Is she here?"

We were both crying by the time I was telling her the truth about Priscilla's Famous Organic Sauerkraut. "It's Magda's recipe, the woman Ernst Eberhardt loved before the war. I hoped Priscilla might see the label and know everything has changed, but I haven't found her. I looked everywhere and I don't know any more today than I did in New Jersey."

We retreated to the wicker furniture in the sun room and drank from a pitcher of water as Betty spoke to me of how she'd passed these years apart. We'd been through so much together, she thought I deserved to know. She said our old neighbor Neal had been a fat activist, and that when she'd gone to see him that night we all heard the Sweetness #9 origin story, he told her she shouldn't hate herself, that she should embrace her body for what it was and reclaim the word "fat" as homosexuals had reclaimed the word "queer."

"Fat is beautiful," he said, and if she couldn't see that, she should live in a foreign country where the average citizen made no more than two hundred dollars per month. "Live like they do for a year. Walk everywhere, go to sleep hungry, don't take a vacation. Try Ukraine."

That's where Neal had gone. In the summer of 1992, when few Americans other than missionaries and documentary filmmakers were bold enough to trek that far behind the Iron Curtain, he'd traveled to Kharkov, in Ukraine's Russian-speaking north-east. He went to meet a woman, a mail-order bride he'd corresponded with after finding her picture in a crudely printed catalogue that a friend of a friend had given him. He was thirty-seven and he wanted to marry, but when he knocked at the woman's door, he learned the photo and the face didn't match up. A man answered; the woman was a character he'd dreamed up, hoping to convince a few Western men to send valuable gifts or money. He was an engineer for the city, going in to work each day even though he hadn't been paid for more than a year. Neal thought to return home after learning all of this, but he had nothing to go back to: not a close family, not a good job, not a lifelong friend or even a sport he closely followed. So he settled into a one-room flat at the end of the metro's Red Line, in a neighborhood his handheld translator told him was known as "Cold Mountain."

There were no U.S.-style supermarkets in this city of almost 2 million, only small corner stores at which all of the goods were kept on shelves behind a series of counters. To get anything, you had to approach a humorless woman in a blue smock and tell her exactly what you wanted. But Neal didn't speak Russian, and he was too self-conscious to point at all of the many things that he wanted to eat. "Look at the fat American!" he thought they'd say. And so he lost weight because of his shame, and when he returned to the States after a year, still single and lonely, he ran an advertisement in a weekly paper on a lark. "Guaranteed weight loss program! Lose 15 percent of your body weight or your money back!" The response was overwhelming. You only had to promise a secret, he saw, a new way of life, and all the riches in this world could be yours.

Betty told me his program had worked. By the time Ernest and I were traveling north from San Diego, she was already as thin as she had been in college. "I met a man, too." She looked me in my eyes, not ashamed of this, but cautious, perhaps fearing it would come as a shock. She took my hand. "He approached me at the central market, after hearing me lapse into English. I'd forgotten the word for pork." She smiled and her eyes lit up, even though the cancer had made the whites yellow. "He's a professor of philology. A decent man. I moved into his apartment after only a month. It wasn't much bigger than this room. We've been together ever since. When I got sick, he insisted I come back. There was nothing the doctors could do, but Sergei knew I had to see you and the kids. He flew here with me."

"He's with you?"

"He insisted on staying in a motel. In Ukiah. He said he would only come if you approve. We are still married," she reminded me. "He's very old-fashioned that way. Would you mind if he stayed with us? It shouldn't be very long now."

I only then realized her plan: she had come back to die. I held her hand in mine, saying it'd be more than okay. "You think I couldn't benefit from a little female company?" I tried a sort of laugh. "You should hear them whisper about me at the hardware store. I'm the bachelor farmer everyone has questions about."

Ernest withdrew from classes that quarter to spend more time with his mother on the farm, and so all that fall, as the days grew shorter and the evenings more crisp, we took our meals together as a family outside at a long wooden table set up underneath the thick branches of a huge oak tree. I wouldn't call it saying grace, but I did start each meal with the same statement: "Let's be thankful."

Betty died in bed one morning that winter, surrounded by her son and me, Sergei, and one of the hospice workers who'd stayed with us at the end. Priscilla reappeared not even a month later, after Ernest and I had gone out into the rain and thrown Betty's ashes across the empty fields that'd return to life the following spring. She, too, had stopped using the name Leveraux (Mockus was more authentic, she believed) and found me through the sauerkraut I sold. She'd seen a jar of it one day at the North Coast Co-op in Arcata, and after picking it up, stopped by the sight of her own name, she'd read the fine print and found an address for Leveraux's Fine Foods.

When she rang the doorbell, she was wearing a floral-print dress over a pair of blue jeans and had a ring on one of her toes (she wore no shoes). Her nose was pierced in two places, and one of her ears had six or seven silver studs in it. A wildflower was tattooed on the side of her neck, though at first I couldn't see it clearly because of her dreadlocks; I thought it might be a snake.

I almost fell over. I felt a weakness in the back of my legs, a hole opening up in my chest. I grabbed my arm by the elbow and held it close to my side. "Oh, Priscilla," I said.

"I'm pregnant." The words came out like a dare. "Seven months." Like a threat. "Can I stay?"

I stepped out and fell into her as if for support, wrapping her up in my arms and saying of course, she could stay as long as she wanted and tell me as much as she thought I needed to hear. "We all have secrets. I'm just so happy that you're home."

Her daughter was born that spring, when the green peas were beginning to shoot up their runners in the fields. She weighed seven pounds, five ounces, and screamed so loudly you would've thought she was auditioning for a spot in the Juilliard School of Music. That first day in the hospital, I told Priscilla she'd better get used to it, and then I stood there silently, watching as she tried to convince her baby to take her breast.

I've kept up with the Churchill Diet all these years, with only the occasional slip, and though I can no longer say if I started this as an act of penance or in an effort to rid my system of all the many chemicals that had built up in my bloodstream over the years, I do feel I wouldn't have begun this book if it weren't for that one change in my life. I took to writing my memoirs late, in 2009, not long after the U.S. handed over control of the Green Zone to the Iraqi people.[*]

After dazzling some of his writing instructors at UC Davis, Ernest went on to get an MFA in poetry at the University of Iowa, where his mentors were no less impressed by the absence of verbs in his work. He published his first poetry while there (using the pen name Ernesto Martínez), and is currently serving a Fulbright Fellowship in Ukraine, where he's working on a new cycle of poems that I've been told has something to do with his mother.

Priscilla lives with me in Potter Valley, though she has plans to return to Humboldt County when she can afford it. On those nights when she goes into town to take a class at the community college (she's training to become a nurse), I watch after my granddaughter, little Michelle Roosevelt Mockus, and sometimes tell her stories I know she can't understand.

My wife was wearing a cross from the Eastern Orthodox Church when she died, and though I tried to give it to Sergei, he insisted that I take it and wear it as my own. By then, old man Johnson, the World's Oldest Man, was long gone, taking with him his belief in vanilla soda

---

[*] I did not wish to see my memoirs repurposed and marketed as fiction, but sadly this was considered the safest way to avoid possible litigation from the manufacturer of "Sweetness #9." I put up a good fight, you should know, but in the end I was granted only one concession: the right to address the reader in this footnote. I thought it a minor victory, because even if the standard disclaimers—*any resemblance to persons, places, or things living or dead is purely coincidental*—would have to dirty the copyright page of this "novel," I could still advise you to study those resemblances very closely. Then the book's editor read my first go at this footnote, and she wrote to share her excitement with me, saying that rather than help establish the truth, it would only further destabilize it. "'It self-consciously addresses the devices of fiction and systematically draws attention to its status as an artifact in posing questions about the relationship between fiction and reality.'" She was quoting from Wikipedia. "Don't you see? Metafiction doesn't let you forget you're reading fiction—and that's exactly what your footnote does! I love it!" I, it should go without saying, do not. I find myself boxed in by it. But there is no escape, apparently, so let me simply retreat once more to the body of the text.

and cream-filled sponge cake. I didn't even bother to read of his successor. I felt ready for something new, and so when Sergei pushed Betty's cross back into my hands, I wore it and soon found reason to seek out the Orthodox church in Santa Rosa, about an hour south of here.

I visited just that one time, spending a few minutes looking at the brightly painted ceilings. Since then, I've found myself stopping at the place I first noticed on a drive in to the farmer's market one Sunday. It is a beautiful old church, built in the German style, sitting up on a hill off to the side of the valley. On closer inspection, I discovered it was a Lutheran church for the deaf. The first time I entered it, I found the service already in progress. The pastor stood facing the congregants, delivering his sermon like a third-base coach. Everyone kept their eyes to the fore, because in this church you could not afford to look away. I sat in the back pew and fell into the silence, occasionally glancing up at the unadorned cross behind the pastor or off to the stained-glass windows at our sides: a fish, the three kings, the blazing star of Bethlehem.

A team of ushers moved through, passing a basket back and forth. Then it was time for communion, with two lines forming in the central aisle. When I reached the front of mine, I found one man ready to offer me the body of Christ and another with a silver chalice filled with the blood. I accepted the wafer into the cup of my hands, then laid it on my tongue and drank from the chalice. I shouldn't look at this with my old eyes, but no matter how many lives we lead between the cradle and the grave, it is inevitable that one will awkwardly overlap the next. The bread was crisp and without flavor, and it broke down too easily when it came into contact with the wine, which was cloying and overly sweet.

I wish I had the words to explain why I keep coming back.

Acknowledgments

Thanks to:

Ed Salmina, my first writing teacher; the University of Southern California, for providing me a home; Pam Houston, for creating such a wonderful community for writers at UC Davis; the U.S. Fulbright Program, for a life-altering journey to Ukraine; Dave Chariton; Sabrina Tom, Rose Gowen, Josh Bernstein, and Cody Todd, for your feedback and encouragement; Ken Kalfus, Karl Iagnemma, and Ben Fountain, for taking the time to read a book of stories from an unknown writer; Robert Hedin and the Residency Program at the Anderson Center, where I did in a month what I'd been unable to do in ten years; T. C. Boyle, for your many gifts and years of guidance; Augsburg College; Fiona McCrae; Mitchell Waters, agent extraordinaire, Steven Salpeter, and Holly Frederick at Curtis Brown; Nicole Dewey and everyone at Little, Brown, in particular Victoria Matsui, who did what I'd been led to believe editors no longer do — in short, everything; and my parents, for a lifetime of belief, support, and understanding.

About the Author

Stephan Eirik Clark was born in West Germany and raised in England and the United States. He is the author of the short story collection *Vladimir's Mustache*. A former Fulbright Fellow to Ukraine, he teaches at Augsburg College in Minneapolis. This is his first novel.